Resistance

12-14

Resistance

JENNA BLACK

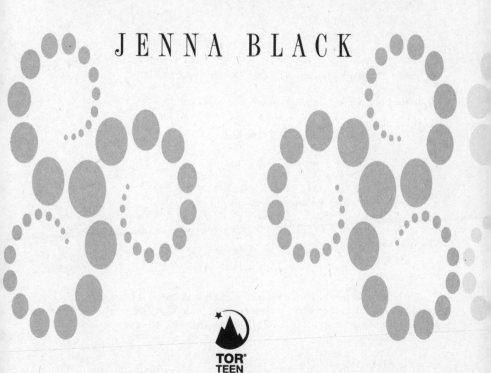

TOR°
TEEN

A TOM DOHERTY ASSOCIATES BOOK
NEW YORK

This is a work of fiction. All of the characters, organizations, and events portrayed in this novel are either products of the author's imagination or are used fictitiously.

RESISTANCE

A Tor Teen Book
Published by Tom Doherty Associates, LLC
175 Fifth Avenue
New York, NY 10010

www.tor-forge.com

Tor® is a registered trademark of Tom Doherty Associates, LLC.

Library of Congress Cataloging-in-Publication Data

Black, Jenna.
    Resistance / Jenna Black. — First edition.
        p. cm.
    "A Tom Doherty Associates book."
    Sequel to: Replica.
    ISBN 978-0-7653-3372-8 (trade paperback)
    ISBN 978-1-4668-0490-6 (e-book)
    1. Science fiction. 2. Friendship—Fiction. 3. Conspiracies—Fiction.
4. Gays—Fiction. I. Title.
    PZ7.B52894Rf 2014
    [Fic]—dc23

2013025954

Tor Teen books may be purchased for educational, business, or promotional use. For information on bulk purchases, please contact Macmillan Corporate and Premium Sales Department at 1-800-221-7945, extension 5442, or write specialmarkets@macmillan.com.

First Edition: March 2014

Printed in the United States of America

0 9 8 7 6 5 4 3 2 1

To Dan,
thanks for everything you do to help me live my dream.

Resistance

CHAPTER ONE

"You can't be serious!" Nadia told her mother.

She tried to keep her voice level and calm despite a stab of panic. She'd known her life would never be the same after what had happened, and she'd known that being summoned to her mother's private study hadn't boded well, but nothing could have prepared her for the bombshell that had just exploded in her face.

Esmeralda Lake sat rigidly on the edge of the sofa. "It will only be for a week," she said, but the promise was hardly comforting, especially when her expression was so forbidding. "Two at the most. Just until some of the . . . furor . . . dies down."

"You don't think sending me to an Executive retreat is going to fuel the fire?" Nadia asked incredulously. Retreats billed themselves as relaxing spas, places a busy Executive might go to for a quick break from the stresses of life. There was no press allowed, and there was no access to the net, or even to telephones, allowing said stressed-out Executive to experience an unparalleled escape from the troubles of the world. Which all sounded nice in theory, but everyone knew Executives went to retreats to escape some kind of scandal. You went to a retreat when the press found out you had a drug problem, or when you'd been caught cheating on your husband, or when you were having a nervous breakdown. You went there to *hide*, because you had something to be ashamed of.

"You were arrested for treason, Nadia!" her mother snapped. "*Everyone* has seen the footage of you being marched through the lobby in *chains*. Our only hope of quieting the gossip is to get you out of the public eye."

"But I was *exonerated!*" Nadia protested. "I didn't do anything wrong." She paced in front of the sofa on which her mother sat, having sprung from her own seat the moment Esmeralda had told her she was being sent away. The idea of being locked in a retreat, away from her friends and family, unable to contact anyone—and unable to find out what was happening in the outside world—made her feel dizzy and slightly nauseous. She had escaped execution only because she, with some help from her sister, Gerri, had recorded the Chairman admitting not only that he'd had his own son killed, but also that he was providing human test subjects for Thea, the world's first true artificial intelligence, to experiment on. But if the Chairman ever located the recordings, she would be in mortal danger, and behind the walls of a retreat, she'd never even know it.

"Don't be such a child," her mother said, showing no sign of sympathy. "Whether you did anything wrong or not is irrelevant, and you know it. It's the perception that matters."

Unfortunately, Nadia *did* know that. Despite her being publicly exonerated, people would want to believe Nadia had done something to bring it on herself. The idea that a completely innocent person might have been arrested and humiliated as Nadia had been didn't sit well with Paxco's elite, and if they could convince themselves Nadia was guilty of *something*, even if it was just stupidity, they would all sleep better at night.

"Please don't make me go," Nadia begged, knowing it was a lost cause. Her mother had decided before Nadia had set foot in the room, and there was no changing her mind.

Esmeralda's eyes softened, but only a little bit. "It won't be so bad. After everything that's happened, a little time away from it all will do you good. And Tranquility is truly a beautiful facility, especially at this time of year. Their gardens are breathtaking."

"How would you know?" Nadia challenged. "Did your family send *you* there to hide you away like a shameful secret?"

A part of her knew she was being unfair to her mother. From Esmeralda's standpoint, sending Nadia to a retreat for a week or two was the obvious choice. Without her presence in the public eye, the press would gossip itself out and then lose interest as soon as the next scandal occurred. There would be murmurings when Nadia reemerged, but nothing like the feeding frenzy that was happening now. If Nadia weren't so painfully aware of how precarious her situation was—and how dangerous it would be for her not to know what was going on in the outside world—she might even have had to reluctantly agree that spending some time at Tranquility was just the thing.

"Enough!" Esmeralda said firmly. "You're going, and that's final. You can be as angry with me as you like, but I'm doing this for your own good. Your whole future is at stake here, and we have to be smart about managing the damage control."

Nadia's eyes burned with tears she refused to shed. Yesterday, she had engaged in a battle of wills against the Chairman of Paxco and his sadistic hatchet man, and she'd won. Against her mother, however, there was no victory to be had.

"Fine," she said as her shoulders slumped in defeat. "When do I leave?"

"I've arranged a car for you at four o'clock."

This just got better and better. She'd hoped she'd have at least a few hours—long enough for Gerri to get home from work so that Nadia could have another conversation with her. They'd spoken briefly this morning, and Nadia had urged her sister not listen to the blackmail recordings. She'd promised to explain the why of it tonight when they had more time, though she was still unsure what she could say to keep Gerri's curiosity in check.

Nadia hoped Gerri would follow her instructions even without knowing why. Knowing the Chairman's terrible secret was just too dangerous, and Nadia *had* to keep the information—and the recordings—deeply hidden. Even from her own family.

"How am I supposed to pack for a week or two in thirty minutes?" Nadia asked.

Her mother looked surprised. "That's not how retreats work, dear. They'll provide everything you need."

"You're telling me I can't take *anything* with me?" Panic was making her light-headed. At least if she was packing a suitcase, she could try to smuggle a phone in with her. Something, *anything,* to keep her in touch with the outside world.

Her mother put her hands on Nadia's shoulders and looked her in the eyes. "It will be all right," she said, and there was true warmth in her voice for the first time since Nadia had set foot in her study. "I know a week seems like forever at your age, but it will be over before you know it. And maybe you'll like it there. You never know."

But Nadia *did* know.

Her mother was making a genuine effort to soften the blow, but she'd never exactly been the nurturing sort, and it didn't come naturally to her. It was not an oversight that

Nadia's father wasn't present for this conversation. He must have agreed to Esmeralda's plan, but he would have had trouble holding firm in the face of Nadia's distress. So he just avoided the whole thing and left it to his wife. Nadia tried not to hate him for it.

She couldn't think of anything to say. Nothing that she wouldn't regret later, at least. Without another word, she broke away from her mother's hold and marched toward her bedroom. She might not be allowed to bring anything with her, but she had some arrangements to make before she left, and she had less than thirty minutes to do it.

The Tranquility Executive Retreat was located on Long Island on thirty acres of beautifully cultivated, ridiculously expensive land. Most Executive retreats were located upstate, the better to isolate their guests, both from the press and from society in general. Executives who went to upstate retreats generally didn't leave, nor did they receive many visitors, having disgraced their families and friends with whatever scandal had caused them to enter the retreat in the first place. Tranquility was for Executives who could still be reclaimed into society, and whose family members wanted convenient access for visits.

Her mother bid her a chilly farewell, and Nadia was hardly feeling warmer herself. Understanding why her mother was sending her away didn't make the sting of it hurt any less. And the fact that she was being whisked away so quickly, without having a chance to say good-bye in person to anyone but her mother, didn't do much for her peace of mind, either.

She managed a quick phone call with Gerri before leaving. "Please remember what I told you this morning," she said vaguely. "Please promise me. I'll explain when I can."

Gerri didn't like it one bit—she had to be dying of curiosity, if nothing else—but she got the message and made the reluctant promise.

Nate hadn't answered his phone, so Nadia was forced to leave him a message. She was just going to have to trust him to protect their secret—and to find a way to contact her and let her know if the worst should happen and the Chairman found the recordings.

When Nadia's limo approached, the small cluster of reporters who'd chosen to stake out the garage entrance perked up, snapping pictures wildly. The limo, of course, had tinted windows, so all they were getting was a photograph of a car, but that didn't seem to discourage them. Several of them charged the limo and knocked on the glass, shouting questions. Another stood directly in the limo's path to block the way. Blocking the car was illegal, and one of the security officers who'd been assigned to control the press started forward to remove the obstacle. However, Nadia's driver was apparently under strict orders not to stop for any reason. When the reporter stepped into his way, he didn't lessen his speed. The reporter had to dive to the side before the security officer could remove him. Nadia wondered how *that* little drama was going to play with the media.

About eighty minutes later, the limo pulled up to the massive iron gates of Tranquility's entrance, and Nadia got her first look at the facility that she hoped would be her home for no more than one week.

The gates were closed and guarded by a security booth, which housed two security guards. Stretching out from both sides of the gates was an iron fence about seven feet tall. Each fence post was topped by a fleur-de-lis, the center of which looked wickedly sharp and forbidding. The decoration did little to hide the reality that the fence was meant to keep unwanted visitors—like the press—out. The limo drove through, and Nadia shivered at the suspicion that the fence worked just as well at keeping guests *in*.

Nadia couldn't see the facility itself from the entrance. The driveway curved shortly past the gates, and a wall of trees that ran parallel to the fence blocked everything beyond from view. No reporter with a zoom lens would intrude on the privacy of those who took refuge behind this retreat's walls.

Nadia swallowed a lump of dread that formed in her throat when she looked over her shoulder and saw the gates closing behind her.

"One week," she murmured to herself under her breath. "Two at most."

The reminder would have been more comforting if Nadia could actually *believe* it. Her parents might think of her stay here as something harmless and temporary, but when Chairman Hayes found out, Nadia was sure he would do his utmost to ensure that the retreat served as a permanent solution to his problem. After all, what damage could Nadia do to him when she was to all intents and purposes imprisoned, allowed no contact with the outside world?

The grounds the limo wended its way through were lovely, as advertised. Flowerbeds bursting with out-of-season blooms lined the driveway and surrounded white gravel walking paths. In the relatively short drive from the gate to the front drive, Nadia saw no fewer than three pristine white gazebos and two artfully placed ponds, one with water lilies, one without. No doubt the decorative gardens and paths continued all the way around the building.

Tranquility's main building was a modern reinterpretation of a classic Gothic mansion. It had all the turrets, peaks, and gables associated with the Gothic style, but they were fashioned of steel and glass rather than stone and wood. The effect might have been cold and sterile, if it weren't for the profusion of flowers growing on trellises and in window boxes. In her present state of mind, Nadia couldn't quite persuade herself to think of the place as inviting, but it was at least making an effort.

As the limo pulled up to the curb at the front entrance, a woman in khaki trousers and a powder-blue shirt adorned with the Tranquility logo exited the building and descended the short set of stone steps, smiling brightly in Nadia's general direction, though of course she couldn't see through the tinted windows.

"Here we are, Miss," the driver said unnecessarily as he put the limo in park. No doubt he was preparing to get out and open Nadia's door for her, but the woman beat him to it.

"Thank you," Nadia said to the driver, feeling awkward. Ordinarily, she would tip him after such a long drive, but her mother had insisted she couldn't bring a purse. He touched the brim of his hat and nodded.

"You must be Nadia," the woman said, her smile so wide and bright it made Nadia's cheeks ache in sympathy. "My name is Marigold, but you can call me Mari. Welcome to Tranquility!"

"Um, thanks," Nadia said, for lack of a better response. She wanted to yell at her driver to hit the accelerator and get her out of here, but that wasn't an option, so she reluctantly climbed out of the car.

"You're going to have a wonderful time here," Mari gushed, taking Nadia's arm and steering her up the steps.

Nadia sincerely doubted that, and she couldn't help casting a longing glance over her shoulder as the limo drove away.

She was now officially stuck here until her parents chose to send for her.

If Mari noticed Nadia's melancholy, she chose to ignore it. "Let's get you checked in, and then I'll show you around and help you get oriented."

Mari led Nadia to an elegant locker room, decorated with brass and marble and more of the ubiquitous flowers. Several of the lockers had electronic key cards sticking out of them, and Mari opened one of those for Nadia, handing the card to her.

"You can change out of your street clothes here," Mari said cheerfully. She pointed into the locker. "You can choose a robe, or a pants and tunic combo, whichever you prefer. Everything's your size and super comfortable."

"You mean I'm not even allowed to wear my own clothes?" Nadia asked in dismay. She hadn't thought through exactly what it meant that she hadn't been allowed to bring luggage.

Mari's smile didn't dim. "The goal here at Tranquility is for our guests to leave the outside world behind entirely. You don't have to dress to impress here. You just have to be comfortable."

Nadia crossed her arms over her chest. She'd hardly call her casual pants and knit top "dressing to impress," although, of course, they were of the highest quality and custom-made by a top designer. "I'm perfectly comfortable dressed the way I am."

She'd kind of hoped her obstinacy would crack Mari's maniacally cheerful demeanor, but it didn't. "Trust me, your spa wardrobe will be even more comfortable. Once you put it on, you'll never want to take it off."

In the past, Nadia had always been dutiful and obedient, as befitted an Executive girl. A girl in her position, slated to marry the Chairman Heir while still not old enough to make a legally binding agreement, couldn't afford to set a foot wrong, and she'd had that drilled into her head for as long as she could remember. Not that long ago, she would have done as she was told without protest, but she was tired of doing what she was told. Being dutiful and obedient hadn't stopped her from being embroiled in this awful mess.

"I prefer to wear my own clothes," she said, putting all the stubbornness in her core into the words.

For the first time, Mari's smile faltered just a little. Her facial expression didn't change much, but her eyes were somehow a shade less warm.

"You will not be allowed into the facilities in street clothes," Mari explained patiently. "Proper attire is required if you want to use the pool, the spa, the gym, or any of our dining facilities. You'll miss out on all the features that make a stay at Tranquility relaxing and enjoyable."

Nadia couldn't care less about the recreational opportunities she might be missing out on. However . . . "Are you telling me I can't get any food if I'm wearing my own clothes?"

"You will not be permitted into the dining hall or into the cafes if you aren't properly dressed, and I'm afraid we don't provide room service." A sharp edge had entered her voice, and Nadia knew she was well on her way to making an enemy.

Giving in was harder than she'd thought it would be, but in the end, Nadia knew she had no choice. If her stay here were only going to be a day or two, she might have gone hungry just on principle, but she couldn't hold out for a week. She refused to contemplate the possibility that it might be longer.

"Fine," she said with a frustrated huff. "I'll change clothes."

"A good choice," Mari commented smugly. "I'll wait outside while you change. You can put your street clothes in the locker for the duration of your stay. Let me know when you're ready and I'll give you the tour, then show you to your room."

Nadia couldn't manage a gracious response, so she settled for saying nothing.

nadia drew the line at changing into Tranquility underwear. She donned the powder-blue tunic and pants, which, as promised, fit her perfectly. Fearing Mari might check and notice that the undies were still in the locker in their sterile plastic packaging, Nadia unwrapped them and stuck them in the generous pocket of her pants. The bra made an odd-looking lump, but she hoped the tunic would hide it sufficiently.

Closing the locker, Nadia rested her forehead against the cool metal, trying to compose herself before she had to face the smiling demon again. There was a part of her that couldn't believe this was really happening to her. She'd always believed that Executives who were forced to hide away in retreats had brought it on themselves, had scorned them for their lack of self-control or social skills. She'd suffered from the quaint delusion that at least some part of her future was under her control. Now she knew how wrong she had been. About everything.

Fighting off her sense of impending doom, Nadia let Mari know she was ready, and they began their tour.

If Nadia had checked herself into the place voluntarily, she might have found the Tranquility Retreat appealing. The grounds truly were beautiful, and the array of spa services available was almost dizzying. She could spend all day every day being shamelessly pampered, without a duty in the world.

She could take a dip in the heated pool, steam her pores in the sauna, take yoga and aerobics classes, or just sit around doing nothing. She could eat in the grand dining hall, or at one of a handful of smaller outdoor cafes with lovely views and impressive menus. There were movies every night— shown from disc, naturally, rather than streamed from the net—and an impressive library brimming with books. But whereas many of the guests at Tranquility probably enjoyed being completely cut off from the outside world, Nadia already felt like she was suffocating.

The main building housed the administrative offices, the guest rooms, the library, and the dining hall. Another building about fifty yards away housed the spa and the entertainment center. There were two other buildings that Nadia could see as Mari dragged her along for what felt like an endless tour. Those buildings were much more utilitarian in form, plain rectangles with regularly spaced windows and only a few embellishments here and there. They were also a considerable distance away, and Mari ignored them as if they didn't exist. Nadia suspected those were the psych and rehab facilities, where the "guests" were literally prisoners, unable to leave of their own free will.

"What are those buildings?" Nadia asked as Mari led her back to the main building at the end of the tour. Although she'd already guessed for herself, she was curious what Mari would say.

Mari kept smiling away, nauseatingly chipper. "Those are for our guests who require extra care," she said breezily. "Everything you need will be in the main building or the spa, so the extra-care facilities aren't included in the tour."

"Could I go there if I wanted to?"

Mari looked at her as if she might be going nuts. "You could go to the lobby during visiting hours, if you wanted to, but there's nothing of particular interest to see. Unless you know someone who is staying there?"

Nadia shook her head. The only person Nadia knew who'd spent any time in a retreat was Nate's mother, and she barely remembered the woman. Nadia had been only six when Eleanor Hayes had entered an upstate retreat as a permanent resident. The Chairman Spouse had not been seen in public since, nor had she communicated in any way with Nate—or anyone else in the outside world that Nadia knew of.

"Speaking of visiting hours," Mari continued, "they are Wednesdays from five P.M. to eight P.M., and Sundays from noon to three. You'll be eligible for visitors after you've been with us for five nights, although we encourage friends and family to give our guests at least two weeks of complete peace before visiting."

Mari beamed, as if the idea of being completely cut off from friends and family for two weeks were her idea of pure bliss. It took everything Nadia had to keep the barrage of scathing remarks that came to her mind from spilling out of her mouth.

CHAPTER TWO

nate awakened from a deep, exhausted sleep to a bedroom that was still dark. The first hints of feeble light peeked around the edges of his curtains, but Nate wasn't an early riser under the best of circumstances, and after the day he'd had yesterday, he was sure he could sleep for a week. He groaned and let his eyes blink shut for a moment before his sleep-fogged mind remembered that *something* had woken him up. A change of pressure, and the soft squeak of mattress springs.

Nate was lying facedown on top of the covers, having fallen into bed last night without even bothering to get undressed. The aftermath of Nadia's arrest and their subsequent standoff with his father was draining the life out of him, and he fantasized about banning all reporters from the planet. They'd been after him all his life, but they were positively *hounding* him now. His neck was stiff as hell from lying in one position too long, but he slowly and painfully cranked it around to the other side.

Without the light on, Nate could only see a shadowy form sitting on the bed beside him, but something deeper than his conscious mind knew exactly who it was, as impossible as it might be.

"Kurt?" he asked in a hoarse croak, blinking a few times to try to force his boyfriend's features to come clear.

Kurt reached out and brushed away a lock of hair that was

plastered to the side of Nate's face, a gentle, familiar touch that immediately made Nate's heart—and other parts of him—ache with longing.

"You look like shit," Kurt said with a shake of his now-bald head. "Your new valet allowed you to go to bed with your clothes on?"

Nate let out a soft snort. The idea that a valet could "let" the Chairman Heir do anything was laughable, though he had to admit, if Kurt had still held the position, he would have undressed Nate by force, if necessary. He was the bossiest valet Nate had ever met. And he was irreplaceable.

"I didn't hire a new valet," Nate admitted. He sat up slowly, wincing from the lingering effects of the beating he'd taken a few days ago. A beating that Kurt had ordered, though he'd paradoxically done it in an attempt to protect Nate. "What are you doing here? And how did you get in? Please tell me nobody saw you."

The deal Nadia had negotiated with the Chairman had included complete amnesty for Kurt, but Nate didn't trust it. When Kurt had been accused of murdering the original Nate Hayes, Nate—who, though he was a Replica, had all the knowledge and memories and feelings of his original—had made it dangerously clear to his father how much Kurt meant to him. If the Chairman could find a way to hurt Nate through Kurt, he'd do it in a heartbeat. The old man was a vindictive son of a bitch, and he wouldn't forgive Nate and Nadia for having won their battle of wills.

"How did I get in?" Kurt asked with an exasperated expression Nate could make out even in the darkness. "Do you really have to ask me that?"

Before he'd become Nate's valet, Kurt had been a Basement-dweller. Basement-dwellers learned thievery, breaking and entering, and drug dealing when respectable citizens were learning reading and arithmetic. Breaking and entering when he already had a key to Nate's apartment and knew exactly where guards and security cameras were located probably hadn't been much of a challenge. Not to mention that the two of them had made a habit of sneaking in and out together for forbidden jaunts to the Basement.

"All right, skip that. Tell me why you're here."

Enough light from the rising sun filtered through the curtains that Nate could now see Kurt's face more clearly, could see the little smile that curved his lips.

"Well, first of all, for this," Kurt said, then put his hand behind Nate's neck and pulled him in for a kiss.

Nate made a little sound of protest. His mouth had to taste disgusting right now, and he and Kurt had about a thousand unresolved issues between them. But Kurt didn't seem to mind the taste of his mouth, nor did he seem to care much about the issues. With anyone but Kurt, Nate was too much of a take-charge kind of guy to give in on even the most trivial matter, at least not without a fight. But giving in to Kurt had always been frighteningly easy, and he did so now, abandoning his commonsense objections and losing himself in the moment. Kurt was the best kisser Nate had ever known, though there were other things he was equally good at.

The kiss ended way too soon, and the possibility of progressing to "other things" faded away. Kurt kept his hand on Nate's neck, kneading the tight muscles there as he stayed intimately close.

"You gotta know that you came first," Kurt said, looking intensely into Nate's eyes. "I was already with you when the resistance asked me to take advantage of it."

So much for ignoring the issues that lay between them.

Nate's chest hurt, and he dropped Kurt's gaze, hardly able to swallow the truth that he had learned: Kurt—his valet, his friend, and his lover—had spied on him for some shadowy resistance movement Nate hadn't even known existed.

"How can you expect me to believe that?" Nate asked, his hands clenching into fists in his lap. "You've obviously lied before."

"You think I could have guessed where things would lead when I hooked up with you at Angel's? I thought you were just some uptight Exec kid looking for a good time. No way I expected us to hit it off and that you'd actually *hire* me."

Nate was glad for the semidarkness, which might help hide the redness of his cheeks. Theirs had not been what you'd call a storybook romance, and he wasn't exactly proud of how it had begun. There was a time not that long ago when he'd treated the Basement—or Debasement, as its residents called it—as his own personal playground, taking advantage of the unfortunates who lived and worked there without really thinking about what their lives must be like. He'd never been cruel or unfair to any of them—at least, not that he knew of—but his well-meaning ignorance was a source of shame anyway. How could Kurt possibly have loved the privileged, self-centered bastard he had been before the rude awakening of his death?

"So you weren't a member of the resistance when we met?"

Kurt looked away briefly before answering, and Nate braced himself for a lie. But Kurt was a master of not doing what was expected.

"I was," he admitted. "But I wasn't active. What's a teenage whore going to do to help bring down a government?"

Nate flinched. "Don't call yourself that!" He had no illusions as to what Kurt's former profession had been, had known it from the moment he'd first laid eyes on him prowling the club, but that didn't mean he had to like it.

"What? A teenager?" Kurt grinned at him. "I suppose I could be as much as twenty, but I'm pretty sure it's more like eighteen."

Just another indication of how different life in the Basement was from the life Nate had always known. He couldn't imagine not knowing how old he was. "You know what I mean," Nate said with a tired sigh.

Kurt patted his thigh. "Yeah. But I'm not ashamed of it, like you are."

"Kurt—"

Kurt silenced him with a brief kiss. "It's all right, Nate. I get it. Really, I do. But I stopped being a whore the day you hired me. And I came to your bed because I *wanted* to, not because it was part of a job. I love you, you idiot."

Even in the midst of his turmoil, Nate couldn't help laughing. "You're such a charmer."

"You want charm, marry Nadia. Oh, wait. You will. My bad."

His words drained every drop of humor from Nate's body. The fact that Kurt might have been using him all along had certainly bothered Nate, but it was a sin he was prepared to forgive, knowing that however things might have started, Kurt's affection for him in the end had to be at least somewhat genuine. Other things he had done were far harder to forgive.

"Dante put a tracker on Nadia, and you *knew*," Nate said, shaking his head in disbelief. "You set her up so your resistance buddies could *kill* her." He wanted Kurt to deny having known, wanted it all to have been Dante's idea, but he knew in his heart that wasn't the case.

Kurt reached for him, and Nate slapped his hand away. He might never be able to love Nadia the way she deserved, but she'd been his friend long before Kurt had come into his life, and the idea that Kurt had been willing to sacrifice her like that . . .

Kurt didn't even have the grace to look particularly guilty. "From what I understand, having that tracker on her probably saved her life."

"That doesn't make it right! But then, you knew that, or you wouldn't have gone behind my back."

Kurt's gray eyes narrowed, and his voice took on a sharp edge. "Uh-huh, couldn't possibly be 'cause you would have pitched a fit if you knew. You'd never do a thing like that, right?"

Kurt's words hurt more than the fading bruises. Both Kurt and Nadia had kept secrets from him. Big ones. And both for the same reason: they didn't trust him. They thought of him as some impulsive, out-of-control child who'd fly off the handle and act without thinking. And the worst part about it, the part that hurt most, was that they'd been right.

"We couldn't let her be interrogated," Kurt said a little more gently. "She knew enough to bring down the entire resistance if she talked, and Mosely has . . . *had* . . . a way of making people talk. Besides, we thought that if she got caught, she was going to die anyway. We *all* thought that, even you."

Nate closed his eyes, as if that could block out the memory. He had tried everything he could think of to stop Nadia from putting herself in danger. Respecting her decision had been one of the hardest things he'd ever done, and when he'd gotten the frantic call from Dante, telling him she'd been arrested . . .

"You could at least have told *her* about the tracker." He opened his eyes to glare at Kurt.

Kurt shrugged. "Who knew how she would react under pressure? I thought knowing about the tracker might freak her out, so I told Dante to keep his mouth shut."

Kurt had no idea what Nadia was really made of. If he'd seen her standing up to the Chairman and to Mosely under threat of death and torture . . .

"You don't know her at all," Nate said, shaking his head at Kurt. Not that he was surprised. Kurt and Nadia had never liked one another. Kurt saw Nadia as a stuck-up aristocrat, and Nadia saw Kurt as a bad influence. But Nadia had the insight to see past her dislike, which apparently Kurt didn't. "She never once doubted you. Even after you had your friends beat the crap out of me and tell me you killed me, she was convinced you did it for a good reason." Kurt had been trying to chase Nate away for his own good, but Nate wasn't sure he could ever shake the memory of Angel jerking the locket off him and telling him Kurt never wanted to see him again.

"I'm not going to apologize for not trusting her," Kurt said stubbornly. "If that makes her a better person than me, then I'm okay with that."

Nate reminded himself that growing up in the Basement must have made it near impossible for Kurt to trust *anyone*. Despite his hard, sharp edges, Kurt was a good guy at heart, and that was an impressive accomplishment, considering his background.

"Her family sent her away to a retreat because of all the things she did to try to help you." Just thinking about it made Nate's blood pressure rise. How could her own family do that to her? She'd said in her phone message that it would only be for a week or two, but he'd heard the doubt in her voice.

"Yeah, I'm sure that's a real hardship."

Nate struggled against his urge to snap back. He was hardly surprised at Kurt's lack of sympathy. When your own life had included not knowing where your next meal was coming from and selling your body to make ends meet, being trapped in a luxurious spa where you were waited on hand and foot didn't sound so bad. Even so, Nate bet Kurt wouldn't like being imprisoned there much more than Nadia would, at least once the novelty wore off.

"So are you gonna stay pissed at me?" Kurt said. "Or are we gonna kiss and make up?"

"Can't I do both?"

Kurt laughed softly. "Are you too pissed to want this back?" He reached into a pocket inside the ratty jacket he wore and pulled out the locket.

Nate's heart squeezed in his chest. Angel had broken the chain when she'd yanked it off him, but Kurt had either repaired the damage or gotten a new one. Nate had worn that locket against his skin every day since Kurt had given it to him, and he'd missed its comforting weight since it had been taken from him. He held out his hand, and Kurt laid the locket in his palm.

"I'm sorry I hurt you," Kurt said, curling Nate's fingers around the locket.

"And I'm sorry I took you for granted," Nate responded, his throat almost too tight to let the words out.

They sat like that for a long moment, their eyes locked, their hands clasped around the locket. Nate yearned to kiss Kurt and drag him down onto the bed, but too many things still lay between them.

Nate slipped the locket on over his head, pressing the skin-warmed gold against his chest. Then he straightened up and met Kurt's eyes again, this time in a challenging stare.

"All right. Mushy time is over. Now tell me why you're *really* here."

Kurt rubbed a hand over his bald head. He'd shaved off his hair when he'd gone into hiding, and he looked older and more sinister without it. Nate hoped he'd let it grow back.

"I'm gonna guess that the news feeds have it all wrong about what happened," Kurt said. "Except for the part about Mosely being a murderer, that is. Thought you might be able to clear some things up."

"*You* thought that? Or your resistance buddies did?"

"Does it matter?"

Actually, it did. Nate was all for opposing Paxco's oppressive governmental practices, as long as that opposition was nonviolent. The problem was that Nate didn't know much about the resistance movement and what they were up to. He had high hopes that when he eventually became the Chairman, he'd be able to make Paxco into a better, more just state, but that would be a lot harder to achieve if the resistance staged some kind of coup in the meantime.

"Probably not," Nate said with what he hoped was a careless shrug. "I can't tell you much anyway. Nadia and I . . . actually, mostly Nadia . . . negotiated a deal with my father. In return for us keeping our mouths shut, he granted you full amnesty."

"He granted me amnesty for something he knows perfectly well I didn't do?" Kurt shook his head, and Nate couldn't blame him. "Your father is a tool, and a crooked one at that."

Kurt didn't know the half of it. "It's not legal amnesty," Nate clarified. "Legally, you were cleared of all charges. I mean he's promised not to come after you off the books."

Kurt frowned. "Why would he do that, anyway? I didn't do anything to him."

"He'd do it because I pissed him off and he knows how much it would hurt me if something happened to you."

Kurt pondered that a moment without comment. "Okay. So I'm free to show my face in public again."

"Yes."

"Do I still have a job?"

Nate ached to say yes. He missed having Kurt so close, missed the opportunities for stolen kisses and shared secrets. But no matter what his father had promised, Nate's gut told him Kurt would present too tempting a target.

"I'm sorry," Nate said, "but no. I don't trust my father, and it's not safe for you here."

A muscle ticked in Kurt's jaw, and there was a hint of hurt in his eyes. "You mean you don't want me here now that you know the truth about me. At least have the balls to say it."

Nate jerked back in surprise. Kurt's involvement with the resistance had nothing to do with it. Nate was near the top of the Executive establishment the resistance wished to topple, but he refused to think of Kurt as any kind of enemy. Hell, he wasn't even sure he disagreed with Kurt's cause, though he suspected he was in a better position to effect eventual change than the resistance ever would be.

"That's not why you can't stay here," Nate said, his voice rising only because Kurt's had. "My father knows about us." Kurt's eyes widened with shock. "Knows, and doesn't care as long as we're discreet. But he also knows how much you mean to me. He can't afford to do anything to *me*." Not when he hadn't had the foresight to follow the old British adage of producing an heir and a "spare." "But I can't tell you how ugly it got between us. He never really loved me, but now he *hates* me." And it was a damn good thing Nadia had forced the Chairman to destroy Thea. Otherwise, he'd have killed Nate again and animated a new Replica, one who knew none of his secrets and would continue his career as a spoiled play-boy without ever getting in the way. "Having you close to me is too risky."

Kurt's face said he wasn't entirely convinced by Nate's argument, but he let the issue drop. "So what exactly *did* happen when Nadia was arrested? How did you and Nadia get the Chairman to agree to anything?"

"I told you: we agreed not to talk."

"That's bullshit. If you and Nadia throwing around wild murder accusations had a chance in hell of making him back down, you'd have been singing to the skies an hour after I told you what happened on the night of your murder."

Nate shuddered, his mind still having trouble dealing with the reality that his father had been present and had ordered Mosely to kill him. It was one thing to believe your father hated you, another to *know* it.

"I said we agreed not to talk. I didn't say what we agreed not to talk about, and it's not the murder." His long habit of trusting Kurt made Nate want to blurt out the whole truth, but this particular truth was like an infectious disease. Nate didn't like the idea that he was helping his father cover up his crimes, but there was enough unrest in Paxco already. He wanted his father out of power, but not at the cost of starting a civil war.

"Well, what then?" Kurt prompted.

"I'm sticking to the agreement and not talking." Nate's

stomach twisted uncomfortably. *At least I'm not lying about it,* he tried telling himself, but that didn't make the secret sit any better.

Kurt stared at him with a combination of anger and suspicion in his eyes. "And that has nothing to do with the fact that I'm a member of the resistance."

Nate wanted to blurt out a quick denial, but Kurt deserved more honesty than that, so he sighed and rubbed his eyes. "I don't know," he admitted. "I don't know if I'd tell you if I knew for sure it wouldn't go any further. I'd sure as hell think about it long and hard before I decided. I wish *I* didn't know."

He thought Kurt would get angry over his refusal to talk, but Kurt surprised him by patting his thigh.

"I'll leave it alone," he promised. "For now, at least. I can't throw stones about keeping secrets. And I need to get out of here before people start waking up, anyway. Unless you've changed your mind about the job."

Nate shook his head, sure he was making the right decision about that, at least. "You've already gone through hell because of me. I won't let that happen again." He wished he were more certain that was a promise he could keep. "Where will you go?"

Kurt shrugged. "Back to Debasement, I guess. Where else?"

It was the obvious answer, but it was one Nate refused to accept. "You are *not* going back to the Basement." The Basement might be Kurt's natural habitat, and he'd managed to take care of himself there for years before Nate had met him, but there was no such thing as safety there. "I might not be able to give you a job, but I can give you money."

Nate was prepared for Kurt to put up the obligatory argument—no Executive or Employee would accept charity without protest. Apparently, Basement-dwellers had no such social convention.

"Money would be good," Kurt said easily. "Dollars would be best, if you're trying to keep your father from finding out. Scrip can be traced to you."

"I'll see what I can do," Nate said drily, rolling stiffly out of bed. "Someone stole all of my dollars not so long ago."

Kurt laughed. "I'd tell you I'd pay you back, but, you know . . ."

Nate wasn't awake enough to think of a good comeback, so instead he trudged out of the room to collect the few dollars he had left to give to Kurt.

"How can I contact you?" he asked when he returned and handed the money over.

Kurt stuffed the bills into his pocket. "If you want to keep me off Daddy's radar, you don't. It's too easy for a guy like him to tap phones."

Nate fought a spike of panic, hating the thought that he wouldn't know where Kurt was and wouldn't be able to contact him. "But I *will* see you again, won't I?" He sounded needy and pathetic, but he couldn't help it.

Kurt gave him a crooked smile and stroked the side of his face. "'Course you will. And I'll see if I can get you a black market phone your dad won't be able to tap."

Grateful beyond words, Nate hugged him tight.

nate supposed there were people he was less eager to sit down and have a private chat with than Robert Dante, but off the top of his head, he couldn't think of one. Dante was a resistance spy who had infiltrated the Paxco security department. He'd then been sent by Mosely to spy on Nadia, pretending to be her father's personal assistant/general servant, so he was a spy times two. As if that weren't bad enough, the asshole was way too familiar with Nadia, and had planted the tracker on her, marking her for death. Somehow, it was a lot easier to forgive Kurt for that than it was to forgive Dante.

However, much as he hated to admit it, Nate needed Dante, or at least his contacts, right now. The tricky part was arranging a meeting without an audience. After Kurt's comment about bugged phones, Nate knew better than to call. But if he showed up at the Lake Towers asking to speak to Dante, he would draw way too much attention to both of them— there was absolutely no legitimate reason why the Chairman Heir would need to talk to a servant in the Lake family's household—so he had to get creative.

Which was how he found himself in the foyer of the Lakes' apartment, making a scene that was drawing the attention of every person in the household.

"Nadia doesn't deserve this!" he bellowed in Esmeralda's face, sure his own face was flushed red with anger. He'd been pissed off at Nadia's mother from the moment he'd received Nadia's message yesterday. An Executive who gave a crap about etiquette would never have stormed in here like this, but as Chairman Heir, he could get away with it.

Esmeralda's face had gone pale the moment he'd started yelling at her, but he wasn't sure whether it was from distress or fury. He'd always been polite to her in the past, and she was always painfully proper. She appeared to be at a loss for how to handle his outburst.

"Bring her home, Esmeralda!" he demanded at the same ear-splitting volume, watching out of the corner of his eye as the peanut gallery of servants continued to grow in size. If he were anyone else, she probably would have had him tossed out by now, but she didn't dare antagonize the Chairman Heir.

"The press—" she started weakly.

"I don't give a damn about the press!"

Finally, Nate caught a glimpse of Dante joining the crowd of observers. He wasn't entirely sure how he was going to draw Dante closer, but it turned out he didn't have to, because Dante waded right in, his fierce scowl saying he was more than happy to volunteer to throw Nate out. He was supposedly just a household servant, not a bodyguard, but he was imposing as hell.

"May I be of any assistance, Mrs. Lake?" he asked, still glaring at Nate while he parked himself between the two as if to shield Esmeralda with his body.

Nice of the arrogant prick to present Nate with just the opening he needed. "This is none of your business," Nate snapped at him while carefully palming the little slip of paper he'd tucked into his pants pocket. The paper that told Dante to meet him in the garage of Nate's building at 1:00 A.M.

"Perhaps you'd like to take a moment to compose yourself, Mr. Hayes," Dante said, before a sputtering Esmeralda could get a word in.

It was the first time in Nate's memory Dante had ever addressed him properly, and it almost startled Nate into losing his head of steam. The asshole usually liked to call him by first name just to get under Nate's skin. He recovered quickly.

"I don't take orders from *servants*," Nate said with a sneer. "Mind your manners or I'll have you fired."

There was a spark of anger in Dante's eyes. He didn't know Nate well enough to realize how out of character the threat was. Nate had never been half as class-conscious as someone of his rank was expected to be, but now was not the time to clarify.

"It's all right, Dante," Esmeralda said. She was holding on

to her composure by a thread, and a hint of unease had found its way into her voice. She was far too politically savvy to risk offending the Chairman Heir, but Nate knew it cost her to keep from telling him off. "I'm sure I'm not in need of protection."

Dante didn't respond, staying stubbornly between Esmeralda and Nate, doing a fine impression of an intimidating bruiser. Mentally crossing his fingers, Nate reached out and grabbed Dante's collar, yanking him forward until he could growl in his face.

"You are being insubordinate," he said as he shoved the little piece of paper under Dante's collar. The servant's livery had no convenient pockets Nate could slip the note into, but he hoped the neatly tucked-in shirt would keep the note in place until Dante had a chance to retrieve it.

They were practically nose to nose, so Nate could see by the slight widening of his eyes that Dante had felt the brush of the paper against his skin. Nate could only hope no one else had noticed.

Nate gave Dante a shove away from him. It didn't exactly break his heart to give Dante a hard time—it had been Dante who had once inspired Nate to throw the first punch of his adult life—and the shove was just barely short of hard enough to knock Dante down. Face red with anger, jaws clenched, Dante fussed with his starched collar, trying to make it lie flat after Nate had rumpled it.

"That will be all, Dante," Esmeralda said sharply.

Still plucking at his wrinkled shirt, Dante made a short bow and left with what Nate thought was exaggerated dignity.

nate leaned against the hood of his car—the car he almost never got to drive, because the Chairman Heir was supposed to travel by limo and leave such plebeian pursuits as driving to the lower classes—trying not to check his watch every thirty seconds. He'd been quite clear in his terse note to Dante, and he was *sure* Dante had felt it slipping under his collar. Of course, just because the bastard got the message didn't mean he would show up. He probably felt like Nate was ordering him around, demanding a meeting when he could have politely asked. Too bad Nate hadn't thought of that *before* writing his little summons.

At 1:35, just as Nate was deciding it was time to give up, the door to the stairwell finally opened and Dante stepped out. Nate was used to seeing him in servant's livery; the only time he'd seen him in anything else was when they'd rendezvoused with Kurt in the Basement, at which time Dante had been disguised as a Basement-dweller. Tonight, he was wearing battered blue jeans and a faded shirt, and for the first time he actually looked comfortable in his clothes. His muscular build had always looked odd for a house servant, and when he'd dressed for the Basement, he'd looked very much like a man in disguise. Nate had no idea what Dante's background was, but the choice of clothes suggested that he was from a lower-class Employee family. He might have built up all those fancy muscles of his doing manual labor.

"You're lucky I'm still here," Nate said, though being antagonistic when he was about to ask for help probably wasn't wise. He should have known Dante would be unruffled.

"And you're lucky I'm here at all. That was quite a scene you caused. Thanks for almost costing me my job."

No, Nate and Dante were never going to be the best of friends. Nate wasn't about to apologize, not when he'd put time and consideration into how to get a message to Dante *without* costing him either one of his jobs.

"Maybe if I were a professional spy like you, I'd have been able to find another way to get you a message," he said. "I figured you might not like it if I called you on the phone or showed up at the Lake Towers and asked to speak to you."

"Very thoughtful of you. Now what is so urgent that you had to make a total ass of yourself to set up a meeting?"

How did Dante manage to pass as a servant in an Executive household when he had such an enormous chip on his shoulder? It had to take some serious acting skills to act subservient to a family of top Executives when he held Executives in such contempt. Nate wondered if he was being overly optimistic in hoping that Dante would be interested in helping Nadia. After all, *she* was a top Executive. Maybe he should be hoping to get help from Kurt instead. But he didn't know how to contact Kurt, and he couldn't afford to wait until Kurt contacted him again. If he wanted to help Nadia, Dante was his best chance.

"Nadia's in danger," Nate said, watching Dante's face carefully for a reaction, which, naturally, Dante didn't give him.

"Mosely's dead. She's been cleared of all charges. And as far as I know, she's no threat to the resistance. So what's the problem?"

Nate swallowed hard at the reminder that the resistance had been willing to kill Nadia to keep her from blowing Dante's cover. These were dangerous people, and they weren't exactly concerned with Nadia's best interests. Dante seemed to like Nadia, but liking someone and being willing to stick your neck out to help them were two different things.

"I can't tell you," Nate said, because if he wasn't going to trust Kurt with the full truth, then he sure as hell wasn't going to trust Dante. "You're just going to have to take my word for it. She's in danger, and that bitch mother of hers has her locked up in a retreat where she's cut off from the outside world and completely helpless."

Dante blinked a couple of times and shook his head. "You want me to take your word for it? You're not actually under the impression that I trust you, are you? Teaming up against a mutual enemy doesn't make us friends."

Nate laughed tightly. "When did I give you the impression I thought we were friends? If I weren't worried you'd finger—" Nate stopped himself from using Kurt's first name just in time. Even someone as casual as he was didn't refer to servants by first name, and doing so would betray an inappropriate level of intimacy. Nate covered his almost-slip with a cough before continuing. "—Bishop during questioning, I'd have turned you in by now."

It wasn't actually true. Nate didn't like Dante and didn't trust his resistance, but there was no way in hell he would turn anyone he knew over for treason. Dirk Mosely might be dead, but Nate had no doubt that whomever the Chairman hired to replace him would be just as brutal and just as morally bankrupt. If Dante were arrested for treason, he'd be tortured until he gave up every resistance contact he knew, and then he'd be executed. Nate had enough black marks on his conscience already without adding one more.

"*This* is how you're planning to persuade me to help you?" Dante asked. "Your technique could use some work. But I suppose you're used to *ordering* people to help you and this whole asking thing is a new experience."

The remark bit a little deeper than Nate would have liked. "You're right," Nate said, and he could see that his words startled Dante. "I suck at asking for help. I don't like you, and you don't like me, and none of that matters. Nadia's in trouble, and we both played a part in getting her there. I'm going to do everything in my power to help her, and I'm hoping you have enough of a conscience to want to help, too. If that's too much to ask for, then just say so and get out of my face."

Dante scowled and looked like he was seriously considering turning around and heading for the exit. Nate wondered if he should have been a little less honest and a little more . . . conciliatory. But it was too late to change his tone now, so he merely held his breath and waited.

Dante let out a frustrated grunt and shook his head. "What is it you want me to do, exactly?"

Nate allowed himself to breathe again. "I was hoping you have or could get a contact inside the Tranquility Retreat. Someone who could get a phone to Nadia. I need a way to contact her, a way to warn her if . . . something goes wrong."

Dante stared at him as if he was trying to read all of Nate's secrets in his face. Nate kept his expression as bland as he could and made no effort to avoid eye contact. Sure, he was hiding things, but he had a good reason, and he didn't feel guilty or apologetic about it. Ten to one Dante was hiding secrets of his own.

"I'm pretty sure I can get a phone to her," Dante said after a long, silent standoff. "But you need to tell me what's going on. What really happened when Nadia was arrested? How did she end up free and Mosely end up dead?"

"I can't tell you that."

"Then I can't help you."

Nate had hurt his own hand far more than he'd hurt Dante's face when he'd punched him, but the memory did nothing to quell his desire to do it again. "You'd abandon Nadia to the wolves because there's nothing in it for you? You'll make a great spokesman for freedom and democracy, or whatever it is your resistance is hoping for."

"I don't personally know anyone at Tranquility," Dante said patiently. "I'm sure the resistance leadership has someone there, what with all those Executives feeling relaxed and talkative out of the public eye, but they're not going to help Nadia out of the goodness of their hearts. And believe me, they're already far from happy about me having revealed our existence to the two of you. They won't be looking to do you any favors. Unless doing you favors turns out to be beneficial to them. Like, for instance, if you give me some good inside information in return."

Nate hated to admit it, but it made sense. Still, there was no way he was telling Dante and the rest of the resistance what he and Nadia had learned. It sure as hell wasn't because he was protecting his father, but if news about Thea and the Basement experimentation program got out, there would be rioting at the very least, and very possibly a civil war. The government of Paxco needed an overhaul, big time, but that wasn't the way to go about it. Still, there were plenty of things Nate knew that the resistance didn't. There was a reason they'd planted a spy in his household, after all.

Nate wished the resistance weren't so damn shadowy so he could know more about them—like who was in charge. Kurt seemed to think they were the good guys, and Nate trusted Kurt . . . But Kurt, like Dante, was just a foot soldier, and if the leaders of the resistance were preparing for some bloody coup, he wouldn't necessarily know about it. And helping them in any way would be a bad idea. Not that that would stop him if it was the only way he could help Nadia.

"I can't tell you what happened when Nadia was arrested," he said, "but I do have information I'm sure your leaders would want. Give me proof that you've gotten a phone to Nadia, and I'll make it worth your while. *Their* while."

"You're the Chairman Heir," Dante said, regarding him suspiciously. "You're really going to inform on the government you're going to inherit someday?"

Nate searched inside of himself for moral qualms. This was out-and-out treason he was talking about. Surely it should bother him, at least a little bit. But how could he possibly feel bad about betraying his father when the man had had the original Nate Hayes killed? "You have no idea how much I hate my father right now. Anything I can do to make his life difficult is all right by me. If I thought your resistance would have me, I'd sign up in a heartbeat."

Gee, he was just full of exaggerations today. He'd never been the most cautious person in the world, but that didn't mean he was about to run out and join a resistance movement he knew so little about. But at least it sounded good, and Dante seemed satisfied with the response.

"All right," he said. "I'll see what I can do. But you'd better have something good for me."

Or what? Nate wanted to ask, but for once he managed to keep the smart-ass comment to himself. He knew exactly what inside information he would give Dante if he succeeded in getting a phone to Nadia. Since Nadia had strong-armed his father into destroying Thea, there would be no more backup scans performed or Replicas made. Thanks to the exorbitant fees Paxco charged for the service that was available nowhere else in the world, the entire state was dependent on the income from the Replica technology. Eventually, the Chairman would have to go public with the news that the state's primary source of income had dried up forever, but he was going to put it off as long as he could. Nate had no clue what the resistance would do with the information once they had it, but he was damn sure they would want it. And if his conscience woke up and gave him a hard time, Nate could console himself that the information would have gone public eventually anyway.

"Work fast," Nate said out loud. "Please," he amended when he saw Dante's annoyance at what had come out sounding like an order. "You have no idea what she's had to endure already, and she doesn't deserve any of this."

"She's the only Executive I've met who I've actually liked," Dante said. "I don't want her to get hurt any more than you do."

Nate swallowed a caustic remark, wondering if all this restraint was going to give him an ulcer. He might not have a romantic interest in Nadia, but he'd been unofficially engaged to her since he was six, and she had always been his best friend. There was no way Dante, who had known her for about a week, was even half as committed to her safety as Nate was.

"Don't contact me again," Dante continued. "You probably got away with the stunt this afternoon, but I wouldn't count on getting away with it again."

"If I can't contact you, then how am I supposed to know when Nadia has the phone? Or to tell you state secrets?"

"Let me take care of that. I'm a professional."

Nate couldn't hold back a soft snort. Dante might be a professional spy, but he was no older than Nate, and if he had a year's worth of experience at the job, Nate would be shocked.

Dante made a face. "I don't know what the hell Bishop sees in you," he muttered.

Nate tried not to squirm or otherwise look uncomfortable. There was no reason to assume from that comment that Dante knew more than he should about Nate's relationship with Kurt. He could easily have said the same thing under the assumption that they were just friends. If Dante knew about them, then Nate would expect him to have played the blackmail card by now. But it wouldn't be good to have him *suspect* it, either, even if he didn't know.

Dante paused a beat, likely waiting for a comeback, but Nate didn't have one.

CHAPTER THREE

FOUR days at the Tranquility Retreat, and Nadia was climbing the walls. There were numerous ways she could occupy her time, but seriously, how many spa treatments could one person have? And Nadia considered playing bingo to be a form of slow torture, despite the retreat's great fondness for the game. She wondered if the men's retreats—of which there were considerably fewer—were equally boring.

The majority of the inmates were matronly women whose children were grown and who didn't feel like they had a place in Executive society anymore. There were a few younger women suffering from some social disgrace or other, but there was no one even close to Nadia's age. It wasn't unheard of for teens to spend time in retreats, but it wasn't all that common, either. Not that Nadia related that well to girls her age anyway, not having a great fondness for sycophants who were outwardly nice while secretly hating her for her exalted status.

She missed Nate. She missed Gerri. She missed her own clothes. She missed the city, and the freedom to go out when she wanted. She even missed her parents, angry though she was with them for sticking her here.

Every day, Nadia prayed that her mother would have a change of heart and would send for her. Not that she harbored any real hope of that. The soonest she was likely to get out was Friday, and the day couldn't come fast enough. If her mother tried to keep her here for more than a week, Nadia swore she would stage an escape attempt.

At home, Nadia rarely went to bed before midnight, but here at the retreat, boredom was driving her to her bed a little bit earlier each night. After yawning her way through some ridiculous card game that required absolutely no skill or attention at the recreation center, Nadia fled the bingo game that was forming and returned to her room in the main building. It was barely nine o'clock. Too early to go to bed, but she couldn't stomach any more "fun." At least she'd gathered a stack of books from the library. Reading the dullest book in the universe was more fun than playing bingo.

Nadia's room in the dormitory wing was pleasantly cozy. Or might have been, if it were more private and contained anything that actually belonged to her. Every time she set foot inside, she was painfully aware that someone had tidied up while she was gone, whether the room needed it or not. It was strangely disturbing to return to her room at night and find that someone had stacked the library books so that their bottom and left edges were all perfectly aligned, and that her bed had been smoothed out so you couldn't see that she'd sat on it when putting on her shoes. At home, she'd never found the idea of servants cleaning her room even mildly invasive, but it was different here.

On her first night, Nadia had rinsed her bra and underwear in the sink and let them dry over the shower bar overnight. They were still damp in the morning, so she'd tucked them into a drawer that contained her spa clothes to hide them. When she'd come back from breakfast, the undies were gone, replaced by a fresh set in the ubiquitous spa blue.

Nadia made it till almost ten before boredom got the best

of her and she heeded the siren call of her bed. She changed out of her tunic and pants, leaving them crumpled on the floor on the off chance it would annoy someone, and into the soft blue nightgown that had been left folded on her bed. She hated the feeling of being so firmly under control that she wore the clothes that were laid out for her like a little kid. She'd tried sleeping in her clothes one night, but couldn't drift off. Then she'd tried sleeping naked, but that hadn't worked, either. She felt too vulnerable.

She pulled back the covers and, to her shock, discovered a folded sheet of paper there. Nadia hurried to the door to make sure it was locked, because it would be just her luck if housekeeping was making another sweep at just this moment.

No longer feeling even remotely sleepy, Nadia grabbed the sheet of paper, eyes darting to the end to read the signature first. The note was from Dante, and he asked her to meet him at the fence at midnight. He'd drawn a rough map of the retreat and marked the spot where he wanted to meet, then told her to tear up his note and flush it.

Nadia read the note three times, looking for subtle nuances that would let her know what was happening. Had the recordings been found? Was Dante contacting her on Nate's behalf in a last-ditch effort to save her before she experienced some kind of unfortunate accident? Surely if he'd gone to the trouble of smuggling this note to her and driving out to Long Island at this time of night, it meant something bad had happened.

Checking the clock, willing midnight to hurry up and get here so she could end the suspense, Nadia changed out of her nightgown and back into her spa uniform once more.

• • •

nadia's pulse raced with nerves as she slunk through the dormitory halls. There was no curfew at the retreat, and she was free to wander the grounds at any time of night she wished. However, wandering around for a clandestine meeting with a friend from the outside was very much against the rules. If no one saw her leaving, then no one could ask her where she was going and what she was up to. She wasn't sure what the consequences of breaking the rules would be—it wasn't like the retreat staff could out-and-out punish one of their paying guests—but they surely had something in place to discourage such behavior, and she had no wish to find out what it was.

There were no formal retreat activities available after 10:00 P.M., so most of the guests were in their rooms, either in bed or preparing for bed, as Nadia hurried toward the fire stairs that were the exit closest to her room. She wasn't supposed to use them unless there was a fire, but there was no alarm, and the less time she spent in the hallway, the better. She winced at the sound the door made thunking closed, but no one came running to investigate.

Phase one of her nighttime escapade had been successfully completed, and Nadia felt a little calmer. The hardest part should be over. Moving as silently as possible in her spa moccasins, which really wanted to squeak with her every step, she made her way down the stairs until she reached the fire door at the bottom. There *was* an alarm on this door, but Nadia took advantage of a manual override and slipped out into the night.

The moment Nadia stepped outside, she realized she should have put on one of the sweaters the retreat had conveniently provided. It was late March, and the weather was usually temperate and comfortable during the day. Nighttime was a different story, and the spa uniform wasn't exactly toasty warm. Nadia shivered, but she wasn't about to press her luck by going back to get a sweater.

The walking paths around the retreat were all lighted, though only with small, dim bulbs discreetly marking the way. Nadia didn't like the idea that someone looking out a window might see her in that dim light, so she avoided the paths, trying not to trample the flowers as she wended her way toward the rendezvous point Dante had marked. Her sneaking around would probably make her more conspicuous if someone spotted her, but there was no one out and about at this time of night, at least not that she could see. Every once in a while, she glanced over her shoulder at the main building, checking the lighted windows to reassure herself that no one was looking out.

Eventually, she came to the wall of trees that hid the interior of the retreat from view. It also hid the fence from the view of the guests, but for Nadia out of sight had never been out of mind.

The rendezvous point Dante had marked on his makeshift map was, naturally, a long way from the lighted, guarded front entrance. The wall of trees Nadia had to fight her way through was not as carefully pruned and weeded here as it was at the entrance, and she wished she had a machete-wielding guide to help her through. But the weeds and underbrush provided extra assurance that no one from the retreat would witness her clandestine meeting.

Nadia moved slowly through the trees, trying not to betray her location. There was no reason to suspect there was some kind of trap waiting for her, but after all that had happened to her in the past weeks, she didn't think paranoia was at all unreasonable. She came to a dead stop as soon as she could see the fence through the trees, and she crouched down to examine her surroundings more closely while keeping under cover.

The line of trees ended about ten yards short of the fence, giving way to a strip of neatly mowed grass. Nadia feared she would be terribly exposed out there, but exposed to *whom* she didn't know. There were no guard posts, and no one patrolled the perimeter of the retreat. The place might feel like a prison to her, but it *wasn't* a prison. And there was nothing but woods on the other side of the fence, so there shouldn't be anyone on that side who could see her. She stared into those woods until her eyes hurt, trying to find Dante in the darkness, but he either wasn't there yet or was well hidden.

Taking a deep breath for courage, Nadia rose from her crouch and stepped cautiously onto the grass, ready to bolt at the first sign of trouble.

No sirens blared, no angry voices shouted at her to halt, and Nadia told herself there was such a thing as too much caution. She was going to give herself a heart attack if she didn't stop jumping at shadows.

"Dante?" she called out, not daring to do so very loudly.

"Here," Dante's voice answered from the shadowed trees on the other side of the fence. She moved toward the voice as a weedy bush rustled and Dante emerged from it.

Her desire to rush forward and throw her arms around Dante was almost embarrassing in its intensity, the sight of a familiar face bringing tears to her eyes. Of course, there was a seven-foot-tall iron fence between them, so throwing her arms around him might have been awkward.

Nadia hurried to the edge of the fence, grabbing the bars that separated her from him to keep from doing something inappropriate with her hands. She barely knew Dante, and she wasn't sure how much she trusted him, but she was ever so glad to see him, even if she worried that he came with bad news.

"Has something bad happened?" she asked without pre-amble, her voice coming out breathless as if she'd just run from the main building rather than walked.

Dante blinked in surprise. "Hello to you too. And no, nothing bad has happened."

Nadia let out a shaky sigh of relief, her knees suddenly feeling wobbly. "Then what are you doing here?" she asked. Too late, she realized how rude her question sounded, and she mentally snarled at herself to calm down and think before she spoke. "Sorry. I didn't mean that how it came out. I'm glad you're here. I'm just . . . surprised to see you." One thing she was sure of: he wasn't here for a social call. He'd gone to too much trouble to arrange this meeting for there not to be weighty reasons behind it.

"No worries," Dante said with a wry grin. "I don't take offense that easily."

Nadia raised an eyebrow at him and couldn't suppress a hint of a smile. "That so?" She'd managed to offend him pretty badly on more than one occasion. Of course, she'd been trying to browbeat him into revealing his true identity at the time, so one could argue she'd been working pretty hard at it.

Dante chose to ignore her teasing, looking her over from head to toe. "You look . . . different."

"You mean because I'm wearing a uniform and they won't even let me put on my own makeup here?" You could schedule a makeup application session at the spa, and many of the women did so every day, but the idea brought the stubborn out of her, and she decided to do without.

"I suppose," he said, frowning.

Nadia wondered if what he was really reacting to was the

stress and frustration that were eating away at her insides. She felt like someone had blindfolded her, shoved her into a minefield, and ordered her to walk. Every step could be her last, and she'd never see the danger coming. She shivered, hugging herself in a futile attempt to stay warm in the nippy air.

"You haven't answered my question," she said. "If nothing bad has happened, then why are you here?"

Dante reached into his pants pocket and pulled out a phone small enough that he could hide it in the palm of his hand if he wanted to. "Nate . . . Nathaniel . . . wanted you to have this." He passed the phone through the bars, and Nadia grabbed it as if it were a life preserver and she was drowning.

"OhmyGod!" she cried. "Thank you!"

The sense of relief that surged through her was out of proportion. Thanks to Nate's thoughtful gift, she was no longer wearing the blindfold, but the mines remained.

"What is going on with you two?" Dante asked, and he sounded exasperated. "I expected you to be back to your old selves now that Mosely's gone, but you and Nathaniel both are acting like the world could end any moment."

Nadia wished she could have heard the conversation between Dante and Nate. She suspected it had been colorful, and she was pleasantly surprised they were able to get along well enough to work together and smuggle her the phone. She was also pleasantly surprised that Dante didn't seem to know the details of the trouble she was in. She hadn't been sure Nate would be able to resist telling Bishop everything, and Bishop would have shared the information with the resistance, including Dante. Maybe Nate was finally learning discretion.

"I can't tell you," Nadia said regretfully.

"Because I'm a member of the resistance?" There was a spark of challenge in his eyes, and he lifted his chin ever so slightly.

That was certainly part of it, but she saw no reason to say so. "I can't tell *anyone*. Not even my parents. Believe me, it's better that way." Maybe Dante would even agree, if he knew what she was hiding. He wanted to see Chairman Hayes out of power, and he was obviously willing to go to great lengths to help bring that to pass, but would he think it worth a potential civil war? Nadia didn't know him well enough to answer that one way or the other.

"Better for who?" Dante asked sharply, still challenging her with his eyes. "Your people, or mine?"

He was deliberately goading her, she decided. Hoping she'd trip up and give him information in an effort to defend herself. "Better for everyone. And may I remind you that I stuck my neck out for Bishop more than once. *I'm* not the one who has trouble respecting people of different classes." She shivered again, wishing she'd had the guts to go back to her room and grab a sweater.

To her surprise, Dante looked sheepish and backed down. "Sorry," he mumbled, taking a moment to look down at his feet. "I didn't mean to pick a fight."

Yes, he had. But Nadia wasn't going to call him on it.

"You look like you're freezing," he continued, looking up once more. "Here." He slipped off the faux-leather jacket he was wearing and tried to hand it to her through the bars.

Nadia raised her hands in refusal. "You don't have to do that," she said, despite the serious appeal the idea held. "If one of us has to be cold, it should be the idiot who left her room without a sweater."

"I'm not trying to make a class statement or anything,"

Dante said, completely misinterpreting her refusal. "You're shivering, and your lips are turning blue. Take the jacket."

Now that he'd made it into a class issue by saying it *wasn't* a class issue, there was no way Nadia could accept his jacket. She was *not* the pampered Executive who always looked out for her own comfort at the expense of others'. She never had been, no matter what Dante thought.

"I'm fine," she said as she tried not to stare longingly at the jacket.

With a grunt of annoyance, Dante folded his jacket into as small a bundle as he could and hurled it over the top of the fence. It landed on the grass about five feet behind her.

"Just stop being difficult and put on the jacket already."

Nadia thought of herself as having a pretty strong will, but it was hard to exercise that strong will when she wanted what he was offering so badly. She bit her lip in indecision. Dante crossed his arms and fixed her with a commanding stare. She didn't like giving in to his high-handed tactics. However, there was no reason for *both* of them to be cold.

She picked up the jacket and draped it over her shoulders. Thanks to her playing hard-to-get, most of his body heat had dissipated from the inside, but it still felt deliciously warm. Best of all, it wasn't spa-issued.

"Thank you," she said, drinking in the warmth—and taking a moment to admire how Dante looked without the bulky jacket hiding his form. Even when she'd thought him an enemy spying on her for Dirk Mosely, she'd always been reluctantly aware of how nice he was to look at. He was unlike anyone Nadia knew, the complete opposite of the polished Executive teenager. His good looks had not sprung from a pampered life, an expert tailor, or a professional stylist. His skin was tanned, his nose freckled, his upper body solidly muscled, but with muscles that had been earned by hard work, not carved and cultivated in a gym. And yet the coarse appearance looked right on him, and Nadia suspected he'd lose a lot of his appeal if an Executive stylist tried to polish him.

Nadia realized she was staring and quickly looked away. She hoped Dante hadn't noticed, but he *was* a spy. He didn't miss much. Luckily, he didn't have Nate's ego, so he didn't start preening—or tease her.

"They won't let you wear your own clothes here?" Dante asked.

Nadia clutched his jacket more tightly over her shoulders. "No. The place is a living hell, where everyone smiles and tells you to relax and have fun." She gave a dramatic shudder. "If I don't get out of here soon, they're going to have to lock me in the mental ward."

Nadia had meant her words to be flippant, but the terror she was expressing was very real and must have shown in her voice. Dante reached through the bars and took one of her hands, giving it a warm squeeze.

A proper Executive would have jerked her hand away and reminded him of his place. Even here, in the middle of the night, with no one to see, she should have demanded he respect her status and not do something so familiar as holding her hand. But instead of doing what she should, she curled her fingers around his and hung on.

"I'm scared, Dante," she admitted. "I've been here less than a week, and I'm miserable already, and I know they might never let me out."

Dante squeezed her hand again. "They won't keep you here forever," he assured her, though he had no way of knowing that. "The media storm is already beginning to die down.

They're starting to sniff around someone else's skirts, and you know how much they love to jump on whatever's newest."

Nadia felt sorry for whomever the press had descended upon now, but she was grateful nonetheless. If someone else would make a big enough splash, the press would forget about Nadia altogether and she'd be able to get out of this godforsaken place.

"Who are they picking on now?" she asked. She wasn't as fond of gossip as other Executive girls her age, but she had to admit to a certain amount of curiosity, especially when she was so cut off from the news. And she couldn't help hoping the media's victim would be someone she despised, like the Terrible Trio of Jewel, Cherry, and Blair.

Dante grinned at her, his eyes glinting with mischief, and she figured he knew exactly what she was thinking. To her knowledge, he'd never met Cherry, but he'd had to wait on Jewel and Blair before, so he knew exactly how much they deserved to be knocked down a peg.

"No one you know, I'm afraid. There's a delegation from Synchrony making a state visit this week. Chairman Belinski brought the whole family, including his daughter, Agnes. Either the press in Synchrony isn't as aggressive as ours, or poor Agnes doesn't get out much. Let's just say her answers to some reporters' questions haven't been terribly articulate."

Nadia cocked her head. It sounded to her like Dante felt genuine sympathy for Agnes Belinski. "Let me get this straight: you're cutting an Executive girl some slack instead of chortling about her misfortunes?"

"I do not *chortle*," he replied in tones of offended dignity, but he quickly lost any sign of humor. "Yes, I feel sorry for her, even though she's an Executive. She doesn't seem to have the . . . advantages the rest of you have."

"Like what?"

He shrugged. "I don't know. She's not as polished, or as self-assured." He met her eyes, and his voice dropped lower. "And she's not beautiful, either."

The words traveled through her like an electric shock, raising goose bumps on her skin. For the first time, she realized that she was still holding Dante's hand, and that his thumb was rubbing back and forth over her knuckles. Her breath froze in her lungs as she met his gaze. For a fraction of a second, she thought perhaps she was reading things into his words, misinterpreting the cues. But no. The look in his eyes told her quite plainly what he meant.

"You think I'm beautiful?" she asked in a breathless whisper.

One corner of his mouth tugged up in a small smile. "You know you are."

Nadia shook her head. She couldn't count how many times she'd been told she was beautiful or read a rhapsodic description of herself in the society columns, but those were just empty words, meant to flatter the daughter of a powerful Executive family. Nate had called her beautiful more than once, but it didn't mean much coming from him, either, since he wasn't that interested in female beauty. Hearing the words from Dante was something altogether different, and she didn't know what to say. She *did* know she should let go of his hand and put a little distance between them, but she couldn't seem to make herself do it.

Dante reached through the bars and took her other hand, and she let him. Her heart was beating double time, and she couldn't seem to take in enough oxygen.

"When I heard you'd been arrested—" he started to say, then had to stop to clear his throat. "I'm sorry I had such a chip on my shoulder when we first met. It didn't take me long to realize you weren't like the rest of the Executive girls, but it wasn't until you were arrested that I realized how much I'd come to . . . admire you. I told myself that if I ever saw you again, I'd let you know. So here I am. Letting you know."

She couldn't tell in the darkness, but Nadia suspected he was now blushing. He shifted awkwardly from foot to foot, and she worried that her silence was giving him the impression she was offended or uncomfortable. She was neither.

"Thank you," she said, and it was her turn to squeeze *his* hands. "It means the world to me that you came all the way out here to see me, even if it was just to bring me the phone. I feel a lot less alone now than I did before I got your note."

Dante smiled at her, but he let go of her hands. She tried not to let her disappointment show. It was certainly for the best. If someone were to catch her holding hands with a servant in the middle of the night, it would be just the kind of scandal that could land her in a retreat permanently.

"The phone is secure and untraceable," he said, turning businesslike. "Nate has a secure phone, too, so he can call you if there's trouble. You only want to use it in case of emergency, though. Don't call him because you feel blue."

She had no trouble reading between the lines, and she laughed a little. "I'll assume your resistance leaders are listening to every word I say if I ever use the phone."

This time, she was sure he was blushing, but he didn't tell her she was wrong. "I'm sure you'll be getting out soon, but just in case you need to see a friendly face, I'll come hang out here at midnight every night. You don't have to come meet me, but I'm here if you need me."

Nadia's eyes widened. "You don't have to do that!"

"But I will anyway."

Because his resistance bosses wanted him to? Or because *he* wanted to? Nadia didn't have the guts to ask.

"You'll waste almost three hours driving back and forth from Manhattan," she protested. "And you still have a job to go to, don't you?"

"I'm still acting as your father's 'assistant,' if that's what you're asking. But he doesn't trust me, so it's not like he gives me anything important to do. I won't collapse of exhaustion if I lose a little sleep each night."

There were other protests Nadia could have tried. She could have pointed out that someone might notice him leaving his room in the servants' quarters every night and wonder what he was up to. Or that every time he visited the retreat was another chance of getting caught. Obviously, he had to be borrowing someone's car to get out here, because an Employee of his rank would have to scrimp and save for years to afford one. Which meant there was yet another chance of getting caught, one more person in the loop who might talk.

But the idea of having a lifeline waiting outside the fence for her every night, the idea of having someone to talk to, of having a familiar face who could keep her up-to-date on what was going on in the world, was too much to resist.

"Thank you," she said for what felt like the millionth time.

Her eyes got misty when she finally had to leave and get back to her bed.

CHAPTER FOUR

On Wednesday morning, Nate received his first ever message on the secure phone Dante had acquired for him. It was a photograph of Nadia, holding a similar phone. Proof that Dante had held up his end of the bargain. Nate should have found the photo reassuring. Nadia was no longer so completely cut off from the outside world. But instead, the photo made Nate wish he could ride in there on a white horse and sweep her away.

The girl who would one day be the Chairman Spouse of Paxco stood behind bars, dressed in a shapeless tunic and pants that were obviously a uniform of some sort. Better than a prison jumpsuit, to be sure, but still strangely ominous to his eyes. She was smiling for the camera, but she wasn't putting much effort into it. She knew how to paste on a smile for the public to see no matter what she was feeling inside, but for this photo, she wasn't bothering. It made her seem even smaller and more vulnerable, but maybe that was just Nate's guilty conscience dragging him down. If it weren't for him and his stubborn insistence on carrying out a secret rebellion at a very public wedding reception, none of this would have happened.

Of course, if none of this had happened, Thea would still be operating on "expendable" victims in the basement of the Fortress, vivisecting them in an attempt to understand the connection between a person's body and mind. The A.I. had learned how to re-create a human body and a brain with all its personality and stored memories—Nate was living proof of that—but that hadn't satisfied her. Her ultimate goal was to re-create a human mind in a body of her choosing, so that she could make the Chairman—her protector and benefactor—quasi-immortal by re-creating his mind in a younger body whenever old age started to degrade his current one. In the grand scheme of things, destroying Thea had been for the greater good—certainly the helpless Basement-dwellers and prisoners Thea had used as test subjects would say so—but it remained to be seen how brutal and far-reaching the consequences would be, especially if the Chairman ever found the recordings.

Nate frowned at the photo when he noticed for the first time that the jacket draped over Nadia's shoulders wasn't part of her uniform. At first, the dark jacket had blended in with the dark background of a nighttime shot, but when Nate stared at it more closely, he could clearly see it was much too large to be Nadia's own, and its design was unmistakably masculine.

"Dante," Nate muttered with a muffled curse, fighting the surge of territorial aggression that made him want to throw the phone across the room. He closed his eyes and mentally shook himself by the scruff of the neck. He had already established that he had *no* right to feel possessive toward Nadia. She would never be more than a friend to him, even when she was his wife. She had never liked Kurt, but it had never seemed to bother her that her husband-to-be was in love with someone else, and Nate wanted to be just as mature and accepting of her. Unfortunately, he couldn't seem to make himself feel the way he *wanted* to feel, and he didn't like the idea of Dante taking a special interest in Nadia.

Shaking his head, Nate turned off the phone and tucked it into his pocket so he didn't have to see the offending photo anymore. He was making something out of nothing, even if he *had* had the right to be jealous. So Dante had given Nadia his jacket. So what? He was just being a gentleman when Nadia was cold. Harmless and inoffensive.

And yet he had chosen to take the photo while Nadia was wearing the jacket. Nate couldn't help suspecting it had been a deliberate attempt to get under his skin.

"And you're letting him get away with it," Nate admonished himself with another surge of annoyance.

It was time to stop thinking about what designs Dante might have on Nadia and start concentrating on getting through what was sure to be a tough day. *Any* day that included being in the same room with his father was a tough day, but today would be worse than most, because his father had demanded a meeting first thing in the morning. Nate suspected it had something to do with the ad for Replica technology he had shot the previous week. Obviously, the ad was now obsolete, but since the public didn't know that, it was still airing on the net. Nate had been in rough shape when he'd shot it, and he'd done a terrible job—he cringed and hit the mute button whenever it came on—and he suspected his father wanted him to do a new and improved version. Kind of a waste of money, except Nate was beginning to think his public image needed some serious rehabbing. The fact that he was a Replica made people uneasy, and there was more than one crackpot on the net trying to convince everyone he was some kind of danger to society. Getting some positive images out there might help.

In the old days, there was a good chance he would have blown the meeting off and weathered the storm of his father's temper later. Pissing off his father had been one of his favorite pastimes, after all. That was before he knew his father could murder him in cold blood without missing a beat. And before Nate realized how badly he was shirking his duties as the Chairman Heir.

Long habit had Nate arriving at the Paxco Headquarters Building—formerly known as the Empire State Building—about a half hour late, despite what had started out as reasonably good intentions. Nate had vowed to himself that he would start being a more responsible heir and spend more time at work, learning the ropes so that he'd have a clue what he was doing when he became Chairman. He hadn't quite lived up to that vow yet, but he was still reeling from everything he had learned about his father's secret activities and about his own murder.

Nate didn't feel like prolonging the inevitable, so he didn't even stop by his own office before heading up to the top floor. He fully expected to be kept waiting even though he was already late, and when his father's secretary told him to go right in, a chill of unease traveled down his spine. Maybe his father had decided to dispense with the mind games, now that he and Nate had all their cards on the table.

Nate dismissed the possibility as soon as it crossed his mind. The day the Chairman stopped playing mind games would be the day he died. Letting Nate come in immediately when he was used to having to wait was just one more, designed to put him off balance from the start.

The Chairman was standing in front of his floor-to-ceiling windows, holding a steaming cup of coffee in one hand while gazing out at the city majestically. The Empire State Building had once been the tallest building in the world, and though many other buildings had eclipsed it in size, the view from the top was still spectacular. Not that the Chairman was really admiring the view; he was just posing for effect.

The Chairman held the pose for a handful of seconds before taking a seat behind his desk. Usually, he had papers scattered all over his desk, but today it was meticulously neat, the dark leather blotter free from its usual clutter.

As was no doubt his father's intention, Nate's eyes were drawn immediately to the stack of stapled papers sitting in the middle of the blotter with a thick gold pen perched on top. The print on those papers was small, and Nate wasn't very good at reading upside down anyway, but if he had to guess, he'd say they were contracts of some sort.

"You wanted to see me?" Nate said, hoping he sounded more nonchalant than he felt. His every instinct told him that something bad was about to happen, and the satisfied glint in the Chairman's eyes reinforced those instincts.

"Yes," the Chairman said with a predatory smile. "Please, have a seat." He gestured toward the pair of chairs in front of his desk.

Nate didn't want to sit, and if it weren't nine o'clock in the morning, he might have invited himself over to his father's liquor bar for a drink. Not that the delay would have gotten him anywhere. He forced his feet forward and lowered himself into a chair.

"What's this about?" he asked. He tried not to stare at the pile of contracts, not wanting to give the Chairman any satisfaction.

Nate's father leaned back in his chair and took a sip of coffee before answering. "You know that we've been hosting a delegation from Synchrony since Monday?"

Of course Nate knew that. He might be a little lax about his duties, but he wasn't living in a cave. He frowned. "I think I heard about that in the news somewhere."

Nate was pleasantly surprised to find he could still make

wise-ass comments, considering what he now knew about his father. It felt almost normal, except for the way he tensed up on the inside after the words were out.

"I thought maybe it had escaped your attention, seeing as you failed to attend the dinner and cocktail party that were held in their honor. Did your majordomo misplace your invitation?"

Nate snorted in disdain. He attended at most one out of every five social events he was invited to, and most of those were only brief appearances, photo ops for the press. His father could hardly be surprised that he had chosen not to attend a dinner or cocktail party with a bunch of visiting dignitaries.

"If you called this meeting just to scold me for not coming to the party—" Nate started, leaning forward as if to rise to his feet.

"Of course not," the Chairman said. "I know from experience that would be about as useful as scolding an infant for wetting its diaper."

Nate gritted his teeth against the urge to defend himself. His father certainly had some justification for thinking of Nate as childish and irresponsible, and if he was going to turn over a new leaf, he would have to start getting more involved in both business and social politics. He settled back in his chair once more and waited for the Chairman to continue.

"As I'm sure you know—despite an astounding lack of firsthand experience—events of this sort are rarely the social occasions they appear to be to the general public. Chairman Belinski and I have had some very fruitful meetings about how to strengthen the bonds between our two states."

Nothing surprising in that. Paxco had been courting Synchrony for some time, hoping to improve trade relations and gain better access to Synchrony's low-cost, high-quality tech products. Paxco had sunk all of its R&D and manufacturing money into the Replica project, and now that Thea was gone, the Chairman must be desperately looking for new revenue streams to tap into. Most of the Synchrony tech was designed with military applications in mind, but it could easily be adapted to civilian use.

Of course, Paxco and Synchrony had already taken a significant step toward becoming bosom allies when Chairman Belinski's niece had married into one of the top Paxco Executive families. It had been at the wedding reception for the happy couple that the Chairman had ordered his hatchet man to stab Nate to death because he'd overheard an incriminating conversation.

"You know," Nate said, unable to keep his mouth wisely shut, "I don't actually remember the wedding, seeing as you had me murdered and I only remember events up to my last backup, but I'm pretty sure one did actually take place and that it does create a bond between our states."

His father's smile was hard and cold.

"An apt observation," the Chairman said. "There is nothing that unifies two states better than a marriage. And it just so happens that Chairman Belinski has a marriageable daughter. And I have a marriageable son."

The blood drained from Nate's face so fast it left him dizzy. He'd have leapt to his feet and shouted a protest, only he was afraid his knees wouldn't hold him. The Chairman turned the stack of contracts around so that Nate could read them and see the words "marriage agreement" featured prominently at the top.

"I'm engaged to Nadia," Nate said, but his voice came out sounding thin and tentative.

"Not by any legal definition of the term. Nadia Lake is too young to sign a legally binding marriage agreement. Agnes Belinski, however, will turn eighteen a week from Saturday. At 12:01 on that morning, she will sign her copy of the agreement, and your engagement will be official."

Nate was shaking his head, his pulse racing. "You'll destroy her," he said, hardly able to absorb the cruelty of his father's decision. Nate and Nadia had been unofficially engaged since he was six and she was four. Partially to scandalize people, and partially to help camouflage his sexual preferences, he'd given the press and the rest of Executive society the impression that he was already sleeping with her. And she'd just been a victim of a media storm that had her family hiding her away in the equivalent of a medieval convent. Everyone would assume she had done something terrible. Something so shameful that the Chairman could no longer countenance letting her marry his son. She would be seen as damaged goods, and no respectable Executive would be willing to marry her. Ever.

"Perhaps the two of you should have thought of that before you forced me to destroy the heart and soul of our economy," the Chairman said acidly. "As long as we had the revenue from the Replica program, you could marry within our state. Now, however, I have no choice but to use your marriage in a more politically advantageous manner."

The explanation was pure bullshit. The Chairman's intention was to punish Nate and to ruin Nadia's life.

"I won't do it!" Nate said, mining the fury that lay beneath his dismay. He stood up and found that his knees would hold him after all as he glared down at his father. "You can't drag me to the altar at gunpoint."

The Chairman, unaffected by Nate's declaration, rose

from his seat. "You will marry Agnes Belinski, or I will have you put in reprogramming to correct your sexual deviance. I'll make certain Miss Belinski will still be waiting for you when they're done with you. And I will, of course, suggest to the public that your deviance is due to Nadia's inability to inspire you to correct your behavior. I don't think that will do her marriage prospects much good either, do you?"

It took everything Nate had to hold himself together. He felt like he was literally going to explode, and he wanted to ram his fist through his father's face. He should have known something like this was up as soon as he'd heard the Belinskis were visiting.

"Shall I call security to take you to a reprogramming facility? Or will you sign the contract?"

Nate wished he could believe his father was bluffing. Wished he had the guts to storm out of the office without signing the papers. But the Chairman was right. If Nate's sexual preference was revealed, it would destroy Nadia's reputation as surely as breaking the marriage agreement would. And he would come out of reprogramming a changed person, his spirit crushed. The only person Nate had ever known who'd gone through reprogramming had come out the other end a shell of himself, a broken man who was no longer interested in men—or in life in general. It had been years ago, but if Nate remembered correctly, the guy had checked himself into an upstate retreat within three months of returning to society, and he'd been there ever since.

"You can't do this," Nate said, but the words came out sounding more like a question than a statement. "The recordings . . ."

The Chairman raised an eyebrow. "What about them?"

"We won't let you do this." But the uncertainty in his voice undermined any chance of being convincing.

"You're suggesting the two of you will release the recordings if I change the marriage agreement?" The Chairman sounded in equal parts amused and condescending. "Here's the thing about blackmail, son: it only works if I believe you're going to follow through on your threat."

Nate tried to dredge up some fire and conviction. "I'll do whatever it takes to protect her."

"And you think releasing the recordings would protect her?" His father actually had the nerve to laugh. "Blackmail is like chess—you have to look past your next move and all the way to the end game. So let's say I refuse to honor your demands. You then have to choose whether or not to release the recordings. What's the upside to releasing them?"

Nate couldn't have answered if he'd wanted to, his teeth clamped together so tightly his jaw ached. But his father wasn't really interested in what Nate had to say anyway. This was a lecture, not a dialog.

"You'd probably get a little glow of satisfaction from sticking it to me, maybe even feel proud of yourself for proving me wrong. But I can't see anything else good coming out of it, and that's not whole lot of upside when you know releasing the recordings will cause riots at least, a war at worst. Now what's the downside? Other than those thousands of people who might die if the worst happened?"

This time, the Chairman made no pretense of waiting for Nate's response.

"The downside is that once those recordings are out, I no longer have any reason to keep Nadia alive. No reason to keep your boyfriend alive, either. So tell me, Nate: are you going to release those recordings?"

Nate was speechless, his mind searching desperately for a way out, a way to counter his father's relentless logic.

"Nadia's blackmail worked at the Fortress because with her life and yours both already forfeit, there wouldn't have been much of a downside to releasing the recordings, and—in her starry-eyed worldview—there would have been the upside of stopping Thea's experiments. I had reason to believe she would think that releasing the recordings was the 'right' thing to do. I don't believe either of you would think that's the case now.

"You're going to sign the marriage contract," the Chairman concluded, "and you're going to do it *now*. We won't make the announcement publicly until Agnes has come of age and signed as well, but I have already scheduled some time with Esmeralda and Gerald Lake to inform them of the change in plans."

"Please—"

The Chairman picked up the phone. "If you haven't started signing by the time I get security into this office, you're going into reprogramming."

He hit two buttons on the phone before Nate grabbed the pen. His hand was shaking with rage as he signed the contract, but he refused to accept the defeat. He had a little more than a week before Agnes would be old enough to sign the contract herself and seal their fates and Nadia's. Somehow, he would have to find a way to get out of it before then.

There was no way he was changing his father's mind. However, Chairman Belinski might be another story. Nate would learn as much as he could about his would-be father-in-law. And then he would find a way to convince the Chairman and/or his daughter that he was not the great catch they thought him to be.

CHAPTER FIVE

nate left Headquarters as soon as he escaped his father's office, his resolution to be a good heir blown out of the water. How could he possibly get anything done when the whole course of his life and Nadia's had just been changed for the worse? Knowing that Nadia, his best friend, would one day be his wife had been a blessing. She knew about his secret life, and despite the expectations of Executive society, she had never condemned him for it. Certainly she'd never called it "sexual deviance," as the Chairman just had. He'd never loved her as a man was supposed to love a woman, but she would have been the perfect wife for him, one who would never judge him or reveal his "shameful" secret to the rest of the world. Nate knew next to nothing about Agnes Belinski except that she had an old-lady name and had not made a good impression on the media, either with her looks or her demeanor. He didn't have to know her to be certain she'd be far less accepting of him than Nadia.

But as bitter a pill as Nate had to swallow, it was nothing compared to the devastation the change of marriage plans would bring to Nadia's life. The public humiliation she would suffer was something he wouldn't wish on his worst enemy. And it wasn't the kind of thing that would blow over someday when the media found something more interesting to harp on. Her reputation could have been rebuilt after the scandal of her arrest, though not without difficulty, as evidenced by her stay at the retreat; but a second scandal, especially one of this magnitude, was a death blow.

Nadia wouldn't be able to set foot in public without the media rubbing their hands together with glee as they dredged up her history. Not that she'd have much cause to set foot in public anyway. Executive society would ignore her as if she didn't exist. She wouldn't be welcome in anyone's home, would receive no invitations, no visitors, no friendly phone calls. The ostracism would be complete, and Nate could only pray that she wouldn't be bustled off to one of the upstate Executive retreats, never to be seen again.

Nate seethed for the entire ride back to his apartment, but there was a fair amount of dread mixed in with his fury. *Someone* would have to tell Nadia the news, and he feared that task would fall to him. Nadia would be allowed visitors at the retreat for the first time later this evening, and Nate had already made arrangements for a car to get him there the moment the gates opened. He'd assumed he'd be sharing the visiting hours with her parents and maybe her sister, but after his father told the Lakes about his change of plans . . . Nadia's mother would be too devastated by the news—and too angry at Nadia, even though none of this was her fault—to go through with the visit. And if Esmeralda stayed home, her husband and Gerri would, too. Leaving Nate as the only person who could tell Nadia that her world was coming to an end.

Unfortunately, Nate had once again underestimated his father's capacity for cruelty. When Nate entered his apartment, he was immediately accosted by Hartman, his major-domo.

"The Chairman called," Hartman told him, and Nate's insides froze.

"Whatever he wanted, I don't want to hear about it," he said, giving Hartman his fiercest glare. Hartman often seemed to be at a loss for how to handle Nate's petty rebellions, but he apparently had no doubts this time. When Nate strode away, Hartman followed on his heels.

"I'm afraid he was quite insistent, sir," Hartman said.

"Ask me if I care." Nate wondered if he should indulge his new enthusiasm for punching people by bashing in his major-domo's nose. That would shut him up.

"Oh, you'll care all right," Hartman said ominously, and Nate came to a stop with a curse so foul it made his major-domo wince.

"What is it, then?" he snapped, feeling like he would go crazy if he heard any more bad news.

"Your father invites you to join him for a private dinner with Chairman Belinski and his daughter this evening."

Nate blinked and shook his head. "Wait. *That's* what you think is so important? A dinner invitation?" One Hartman had to know Nate would refuse out of hand.

"It conflicts with your currently scheduled plans," Hartman said. "The dinner is scheduled for six o'clock."

Of course it was. Right during the heart of the retreat's visiting hours, so that Nate wouldn't have time to drive out there either before or after the dinner. "You can send my father my *sincere* regrets," Nate said, but he knew it wouldn't be that easy. The Chairman was a bastard, but he wasn't stupid, and he knew exactly what kind of response his invitation would elicit.

Hartman nodded. "He told me you would say that. He said to tell you your mother might appreciate some company. He said you would know what that meant."

At first, he didn't. What did his mother have to do with

any of this? But it only took a moment for it to make sense. If Nate didn't show up for the dinner tonight, the Chairman would recommend to the Lakes that they send Nadia to the Preston Sanctuary, the upstate retreat his mother had holed herself up in for the past decade. It was the kind of place where visitors were as rare as four-leafed clovers, and from which Executives rarely emerged. In one of those places, Nadia might well disappear from his life as thoroughly as his mother had. She might be destined for such a place anyway, but if his father "recommended" it, the Lakes would surely obey.

"Do you still wish me to send the Chairman your regrets?" Hartman asked. There was a disquieting glint of satisfaction in his eyes. He wasn't used to winning arguments with Nate, and it seemed he was enjoying the novel experience.

Nate was angry enough—and felt helpless enough—that he was tempted to fire Hartman on the spot just because of the look on his face. He controlled the impulse with embarrassing difficulty. Hartman didn't understand the threat he was making on the Chairman's behalf, and Nate had to admit he wasn't the easiest person in the world to work for. He suspected Kurt was the only person who'd ever been on his household staff who *didn't* want to smack him every once in a while.

"Tell him I accept," Nate said, because he had no other choice. But he was going to do his level best to make Chairman Belinski think twice about the marriage arrangement. His own father didn't give a rat's ass about Nate's happiness and well-being. Nate could only hope Chairman Belinski was a more loving and protective parent.

wednesday was the closest thing Nadia had had to a good day since the moment she'd first set foot in the retreat.

Thanks to the phone Dante had smuggled to her, she had a connection to the outside world, even if she could only use it in case of emergency. And she knew he would be waiting for her outside the fence again at midnight. She probably wouldn't be as desperate for a friendly face today as she had been in the past, because it was an official visiting day, but she would sneak out to meet him anyway. If he was going to go through all the bother to come to the retreat every night, the least she could do was to show up, if only to thank him again.

Nadia occupied her morning with a number of spa appointments, picking services where she didn't have to undress. Having learned her lesson when her underwear was whisked away that first day, she wasn't leaving the phone out of her reach for an instant.

The afternoon, she spent reading on the spa's rooftop veranda, which provided a panoramic view of the grounds. It was a beautiful spring day, and there were moments when Nadia was actually able to take a deep breath and relax for the first time in weeks. Those moments never lasted long, but she appreciated them anyway.

She was down in the visitors' lobby at exactly five o'clock. She didn't know who was planning to show up or when, because that would have required communication with the outside world, and she wanted to make sure she didn't miss a single minute of her time with her loved ones.

The visitors' lobby was festive and comfortable. Chairs and tables were arranged in intimate clusters so that people could visit in a semblance of privacy. There was a table of hors d'oeuvres set up near the entrance, and retreat staff prowled the room to take drink orders. A merry wood fire crackled away in a recessed area in the middle of the room, and Nadia could see the carpeted stairs leading down to the fireplace were a popular seating choice, the room being surprisingly chilly considering the outside temperature.

Except for the fireplace with its enormous mantel and the chimney that disappeared into the ceiling, the lobby had an open floor plan. Standing in the doorway from the dormitory wing, Nadia could see practically the whole room without having to move. The visitors hadn't been granted entry yet, so all she could see were retreat employees and fellow inmates like herself. It was a veritable sea of powder-blue uniforms, and Nadia swore that when she got out of here, she would never again wear so much as a hair ribbon in that color.

The visitors began to trickle in within a minute or so of Nadia's arrival, and she waited and watched breathlessly as people in street clothes entered the room. There were some enthusiastic greetings, complete with hugs and kisses, but mostly everyone was quiet and reserved, as if they were meeting at a funeral. Nadia supposed the circumstances that had driven most of the guests into the retreat cast a pall on their relationships with friends and family.

By six o'clock, the steady stream of visitors had slowed to a trickle, and no one had come for Nadia. She circled the room restlessly, feeling like a lost soul. Of course, she reminded herself, the retreat was almost an hour and a half's drive from Manhattan, so it would take a while for any of her visitors to arrive. Neither her father nor Gerri would leave work early for anything short of a crisis, and her mother would wait for them before coming out herself.

Nate's absence was a little harder to explain away, as he was liable to duck out of work on the flimsiest of excuses. She knew he was trying to become more responsible, but she didn't think his newfound sense of responsibility would keep him in the office when he had a chance to visit her, especially when they hadn't seen each other before she'd been spirited away. He would want to put in an appearance to give her some moral support, if nothing else.

Nadia finally got tired of her restless pacing and plunked into a seat where she'd have a good view of the entrance. She wasn't the only retreat guest not to have any visitors yet, and she supposed she could go sit with some other lonely guest so they could keep each other company. But the guests were far from the most social bunch, and Nadia was so much younger than everyone else it was hard to find common ground. She felt like a complete pariah sitting in the corner by herself, but that wasn't enough to motivate her to move.

The hollow feeling in Nadia's stomach worsened as every minute ticked by. She checked the time compulsively, deciding that she couldn't reasonably expect anyone to show up until 6:30 if they didn't leave Manhattan until 5:00. When 6:30 rolled around and there was still no one, she told herself they probably didn't leave work until 5:30, and therefore she shouldn't expect anyone until 7:00.

When 7:00 came and went and she was still alone, Nadia ran out of hopeful excuses and started entertaining the possibility that no one was coming. At first, she could hardly believe that was the case, but as the hands on the clock continued their relentless circling, it became harder and harder to deny it. She considered fleeing the visitors' lobby and heading back to her room before visiting hours officially came to the end, just to escape the humiliation of being so thoroughly abandoned, but a stubborn kernel of hope refused to die. She would stay and wait until the retreat staff kicked the visitors out, just in case someone was running terribly late and would show up at the last moment.

No one did.

Visiting hours were over, and everyone was saying their good-byes. Most of the guests were gone already, and those who remained were outnumbered by the staff. When Nadia noticed Mari of the manic smile heading her way, she quickly vacated her seat and practically ran for the exit. No doubt the woman was coming to offer consolation of some sort, but Nadia couldn't have stomached it even if she'd believed it sincere. She fled back to her room and locked the door behind her, sitting on the edge of her bed and urging herself not to cry.

She'd only been away five nights, though it felt like forever to her. She had certainly gone longer than that without seeing Gerri before, as her sister had her hands full with work and two young children. Her mother had never been warm and nurturing, and she might have taken the retreat's suggestion that visitors stay away for the first two weeks to heart. Or maybe she was planning to bring Nadia home in the next couple of days, making a visit unnecessary.

But Nate . . . How could *Nate* not have come? He *had* to know she was climbing the walls, *had* to know she was desperate for company. Obviously, he *did* know, or he wouldn't have sent Dante to deliver the phone.

Nadia swallowed the lump in her throat. There was a logical explanation for his failure to appear. He certainly hadn't done it to hurt her, or even out of carelessness. Nate might not be the most considerate and responsible of people, but he had always been her best friend. If he hadn't come tonight, it was because, for some reason, he couldn't.

Nadia reached into her tunic and withdrew the phone she had tucked in her bra. The temptation to dial Nate's number, to find out if he was all right, to hear his explanation for why he hadn't come, was almost overwhelming. But as hurt and as abandoned as she was feeling, the phone was only for use in emergencies, and this was *not* an emergency. Using the phone involved risk, and wouldn't she feel like the world's biggest idiot if she lost her lifeline just because she felt lonely?

Reminding herself that Dante would come tonight, that she wasn't completely isolated no matter how she felt, she tucked the phone back into its hiding place.

CHAPTER SIX

The media had been overly generous when they labeled Agnes Belinski "plain," Nate decided the moment he set eyes on the girl his father meant to shackle him to for the rest of his life. Her body was pear-shaped, and the clingy blouse and flowing skirt she wore made that shape more obvious, rather than camouflaging it as she probably hoped. Puffy cheeks and a receding chin made her face look round as a soccer ball, and her thin, fine brown hair was cut in an unflattering bob. Even if he liked girls, he wouldn't want *her* in his bed.

Nate made little effort to hide his distaste when his father introduced him to Chairman Belinski and his homely daughter. He made his handshake as brief and limp as possible, and after looking Agnes up and down once, refused to meet her eyes. He wondered idly why Mrs. Belinski hadn't come to dinner—he knew she had come to Paxco with her husband and daughter—but he wasn't interested enough to bother asking.

"Chairman Belinski and I have some important matters to discuss," Nate's father said. "We'll leave you young people to get to know each other, then we'll rejoin you when dinner is served."

Though he wasn't looking straight at her, Nate could see the look of near-panic Agnes shot her father; he could also see the reassuring smile Chairman Belinski gave her.

Nate grimaced. So not only was Agnes homely, but she didn't have the grace and self-assurance to fulfill her social obligations without her daddy holding her hand. She was probably the kind of girl who burst into tears if anyone said anything even remotely unkind to her.

In short, she was nothing like Nadia, who would have been as close to the perfect wife as it was possible to get.

The two Chairmen left the room, both looking pompous and self-satisfied—Nate's father because he knew just how poorly Agnes stacked up against Nadia, and Chairman Belinski because his daughter would be marrying well above her station. Synchrony was one of the smaller states, and not a particularly wealthy one. They produced great tech, but they kept too much of it to themselves to realize anything close to their earnings potential. Their elite and exceptionally well-equipped military was envied worldwide, but in the hierarchy of states, rich outranked well-defended by a mile. Paxco could have gotten a bigger financial boost by creating an alliance with a much wealthier state, and Nate was convinced his father had picked Synchrony because he knew just how Nate would feel about Agnes.

Nate had never thought of himself as a mean or cruel person. He was careless of people's feelings sometimes, but it was rarely out of malice. But the anger and resentment burning inside him were almost too much to bear, and he just couldn't bring himself to make friendly with Agnes in even the most superficial way. She was the enemy, and he would give her exactly the kind of consideration an enemy deserved. When their fathers left the room, Nate stood rooted to the floor in stony silence, daring Agnes to break it.

Agnes licked her lips nervously. A couple of times, it looked like she was going to say something, but she either thought better of it or just plain didn't have the nerve. Nadia would have handed Nate his ass on a silver platter if he'd treated her like this, but Agnes just stood there. He might have hoped that if he was being forced to marry a homely stranger, she might at least have a decent personality to make up for her shortcomings, but it seemed she had the personality of a frightened mouse. Maybe Nate would get lucky and she'd start begging her father to cancel the engagement plans the moment Nate was out of her sight.

Giving Agnes one more disdainful look, Nate walked past her and plopped himself down in an armchair near the fireplace. If there had been a fire he could stare broodingly into, he would have done it. Out of the corner of his eye, he saw Agnes still standing in the same spot, shifting from foot to foot. If she couldn't even make a show of standing up for herself with *him,* how the hell was she going to handle people like the Terrible Trio, who so loved to publicly embarrass other girls to make themselves feel more important? *This* was the girl his father wanted to be Chairman Spouse of Paxco someday?

The awkward silence eventually became so uncomfortable that Nate was forced to break it himself. If he were being extremely generous, he might think that had been Agnes's plan all along and she'd actually won a battle of wills against him. But he was hardly in the mood to be generous to anyone, much less the girl his father would force him to marry.

"What kind of a name is Agnes, anyway?" he asked out of nowhere. Agnes jumped at the sound of his voice, her eyes going wide. No, she definitely had not been engaged in a battle of wills. She'd just been incapable of speech. "I don't think I've ever heard of anyone named Agnes who wasn't at least eighty years old."

Splotchy color rose in Agnes's chipmunk cheeks, and she

looked at the floor instead of at him when she answered. "I was named after my grandmother." Her voice was high and thin, almost like a little girl's. It was a voice Nate knew would grate on his nerves in no time flat. Not that everything about Agnes didn't grate on his nerves already. "She was the first Chairman of Synchrony."

The first Agnes Belinski must have had an impressive backbone to have been Chairman of a corporate state, even a small one like Synchrony. Too bad her namesake seemed to have inherited none of it.

No, *not* too bad, Nate reminded himself. If Agnes were a girl like Nadia, the kind of girl who always stubbornly fought back, he'd have no hope of frightening her out of the marriage. After all, the status and money and power she would get out of being Chairman Spouse of Paxco were well worth fighting for. Nate knew any number of Paxco girls who would stab their grandmother in the back if that meant they got to marry him, and it wasn't because they were so all-fired fond of him. Better for him that Agnes be a wimp.

Walking gingerly as if to keep her shoes from clacking against the hardwood floor, Agnes proved herself capable of movement and took a seat on the sofa. She sat straight and primly, with her knees locked together and her hands folded in her lap. Nate thought she was going to give him more details about her grandmother, to try to fill the silence with meaningless chatter, but she didn't. He imagined Nadia, sitting alone at the retreat, waiting patiently for visitors who would never come. She wouldn't know why, and she'd be both hurt and angry.

"You're going to ruin an innocent girl's life," he blurted, glaring at Agnes. She just blinked at him stupidly, as if she had no idea what he could possibly be talking about. But unless she'd been living in a cave, she had to know Nate had already been informally engaged before she'd entered his life. If she hadn't known it by the time she first set foot in Paxco, then someone had certainly told her by now. He kept glaring at her until she bowed her head.

"I'm sorry," she said, proving she *did* know.

Nate waited for more, but obviously Agnes wasn't much of a talker. "You're sorry? That's all you have to say for yourself?" He looked for some hint of spirit and defiance in her, but there was none. If he hadn't despised her so much, he might have felt sorry for her.

"When your father's a Chairman, you don't get to pick whom you marry," she said. It was a statement of fact, not a complaint. If her lack of choices bothered her, she certainly wasn't letting it show.

"Tell your father you won't do it."

She looked shocked by the very suggestion, as if he'd told her to fly to the moon. "What?"

"You heard me."

"Why would I do that?" she asked, sounding genuinely perplexed. "Solidifying the bond between Paxco and Synchrony will be advantageous to both our states, and—"

"Because if you don't fight it, you'll be stuck with me," Nate said as ominously as he could. "You won't like that."

He thought he detected a hint of unease in Agnes's eyes, but she shrugged as if it hardly mattered to her. "You're the Chairman Heir of Paxco. Surely you know that what you and I would like is irrelevant. I didn't much like it when it looked likely I'd marry a fifty-two-year-old marketing director with two children older than I am, but the match made political sense and I didn't complain about it. I know my duty."

Nate sneered at her. He didn't care if she married a

ninety-year-old geezer with no teeth or a nine-year-old boy who was years away from shaving. Anyone but him.

"Of course you don't want to fight it," he said. "It's a sweet deal for you, isn't it? You'll go from being a little nobody from a little nothing state to the Chairman Spouse of the richest, most powerful state there is. You don't give a shit how many lives you have to ruin to get what you want."

Nate had the satisfaction of seeing Agnes flinch at his language. He had the brief thought that if Nadia could see him now, she'd tear into him for being such a bastard to a girl he didn't even know. He certainly wasn't playing his preferred public role of the charming rake. But if being a bastard was what it took to get rid of Agnes and save Nadia's reputation, then he had zero qualms about it.

"I'm doing what's best for my family and my state," Agnes said, with all the spirit and fight of a lump of clay. "I'm sorry if it means someone will get hurt, but—"

"What if I tell you I can make your life far more miserable than your fifty-two-year-old marketing director would?" He fixed her with the coldest look he could manage, letting every bit of his fury show in his eyes.

She quickly averted her eyes, but instead of fleeing in terror she merely shrugged again. "People are mean to me all the time." She made a sweeping head-to-toe gesture. "Look at me and ask yourself how much joy I'm expecting from a marriage."

For the first time, Nate felt the tiniest twinge of genuine sympathy. He'd seen the way other Executive girls treated Nadia, who was beautiful and poised and strong. They were jealous of her status, eager to stab her in the back whenever they had a chance. Even if Agnes wasn't prime marriage material outside of Synchrony, she was the daughter of the Chairman, in the top echelon of the Synchrony elite. She'd have been the object of the same kind of jealousy, and so far he'd seen no hint that she had the tools or the confidence with which to defend herself.

But just because Nate felt a little sorry for her didn't mean he had the least interest in marrying her, even if the marriage arrangement *wouldn't* have destroyed Nadia. She was a sacrificial lamb, being offered up for the slaughter by her power-hungry father. And the worst part about it was that she didn't even seem to mind.

Threatening Agnes with the prospect of a miserable marriage wasn't going to work, if that was what she'd expected all along. Nate was going to have to find some other way to sabotage the arrangement—preferably in such a way that his father wouldn't see his hand in it—before Agnes turned eighteen and signed the papers to make it legally binding.

If only he had the faintest idea how he was going to pull it off . . .

nadia had pulled out the phone Dante had snuck to her three times while she waited in her room for midnight to come. The lack of visitors had filled her with a sense of foreboding, and the temptation to call Nate and ask him why he hadn't come was almost overwhelming. But there was always the remote chance that someone might hear her talking, that the staff would find out she was in possession of a contraband phone and take it away from her. It was a chance she wasn't willing to take, and so each time the temptation hit, she managed to fight it off.

Nadia bundled up in a sweater before slipping outside for her midnight walk. Her nerves were even more fraught this time, and she found herself jumping at every sound, startled by every shadow.

What if Dante didn't show up? No one else she'd been expecting had come for her today. What if everyone she knew had now abandoned her, leaving her to rot here in this gilded prison?

Nadia battled against the worries as she made her way through the lawns and flowerbeds toward the wall of trees. She was probably making something out of nothing. There was probably a benign explanation for why she hadn't received any visitors today, and she was going to drive herself insane if she didn't stop speculating. She should ignore the squirmy, uncomfortable feeling inside her that told her something was horribly wrong.

Her attempts to calm herself met with little success, and by the time she emerged from the trees into the clearing before the fence, her pulse was racing and her hands were clammy. If Dante didn't show up, she didn't think she could possibly resist making a phone call. There was no one to hear her out in the woods, and she needed that sense of connection as much as she needed to breathe.

"Dante?" she called out softly, already half-convinced that he wouldn't be there. She peered into the trees beyond the fence, crossing her fingers and holding her breath. There was no sign of movement, no man-shaped shadows hidden among the tree trunks. "Dante?" she called again, a little louder, though her voice was shaky with nerves. He had *promised* to be here, and even if unforeseen circumstances had somehow prevented her family and Nate from visiting her, surely those circumstances wouldn't affect Dante.

"I'm here," Dante's voice answered, and Nadia feared for a moment she was going to burst into tears of relief. She now saw the man-shaped shadow she'd been looking for—*inside* the fence.

"How did you get in here?" she asked, then wanted to slap herself for the silly question. It wasn't like the fence was electrified or topped with barbed wire or anything. The spiky fleurs-de-lis at the top looked intimidating, but they wouldn't stop a determined intruder.

"I climbed the fence," he answered simply, as if her question hadn't made her sound like an idiot. "It's more for show than to actually keep people out. People stay away because they don't want to be sent to prison for trespassing on an Executive retreat, not because they can't get in."

Nadia bit her lip as Dante came closer, close enough that the moonlight illuminated his face. "You should go back to the other side," she said, looking nervously up and down the strip of grass. "If someone saw you . . ." The wheels of Paxco justice had never turned fairly, and a low-level Employee like Dante, caught trespassing on an Executive retreat with an underage Executive girl, would be ground into dust.

Dante dismissed the threat with a careless wave of his hand. "I'm a spy for Paxco security, remember? If I get caught, I can talk my way out of it."

Nadia wasn't as confident of his safety, and standing out on the grass where anyone could spot them—if anyone actually wandered around this part of the grounds at this time of night—struck her as tempting fate. She glanced over her shoulder at the trees behind her.

"Come on," she said, putting a hand on Dante's shoulder to urge him forward. "Let's at least get you into some cover." Touching him like that was an overly familiar gesture from an Executive to a servant, but it felt right and comfortable, and Dante seemed to have no objection.

Together, they entered the protection of the trees. Nadia led Dante to a fallen tree she had noticed on her way to the fence. It would give them something to sit on, and the gap in the canopy allowed moonlight to filter through. She wasn't sure what she was going to say to him, or what they were going to talk about. Whining about her lack of visitors seemed petty, and Dante was unlikely to know what any of them had been thinking when they'd failed to show up. In fact, she wasn't sure *what* she was hoping to get out of this encounter, except that she'd longed for contact when she felt abandoned.

As they sat together on the fallen tree, Nadia felt suddenly and surprisingly awkward. None of her highly polished Executive social skills had prepared her for a situation like this, for having a clandestine conversation with someone who was of such a different social class that it was almost as if they were from different worlds. He probably thought living in a retreat where you had no responsibilities and were waited on hand and foot was the pinnacle of luxury and Executive excess. No doubt he thought it was whiny and childish of her to complain about a life so many others would envy.

But when she looked Dante full in the face, with moonlight chasing away the shadows that had hidden his expression, she realized with a sinking feeling that he wasn't here for social reasons of any kind.

"What's happened?" she asked, dreading the answer. If something bad had happened to one of her family members, that would explain why they hadn't shown up for visiting hours. Though it wouldn't explain why Nate hadn't come. Unless something had happened to *Nate* again.

Dante didn't answer immediately, and the look on his face was far from comforting.

"Dante, please! Tell me what's wrong. You're scaring me."

He cleared his throat nervously. "I'm not supposed to know about this, and I'm not sure I should be the one to tell you."

Nadia would have reached out and shaken him if she had any reason to suspect that would make him cough up the news sooner.

"Is someone hurt?" she asked, her voice going rough and tight. She remembered all too clearly the threats Dirk Mosely had made against Gerri's children, and she couldn't help worrying that he'd somehow reached out from beyond the grave to get his revenge.

"No, no. Nothing like that," Dante hastened to assure her, and Nadia let out a breath of relief. As long as Nate and her family weren't hurt, she could survive anything else he had to tell her.

"Then what?"

"I, um, overheard your parents arguing."

Even under the circumstances, Nadia couldn't help a small smile. "I'm sure it was entirely accidental on your part." She doubted a professional spy and double agent would be able to resist investigating the sounds of an argument in the household where he was employed.

Dante ducked his head and looked uncomfortable, but he didn't deny her assumption. "It's not public knowledge yet, but apparently the Chairman notified your family in advance as some kind of supposed courtesy."

"Notified them of *what*?" Nadia asked, losing patience with the slow buildup. "Just spit it out already!"

"All right," he agreed softly. He raised his head and met her eyes, and the sympathy in his scared her even more. "Sometime next week—I didn't catch exactly when—the Chairman is going to announce the official engagement between Nate and Agnes Belinski."

The floor dropped out from beneath Nadia's world. She'd been unofficially engaged to Nate for literally as long as she could remember. Her entire life, she had striven to be the perfect Executive, her behavior always exemplary, her every decision colored by the knowledge that a misstep could ruin her and her family. Her family's entire future had rested on her shoulders, and she'd lived in constant fear of letting them down. She'd done everything she possibly could to protect her reputation—a sometimes difficult task with someone like Nate in her life—and to fulfill her every duty.

Until the original Nate Hayes had been murdered, and Nadia had allowed herself to become embroiled in the quest to clear Bishop's name. She had defied Dirk Mosely, and defied the Chairman himself. And now she was paying the price.

Tears burned in her eyes, and there was a tremor in her hands she tried to hide by tucking them under her arms and hugging herself as if she were cold.

It came as no surprise that the Chairman was a vindictive son of a bitch, and she probably should have foreseen this the moment she'd made an enemy of him. Maybe she should have extended her blackmail to protecting the marriage agreement. Maybe she still could, although locked up here in the retreat, it wasn't like she had access to the Chairman to threaten him, or to the recordings to release them. She'd need Gerri's help for that. And Gerri hadn't shown up.

"They were arguing about sending me away for good, weren't they?" she asked, holding herself together through sheer force of will. No wonder no one had come to visit her today. She had destroyed the ambitions of her entire family. Her father would never be promoted to the board of directors, and the stink of scandal would cling to the Lake family name for years to come. Her mother would host no more dinners or parties in the foreseeable future, nor would she be invited to social events other Executives hosted. The same was true of

Gerri. Even their closest friends would shun them, afraid the taint of scandal would rub off on them. And, fair or not, the blame would rest squarely on Nadia's shoulders.

Dante nodded. "Your father is against it. Adamantly."

Nadia stifled a half-laugh, half-sob. "Like that'll do me any good."

Dante hadn't been with their household long, but he surely already knew that Esmeralda always got her way. If she thought sending Nadia away to some upstate retreat where she would never be seen again was necessary to salvage the shreds of the Lake family's reputation, then that was where Nadia would end up. Regardless of what her father thought about it.

"Maybe it will," Dante said, reaching out and squeezing her hand. "He fought for you. I've never heard him get so worked up about anything before. I've never heard your mother back down from anyone before either, but she did this afternoon."

But they both knew that her father had only won the first battle of the war. There would be more to come, and long experience led Nadia to believe she and her father would end up on the losing side. Her life as she knew it was now over.

A tear trickled down her cheek. Ordinarily, she would have tried to hide any sign of weakness, especially in the presence of a social inferior, but she supposed there was no reason to keep up appearances right now. Thinking about what her future might hold made her want to curl up in a hole somewhere and die. Dante squeezed her hand a little tighter, but he didn't have any more comforting words to offer.

"What happened when you were arrested, Nadia?" Dante asked. "There's no way Chairman Hayes thought Agnes Belinski was a better match for Nate than you. The change in plans has spite written all over it. What I don't get is, if he hates you so much, why did he let you out of Riker's?"

Nadia shook her head at him even as tears continued to fall and she clung to his hand. "You never take off your spy hat, do you?"

It was hard to tell in the darkness, but she thought he might have blushed. "Sorry," he mumbled, scuffing at the ground with one foot. "I can't help noticing this stuff. And wondering about it."

For a moment, Nadia was sorely tempted to tell Dante everything, to tell him about Thea, about her experiments, about Mosely's mission to procure test subjects from among the lowest, most powerless citizens of Paxco. She wanted to thrust a dagger through the Chairman's heart and laugh while he bled.

But it wouldn't be the Chairman who bled if word of his crimes got out. Dante's resistance movement claimed to want to change the government slowly and peaceably—or at least that was what Dante thought the eventual goal was—but despite the Chairman's ruthless quelling of protests, there were plenty of malcontents out there who would gladly turn to violence if given sufficient cause. Triggering a rash of riots that could potentially escalate into full-out civil war was *not* the way to punish the Chairman for his sins. Which meant, she realized with a sinking feeling, that she wouldn't be able to blackmail her way out of this even if she *could* reach the Chairman. Any threat she made to release the recordings would be a bluff, and he was too savvy not to know that.

"I can't tell you what happened," she said. "But you're right that the Chairman hates me. He can't kill me or put me in Riker's." As long as the recordings existed and were hidden. Nadia had arranged for them to be released to the public should something happen to her. "But he can—and obviously will—hurt me in other ways."

Just as he would hurt Nate, in any way he could.

The thought of Nate made her chest ache, and the tears flowed more freely. Why hadn't he come to tell her the dreadful news in person? How could he leave her here in ignorance?

How could he let the Chairman marry him off to someone else?

The tears burst from her in an uncontrolled gush, no longer demure and ladylike. Dante drew her into his arms, cradling her head against his shoulder, and she didn't even think of resisting.

"I'll spend the rest of my life locked up in a retreat somewhere up north," she sobbed, not sure how she would bear it. Five nights at Tranquility had her wanting to scream. How could she live in a place more restrictive and more isolated than this for the rest of her life?

"Maybe not," Dante whispered soothingly, holding her tightly to him. "Your father may win in the end. And even if they do send you away, it might not be forever."

She appreciated his attempts to comfort her, but it could never work. She could see her fate stretching out before her all too clearly. She would be sent to a distant retreat, where everyone was way older than her and female. She would never be seen in public again, might never see her family or Nate again. They could keep her at the retreat against her will until she was eighteen, and then they could keep her there by refusing her access to the family's funds so that she had nowhere else to go. She would never marry, never have children. Hell, she would never even know love, because there would be no boys or men in her life.

"You don't understand," she hiccuped against Dante's jacket. An Employee like Dante would never have had to face the specter of a retreat, couldn't possibly comprehend what such a gilded cage was like.

Dante sighed and stroked her hair. "I *do* understand," he said softly. "And I'll do whatever I can to help you. I'm sure Nate will, too."

Nadia shook her head and tried to pull away from Dante's arms, but he wouldn't let her. She went limp against him. Propriety didn't matter anymore, and if she wanted to let a male servant hold her and comfort her, then she would. His arms felt solid and strong around her, and she liked hearing the steady thump of his heart when she pressed her head to his chest.

"Nate can't help me," she said, feeling the truth of her words down to her bones. She didn't know how the Chairman had convinced Nate to agree to the match with Agnes Belinski, but she knew he hadn't done so willingly. Somehow, his father had gotten a hold on him, and if he was determined to make both Nate and Nadia suffer, then he would be sure to keep them apart.

"Probably not directly," Dante agreed. "I don't know what's going on under all this, but I do know the Chairman will be watching Nate's every step. But he won't be watching *me.*"

He finally released her from his embrace. Nadia would have regretted the loss, if he hadn't cupped her wet cheeks in his hands and stared intently into her eyes.

"We'll find a way, Nadia," he said, with such certainty that she could almost believe him. "Nate and I don't like each other, but we both like you. A lot. We can work together to help you."

"Help me *how?*" It wasn't like she was in some kind of physical danger they could save her from.

"Help you escape, if it comes to that."

"Escape." Somehow, the thought had never occurred to her. Maybe because it was so wildly impractical. "Where would I go? How would I live?" She would have no money, and no way of getting access to money if her family didn't want her to. It wasn't like she could just get a job somewhere. Jobs went to Employees, not Executives, and it wasn't as if she could hide her identity. Especially once the latest scandal broke. Her picture would be plastered over news feeds and gossip columns everywhere.

Dante made a face. "I don't have the answers, at least not now. But we'll figure something out. It might take time, but if you get sent upstate, we'll find a way to get you out. I promise."

Nadia fervently wished she could believe him. Maybe someday, when Nate became Chairman, he would have the power to free her, but not before. Not when the only place she could flee to was the Basement, where she could have food and shelter for free, if she didn't mind living among drug dealers, prostitutes, and gangs who would see her as fresh meat.

"Thank you," she said, because she really did appreciate his kindness and his intentions, even if she didn't believe he could succeed.

Dante nodded gravely, then put his arm around her, snugging her close against his side. Her tears were drying—for now—so she didn't technically need his shoulder to cry on anymore, but she leaned easily against him anyway. His body felt warm and solid and safe against hers, and right now she needed warm, solid, and safe.

There was a long, companionable silence, until Dante suddenly broke it.

"Do you love him?"

She'd been asked that question by reporters dozens of times, and she'd always refused to answer on the grounds that it was private. However, her refusals had always been phrased in such a way as to make the interviewer believe the answer was yes. It was on the tip of her tongue to answer Dante the same way, but he wasn't a reporter. He was a friend and a confidant—the only one she had left to her—and he deserved honesty from her, at least when she could afford to give it.

"He's my best friend," she said, "and I love him like a brother." Even as she said it, Nadia wasn't sure she was being entirely honest after all. There had never been any hope of a romance between her and Nate, but sometimes she suspected she was at least a little in love with him anyway. "But if we were Employees and could marry whom we chose, we never would have ended up with each other." And that part *was* entirely true. "Does that answer your question?"

"Yeah. And sorry if that was too personal."

"If it'd been too personal, I wouldn't have answered." She angled her head so she could see his face. Moonlight limned one side of it while leaving the other cloaked in shadows. The freckles over his nose had faded since he'd started working for the Lake family and spent most of his time indoors, but they were still faintly visible, even in the moonlight. They would be considered an unsightly blemish on an Executive, but Nadia found herself fighting the urge to reach out and touch them.

She licked her lips, aware of how close she was to Dante's sensual mouth. She and Nate had kissed many times, but they had always been sham kisses, meant to help strengthen the illusion that he was into girls. Nadia had no idea what a *real* kiss felt like, and she suddenly wanted to find out in the worst way. She looked into his eyes and saw the answering spark there, but he didn't take her up on what she felt certain was a blatant invitation. He smiled at her and stroked one hand lightly over her hair.

"You've just had some bad news and are in an altered state

of mind," he said gently. "I'm not the kind of asshole who'd take advantage of that."

"Oh, *now* you're going to turn all gentlemanly on me?" she asked, her cheeks heating at the rejection. He'd worded it nicely enough, but why should she expect a guy who thought Executive girls were akin to pampered poodles to want to kiss someone like her? Sure, he seemed to like her just fine now that he'd decided she wasn't cut from the same cloth as most of her peers, but that didn't mean he'd forgotten what she was. What she would always be, even though she would live the rest of her life in disgrace.

It was embarrassingly hard for her to stop leaning against him and put some distance between them on the log, but she managed it, wishing she could sink through the ground in her humiliation. Dante's eyes widened, and he took her hands before she could jump to her feet.

"I'm not saying no," he told her earnestly. "I'm just saying not now."

She appreciated his attempt to spare her feelings, but she knew a rejection when she heard one. And it probably served her right, anyway. Kissing Dante as some kind of secret act of rebellion, or just because he was there, didn't say much about her strength of character. Even if the yearning in her belly suggested there was more to it than that.

"I mean it, Nadia. To tell you the honest truth, I've wanted to kiss you ever since the first time I met you."

She gaped at him. "You thought I was a spoiled, privileged, self-centered Executive bitch, remember?"

One corner of his mouth lifted in a sexy smile that revealed a dimple on his cheek. "No, that's what I thought of the *others*. I knew you were different from the moment you ever-so-politely tore Jewel to shreds with your words."

Nadia smiled a little at the memory. She lost almost as many verbal skirmishes with the Terrible Trio as she won, but the victories were sweet. And she remembered how Dante had visibly fought off a smile when Nadia cut Jewel down to size.

"If you still want to kiss me when I come visit you tomorrow, believe me, I'll be more than happy to let you."

Nadia swallowed hard, realizing he meant it. "You really mean to keep showing up here at midnight every night?"

"Of course I do. I told you I would." Once again, he cupped her face in his hands. "No matter what it feels like, you're *not* alone in this. Okay?"

Damn if Nadia's eyes weren't stinging again, but for very different reasons. No doubt she *should* be trying to talk Dante out of coming. There was risk every time they met, and he had to be running himself ragged. But she needed him too much to do the right thing. And besides, she doubted she was capable of talking him out of it anyway.

Words couldn't express how grateful she felt, so she recklessly threw her arms around him and hugged him.

CHAPTER SEVEN

nate buried his head in his pillow and willed himself to fall asleep. It didn't work this time any better than it had worked the last fifty he'd tried. He flopped over onto his side and glared at his clock, which told him it was almost four A.M. His body felt sluggish and heavy with exhaustion, desperately in need of sleep, but his mind had other ideas, circling endlessly around his fears for Nadia and for his own bleak future with Agnes. He *had* to find his way out of the engagement.

But even if he did, his father could easily find another would-be bride for him, one with as few redeeming features as Agnes. And Nadia's reputation would still be destroyed.

It was all so unfair he wanted to scream.

Nate forced his eyes closed and took a deep breath, searching for a sense of calm or peace, but there was none to be found.

If his nerves hadn't been so taut and his mind so hyperactive, he probably never would have heard the very soft creak of his bedroom door opening, or the even softer sound of footsteps on the carpet as someone entered the room.

Adrenaline jolted through his already-wired system, and he sat up with a startled yelp, suddenly convinced his father had decided to dispose of him once and for all instead of forcing him into marriage.

"Easy," the intruder said, holding up his hands in a calming gesture. "It's just me."

At the sound of Kurt's voice, Nate let out a shuddering breath. His heart was still galloping, and he wondered if maybe he'd been closer to sleep than he'd realized, his mind right on the edge of a nightmare that Kurt had interrupted.

"Sorry to scare you," Kurt said as he approached the bed.

Nate would have liked to pretend he hadn't been scared, but Kurt would never buy the act. "We have to stop meeting like this," he responded instead, making room so that Kurt could sit on the bed beside him.

Kurt snorted. "It's like this or not at all. Which would you rather?"

"Don't be a bastard."

"But I *am* a bastard."

Nate sat up and rubbed his bleary eyes. His mind was too slow and his heart too heavy for banter. He turned on the light beside his bed, though he quickly dimmed it to its lowest setting, to keep his eyeballs from searing.

Kurt was dressed in his full Basement regalia, black leather pants hugging every curve of his ass and thighs, a red mesh shirt displaying the tattoos that covered his chest and abdomen. A silver bar pierced his eyebrow, and Nate could tell by the slight lisp that Kurt was wearing the little silver ball in his tongue. His eyes were lined with kohl, and his head was covered in a dark fuzz that suggested he was letting his hair grow back. He looked wild, and sexy, and mouth-wateringly tempting. And yet . . .

"You're wearing this getup for me, right?" Nate asked with narrowed eyes. "Not because you're living in the Basement and have to blend in. *Right?*"

Kurt's smile looked almost sheepish, which was a rare expression for him. "I'm not gonna lie to you."

Nate resisted the urge to point out how many times he already had. "I thought we had a deal. I give you dollars, you don't go back to Debasement."

Kurt reached out and brushed a caress over Nate's cheek. "I love that you think you're a man of the world and that you're really so naive under it all."

Nate felt the color burning in his cheeks, but the affection in Kurt's voice took a lot of the sting out of his words. "I'm not as naive as you think," he said, because he couldn't resist trying to defend himself.

Kurt raised his pierced eyebrow. "And you thought an unemployed Basement-dweller could find a place to live somewhere *other* than in the Basement? They check ID if you try to rent or buy Employee housing, you know. Even if I showed up in the system as employed, you wanted me to keep my head down. If I rent a legitimate place, then I'm out there for anyone to find."

Nate felt like an idiot. He'd never in his life had to fend for himself, and it had never occurred to him that a Basement-dweller like Kurt couldn't rent himself an apartment just because he had dollars.

Kurt stroked his cheek again. "It's okay, Nate. I lived most of my life in Debasement. I know how to stay safe there."

Nate swallowed hard. "At least tell me you're not working."

Kurt showed no sign of being offended. "I'm not working. That's what your dollars are for."

Of course. If those dollars weren't going into rent, as Nate had originally intended, then they were buying Kurt some modicum of safety and security in Debasement. Allowing him to pay off whatever drug lords or gang leaders demanded as "rent" or "dues" or protection money. Food and shelter might be free in Debasement, but that didn't mean a Basement-dweller didn't need cash. There was a reason Kurt had sold himself before Nate met him, and it wasn't because he enjoyed the work.

Kurt's lips lifted in a sudden, wicked smile. "'Course, not working means I'm not getting any." He raised his hand to the V of Nate's pajama top, fingers brushing over the exposed skin there.

The touch peppered Nate's skin with goose bumps and awakened an instant ache. One he had no right to be feeling under the dismal circumstances.

"We shouldn't—" he started to protest, but Kurt silenced him with a finger on his lips while his other hand slipped the first button of his pajamas free.

"Forget that shit for a moment," Kurt murmured. "You look like you could use some serious stress relief. Let me give it to you. We'll talk after."

Nate found he didn't have the strength of character to resist.

ONE thing Nate could say about Kurt: he knew how to deliver stress relief.

Nate stretched languorously and wished they could stay in bed like this forever, never inviting the outside world back in. A little voice in the back of his head whispered that it was disloyal of him to be experiencing pleasure when, thanks to him, Nadia's life had been ruined. He cuddled closer into Kurt's arms in hopes of drowning that voice out, but as the sweat cooled on his skin and real life insisted on intruding, the afterglow dimmed.

"Do you know about the engagement?" he asked, wondering if it was a coincidence that Kurt had made an appearance tonight, when Nate was reeling from his father's cruelty.

"Yeah." Kurt gave him one more rib-crushing squeeze, then put a little distance between them on the bed and propped his head on his hand. "Dante overheard her folks fighting about it."

Nate frowned in puzzlement. Dante and Kurt obviously knew each other from their mutual resistance activities, but Nate was a little surprised that Dante found the engagement news so vital that he had to report it to Kurt on the very day he overheard the argument about it.

Grinning, Kurt reached out and smoothed away the frown line between Nate's eyebrows. "No, he didn't rush out to tell me the moment he heard the news." The grin faded. "He went to visit Nadia earlier tonight."

"What?" Nate yelped, sitting up in a hurry.

Kurt sat up more slowly. "He meets her at the fence line every night. Not anything official—I didn't know about it until he called me earlier. Says it's for moral support."

Kurt was looking into Nate's eyes searchingly. Nate tried not to show the irrational anger that spiked through his heart at the thought of Dante having secret nocturnal meetings with Nadia.

"You have a problem with that?" Kurt asked, that pierced eyebrow of his arching higher than ever.

"No!" Nate said, a little too sharply to be convincing. He blew out a deep breath. "I'm being stupid," he admitted. "I don't like Dante, and I don't like the idea of Nadia leaning on him." It should have been *Nate* she leaned on, *Nate* who was there when she needed him. For most of his life, they had been each other's only true friends, their friendship untainted by jealousy or politics or ambition. He *hated* that Dante had been out to see her, and he had not.

"You're jealous."

"No, I'm not." Nate mentally rolled his eyes at himself for the childish—and even less convincing—response.

"Yes, you are," Kurt said with a laugh, ruffling Nate's hair affectionately. Nate batted his hand away, not in the mood for playful gestures. Though at least the playful gesture told him his irrational jealousy wasn't hurting Kurt's feelings.

"Like I said, it's stupid. I don't want her like that."

"But you don't want anyone else to want her 'like that,' either."

The twinkle in Kurt's eyes said the teasing was still good-natured, but Nate was uncomfortably aware that Kurt didn't exactly see in him a pinnacle of maturity. Kurt could have been describing a child throwing a tantrum because some other kid was playing with his discarded toy.

"Maybe there's a part of me that doesn't," he admitted reluctantly. "But I don't want Nadia to be facing this alone." Nate wondered if there was some way he could tag along with Dante to one of these secret meetings of his, but quickly dismissed the idea. First of all, they'd probably kill each other before getting to the retreat. Second of all, Nate would probably end up feeling like a third wheel, and a jealous one at that. And third, he had to be extra careful with his movements, sure his father had eyes watching him all the time. If he snuck off to visit Nadia in the dead of night, the Chairman would retaliate by making sure Nadia was moved out of his reach.

"Well, looks like you don't have to worry about her facing it alone after all."

"You can stop teasing me anytime now."

"Why would I want to do that?"

Nate couldn't help smiling. It had only been a couple of weeks since Kurt had been by his side day and night, but it felt like a lifetime ago, and he sorely missed the easy camaraderie between them. Their lives were so different that it was almost impossible to imagine that they could relate to each other in any meaningful way, and yet there had always been a palpable connection between them.

"I miss you," Nate said softly, his heart aching with the loss.

"Then hire me back. You don't want Nadia to be alone, and *I* don't want *you* to be alone."

The temptation to say yes was almost overwhelming. If he had Kurt back in his life, available whenever he needed him, maybe the situation with Agnes would become more bearable. But Nate had just seen a perfect example of how the Chairman could shatter lives, and he didn't dare put Kurt at risk.

"The guy I was before would have been selfish enough to do it," he said. "Maybe something got lost in translation when I was made into a Replica, but I feel like that guy, the original Nate, is a total stranger to me. I can't put you in danger just because I'm lonely. I *won't*."

"You're the same guy," Kurt countered. "You're so much the same I keep forgetting you're a Replica. You were never selfish. You were just . . . careless, sometimes."

"Careless" didn't sound much better to Nate, but he wasn't going to argue about word choice.

"Everything that's happened . . . It's kinda opened your eyes. So you're different, but you're still the same guy."

Nate allowed himself a little snort of laughter. Maybe Kurt was right. Maybe the changes in him had nothing to do with being a Replica and everything to do with the crap life had thrown at him recently.

"Does it ever weird you out?" Nate asked, unable to look into Kurt's face for fear of the answer. "Me being a Replica?"

He saw Kurt's shrug out of the corner of his eye. "Yeah, if I think about it. But I don't think about it unless you make me."

Nate supposed that was one way to handle it.

"So anyway," Kurt said in an unsubtle change of subject, "Dante's seeing Nadia every night, and I can meet with Dante without either of us being watched. Dante thought you might want us to pass a message to her."

Nate thought he heard a hint of disapproval in Kurt's voice, but he chose to ignore it. "So he told her about Agnes?"

"Yeah."

Nate made a conscious effort to relax his tight jaw muscles before he ground his teeth into dust. Nadia should have heard the news from him, or at least from her family. Not from some resistance double agent with questionable motives.

"You okay?" Kurt asked, laying a hand on Nate's shoulder.

Nate rested his head in his hands, hating the feeling of helplessness that had plagued him from the moment his father told him the news.

"No," he said hoarsely. "I'm not okay. My father's going to force me to marry a girl with the looks and personality of a wet sponge, and Nadia's whole life is being ruined because of me."

"It sucks. But you could have been born in Debasement. So could she. How many Basement-dwellers do you suppose would kill to have your problems?"

Nate almost lashed out, stung by Kurt's apparent lack of

sympathy. Neither his problems nor Nadia's were petty, and even a Basement-dweller might not be so eager to take them on if they knew what was really at stake, if they knew just what kind of threat hovered over their heads. But of course, Kurt *didn't* know, and Nate wasn't planning to tell him.

It wasn't until he saw the searching look in Kurt's eyes that he wondered if the comment was meant to annoy Nate into telling him more. There was a time when Nate had felt he could tell Kurt anything, but those days were past.

Kurt sighed, perhaps disappointed with the failure of his fishing mission. He leaned over the side of the bed and rooted around in the heap of clothes he'd left there. Nate took a moment to admire the curve of his hip and the Chinese calligraphy tattooed right above his butt. Kurt had told him the characters said the equivalent of *fuck you,* though he'd had to take the tattoo artist's word for it. Who knew that crude words could look so elegant?

Kurt made a sound of satisfaction and rolled back over, a phone in his hand. "I know Dante gave you a secure phone already, but if you want to call me, use this one."

Nate gave a humorless laugh. "You mean your resistance buddies won't be listening in on this one?" Despite the little flare of bitterness, he took the phone, relieved that he would finally have a way to get in touch with Kurt rather than having to wait for him to drop by in the dead of night.

"Don't be a dick. What did you expect Dante to do? Go buy you a black market secure phone with his own money and no strings attached? He convinced the resistance to provide two fucking expensive phones. You'd better cough up some good information for it and quit complaining."

Nate rubbed his eyes. He'd almost allowed himself to forget that he'd promised information in return for the phone.

He'd also forgotten what it was like to be with someone who didn't hesitate to tell him when he was being an asshole.

"Message received," he said, though he still found it hard to be all that grateful for a bugged phone. "How much do I owe you? Oh, wait. You bought it with my money, didn't you?"

"Smart-ass," Kurt said, punching him on the shoulder. "Now it's time to spill. And if you're tempted to screw Dante because you don't like him, remember, he's your path to Nadia. You need to get a message to her without making her use her phone and maybe lose it, you give me a call, and I'll get it to her through Dante."

Nate didn't need the reminder. No, he didn't like Dante, but he needed him, and he knew it. He wasn't stupid enough to antagonize someone he needed.

Hoping he wasn't making a big mistake, starting some kind of trouble that would come back to bite him, Nate told Kurt that he was talking to the last Replica that would ever be made.

CHAPTER EIGHT

Тнє news hit the net first thing Friday morning. *The resistance works fast,* Nate thought sourly as he flipped from story to story. It seemed every member of the media, plus a host of online "personalities," had rushed to share their opinions and their predictions of doom.

None of them had any real facts. Nate had told Kurt only that there would be no more backup scans performed or Replicas created. He had steadfastly refused to explain why. He hadn't liked keeping secrets from Kurt, but the media frenzy was clear evidence he had done the right thing. Stock prices had already plummeted, and he imagined there would be demonstrations all around the state as opponents of the Replica technology declared victory and those who feared for their livelihoods took offense. Nate didn't want to imagine the shock wave that would rip through the state if people knew what the true cost of the Replica technology had been.

The news hadn't been out for more than an hour before the Chairman held a press conference during which he assured the people of Paxco and the world that the Replica program was not, in fact, defunct, but was merely on a temporary hiatus while some technical difficulties were resolved. He accused the press of exaggeration and sensationalism. Funny how, afterward, the members of the Paxco press corps bought the Chairman's story hook, line, and sinker, while the foreign press remained skeptical.

The Chairman's statement had gone a long way toward slowing the bleeding, although stock prices were bound to be depressed for a while. But he couldn't pretend the situation was temporary forever, and if today's preview was anything to go by, the day of reckoning was going to suck. Nate might have felt bad about leaking the news, except it had to come out eventually.

Still in his robe and slippers, Nate got off the net about thirty minutes after he had planned to arrive at work. As usual, he had an endless series of meetings he was supposed to sit in on, but his role in those meetings was always just to sit there and listen quietly. He had no official job duties—at least none of even moderate importance—and his participation was all part of one long training exercise for when he would be Chairman someday. He was trying to be more responsible about his training, he really was, but setting foot within ten miles of Headquarters today was probably a terrible idea.

There was one consequence of sharing state secrets with the resistance that he had anticipated—and dreaded—from the very beginning. The number of people who knew that the Replica program was now defunct could be counted on one hand, and with Nadia hidden away in her retreat with no access to the outside world, the only person the Chairman could possibly suspect of leaking the information was Nate. Somehow, Nate didn't think his father would take it very well, even if the Paxco PR machine convinced everyone the situation was only temporary.

You did the right thing, he told himself, but he wished he felt more convinced. Getting that phone to Nadia had been vital, and if he hadn't followed through and given the resistance the information he'd promised, he would have lost any chance of making them into allies when he needed them. But their haste to broadcast what he'd told them made him even more aware that he needed to tread cautiously. He couldn't see how releasing the information to the public prematurely was going to help their cause if they were aiming for peaceful reform. Now, if they were hoping to destabilize the government to make it more vulnerable to a violent takeover . . .

Nate commanded his majordomo to intercept all phone calls and potential visitors—an order that Hartman accepted with one of his looks of long-suffering patience—and spent the day pretending he was in an Executive retreat himself. Once he switched off the net, he kept it off. He ignored phone calls that came through to his private line, and he didn't even look out his windows, much less step outside. Perhaps it was childish of him to insist on living in the land of denial, but he would take whatever reprieve he could get.

He was able to keep his head buried in the sand until almost three o'clock. That was when Hartman told him his father had called and ordered Nate to appear in his office in fifteen minutes. If Nate dropped everything and ran, he might be able to make it to Headquarters in that amount of time, but he didn't see much point in it. His father couldn't get any more pissed off at him than he was now, and if he had figured out a way to punish Nate for his latest transgression, Nate didn't want to know about it.

"You're not going, sir?" Hartman asked when Nate made no response to the demand.

It was Nate's turn to put on the long-suffering expression. "How long have you worked for me, Hartman?" It was a rhetorical question. Hartman had been with him since he'd moved into the apartment, the day after he'd turned eighteen.

More than long enough to be intimately familiar with Nate's propensity to shirk meetings.

"He's not going to take no for an answer," Hartman said grimly.

"Next time he calls, tell him he can send security to march me over there in chains if he wants to. That might give the press something new to drool over for a while."

"Sir—"

"I said no," Nate snapped, then mentally smacked himself for being an asshole. Not that it was the first time he had put Hartman in the unenviable position of being stuck between him and his father, but he was trying to be more considerate of other people, and this was a serious case of backsliding.

Nate huffed out a breath. "Sorry, Hartman. It's not your fault my father and I are both pig-headed assholes. I shouldn't have snapped at you."

Hartman looked like he was about to faint with shock. Nate wondered guiltily how many other times he had carelessly snapped at the man without ever bothering to apologize.

"Next time he calls," Nate said, "put him through to me. I'll tell him no myself."

"Yes, sir," Hartman said in obvious relief. "Thank you, sir."

"No, thank *you* for putting up with me."

Hartman cracked a small smile. "I have two teenagers at home. Believe me, I'm used to it. Sir."

Nate laughed and made a mental note to ask Hartman about his children sometime when things weren't so . . . tense. He should at least know the names and ages of his staff's kids.

Now all that was left for Nate to do was wait for the explosion and hope the shrapnel didn't kill anybody.

• • •

contrary to Nate's expectations, the Chairman didn't call when Nate failed to answer his summons. Nate had an uneasy feeling in his stomach when his father's fifteen-minute deadline expired and the phone didn't ring. The unease grew deeper as another fifteen minutes passed with no call. It wasn't like Nate *wanted* him to call, of course, but he couldn't help thinking the Chairman was up to something. Planning another way to make Nate's life miserable.

The phone rang plenty of times in the next hour, Hartman diligently answering, but never was it the Chairman. Nate paced his apartment, the tension in his body making him feel like he'd drunk too much coffee.

At five, Nate was standing in front of his living room windows, staring out at the city while sipping from a glass of scotch, a fine single malt that Nate's less-than-sophisticated palate couldn't distinguish from the cheapest rotgut money could buy. He'd only gotten a couple of sips into his system— nowhere near enough to calm him—when there was a commotion in the vestibule, which was discreetly concealed from view so Nate didn't have to feel like his guards were watching his every move.

It wasn't the commotion of someone trying to get in without permission; it was more like a ripple of shock and uncertainty. The hairs on the back of his neck rising, Nate turned from the window in time to see his father clear the entryway. Both Hartman and Nate's butler came running, no doubt summoned by the guards to see to the Chairman's every need, but he waved them away. Nate fought a prickle of irritation that neither of his servants thought to look at him for confirmation that they could leave, but of course the Chairman outranked him in all things.

Nate took another sip of his scotch, hoping to moisten his

dry mouth. His father almost never came to his apartment. Certainly Nate wouldn't have expected him to show up in person to chew him out. When he wanted to see you, you came to him, not the other way around.

Nate searched the Chairman's face as he entered the living room, expecting to see the fury and disdain his actions had triggered. Instead, he saw something that looked suspiciously like sadness. It was not an expression Nate could ever remember seeing on his father's face before, and he gripped the tumbler more tightly as tension coursed through his body.

"I had meant to talk to you about the trouble you caused by leaking information that wasn't ready for public consumption," the Chairman said, with only a small spark of heat in his voice, as if the issue were of only minor importance. "But that will have to wait for another time. I'm afraid I've had some bad news."

Nadia! Nate thought, his heart nearly stopping. *Something's happened to her.* Nate swallowed hard, keeping his panicked thoughts to himself. If something had happened to Nadia, the Chairman wouldn't look so sad. Hell, he'd probably be gloating—or worried about the recordings being released due to her death. So it wasn't that. But Nate couldn't imagine what could make a man who had murdered his own son sad.

"It's your mother," the Chairman said, and if Nate didn't know better, he would swear his father was a little choked up. "I'm afraid she's passed."

The news was so unexpected it took Nate a few seconds to absorb what he'd just heard.

His mother was dead.

There was a tight feeling in his chest and in the back of his throat as he remembered the bright-eyed, laughing woman of his childhood. The woman who had always loved him unconditionally, or so he'd thought at the time. Many of his illusions about her had shattered when she'd abandoned him and his father to spend the rest of her days behind the walls of a retreat. Not once in all the years she'd been there had she ventured out. Not once since she'd entered the retreat had Nate seen her face in anything but a photograph or even heard her voice.

Ellie Hayes had effectively been dead to him for going on ten years now. So why did he feel like there were a thousand rubber bands constricting his chest, making it hard to breathe?

Breathing became even harder as Nate considered the timing of his mother's demise. His head snapped up, and he squeezed the tumbler in his hand so hard he was lucky he didn't shatter it and cut himself.

"You did this," he growled at his father, taking an aggressive stride forward. "This is part of your vendetta, isn't it? Or is it my punishment for leaking the information?"

Nate expected his father to respond in kind, with the anger Nate was always so good at triggering. Instead, the Chairman sighed and rubbed his eyes.

"There's no vendetta, son."

"Oh, sure. That's why you're forcing me to marry Agnes. And it's just a coincidence that my mom died today."

"It *is* a coincidence," the Chairman said with a hint of heat in his voice. "She's been fighting cancer for more than two years, and her condition had been steadily deteriorating for months."

Nate shook his head as his face went cold. "No. You killed her. I know you did."

"I can show you the medical records if you want. We were obviously estranged, but I still served as her next of kin."

"I don't believe it!" Nate insisted, wondering if sheer will could make it so. "If she knew she was dying, she would have . . . She would have . . ." He couldn't force the words out past his hurt. "You killed her," he finished lamely.

"I know it would be easier for you to believe that, but I'm sorry, Nate. Cancer killed her, not me."

Nate blinked in surprise. His father *never* called him "Nate." It was always "son" or "Nathaniel." Only people who actually *liked* him called him "Nate." It felt downright weird, and almost invasive, to have the Chairman call him that.

"I may be angry with you," his father continued, "but you're still my son. And though I know you don't believe it, I do love you. The marriage arrangement is a political and economic necessity, not a punishment."

"Why should I believe a word that leaves your mouth? And if Mom has had cancer for two years and you knew about it, why didn't you tell me?"

"I didn't think it would serve any purpose. She refused to see anyone. I wouldn't even have known she was sick myself if the staff hadn't contacted me.

"Your mother became . . . unbalanced after our falling out. I thought entering the retreat would be good for her, that maybe if she spent a few months there, she would heal. In the end, though, I think it was the worst thing she could have done. She could live there in perfect denial, and the more time passed, the more attractive that life of denial became. I have no doubt that in her heart, she loved you until the end, but she'd broken from her old life so thoroughly there was no coming back."

There was a sheen in his father's eyes, and he was breathing extra deep, as if to keep grief at bay. Even so, Nate didn't believe him, sure the Chairman could summon the trappings of grief on demand if he wanted to.

"What really happened between you two?" Nate asked.

He remembered the coldness and the distance entering his parents' marriage, and toward the end, he remembered hearing them shouting at one another—always behind closed doors, and never quite loud enough for Nate to understand what they were fighting about.

When Ellie left for the retreat, she did so with minimal fanfare. The press—and Nate—had been told nothing about why she was leaving, beyond that she and the Chairman had had a "falling out." There was rampant speculation, of course, the most popular theory being that there'd been infidelity involved. However, speculation was not fact.

Nate had asked his father countless times over the years about the disintegration of the marriage. His father had never answered, and Nate didn't expect things to be different even now. But for once, his father surprised him.

"I was unfaithful to her, and she was incapable of forgiving me for it."

The very personal admission was so surprising, Nate didn't know what to say. He certainly had no interest in even *thinking* about his parents having a sex life, with each other or with anyone else. Theirs had, of course, been a marriage of state, and any happiness they may have experienced in the union was purely coincidental. Nate had the vague sense that they had loved each other once, but his only concrete memories were from the time after the strain entered their marriage, when the most positive word he could use to describe their feelings toward one another was *indifferent*.

If his mother really had fled to the retreat for the rest of her life over an infidelity, that spoke to a much deeper relationship between his parents than Nate had ever imagined.

The Chairman cleared his throat. "Your mother made it clear in her will that she did not want a full state funeral.

Even in death, she wished to remain out of the public eye. The funeral will be held on Monday, at the retreat. Her wishes were that only friends and family attend, but I cannot afford to offend my top Executives during these difficult times. I'll keep the guest list as small as possible, and of course the press will not be allowed on the grounds of the retreat. That is the best I can do to honor her wishes."

Nate nodded, his feelings a jumbled mess. His father's explanation that his mother had been "unbalanced" did nothing to lessen Nate's hurt and anger over the fact that she hadn't tried to see him, or even talk to him on the phone, before she died. He hadn't realized until now that a part of him had always held out hope that she would eventually end her self-imposed exile. That she would leave the retreat and beg Nate's forgiveness for having left him motherless for so long. That she would realize her love for her son was stronger than her hatred for her husband.

But that pleasant fantasy had died with her.

If ever he missed having Nadia in his life, it was now. She would understand his feelings in a way that no one else would, not even Kurt. She had been there for him when his mother had first left, and she had consoled him through the early years when he had stubbornly continued to hope his mother would come home, only to have those hopes dashed again and again.

"Will you make sure Nadia's parents let her come to the funeral?" he asked, knowing he was tempting fate. No matter what his father said, Nate was convinced there was a vendetta in play, and revealing his desire to have Nadia there might be the best way to guarantee she wouldn't be allowed to come. "No one knows that she's not my fiancée anymore, and the press won't be there. There's no reason—"

"I'll make sure she's there." If Nate didn't know better, he would swear the look on his father's face was one of concern, even care. "But try not to grow too dependent on her, son. We both know she will no longer be a part of your life once the engagement to Agnes is made official."

Nate swallowed several angry responses. His father might be able to control whom Nate married, but Nate was damned if he'd allow him to control who was a part of his life. If Nadia's family sent her away, he would find a way to bring her back. Whatever it took. And if his father and Agnes didn't like it, well . . . all the better.

CHAPTER NINE

Having spent all day alone with her gloomy thoughts, Nadia couldn't wait to get out of her room and meet Dante on Friday night. Leaving well before their midnight rendezvous time, she was so impatient that her sense of caution failed her. The moment she stepped out of her room, she practically collided with Mari, who was patrolling the hallway. Not *really* patrolling, of course. Just making herself available for any guests who might need something.

"Is there something I can do for you, Miss Lake?" Mari asked, glancing pointedly at her watch. Most retreat guests were in bed by now.

Nadia smiled and hoped she didn't look as anxious as she felt. The last thing she needed was to make Mari suspicious.

"No, thank you," she said. "I couldn't sleep, so I thought I'd stop by the library and get a new book."

She couldn't tell from Mari's expression whether she was buying it or not.

"Poor dear," Mari said, still with the same expression of false cheer. Her face had probably frozen that way. "Would you like a cup of chamomile tea? Works great for me when I have trouble sleeping."

"No, thanks." God, this woman was annoying. Nadia wasn't sure if she was genuinely trying to be helpful or if she was just nosy. "Curling up with a good book is what does it for me."

"All right. You let me know if you change your mind."

"I'll do that," Nadia promised, then practically bolted from the hall.

Shaken by what felt like a close call, Nadia dutifully stopped by the library and picked up a book. At least this way if she wound up bumping into Mari again on her way back in, she'd have evidence that she'd been to the library as she'd claimed. How she would explain being gone so long—especially if Mari asked the librarian how long Nadia had been there— she wasn't yet sure.

Book tucked under her arm, Nadia slipped out of the building and made her way across the grounds. Clouds had rolled in since last she was outdoors. The grass was damp, and the air smelled of wet earth. Nadia hadn't noticed it raining, but she supposed that wasn't surprising when she'd been lost in thought. A quick glance up at the sky revealed no hint of moon or stars, but she had no way of knowing if those clouds portended more rain.

Dante was waiting for her when she arrived at their rendezvous, and once again, he was inside the fence. She would have scolded him for taking unnecessary risks, except she was so glad to see him she found herself greeting him with a hug instead. She accidentally thumped him on the back with the book, and he laughed as he obliged her by slipping his arms around her.

"Is that a book in your hand, or are you just glad to see me?" he teased, and Nadia smiled against his chest, surprised at how natural it felt to hold him like that.

"I didn't realize the two were mutually exclusive."

Keeping an arm around her shoulders, Dante guided her into the cover of the woods. He impressed her with his sense of direction by heading straight to the fallen tree they'd sat on the previous night. Like everything else around them, it was damp from the rain, but Dante opened up his raincoat and invited her to sit intimately close beside him.

"You're early," Dante commented.

"So are you." She'd expected to have to wait for him, but she certainly wasn't unhappy that she didn't have to. "How long have you been here?"

She felt his shrug. "A while. I parked closer tonight than I have before. I don't want to leave the car in the same place every night. Someone might notice."

His words reminded her once again how much of a risk Dante was taking by coming here every night. Maybe he was right, and his position as a security spy would allow him to talk himself out of trouble, but she didn't imagine his superiors in the department would be too happy about his extracurricular activities. She wasn't even sure his *resistance* superiors would be happy about them. What vital information could he possibly learn from a girl who was completely cut off from her Executive life?

"You shouldn't keep coming here," she said, though even she could hear how halfhearted her protest was. She *wanted* to do the honorable thing and urge him to protect himself, but she wasn't sure how she could face her current situation without his visits to look forward to.

"I want to," he said simply. "I always thought Executives lived the good life, but I can see with my own two eyes that they're treating you like shit. Um, I mean dirt."

She glanced up at his face and saw his wince. It made her smile. "You think I've never heard the word 'shit' before?" she teased. "I've also heard 'fuck,' and—"

Dante laughed and covered his ears. "Stop! You're shattering my illusions!"

She gave him an answering grin, even as she thought to herself sadly that with her fall from grace, she would never have to censor her language again. Her fellow inmates at the Executive retreat might look down their noses at her if she let something "unladylike" slip out of her mouth, but it would be nothing compared to the reaction she'd have gotten out in the public world. Executive girls did *not* swear. That didn't mean she'd never been exposed to bad language, both on the net and from real people. Bishop, in particular, had gone out of his way to be offensive whenever he thought he could get away with it.

She snuggled more closely against Dante's side as the humor drained out of her. "You haven't by any chance heard anything else about what my parents are going to do with me, have you?" Perhaps it was disloyal of her to encourage Dante to spy on her parents, but since she figured he'd be doing it anyway, it couldn't hurt to try to find out what he'd learned.

Dante rubbed up and down her arm in a comforting gesture. "I don't think they've even spoken to each other since yesterday. They were both pretty angry. Your mother and your sister went a couple rounds this evening, I think, but by the time I got close enough to hear what they were saying, they'd stopped. Don't give up hope. You've got people in your court."

Nadia made a vague sound of agreement, but she wasn't what you'd call convinced. Gerri was a more formidable opponent than their father, but even *she* had trouble standing up to their mother. And, of course, she had her children to think about. If Nadia remained in the public eye, the taint of her scandal would trickle down to every member of her family. Right now, her niece and nephew were too young to understand and be hurt by it, but when they got older, they would be subject to the taunts of jealous peers.

Nadia was already feeling gloomy enough that the first drop of rain spattering on the tip of her nose seemed only fitting. More drops quickly followed.

"Damn it!" Dante cursed, then started wriggling around. Nadia had no idea what he was doing until he managed to work one of his arms out of the sleeve of his coat. "Put this on."

Nadia shook her head and put her hand on his arm to stop him before he could go any further. "I won't melt," she told him as it started raining harder.

She read the stubborn jut of his chin before the next words left his mouth. "You can't go back to the retreat all wet."

She didn't let go of his arm, and with her sitting on part of his coat already, she had him fairly well hobbled. "It's a lost cause. Even if I put your coat on and raise the hood, my feet and legs will still get wet. If someone sees me coming in, they'll know I've been outside." Not to mention that the book she'd taken from the library was already starting to feel soggy.

Dante looked so stricken she couldn't resist reaching up and running her fingers down his cheek. "There's no rule that says I can't go out wandering in the rain at midnight if I want to," she assured him. "I'm not going to get into any trouble."

She would have to be extra careful about any future midnight forays, because the staff would probably be suspicious of her explanation. She'd definitely be worried that someone was watching her. But that wasn't the same as getting in trouble, and she only had to worry about it if someone actually saw her.

Dante went back to looking stubborn. "If you think I'm going to sit here in my coat while you get soaked, you're nuts."

"Out here in the middle of the night with no one to see,

you're not a servant, and I'm not an Executive, and you have the right to wear your own coat."

The muscles in his jaw worked. "For your information, I'm not a real servant anywhere else, either. And I'd offer my coat to an Employee girl just as fast, so it's not some stupid class thing."

He tried to slip his other arm out of his sleeve, but Nadia held on tight, wondering if she looked as stubborn as he did. "You mean it's some stupid sex thing instead, right? As in the big, strapping man can't let the helpless little girl get rained on?"

"Are you always this difficult?" he asked in exasperation.

"I try." She wasn't quite sure where she was finding the guts from, but she actually winked at him. Apparently, she was channeling her inner Nate, though she somehow doubted Dante saw it that way.

The rain was steady now, and her hair was plastered to the top of her head. Her sweater was so far keeping the rain from soaking through, but the same could not be said of her spa pants, which were beginning to cling to her legs. Dante's arm around her shoulders was keeping her partially dry there, despite the way the empty sleeve drooped, and her side where she was pressed up against him was still deliciously warm.

Dante rolled his eyes dramatically. "Fine. Put your arm in this sleeve." He wriggled the empty sleeve, as if she might have some doubt about which one he meant. "We'll share."

It seemed like a fair compromise, especially when she didn't think she could possibly convince him to put his own arm back in the sleeve. She quickly discovered, however, that the coat wasn't all that roomy, and to get her arm in the sleeve, she had to do some odd contortions.

"Here," Dante said, "this'll make it easier."

Nadia let out an undignified little squeak as Dante hauled her onto his lap. Since his coat had been open, his pants were wet, but she didn't mind a bit. Her cheeks burning, she got her arm into the sleeve. The coat strained across Dante's broad back, but the strain lessened when she slipped her other arm around him under the coat. He held the coat as close around her as he could, but Nadia hardly felt the chill of the rain anymore. ~

Nadia felt the beat of Dante's heart where her body pressed against his, aware that his pulse had quickened—as had hers. Rain ran in rivulets down his face, trickling under the collar of his coat and dripping off the tip of his nose. His hair, darkened by rain and night, hung in damp tendrils against his skin, and his eyes looked huge and hungry. But most shocking— and thrilling—of all was that sitting on his lap, she couldn't help but notice the way he stirred beneath her. It made her pulse trip and her breath hitch, this oh-so-tangible evidence that he wanted her in a way Nate never had, never *could*.

Dante cleared his throat. "Maybe we shouldn't—" he started in a still-hoarse voice, but Nadia was dead tired of doing what she *should* do. Just this once, she was going to do what she *wanted* to do. She raised her free arm to wrap her hand around the back of Dante's neck, then pulled his head down toward hers. Meeting him halfway, she kissed him.

She thought perhaps that he'd offer up at least a token resistance, that his sense of propriety might put up barriers she'd have to work harder to knock down, but the moment her lips touched his, it was like a circuit was completed. He made a soft, sexy groaning sound deep in his throat and immediately deepened the kiss, angling his head for the best fit. His lips were deliciously soft, and yet demanding at the same time. Nadia's body thrilled in a way it never had before, showing her just how much she had been missing during the chaste kisses she and Nate had staged.

Dante's tongue brushed against the seam of her lips, and without thinking about it, Nadia opened her mouth and invited him in. The first touch of his tongue against hers was both incendiary and . . . strange. She'd never really thought about what another person's tongue might feel like, so soft and hot and pliant. She wondered at the new sensation for about half a second before she lost herself again, feeling without thinking.

Rain continued to patter, and if Dante's kiss hadn't been warming her from the inside out, Nadia would have shivered in the damp chill. Rainwater had soaked through her sweater wherever it wasn't protected by Dante's coat. Drops pattered against her exposed cheek. And she didn't give a damn. Dante was kissing her, and he *meant* it, and that was all that mattered. It was the most glorious thing she'd ever felt, and she wanted it to go on forever.

Dante pulled away long before she was ready. He was breathing hard, and she could feel the tension in his body, tension that spoke of a desire and longing that matched her own.

"We have to stop," he whispered, his lips still within kissing distance of hers.

"Why?" Nadia asked, trying to close the distance, but Dante cupped his hand around her cheek and held her off.

It was so dark, Nadia could see little more than shadows, and yet she was intensely aware of his gaze burning into her, and there was a slight tremor in the hand against her cheek. He took a deep breath, then swallowed hard before he answered.

"Because if we don't, this is going to go too far." He shifted beneath her, making her even more aware of his obvious arousal.

By the values of Executive society, they had already gone *way* too far, mostly because of the difference in their social status. But even if Dante were a respectable Executive, going any further than heated kisses would be unacceptable. An Executive girl was expected to maintain her virtue for the man she was destined to marry. Once she became a full adult in the eyes of society—which wouldn't happen until she was in her twenties—the rules of conduct would relax slightly. But a girl of Nadia's age would be ruined. Of course, Nadia already *was* ruined in the eyes of society, because everyone assumed she'd been sleeping with Nate. The fact that it wasn't true was of no importance.

"It seems to me that since I'm ruined anyway, I can decide for myself how far is too far," she said, trying to convince herself that this, at least, was a good thing.

"You're not ruined yet," he murmured as his thumb caressed her cheek, his hand still burning hot against her skin. "The new marriage arrangement hasn't been made public, and it's always possible it will fall through before anyone but your family knows."

Technically true, she supposed. But if the Chairman decided she wasn't a fit bride for his son—or just that he wanted to punish her for having blackmailed him into destroying Thea—it seemed unlikely her arrangement with Nate would be allowed to stand even if Agnes were somehow removed from the picture.

"Besides," Dante continued before she could voice her opinion, "if we were going to take this any further, I'd rather it be sometime when it isn't cold and raining and generally miserable out."

That point was considerably harder to argue, and some of the starch left Nadia's spine.

What was she *thinking,* anyway? She was not reckless. She was not impulsive. She didn't dive into things without examining the consequences carefully in advance. She'd felt a reluctant attraction to Dante since they'd first met, but that attraction hadn't truly caught fire until she'd been locked away in this forsaken retreat, cut off from all men and boys.

Was any of it real? Or was she just using Dante because he was convenient? Could she possibly trust herself when her life was crumbling around her and her emotions were in a constant state of turmoil and confusion?

Nadia shivered, and Dante cuddled her closer. The rain was starting to let up, but she was already soaked through. Even if no one saw her sneak back into the dorm, her clothes wouldn't be dry by morning. Whoever came in to tidy up would find the wet clothes and know she'd been out in the rain. Not to mention that the book she'd been carrying with her was probably ruined for good. Maybe that would cause nothing more than a few raised eyebrows, but she would have to assume her "guardians" would keep a closer eye on her from now on, wondering what she was up to wandering around in the rain late at night.

"I might not be able to come tomorrow night," she said, deciding to ignore the issue of what she and Dante might do if they met again in better weather. "They're going to know I snuck out tonight, and I don't want anyone to get curious. The staff here are so nosy, I wouldn't put it past them to have someone follow me."

Dante nodded. "I understand. I'll be here anyway, just in case. And if you think someone might be watching you, you probably should sneak out as usual and then just take a nice long stroll around the grounds. If they think that's what you're doing every night, they'll lose interest real fast."

Nadia couldn't help but smile. "I'm lucky I can get advice from a real live spy."

"Don't take chances," he warned. "I'm here if you need me, but don't give them any more reasons to watch you too closely."

"I won't," she promised.

She had a feeling that by the time the next night rolled around, she'd be longing for company once again, and the urge to meet Dante would be hard to resist. But he was right. If she wanted to make sure he could continue to visit like this, she had to exercise a little restraint. No matter how hard it was.

CHAPTER TEN

nadia saw no sign that her midnight walk in the rain had caused more than a raised eyebrow from her keepers. No one questioned her about the wet clothes, nor about the ruined book, which was removed from her room while she was out at breakfast. Even so, she felt as if eyes were on her at all times. A paranoid delusion, maybe, but she forced herself to humor it anyway, just in case it wasn't so paranoid after all.

Her mind kept replaying the sensation of Dante's kiss, and sometimes she could almost feel the tingle in her lips.

He was an impossible dream, of course. Even if she didn't end up spending the rest of her days hidden behind the walls of a retreat, she could hardly be with someone like him. Even ruined as she was, she would be expected to consort only with "her own kind," and Dante would not qualify. Never mind that "her own kind" would do nothing but sneer at her for her scandalous past.

When Sunday afternoon rolled around, Nadia wasn't at all sure what to expect. She wasn't sure she could face a repeat of the last visiting day, but surely her family would relent now that the initial shock of her fall from grace had worn off.

Now if only Nadia could figure out whether a visit from her family would be a good thing or a bad thing.

She missed everyone, of course. Even with Dante's visits, her loneliness at the retreat was palpable and oppressive. But how could she possibly face her mother, knowing what she knew? And how was she supposed to pretend she *didn't* know? She was a reasonably good actress, skilled at hiding her true feelings—a survival trait for an Executive who spent so much time in the public eye—but she wasn't sure her acting skills were up to the task.

The possibility of having to face her mother almost convinced her not to make an appearance at the visitors' lobby at all. Staying away provided the additional benefit of not knowing if no one showed up to visit.

However, Nadia wasn't a coward, and she wasn't going to let the situation turn her into one. So at three o'clock sharp, her pulse pattering and her palms sweaty, she marched herself to the visitors' lobby.

Too restless—and nervous—to sit, Nadia paced. She would have loved something alcoholic to soothe her nerves, but apparently retreats were the one place where the legal drinking age was enforced for Executives, and the oh-so-helpful servers who wandered the room brought her fruit punch so sweet it made her teeth ache. She carried it around with her anyway, taking an occasional sip just because it gave her something to occupy her attention.

The good news was that Nadia didn't have long to wait before the suspense was ended. When the first group of visitors was escorted into the lobby, she immediately spotted Gerri among them. She quickly scanned the rest of the group, but there was no sign of her mother or her father. She tried not to think too much about the bizarre mix of relief and hurt that churned inside her. Her hand was shaking just a little, so she put down the drink she didn't want anyway and tried to walk calmly across the room to meet Gerri halfway.

The "calmly walking" thing lasted about two steps, and

then Nadia's feet developed a will of their own and propelled her across the remaining distance at a pace just short of a run. With a choked-off sob, she flung herself into her sister's arms, so glad to see her she felt she might explode with it. Gerri hugged her back fiercely, showing no sign that she was annoyed by the undignified display.

"Glad to see you, too, kiddo," Gerri said, and it sounded like she was fighting tears as hard as Nadia was.

Nadia sucked in air, trying to loosen the aching knot in her throat. Hurtling across the room and throwing herself into Gerri's arms was undignified enough. She was *not* going to let herself cry. Public emotional displays were frowned upon in Executive society and also tended to attract unwanted attention from the press. There was no press here to take embarrassing photos, but Nadia was sure gossip could and would make its way out into the world if she made anything like a scene.

Reluctantly, she pulled away from Gerri's arms, though somehow their hands became linked in the process. Nadia searched her sister's face, looking for signs of disapproval, or anger, or disappointment. Gerri was every bit as good as their mother at conveying her unflattering assessment with nothing more than a facial expression, but the look she was giving Nadia now seemed suspiciously like pity. Which made Nadia's battle against tears just that much harder.

"Let's find a quiet corner to talk, shall we?" Gerri asked with a forced smile.

Nadia, uncertain of her voice, merely nodded and led Gerri to a cozy love seat in a secluded corner. She could read the tension in every nuance of Gerri's body language, and she realized her sister was bracing herself to tell Nadia the terrible news about Nate's new engagement. Acting uncommonly impulsive, she decided to save Gerri the trouble.

"I know about Agnes Belinski," she whispered, and saw Gerri's eyes widen in shock.

"How could you possibly . . . ?"

"I have my ways," Nadia answered, feeling a hint of satisfaction at having resources Gerri didn't know about and couldn't expect her to have. "I can't tell you what they are, and you'd better not let *anybody* know that I've already heard."

Gerri cocked her head, regarding Nadia with unbridled curiosity—and maybe a hint of respect, as well. "You're full of surprises, aren't you?"

Nadia summoned a smile she didn't really feel. "You have no idea." Even the fake smile was almost impossible to maintain, so she quickly let it fade away. "Mom sent you in to be the bearer of bad tidings, didn't she?"

It wasn't like Esmeralda had a problem with confrontation. Nor did she have a problem with detailing Nadia's inadequacies to her face. But perhaps sending Gerri had been something of an act of compassion. Maybe their mother thought the blow would be softer coming from her. Which was almost certainly true. No matter how unfair her mother thought Nadia's disgrace might be, she would still consider it to be Nadia's fault. Nadia had had one job in life: to be perfect, at least until her engagement to Nate was finalized. She had failed, and her mother would never be able to hide her disappointment and anger.

Gerri sighed and patted Nadia's shoulder gently. "Actually, it was my idea. Mom is . . ." She shook her head. "I was going to say she isn't herself, but that's not true. It's like she's herself times two million."

Nadia knew exactly what her sister meant.

"I figured getting the news would be bad enough without having to deal with the critique that would come with it if she told you," Gerri continued.

Nadia nodded, certain that Gerri had made the right decision. Nadia knew exactly how her mother felt about her right now, but at least she didn't have to have that disappointment shoved in her face. And she wouldn't have to fight her desire to express her own feelings in return. Her relationship with her mom might never recover from such a confrontation. It might not even now, but as long as Nadia didn't have the opportunity to say the ugly things she was thinking, there was a chance.

"And Dad . . . ?" Nadia inquired.

Gerri made a face. "Had some kind of important meeting he just couldn't miss."

It was not impossible for a man of their father's rank to have important, can't-miss meetings on a Sunday afternoon, but Nadia could easily read between the lines. "In other words, he's had it up to here"—she held her hand over her head—"with confrontation and he can't face one more."

Gerri nodded. "That's the gist of it, I'm afraid. I think he and Mom are just short of meeting at dawn with pistols."

Nadia would have laughed at the image of her parents dueling if the whole thing hadn't been so depressing. And if she hadn't felt so sure her mother would win the duel. She looked into Gerri's eyes.

"I can't live the rest of my live in a retreat, Gerri. I just can't." A hint of panic tinged her voice, and she made no attempt to hide it.

Gerri reached out and squeezed her hand. "It seems to me there's an obvious solution to all your problems."

Of course it seemed that way to Gerri. She knew Nadia had powerful blackmail material against the Chairman, and not knowing what that material was, it would seem to her that using it to force the Chairman to reinstate the agreement between their families was a no-brainer.

"Please tell me you kept your promise," Nadia begged, side-stepping the issue for the moment.

Gerri frowned. "I haven't retrieved the recordings," she said. "Yet. You promised you would explain. Now might be a good time."

Too bad Nadia had never quite figured out *how* she was going to explain. She would love to unburden herself, tell Gerri everything. But the fact was she didn't dare. Knowing the truth about Thea was like having a death warrant with your name on it, which was why neither Nadia nor Nate could tell anyone, even—or maybe *especially*—the people they loved the most. If the Chairman ever caught the slightest hint that they weren't upholding their end of the bargain, he would stop upholding his.

The problem was that if Nadia didn't tell Gerri what was on those recordings, Gerri could just go listen to them herself—which ran the risk of leading the Chairman's spies to their location, which would be even worse.

"You can't listen to those recordings," Nadia said, glancing around the room to make one hundred percent certain no one could hear what they were saying. "Having them safely hidden is the only thing that's keeping me alive, and the Chairman would do anything to find them and destroy them—including putting you under surveillance and bugging your phones and computers. If you go anywhere near the recordings, either physically or electronically, he'll find them."

Gerri's eyes widened. "What the hell is on those recordings that's worth all that?"

"Nothing," Nadia said, the lie falling glibly from her tongue. It was the perfect solution to her problem, making it seem not worth the risk for Gerri to listen to the recordings. "He *thinks* I have something, but I don't. When he found the transmitter, he assumed I'd been sending the whole time and had caught everything he said. But I didn't. As long as he doesn't know that and doesn't find the recordings, I'm safe."

Of course, thinking the blackmail was a bluff did nothing to stifle Gerri's curiosity. "So what did he say that he's willing to kill to keep quiet?"

Nadia wished she had come up with this solution earlier so she'd have had time to think all the possibilities through. Making up an elaborate lie on the fly was fraught with danger, especially when she was faced with a sharp mind like Gerri's. Which meant that keeping the lies to a minimum was her safest strategy.

"I can't tell you," Nadia said, looking her sister straight in the eye. "The information is useless without proof, but if the Chairman ever so much as *suspected* I told anyone . . ."

"How would he find out? It's not like I'm going to say anything to him."

Nadia shook her head. "Maybe all it would take is having you look at him the wrong way." Gerri opened her mouth to protest, but Nadia kept talking. "As long as you can't do anything with the information, there's no reason for you to know. Except curiosity, and that's not good enough."

It was obvious Gerri wanted to argue, and Nadia couldn't blame her. In her sister's shoes, she'd be dying to know what the big secret was, too.

"Please trust me, Gerri," she said. "It's better for everyone if you don't know what I heard."

Gerri's narrowed eyes said she still didn't like it. "Well, I don't suppose I can beat it out of you. But I still wish you'd tell me. If I know what the Chairman's hiding, then maybe I can persuade him to—"

"No!" Nadia said, too fast and too sharply. She forced herself to lower her voice. "Don't even *think* about trying to black-mail him. I mean it, Gerri."

"Why not?" Gerri challenged. "Don't you think it's worth getting our hands a little dirty to save our family from complete ruin?"

"Of course. But do you think for one moment the Chairman didn't consider the possibility when he decided to break the marriage agreement?" Gerri's shrug was as close to an agreement as Nadia was likely to get. "He wouldn't have done it if he weren't fully prepared to call my bluff. And if he calls my bluff and finds out it really *is* a bluff, I won't just be ruined, I'll be dead—and probably you, too."

Gerri leaned back in the love seat, her nails tapping restlessly against the padded arm as her face furrowed in thought. "He's a devious bastard," she said under her breath. "Maybe he guessed you'd be too afraid to try to blackmail him again. Maybe you're playing right into his hands."

It was possible Gerri was right, but Nadia didn't think so. If the Chairman were prepared to give in to a blackmail attempt, then he never would have changed the marriage agreement in the first place. Backing out of the agreement would mortally offend Chairman Belinski and the entire state of Synchrony, and he would not have put himself in that position. Wars had been started over lesser offenses, and though Paxco was much larger and richer than Synchrony, Synchrony's high-tech military made them a bad enemy to have.

"I'm not going to do it, Gerri," Nadia said, putting every bit of her conviction into her voice. "I'm not going to blackmail him, and I'm not going to tell you what I heard. Period."

"Fine," Gerri said. "For now. As long as the marriage agreement isn't signed, and as long as Mom hasn't as good as publicly admitted your guilt by sending you upstate, there's a chance that we can get out of this. But if they start hammering nails into our social coffin, you and I are going to have another talk. I am not going to let the Chairman destroy our family without a fight."

If it came to that, Nadia was going to have to tell Gerri the whole truth, no matter how much she didn't want to. Her sister was ordinarily levelheaded and practical, and she had to hear the sense in what Nadia was saying. But she was also fiercely protective of her family, especially her kids, and she might well be willing to risk both her own life and Nadia's if she thought it would save the rest of the family from ruin.

Gerri sighed. "I wish I could segue from that into something better, but I also have some bad news I have to share with you."

Nadia listened with a heavy heart as her sister told her about the death of Nate's mother. News of Eleanor Lake's passing didn't exactly break her heart, but she knew Nate had to be hurting, no matter how many mixed feelings he had toward his mother. She was grateful that she would be allowed to leave the retreat to attend the funeral. It might be the only chance she got to see or talk to Nate in the near future, considering the difficult position his new unofficial engagement put him in—and the pleasure the Chairman no doubt felt in keeping Nadia as isolated as possible.

Just as Nadia thought this, she saw Nate, standing in the entryway. A smile of greeting began to curve Nadia's lips. Until she saw the girl who stood a couple paces behind him, just in front of his bodyguard. The girl who looked to be about Nate's age, and who was, as Dante had described her, "not beautiful."

The girl who Nadia knew at once was Agnes Belinski.

CHAPTER ELEVEN

meeting Nadia's eyes across the crowded visitors' lobby was like a punch to Nate's gut, made about a thousand times worse when he saw her notice Agnes. Nadia was a pro at hiding her feelings when she wanted to, but she couldn't hide her hurt and dismay at the sight of the girl who would replace her by his side. Nate cursed his father under his breath for one more act of casual cruelty. Instead of forbidding Nate to visit, or arranging some activity that would prevent Nate from doing so, he had merely declared that Nate and Agnes should spend the day together "getting to know" each other. Nate's choices had been to bring Agnes along or to not visit at all. He hoped he'd made the right one.

Nadia was sitting with her sister, Gerri. When he first caught sight of them, they'd been leaning toward each other in earnest—and obviously private—conversation. As soon as Nadia noticed him, Gerri followed her sister's gaze and noticed him, too.

Gerri was like a younger, marginally softer version of her mother. Not quite the cast-iron bitch that Esmeralda was, but plenty formidable nonetheless. Which was only natural, with her being the heir to her father's presidency.

Nate had always had the impression that Gerri didn't like him, though he'd never had any concrete evidence to support that impression. She was properly respectful and polite when they ran into each other at social functions or when Nate had attended business meetings with her. There had never been any warmth in their interactions, but then neither had there been noticeable coldness. Until now, when Gerri was glaring at him so fiercely he could almost feel it as a physical slap across his cheek.

Nate's temper stirred, but he quickly leashed it. Gerri had no way of knowing how the Chairman had managed to force him into this marriage arrangement. Nor did she know that Nate hadn't brought Agnes with him to the retreat by choice. In her place, he'd have been staring daggers, too, and he was glad at least one member of Nadia's family seemed to be standing by her. He glanced over his shoulder at Agnes, who had spoken maybe five or six words during the ride over, and those only when absolutely necessary.

"Stay here!" he ordered her, and he had no doubt she would obey. She was very likely the mousiest girl he'd ever met, which made her about the worst match for him he could imagine.

He started across the room, and, as expected, there was no pitter-patter of footsteps indicating Agnes was following. Meanwhile, Gerri and Nadia exchanged a few more words and a hug. By the time he reached the love seat where they were sitting, Gerri was on her feet. The look on her face had not warmed, and Nate was half-surprised his bodyguard hadn't gone on red alert. He checked over his shoulder to make sure, but Fischer was still standing at attention in the entryway while Agnes stood a little ways off, looking lost and uncomfortable.

"You have some nerve," Gerri said to him when he was within earshot. She looked like she wanted to skin him alive.

Nadia put her hand on Gerri's arm. "Gerri, please."

The soft plea did nothing to calm Gerri's obvious rage. "It

wasn't bad enough that you ruined my sister? You had to bring *that creature* here?"

"Gerri!" Nadia said more sharply. "It's not his fault. And we aren't alone."

Nate saw Gerri do a quick visual sweep of the room, checking to see if anyone was watching them. Which, of course, they were. Nate was the Chairman Heir, and when he walked into a room, he could be sure his every move was being observed.

Gerri shook her head and lowered her voice. "You never deserved her. And she deserved way better than you."

Once again, Nate had to wrestle with his temper. He was the Chairman Heir, and people just didn't talk to him like that. Not only that, the words fucking *hurt*. Nate tried very hard to swallow that hurt, because Gerri was more right than she knew. And until now, he'd never really appreciated just how lucky he had been to have a friend like Nadia.

"I know," he told Gerri in a tight voice.

She blinked in surprise, but otherwise made no response. She gave him another contemptuous look, then brushed past him, bumping his shoulder on the way by like a pissed-off guy might do. Nate ground his teeth and took it without complaint, watching her stride angrily away from him. She paused for a moment to give Agnes a sneer, making the girl's face turn a mottled red; then she left the room.

Nadia sighed. "Sorry about that," she said. "Obviously, she doesn't know the whole story."

Nate turned back to Nadia and took a really good look at her for the first time. She was as beautiful as ever, though the powder-blue uniform leached much of the color from her face and he thought she might have lost a little weight. A glance at her hands showed she'd been chewing her nails, a habit she'd broken long ago, and there was a hint of a slump to her usually proud shoulders. She was not flourishing here at Tranquility, and everything she was suffering was because of him.

Guilt ate at him as he enveloped her in a hug, wishing he were smart enough to think of a way to fix things.

"I'm so sorry, Nadia," he murmured into her hair, and to his shame his eyes were burning. "You know I had no choice, right?"

Nadia hugged him harder. "I know. And we both should have seen it coming. Not that seeing it coming would have helped any." She tried to end the hug, but Nate wouldn't let her go. She probably hadn't had a proper hug since she'd set foot in the retreat, Gerri being too reserved to be so demonstrative in public. He refused to think about the possibility that Dante had laid hands on her.

"Cut it out, Nate," she protested, pushing against him. "Your fiancée is watching us."

"Fuck her," he snarled, still not letting go. He was being an ass, and he knew it. He couldn't count how many times he'd chided Kurt for swearing around Nadia, and here he was doing the same thing. But there was so much anger coursing through his blood, and he had nowhere to turn to let it out.

Once upon a time, Nadia had been reluctant to criticize him with any real heat. Not because he didn't deserve it, but because she thought letting things slide—or being excessively subtle in her criticism—was part of her duty as his presumed fiancée. Things had changed between them since the death of the original Nate Hayes.

"I don't know who you think you're impressing," she said crisply, "but it definitely isn't me. Now let go and show a little class."

"Bossy," he teased, though he doubted there was much humor in his voice. However, he'd created enough of a spectacle already, and Nadia was the one who would have to live with any consequences. He suspected gossip was like a national pastime at an Executive retreat—even more so than it was for Executives in the public eye. What else was there to do in a retreat, after all?

Reluctantly releasing Nadia, he took Gerri's recently vacated seat and patted the spot beside him. Brow furrowed, Nadia looked across the room at Agnes. Their eyes met for a moment, and Agnes turned that particularly unattractive shade of mottled red Nate was already growing accustomed to. He felt his lip curling into an involuntary sneer as Nadia slowly took the seat beside him.

"I take it you and Agnes aren't like this yet?" Nadia asked, crossing her fingers.

Nate snorted. "I'd rather marry Jewel, and you know how much I hate Jewel. But at least she has a personality, however loathsome."

"And she's prettier than Agnes," Nadia said, and though he heard the tone of reproach in her voice, he chose to ignore it.

"I've seen cows prettier than Agnes." He crossed his arms over his chest and slouched more comfortably into the love seat. "Even her *name* sounds ugly."

"That sounds like something Jewel would say," Nadia pointed out, the reproach in her voice growing sharper.

He was sure Jewel and her bitchy friends had said worse about Agnes already. As far as he could tell, Agnes's only redeeming feature was that she was the daughter of a Chairman, and that would buy her very little slack with the Executives of Paxco. Particularly the teenage ones, who had such a propensity for playing games of one-upmanship anyway.

"Just wait till the press gets wind of the engagement," he said. "I'll sound positively flattering by comparison."

Nadia's eyes softened with pity. "The poor thing," she murmured, and Nate felt that damn sneer twisting his lips again.

"This is a better marriage than she could have hoped for in her wildest dreams. And she doesn't give a shit who she has to walk over to get what she wants." He'd told her flat-out that she'd be ruining Nadia's life, and it hadn't seemed to bother her.

Nadia's gaze turned positively fierce. "I know you think you're the greatest prize in the history of the universe, but I can tell you from personal experience that you're not as much of a prize as you think."

Nate flinched at the anger in her voice—and at the truth of her words. Recent events had forcefully opened his eyes to how poorly he had treated her over the course of their friendship, of how he had taken advantage of her kind nature—and of the burden of responsibility that made her unable to protest his treatment.

"You haven't the faintest idea what it's like to be powerless over your life," Nadia continued. "I doubt anyone sat down with Agnes and asked her if she'd like to marry a spoiled, selfish, mean-spirited ass who just happens to be the heir to Paxco. No one ever asked *me*."

Ouch! He couldn't blame Nadia for being angry at him, not after the direction her life had taken lately. And he couldn't argue that he hadn't been spoiled and selfish through much of his life. If he'd grown up as much as he'd like to think, he'd have kept his mouth shut and taken the criticism like a man, but he just couldn't refrain from trying to defend himself.

"I am *not* mean-spirited." It seemed like a puny defense against her assessment of his character, but it was the best he could do.

"I wouldn't have said so before today," Nadia agreed, crossing her arms and glaring at him. "But without having spoken a word with her, I can tell from across the room that Agnes is painfully shy, and that you've been making her miserable. And you just described her as a cow with no personality. I hate to break it to you, Nate, but that's the very definition of *mean-spirited*. It's not her fault your father chose her as his instrument of revenge."

Nate sank a little lower into his seat. "I'm hoping she'll hate me and try to talk her father out of the marriage." And if that wasn't a rationalization, he didn't know what was. Agnes had already made it clear she had no intention of opposing the marriage, so being unpleasant to her served no purpose. Other than to vent his anger, that is.

Nadia snorted. "You're so used to getting your own way you have no idea what it's like to be one of the rest of us. She's an Executive girl, and from what I understand, she's not her father's heir. She's been raised since birth to believe her purpose in life is to bring more power and money to her family by marrying well. She'll do whatever she thinks is best for her family, no matter how personally miserable it will make her."

"It's not like *I* have a choice in this," he retorted.

She raised her chin. "Yes, for two or three days, you've known what it's like not to have choices in your life. Obviously, you understand exactly what it's been like for Agnes and me to live with that our whole lives."

This was not exactly how he'd been picturing his reunion with Nadia. His head was starting to ache, and his heart was a lead anchor in his chest. "You don't understand, Nadia," he said, staring down at his feet to escape the reproach in her eyes. "It's not just that I have to marry Agnes and that I don't like her." His throat tightened, his voice going froggy. "Every awful thing that's happened to you has been because of me. I was having a hard enough time living with what I'd put you through before, but now . . ." He sucked in a deep breath, because if he didn't pull himself together he was going to lose every last scrap of his dignity. And he was sure people were watching, even if he didn't dare to look up.

Nadia slid closer to him on the love seat and put her hand softly on his back. "Don't use me as an excuse to be mean to Agnes," she said. "I'll agree that everything that's happened and everything that probably *will* happen pretty much sucks. But it's all your father's doing, Nate, not yours. And certainly not *hers*."

Leaning forward and ducking his head, Nate clasped his hands together between his knees, wishing he could whisk Nadia off to somewhere private where he didn't have to work so hard to keep himself under control. Not that he was doing such a great job of it as it was, but he really wanted to punch something right now, or maybe to yell out his frustration at the top of his lungs.

Yes, a yelling, screaming, kicking temper tantrum would feel damn good right about now.

"You have to hate me," he said to his hands, letting his hair and shadows hide his face. "At least a little bit. If I'd listened to you on the night of the reception, if I hadn't insisted on hooking up with Kurt at a public event just for the thrill of secretly giving my father the finger . . ."

Nadia sighed and leaned against his side. "I could have just played lookout for you, like you wanted. I didn't have to choose that particular moment to put my foot down, not after all the other things I'd let you get away with over the years. Besides, we might be blissfully ignorant and safe in our old lives if we'd done things differently, but how many more people would Thea have vivisected by now? We might have screwed up both of our own lives, but we saved a whole lot of other people's. How can we possibly regret that?"

Nadia was a better person than he. She was right, of course, but he suspected if he had it to do over again, he would have done things differently. Once again, he was showing how self-centered he was, even when he was trying to change his stripes. But then maybe if it had only been his own life he'd ruined, he might have been better able to see the whole picture. It was what his actions had done to *Nadia* that kept him up at night.

Forcing himself to sit up straight and stop feeling sorry for himself, Nate took hold of Nadia's hand and gave it a fierce squeeze.

"You are the best, nicest person I know," he told her, "and it's so massively unfair that any of this has happened to you. But I want you to know that I'm going to fight for you, even if I have no choice but to marry Agnes." It took a conscious effort for him not to sneer when he said the name, but being cruel to Agnes wasn't going to get him out of the marriage, and he needed to cut it out. "I won't let them bury you in some retreat."

His mind flashed to an image of his mother, lazing her life away voluntarily behind those retreat walls. Maybe his mother had been satisfied with that kind of life, but Nadia would never be, and he would do everything in his power to make sure she wasn't consigned to such a fate.

"You may not have a choice," she said sadly.

"I refuse to accept that. And Dante will never be my favorite person in the world, but I'm going to see if I can hire him away from your family so that it'll be easier for us to work together. Between the two of us, we'll find a way to get you out, if that's what we need to do."

Nadia's delicate throat worked as she swallowed hard and closed her eyes. "Thank you," she whispered, but he could tell she didn't believe him. He wished there was some way he could convince her she had a lifeline available. It would be a lot easier if he had some concrete idea of how to help her.

Nadia opened her eyes, her expression turning composed as she banished her fear and unhappiness and replaced them with compassion. "I'm sorry about your mother."

He grimaced as a jumble of mixed emotions about his mother fought for supremacy. Anger threatened to win the battle as he wrestled with the knowledge that she hadn't wanted to see him before she died. Then he felt guilty for being angry at her when she was dead.

"Thank you," he said, because what else was he supposed to say? "But if you don't mind, I'd rather not talk about my mother right now."

"All right," Nadia agreed easily. She'd probably known all along he wouldn't want to talk about his feelings, at least not yet. She'd known him a long time, after all. "How about you introduce me to Agnes instead?"

Nate made a face. "Why would you want me to do that? I wasn't exaggerating about her personality. She's about as interesting as—" He shut himself up when he saw the way Nadia was looking at him. He cleared his throat. "Sorry. I, uh . . . I'll just go get her, why don't I?"

She nodded. "Good idea."

Knowing this whole thing was going to be awkward all around, he went to fetch Agnes.

CHAPTER TWELVE

If Nate had to accept the condolences of one more person, or hear the words "if there's anything I can do" one more time, he was going to scream. He wanted to remind every one of his ass-kissing well-wishers that he hadn't seen his mother in ten years, that she had disappeared from his life long ago. He wasn't glad she was dead, but he was hardly prostrate with grief, either. But even he, who laughed in the face of Executive rules of conduct, knew better than to say anything like that. He was almost glad his father had demanded a moment of his time before the service started, because at least then he could stop trying to pretend he appreciated everyone's kind words and sympathy for a while.

Nate was not in the least surprised that his father wasn't there yet when he stepped into the intimate little parlor near the front entrance to the building. It was apparently used as a meeting room, where people who were thinking of fleeing to the retreat could meet with the staff and discuss their options. Which meant it was nicely private and had a door that locked. A sofa and chairs clustered around a coffee table, on which lay several stacks of brochures. Nate glanced at the brochures, then snorted softly when he saw all the photos of people smiling as if they'd found heaven on earth. He wondered if any of them actually lived here, or if they were all models.

Unable to sit still, Nate paced the small room, waiting for his father. He'd been glad to get away from the crowd, but now he felt caged and restless. Maybe it was the low ceiling, or the small windows, or the dim lighting, but the room felt close and stifling. Nate tugged at the tie at his throat, wishing he could just take it off and unbutton the collar of his shirt.

He was wound up enough that he jumped at the sound of the door being opened. He hid his embarrassment by tugging on the cuffs of his shirt to make sure just the right amount of fabric was visible beneath the sleeves of his jacket. He stopped in mid-fidget when he saw that his father had not come alone.

Nate had spotted the woman earlier. She was, after all, rather hard to miss. Tall and slender, with a long neck and killer legs, she'd make any straight male sit up and take notice. Ordinarily, Nate would play his role as the charming rake without a second thought, but something about her made the hair on the back of his neck stand up. He hadn't a clue who she was, for one thing. He knew every single person in attendance at this funeral, except for her. Even if she were some kind of visiting dignitary, he should be at least vaguely familiar with her. He'd never been a diligent heir, but he'd always kept up at least a passing familiarity with all the power players in the Corporate States, and she wasn't one of them. Plus, she was too young to be a real power player.

So what was she doing here?

His father closed and locked the parlor door as the mysterious woman gave Nate a coolly assessing look. She wasn't smiling, but there was something about her, some spark in her eye, that suggested she found Nate's obvious puzzlement amusing. Which raised his hackles just a little more.

"What's going on?" he asked, looking back and forth

between his father and the woman. "Who the hell is *she*, and what is she doing at my mother's funeral?"

He expected his father to reprimand him for his rudeness, but the Chairman settled for giving him a dirty look instead.

"This is Dorothy," his father said, and for one of the few times Nate could remember, he actually looked . . . uncomfortable. "Dorothy, this is Nathaniel."

Dorothy smiled brightly, and there was still that glint of humor in her eyes as she reached out her hand for Nate to shake. "Charmed, I'm sure," she said. There was no hint that she was even aware of the tension in the room, much less that she shared in it.

The undercurrents had Nate's nerves on alert, and he declined to shake Dorothy's hand. She'd spoken three meaningless words so far, and already Nate didn't like her. In his mind, he heard Nadia's rebuke about how unfairly he'd treated Agnes, whom admittedly he'd never tried to get to know, but this wasn't the same kind of snap judgment. He'd disliked Agnes from the start because of what she stood for, because of the harm she was going to do to his life and Nadia's. He still had no idea who Dorothy was, so there was no practical reason that explained his reaction to her.

"Dorothy who?" he asked, hoping his voice sounded cold rather than shaken.

Her smile brightened, and he was sure that gleam in her eyes held a tinge of predatory glee. "Why, Dorothy Hayes, of course."

Nate blinked and shook his head. Had his father remarried? Without telling anyone? And to a complete stranger, only days after his wife had died? Nate had a few cousins scattered about on his father's side, but Dorothy wasn't one of them.

Maybe the Hayes name was merely a coincidence. There were unrelated people who had the same surname within Paxco, and there were certainly more of them in the rest of the Corporate States.

"I'm so glad to finally have the chance to meet you," Dorothy continued, but Nate ignored her, turning to the Chairman.

"What the hell, Dad?" He couldn't remember the last time he had addressed his father as *Dad,* but somehow it had just slipped out.

The Chairman cleared his throat and shifted his weight uncomfortably. "Dorothy is . . ." He cleared his throat again.

Dorothy looked at the Chairman expectantly. What was wrong with him? He *never* showed hesitation or uncertainty in front of people, considered it a dangerous sign of weakness. But for this one brief, unguarded moment, he looked like he'd been backed into some kind of corner. Then he sealed up his defenses, becoming once again the coldly confident father Nate had always known. And he finally finished his sentence.

"She's my daughter, Nate."

From the moment her limo turned a corner and the Preston Sanctuary came into view, Nadia knew the place was more than just a more remote version of Tranquility. Situated on the crest of a hill, the Sanctuary loomed over the surrounding countryside like a brooding, forbidding fortress, and it gave Nadia a chill just looking at it.

It didn't help that instead of her family coming to Tranquility to pick her up so they could all ride to the funeral together, they'd merely sent a driver. As if the thought of arriving at the funeral with her in their midst was embarrassing.

Although maybe she was reading things into it that she shouldn't. Maybe her parents and Gerri had driven up the night before and stayed the night in a local hotel. But if so, it would have been nice if they'd taken Nadia with them, especially since she hadn't been able to meet up with Dante last night. A fierce storm had rolled in shortly before the time Nadia planned to leave the dorm to go meet him. She thought that if any of the staff were keeping a special eye on her, they might be able to understand if she went walking at midnight and got caught in the rain, but plunging out into a torrential downpour would be far too suspicious. Not to mention that visiting with Dante in those conditions wouldn't be a whole lot of fun for either of them. She hoped he hadn't waited for her in the rain for too long.

With no company other than the taciturn driver, the ride upstate seemed interminable. The only bright spot Nadia could find was that for the first time in more than a week she was not wearing a retreat uniform. The driver had brought her a package from her mother, and Nadia had been allowed to change into the simple black sheath dress and the shiny black patent leather pumps before leaving the retreat. There was also a black pillbox hat with a dotted veil that would cover her entire face. It was old-fashioned and not even remotely stylish, and Nadia didn't want to wear it. But her mother had put it in the box for a reason, and the last thing she wanted to do right now was annoy her mother. With a sigh, she'd pinned the hat carefully into her hair, but she'd drawn the line at covering her face with the veil, so she had it flipped up over the back of her head instead.

It was hardly a flattering outfit, and Nadia had no jewelry to give it any spark, but she supposed that was appropriate for a funeral, especially one from which the press was barred and at which there would therefore be no photo ops.

The closer the limo got to the Preston Sanctuary, the more obvious were its differences from Tranquility. Tranquility was surrounded by a tall iron fence; so was the Sanctuary, but its fence had high-voltage warnings posted on it. Tranquility had a guard post at the main entrance; so did the Sanctuary, except the guard post included a tower with a lookout, and she could see more towers in the distance. She'd felt like she was entering a prison when she'd arrived at Tranquility, but the Preston Sanctuary felt about a thousand times worse.

How could Nate's mother have chosen to live out her whole life at a place like this? Nadia didn't care *what* kind of falling out Ellie Hayes had had with the Chairman; *nothing* was worth the kind of existence the Preston Sanctuary offered.

Once the limo had passed through the gates, the place became marginally less oppressive. As at Tranquility, the grounds were nicely groomed, although there were fewer flower beds and more expanses of plain green lawn. There were walking trails, but they were shorter and more self-contained than the ones at Tranquility, and there were no hedges or rosebushes or gazebos to block the view anywhere. The on-again, off-again drizzle must have been keeping everyone inside, because even with her unobstructed view, Nadia saw not a soul taking advantage of any of those walking paths. She glanced over her shoulder at the perimeter, taking in the guard towers, and wondered if it was even possible to relax when you were out walking here. She knew *she* would feel like she was constantly being watched, even though the guard posts were there to stop people—especially the press—from sneaking in. But at a place like this, there would be no chance to sneak out for a quick rendezvous with Dante, even if he were close enough to get here.

Nadia hoped and prayed that a place like the Preston Sanctuary was not in her future.

The limo pulled up to the front of the main building, where a bunch of servants in the Chairman's livery lingered to greet guests and guide them to the location of the service. One of them hurried over to open Nadia's door for her. He held off the drizzle with an umbrella as she got out of the car.

"If you would just come with me, miss," he said, still holding the umbrella above her head. The shoulders of his coat were noticeably wet from using the umbrella to keep other people dry.

The servant led her into the imposing building, which had neither the eye-catching modern design of Tranquility nor the welcoming niches for flower beds. The facade was of dark gray stone, with small, leaded-glass windows set at regular intervals on each floor. It was too elegant to be prison-like, especially with the leaded glass, but it wasn't exactly homey, either. The interior wasn't much better, the decor all staid and somber, and the small windows not letting in much light on this cloudy day. Nadia was glad when the servant led her all the way to the other side of the building and out onto a covered porch.

Black-clad Executives stood in intimate little clumps all around the porch. An awning stretched over a path of black cloth that led to a huge tent pitched on the lawn. Rows of wooden folding chairs were set up in front of a pulpit under that tent, and some of the more elderly of the Executives were taking advantage of the seating to plot and gossip in comfort.

The crowd of Executives was full of familiar faces, naturally. These people were the cream of Paxco high society, and Nadia was highly accustomed to socializing with them, though she had never enjoyed it. Because she was presumed to be the future Chairman Spouse, and therefore a person of great influence, many people made a great deal of effort to ingratiate themselves to her, and that got tiresome in the extreme. Equally tiresome were her jealous and spiteful peers, people like the Terrible Trio, who went out of their way to deliver backhanded compliments and sly insults. Nadia was very good at the verbal sparring, but she didn't take to it with the vicious glee the Trio did.

Nadia scanned the crowd, considering her options and assessing the situation. She'd been escorted onto the porch with no fanfare, so most people hadn't yet noticed her arrival. A quick glance confirmed her assumption that the Terrible Trio were all in attendance, the three of them traveling in a pack as they worked their way through the younger members of the crowd. Nadia took a careful step to the side so that there was a pillar and a cluster of older Executives that would block her from the Trio's view. She doubted she could get through the whole service without having to talk to them, but she'd give it her best shot.

She spotted her parents standing at the far side of the porch, but she would have to pass right by the Trio to get there. Besides, she was so angry at both of them she'd be tempted to make a scene, which was Not Done.

Nadia hoped to spot Nate or Gerri, someone she could comfortably talk with, but there was no sign of either of them. She did, however, see Agnes, standing alone and forlorn in the far corner of the porch.

Nadia had spoken to Agnes only briefly at Tranquility—and that only because she had insisted Nate introduce them.

It had taken no more than a couple of words for Nadia to confirm her suspicion that the poor girl was painfully shy and self-conscious. Nate hadn't made any cutting remarks, but he hadn't gone out of his way to be nice, either, and Nadia couldn't blame Agnes for hunkering down into her shell for protection. She looked like she was doing the same thing now, her obvious discomfort in the crowd acting like some kind of force field to keep people away.

Almost without conscious thought, Nadia found herself wandering in Agnes's direction. Agnes saw her coming and looked alarmed, glancing right and left as if in search of an escape route. Apparently subtlety was not her strong suit. But then, based on Nate's unflattering assessment, Agnes didn't *have* a strong suit.

Nadia should hate this girl who had supplanted her, or a least resent her. But Nadia's ruin wasn't Agnes's fault, and holding it against her was unfair. The girl was doing her duty as the daughter of a powerful Executive, just as Nadia would have done in her shoes. Maybe if Nadia made friendly with Agnes, it would put pressure on Nate to do the same. Besides, Nadia would rather try to get to know a stranger than mingle with the Paxco Executives who would cut her and her family out of their lives as soon as they learned Nadia had been put aside in Agnes's favor.

Nadia smiled in her most encouraging manner. Agnes tried to return the smile, but the near-terror in her eyes made the expression look more like a grimace. Her black dress could have used some better tailoring at the shoulders, and its layered skirt made her look more bottom-heavy than she really was. Her taste in clothes was questionable at best and would give those who enjoyed being cruel extra ammunition.

"So, we meet again," Nadia said lightly as she put her hands on the porch railing and looked out over the grounds, trying not to make Agnes feel cornered.

"Um. Yes."

If Agnes looked any more tense, she might start vibrating. At social events, Nadia was usually a big fan of subtlety, but she decided that perhaps with Agnes a bolder approach might be more effective.

"I don't hold it against you, you know," she said, giving Agnes another smile that she hoped conveyed the sincerity of her words. If anything, Agnes looked even more alarmed. "I know Nate has been acting like an ass toward you, but he doesn't know what it's like to be an Executive girl. I do."

Agnes rubbed her hands together nervously. "I'm . . . sorry about all the . . ."

Nadia waved her off. "You have nothing to be sorry about. It's not like we're Employee girls and can choose whom we marry."

"No one's forcing me," Agnes said with the first hint of heat Nadia had seen. "Nathaniel wants me to talk my father out of it, but I won't." She raised her chin, but the defiant gesture was undercut by her hunched shoulders and crossed arms.

"Of course not," Nadia said easily, hoping that she'd managed to talk Nate out of being such a jerk in the future. "Nate may not be the prize catch he thinks he is, but the strategic match is undeniable. He doesn't quite get that personal happiness isn't as important as taking care of your family and your state. If things had been different, I could very easily have found myself in the same kind of situation."

Agnes looked at her wonderingly. "And if you had . . . ?"

Nadia shrugged. "I'd have done my duty, no matter what. You and I are more alike than you think." After all, hadn't

Nadia done everything she could to protect her engagement to a guy she knew wasn't into girls? She would much rather have married someone she was in love with—and who loved her back—but an Executive had to think about the well-being of her family and her state above her own.

Agnes gave her a look of infinite skepticism. "I'm sure in my shoes you'd be parked in a corner all by yourself just like me." A flush of red instantly warmed her cheeks. "I mean, not all by myself . . . But . . ." She stammered to a halt.

Nadia smiled at her. "It's okay. It didn't even occur to me to be insulted until you started backpedaling. You were talking about *before* I came over."

Agnes still looked miserable, as though she'd put her foot so far in her mouth she'd never be able to get it out. "I always say the wrong thing."

"No, you don't. It's just that you're an Executive and any wrong thing you say gets magnified out of proportion." And it didn't help that Agnes was apparently willing to do some of that magnification without anyone else's input.

"You don't know me."

Nadia raised an eyebrow. "Are you saying it's not true?"

Agnes sighed and shook her head. The flush had receded, and the tension in her shoulders eased away. "It's still better when I keep my mouth shut," she said sadly. "Most people aren't as understanding as you."

Nadia had spent a lot of time feeling sorry for herself lately, but despite her misery, she wondered if Agnes weren't the one getting the worst of it. Nadia had never enjoyed the verbal sparring matches with people like the Trio, and she'd had her feelings hurt plenty of times. But she'd always been good at hiding her hurt—and covering up any moments of awkwardness or uncertainty—so that she didn't give the predators too much satisfaction and encouragement. Agnes would attract the same kinds of social predators, but she didn't have Nadia's armor. When the press and the Trio came after her—as they were sure to do when the engagement was announced—she wouldn't be able to hide her hurt, and she wouldn't be able to smooth over any awkward statements that escaped her.

"Keeping your mouth shut won't be an option when the engagement is announced," Nadia said. "It would be better if you could learn to stop beating yourself up when you make a faux pas."

Agnes's jaw clenched, and though she didn't say anything, Nadia could almost hear her thoughts: *Gee, I never thought of trying that. You just changed my life forever with your brilliant idea.*

Nadia smiled ruefully. "Like, for example, when you offer condescending advice to someone you barely know and you want to smack yourself. You apologize for being an idiot, and then you move on."

That surprised a laugh out of Agnes. "You haven't seen Nate lately, have you?" Nadia asked, figuring this was a good time for a change of subject.

"Not for a while," Agnes responded. "His father said they had something important to talk about and told Nathaniel to meet him inside at the top of the hour."

Agnes glanced at her watch, which managed to look clunky despite its diamond-studded face. Not having a watch of her own—apparently her mother hadn't thought she needed one for the funeral—Nadia craned her head to read Agnes's. If Nate had met with his father at the top of the hour, he'd been gone for more than fifteen minutes already.

"It must be some meeting," Nadia muttered under her

breath. Nate and his father couldn't spend five minutes together without sparks flying.

Feeling like a superstitious child, Nadia crossed her fingers and prayed that there were no more shocks in store. But Nate having a long private meeting with his father before the funeral did not bode well.

CHAPTER THIRTEEN

nate stared at his father, his mind unable—or, more likely, unwilling—to grasp what he had just heard. "Your daughter," he repeated, trying the words on for size.

His father nodded. "By a different mother."

If his father had a sense of humor, Nate would have accused him of playing a spectacularly unfunny practical joke. Surely he was misunderstanding what his father was saying to him. He looked at Dorothy again and noticed that her eyes were the same shade of cold gray as his father's. The curve of her chin and her arrow-straight nose were like softened versions of the Chairman's, as if a craftsman had filed away all the rough edges.

Nate shook his head in an effort to deny what his eyes were telling him. "No."

"I'm sorry, son," the Chairman said. "I couldn't think of any good way to tell you about this."

"She's an impostor!" Nate snapped, glaring at Dorothy, who was obviously enjoying what she was seeing and hearing.

"I can show you the DNA test if you'd like. She's not an impostor. I told you before that your mother and I had a falling out, and I admitted that it was my fault, that I was unfaithful. Dorothy was the product of that infidelity. For many years, I didn't know about her—"

"Oh, and now she just happens to appear in your life after Mom died? How convenient."

"No, son. She appeared in my life about ten years ago, when she was thirteen and her mother was beginning to consider her marriage prospects."

Nate swallowed hard, feeling like he was about to be sick. Ten years ago. Right about the time Ellie Hayes left her husband and her son and shut herself behind the walls of the retreat forever.

"That's when your mother found out about the affair," the Chairman continued. "It was ugly, to say the least. She was so very angry . . ." His eyes lost focus for a moment, as if he were haunted by the memory. "I'm sure you remember what a battleground our home became in the weeks before your mother left. Once the DNA tests came back and confirmed that Dorothy truly was my daughter, I wanted to acknowledge her, and give her all the rights and privileges that the daughter of a Chairman ought to have. Obviously, acknowledging her would cause a scandal, but I would hardly be the first Chairman to have had a child out of wedlock."

"But you *didn't* acknowledge her."

The Chairman shook his head. "Your mother wouldn't stand for it. She threatened to make a public spectacle of our marital difficulties. She even insinuated that Dorothy or her mother might meet with an unfortunate accident if I were to publicly acknowledge paternity."

Once again, Nate shook his head, as if by denying what his father was telling him, he could make it not be true. His memories of his mother had dimmed over time, and he'd been angry with her for so long that he was sure it had colored what memories he had. But no matter what, he couldn't imagine the mother he had known threatening to have an innocent child killed.

"She would never have done that!" Nate said, willing it to be so.

The Chairman pinched the bridge of his nose, a gesture that made him look almost vulnerable. "She was not herself at the time. I honestly don't know *what* she would have done if we hadn't reached a compromise."

"A compromise?"

"I agreed that I would not acknowledge Dorothy as my daughter for as long as your mother lived. And she agreed that she wouldn't attempt to humiliate our family or harm Dorothy. But our marriage was over, and she preferred to spend her time in a retreat than to live with me. Dorothy and her mother have been living abroad ever since, and I have been supporting them."

"And now that your mother has freed him from their agreement," Dorothy said with a gleeful smile, "I can finally be my father's daughter for real."

None of this is true, Nate told himself. He didn't care what the DNA test said, or how much she resembled the Chairman—Dorothy was *not* his daughter.

It wasn't impossible to imagine that the Chairman could have kept a secret for all these years—keeping secrets was one of his most polished skills—but not one like this. Not when he was paying for Dorothy's upkeep. Not when Nate's mother must have had friends she would have poured her heart out to, friends who would have let the secret slip. There would have been at least a *rumor* of Dorothy's existence if there were even a kernel of truth in this whole ridiculous story.

Most damning of all was that Dorothy was older than Nate. Sure, she was illegitimate, and that made Nate legally his father's heir by default. But thanks to the laws of primogeniture, his father could easily bypass the default succession and name Dorothy as his heir. And if his father could have done that, he would have been holding the threat of disinheritance over Nate's head for his whole life.

His father had never once suggested that someone other than Nate would be the next Chairman of Paxco; therefore, there *was* no other potential heir. And that meant Dorothy was an impostor—and his father knew it.

Nate drew himself up into his tallest, most dignified stance and met his father's eyes, dismissing Dorothy from his attention altogether.

"I don't know who that woman is," Nate said, his voice calm and uninflected, "but she isn't your daughter. If she *were* your daughter, you certainly wouldn't be introducing her into society during my mother's funeral. Even *you* aren't that much of an asshole."

Dorothy gave a gasp of outrage, but there was too much satisfaction in her eyes for it to be convincing.

"How *dare* you talk to our father that way?" she cried. "He deserves more respect than that, both as our father and as the Chairman of Paxco."

The Chairman laid a calming hand on her shoulder. "It's all right, Dorothy," he said. "He's understandably upset."

Suddenly, the vibe in the room felt even weirder. Chairman Hayes was not the sort of man to be so understanding—either of Nate's behavior or Dorothy's outburst. But if he was in the mood to pardon bad behavior, then Nate was in the mood to take advantage of it.

Nate sneered at Dorothy. "Why don't you go back to whatever hole you crawled out of and *stay* there. Showing up at my mother's funeral is so far beyond tacky there's no good word for it."

"Daddy invited me," she replied with a smirk. "I'm his *firstborn*, and we've been kept apart for too long."

A chill traveled down Nate's spine as he caught the subtle implications of her words and the emphasis with which she delivered them. Dorothy was fully aware of her potential place in the line of succession. And she had ambitions.

Nate had always been secure in the knowledge that his father needed him, but Dorothy's arrival said the Chairman was doing everything he could to change that. To make Nate as expendable to him as Nadia.

"Is that what this is all about?" he asked his father. "You're so sick of me you're grooming a new heir?"

"Don't be absurd. You're my heir, and introducing Dorothy into society won't change that." Dorothy smiled a we'll-see-about-that smile, then had the nerve to wink when Nate glared. The Chairman either didn't notice the byplay or chose to ignore it. "For your information, the reason I'm introducing her here, even though I know it seems tactless, is that it's the only time I will have so many of the top Paxco Executives gathered together *without the press*. I will, of course, have to notify the press about her, but I believe my Executives should learn about it in a more private manner."

"You're full of shit, Dad," Nate said with disgust. There was no earthly reason why the Chairman would introduce a new potential heir if he weren't planning to use her. It was clear he would never forgive Nate for his role in Thea's destruction. If those blackmail recordings were ever found, the Chairman would kill him and think *good riddance*. And even if they weren't found, Dorothy would eventually be named

Chairman Heir, and Nate's whole future would vanish. Good-bye to his plans to take the reins of Paxco and make it into a better place. He would become nothing but the powerless observer he had always been, while the Chairman pulled Dorothy's strings and molded her into a new and "improved" version of himself.

nadia had never been in the center of a scandal before, so being completely ignored by Executive society was an entirely new experience. She stood in the corner with Agnes, making halting conversation, and not a single person in the milling crowd came over to talk to her. It was as if she didn't exist.

"You should mingle," Agnes said with what Nadia assumed was meant to be an encouraging smile. "It's nice of you to try to keep me company, but I think other people are staying away because I make them uncomfortable."

Nadia imagined that there were more than one or two Executives who *would* be made uncomfortable by Agnes's shyness. Nadia didn't know a single Paxco Executive who hadn't been trained from birth in social graces, and they'd be flummoxed by someone who apparently had none. But that wasn't why no one was talking to them.

"Don't worry," she said, trying to keep her tone light. "It's not you they're avoiding, it's me. I'm in disgrace, and no one wants to be seen talking to me. Like I have a contagious disease." She was sure her bitterness showed through, despite her attempt to sound unconcerned.

To her shock, Agnes reached out and touched her arm lightly. "That's ridiculous!" she said, sounding truly indignant. "I've read the news reports. You didn't do anything wrong."

Nadia smiled at the impassioned defense from such an

unlikely source. Perhaps the Executives of Synchrony were more forgiving than those of Paxco. Nadia had always assumed Executives were Executives everywhere, but perhaps that wasn't the case. Either that, or Agnes was dangerously naive.

"What makes you think *that* has anything to do with it?"

Agnes grimaced, acknowledging the point.

"Cheer up," Nadia continued, not sure whether she meant the words for Agnes or for herself. "It's not all bad. The Terrible Trio spotted us a few moments ago, but they're too afraid they might get my cooties to come over and grace us with their presence."

The corners of Agnes's lips twitched. "The Terrible Trio?"

If Agnes had had any success socializing with Executive teens, she'd have known the moniker already. Even the Trio's closest friends and sycophants called them that, though not to their faces, obviously.

Nadia grinned. "You know who I'm talking about, even if you haven't heard them called that before."

Agnes wrinkled her nose, scanning the crowd until she caught sight of the Trio holding court. She raised an inquiring eyebrow, and Nadia nodded to confirm her choice. Obviously, Nadia's retreat from the public eye hadn't done much to rehabilitate her image yet if the Trio thought her so toxic they didn't dare approach to shower her with backhanded compliments and sly innuendo. She wondered what they would do when they found out she was no longer Nate's fiancée. Would that hold them permanently at bay? Or would they figure she'd sunk so low no one could possibly misinterpret their approach as friendly?

Or would she never see them again because she was locked up behind the walls of a retreat like this one?

"If you're keeping them away," Agnes said, "then I'm going to stick to your side like glue for the rest of the afternoon."

She had visibly relaxed since Nadia had first spotted her, standing alone and forlorn in the corner. Her shoulders weren't so tight, her facial expression was more open and unguarded, and she had actually made a joke, of sorts. Nadia began to suspect there was more personality behind the bland, shy mask she showed the world than most people would ever guess. She hoped it wouldn't be crushed when the engagement was announced and so many eyes focused on her in search of flaws.

Chairman Hayes exited the building, stepping out onto the porch and greeting the Executives who were standing closest to the entrance. Nate wasn't with him.

The Chairman started drifting toward the tent, and the crowd of chattering Executives followed him, still grouped in their little conversational clumps, moving forward almost unconsciously, like he was a magnet and they couldn't resist his pull. People were beginning to take their seats, and there was an aura of expectation in the air. A minister hovered near the pulpit, ready to move into place at a moment's notice.

Nadia frowned when she scanned the crowd for Nate yet again and didn't see him. It looked like the service was going to start soon, so where was he? Agnes was looking around anxiously, too. No doubt she was expected to sit up front, with Nate, but Nadia knew instinctively that she was far too shy just to march up to the front by herself.

"Where are your parents?" Nadia asked, thinking to find Agnes another escort. Certainly *she* couldn't walk up front with Agnes. She wasn't even sure her family wanted her sitting with them—perhaps they expected her to sit discreetly in the back row, veil over her face, to make herself as invisible as possible.

"My father's over there," Agnes said with a jerk of her chin. "Talking with Chairman Hayes. My mom didn't come. She's been down with migraines for the last few days."

Nadia followed Agnes's gaze and found the two Chairmen, who were talking earnestly. Whatever they were talking about, they were deeply absorbed, and Chairman Belinski showed no inclination to come escort his daughter to her seat. Nadia scanned the crowd again, wondering if she could somehow have missed Nate. She didn't see him, but she did catch sight of Gerri, who was turned around in her chair, staring back. Gerri gestured for Nadia to come over, patting the seat beside her. Gerri's husband glanced over his shoulder to give Nadia a haughty, disapproving look, a look that clearly said she should decline Gerri's invitation and sit elsewhere.

Ordinarily, Nadia would have immediately marched over in defiance of her brother-in-law's wishes. He was almost a foot shorter than Gerri and liked to puff himself up with pompous attitude to make up for it. Nadia couldn't imagine how her sister managed to live with him and, even more mysteriously, have children with him. But much as she'd like to inconvenience the man, she couldn't just walk away and leave Agnes hanging, and Nate was nowhere to be seen. People were taking their seats with increasing speed, and soon Agnes and Nadia were going to be sticking out like sore thumbs.

Beside her, Nadia saw that Agnes's hands were clasped together tightly, and her face had lost a little color. If she had to walk up to the front row on her own, every eye would be on her, and she would be painfully aware of it. Worse, she obviously had never learned the cherished Executive skill of hiding her feelings, and she was already wearing her misery on her face.

"Let's go look for Nate, shall we?" Nadia asked, hooking

her arm through Agnes's and urging her away from the tent, into the building.

"B-but the service is about to start."

Nadia noticed that the glossy silk of Agnes's black dress did not hide sweat stains. It certainly wasn't warm enough out for Agnes to be overheated, so the perspiration must have come from nerves. Nadia marched steadily forward, and because her arm was hooked with Agnes's, Agnes had to follow.

"The service won't start until Nate is there. So let's go dig him out of hiding instead of keeping all those people waiting."

Nadia unhooked her arm from Agnes's only enough so she could open the door and give the girl a gentle nudge in the back to move her through. Just in time, too, because she saw that almost everyone was already seated, and a couple of people had turned to look in their direction. Nadia thought Agnes might have had a nervous breakdown if more people turned to look.

By the time Nadia closed the door and they were safe within the gloomy interior of the retreat, Agnes looked like she was near tears, and Nadia wanted to find Nate so she could take him by the scruff of the neck and shake him. He was a nice guy, the kind of guy who should feel naturally protective of a fragile soul like Agnes. For him to just leave her hanging like this was appalling.

"It'll be all right, Agnes," Nadia said softly. She wanted to give the other girl a hug, but Agnes's body language did not invite it. "We'll find Nate, and then we can all go take our seats so the service can begin."

Agnes blinked away tears, her eyes wild and desperate-looking. "It's going to get worse when we're married, isn't it? People will be watching my every move, and Nathaniel will hate me even more, and—"

To hell with Agnes's body language, Nadia thought as she put her arms around the girl and hugged her tightly. Agnes momentarily stiffened in shock, but it seemed she was so desperate for a show of kindness that she couldn't help giving in to it.

"Nate doesn't hate you," Nadia assured her, sidestepping the issue about which she could offer no words of comfort. "He's furious with his father, and he's been taking it out on you because he can't take it out on him."

Agnes squirmed out of the hug, and Nadia reluctantly released her, wishing she could offer more than words.

"I've known him since I was four," Nadia continued. "He's being a world-class jerk right now, but that's not what he's really like."

"And what *am* I really like?"

Agnes squealed in alarm, and though Nadia managed to keep quiet, she jumped just as high.

Standing in a doorway behind them, his tie loosened, his collar unbuttoned, and an open bottle of something amber-colored in his hand, was Nate. And the expression on his face was about as bleak and forbidding as anything Nadia had ever seen.

CHAPTER FOURTEEN

nate lifted the bottle of booze to his lips and took a gulp. It was probably something obscenely expensive, meant to be sipped in minute quantities—he hadn't even bothered to read the label when he'd grabbed it—but all he cared about was that there was alcohol in it. Nadia and Agnes were both looking at him like he'd grown a third arm, which meant he was well on his way to creating the drunken slob look he was aiming for. Though he'd have to work a little harder on the "drunken" part, because he'd only had a couple of swallows so far. He raised the bottle again, and Nadia skewered him with a glare.

"Don't you dare!" she commanded, striding forward and snatching the bottle out of his hand so quickly he didn't even think to resist.

Agnes's eyes looked like they were going to pop out of her head, and Nate would have laughed if Nadia hadn't gotten up in his face. She held the bottle out to Agnes without taking her eyes off him. It was whiskey, Nate noted absently, though he didn't recognize the brand name. Agnes bit her lip and approached like she was crossing a minefield, but she took the bottle from Nadia and then hastily backed up a couple of steps.

"What the hell do you think you're doing?" Nadia asked as she reached for his throat. Actually, she was reaching for the buttons on his collar, but it felt rather like a stranglehold. "Agnes and I have been looking all over for you. The service is about to begin." She gave the collar a harder tug than necessary for buttoning purposes.

"I'm not going," he said, twisting away from her hands. "Now give me back the bottle and leave me in peace."

He was good at hiding his feelings in public, had had to do it for as long as he could remember. But there was no way he could put his public face on right now. Not after the bombshell his father had just dropped on him. Not after looking into Dorothy's smirking face and seeing his future laid out plain and clear. Whether she was the Chairman's daughter or not—and Nate refused to admit she was—she would be accepted by the public as such because the Chairman said so. Hell, the people of Paxco would probably throw a big party when his father disinherited him in favor of Dorothy. The original Nate Hayes had been popular, a true media darling. His Replica, not so much.

"What is *wrong* with you?" Nadia asked, reaching for his collar again. "You can't cause a scene at your own mother's funeral. I don't care *what* issues you had with her."

Nate caught her wrists and held her off. "This has nothing to do with her."

What had happened to his life? Only a couple precious weeks ago, he'd been engaged to his best friend. He'd had a live-in—albeit secret—boyfriend whom he loved. And he had been one hundred percent secure in the knowledge that he would one day be the Chairman of Paxco.

Yes, he'd been a crappy heir. He'd avoided work like the plague and made it clear to everyone that he had little interest in learning how to play his future role. He'd neglected paperwork, dozed off in meetings, been rude to people he should have been diplomatic with. But he was eighteen years old, for Christ's sake. He had *decades* before he expected to become Chairman, and he'd known there would be plenty of time to learn everything he needed to know. And even if they'd been a bit vague and amorphous, he'd had *plans* for his state. Plans to make it a better place. Plans to improve the quality of life among Basement-dwellers, like Kurt. Plans to give them more opportunities to join mainstream society, while putting protections in place for those who couldn't. Plans to winnow out those in the government—and especially in the security department—who abused their power.

He would be a difference-maker. Someday in the future, when he was ready to settle down and put his mind to it.

And now, his father could make it all go away with a snap of his fingers. He'd already destroyed Nate's dreams of a happy home life, with Nadia as the kind and understanding wife who would look the other way and not complain about his relationship with Kurt. How long before he couldn't resist ruining the rest of it, too?

"What has your father done now?" Nadia asked him, her brow furrowed with worry.

Leave it to Nadia to home in on the problem without any input from him.

"Let's go somewhere more private to talk," he said, losing some of his head of steam. He met Nadia's eyes and was sure she saw the hint of panic in his. "I can't go out there," he said, waving vaguely in the direction of the porch. "I'm losing it, Nadia."

She slipped her hand into his and gave it a squeeze, her eyes full of kindness and concern. "Okay. Let's talk."

He nodded and started to guide her toward another little parlor room he'd noticed. Another room with a door that could be closed. She moved with him, but looked over her shoulder and waved.

"Come on, Agnes," she said.

Nate swallowed the first couple of responses that came to mind. Nadia was right, and he'd been treating Agnes horribly. He didn't think anything on earth could persuade him to *like* the girl, but that didn't mean he had the right to be cruel to her. So he went with his third response, which was far less caustic than his knee-jerk ones.

"I really need to talk to you alone."

"Tough," was Nadia's tart reply. "We're not sending Agnes out to the service by herself, and we're not leaving her holding the bag if someone comes looking for us. So she's coming with us. Now come on, Agnes."

She waved to Agnes again, and the girl reluctantly came closer. Nate didn't want this virtual stranger intruding on his time with Nadia, nor did he want her to see him falling apart at the seams as he feared he might. But he didn't have the energy to fight a battle he knew he wouldn't win, so he sighed and started off toward the parlor again.

"Make sure you bring the whiskey," he called to Agnes over his shoulder.

Agnes, of course, didn't answer, but he heard the soft tap of her shoes on the wooden floor of the hall, so he knew she was following. Once upon a time, he'd been fairly good at getting Nadia to agree with him, even when he knew she didn't *really* agree. She hadn't been a pushover, exactly, but he'd always known which buttons to push. Those buttons didn't work anymore, and if she was dead set on Agnes coming along, then Agnes was coming along.

Outside, the drizzle had picked up and become a steady rain, drumming on the windows. The parlor Nate led the girls into would have been dismal on a bright and cheery day, the furniture dark, fussy, and old-fashioned. On this gray and gloomy day, the place was positively depressing. Or maybe that was just Nate's mood. They certainly went together nicely. He closed the parlor door. Anyone who came looking for him would have no trouble finding him, but he doubted his father would hesitate to start the service without him there, and once it started, no one was going to come looking.

Nadia and Agnes sat together on a floral-upholstered sofa with spindly legs, but Nate was too agitated to sit. Agnes was still holding the whiskey bottle, probably unsure what to do with it. He wanted to take it from her, more because he wanted something to do with his hands than because he wanted to drink, but Nadia's forbidding stare made him think twice.

"So, what's happened now?" Nadia prompted.

He hated that he had to talk about this with Agnes in the room. Even when she'd disapproved of him, Nadia had always been easy to talk to. They'd known each other so long, been each other's friends for so long . . . He was trying not to think of Agnes as the enemy anymore, but she certainly wasn't a friend.

Soon, everyone, *friend and foe, is going to know about this,* he reasoned with himself. No doubt the Chairman had already been making discreet introductions from the moment he had arrived.

His voice halting as though every word were being dragged out of him by force, he told the girls everything he knew—which, granted, was very little—about his alleged half-sister. Neither Nadia nor Agnes interrupted him, even when his pauses became uncomfortably long. They sat side by side, quietly listening, and Nate was struck for the millionth time by the contrast between them. Nadia, beautiful and tastefully dressed, sat up straight and proud, her eyes soft with sympathy as she looked him straight in the face. Agnes, plain and with no fashion sense whatsoever, sat slumped with her shoulders slightly hunched, her gaze focused either on the floor or at something across the room, never at his face. He doubted she was much more comfortable sitting in on this conversation than he was having it in front of her.

There was a long silence after he'd finished telling them about Dorothy. He'd seen Agnes start when he mentioned his worry that Dorothy would one day be named heir, and he wondered if by some miracle she was now reconsidering the engagement. It wasn't like he'd made a great impression on her as potential husband material if he didn't come with guaranteed rank, status, and money. She chewed her lip and frowned, looking lost in thought.

"I don't know what to say," Nadia said in a small voice, shaking her head.

Nate shrugged. "There's nothing *to* say. If my dad wants to pretend this girl is his daughter, who's going to stop him?"

He gave Nadia his most challenging stare, daring her to argue that Dorothy really was the Chairman's daughter. But, to his utter shock, it wasn't Nadia who spoke, it was Agnes.

"It doesn't make sense," Agnes said, her voice even softer than Nadia's had been.

Nadia turned to her, obviously as surprised as Nate that she'd spoken up. Nate couldn't remember a time when Agnes had spoken without being spoken to first. She surprised him yet again by raising the whiskey bottle she still held to her lips and taking a swift swig.

"What doesn't make sense?" Nadia asked.

Agnes grimaced at the taste of the whiskey, setting the bottle down on the coffee table. She looked back and forth between Nadia and Nate as if uncertain it was all right for her to speak.

"Go on," Nate urged, trying to keep his voice gentle.

Agnes swallowed hard and looked at him, though her gaze kept darting sideways, as if she couldn't quite stand to meet his eyes for more than a second at a time.

"Even though you're still the legal heir," she said, "your stock goes down when people discover another potential heir is out there."

Nate frowned in confusion, but Nadia understood right away what Agnes meant. "Your stock in the marriage market," she said, and Agnes nodded. Agnes looked at her as if hoping Nadia would continue the thought, but Nadia smiled softly and waited.

Agnes licked her lips and did that not-quite-meeting-his-eyes thing again. "Your prime value right now is that you're the undisputed Chairman Heir. That's why my father wants this engagement so badly, even though he's . . . uneasy about marrying me to a Replica. He expects his grandchild to be the Chairman of Paxco someday."

Nate tried very hard not to shudder or make a face at the idea of providing Chairman Belinski with a grandchild. The idea of trying to perform his conjugal duties with Nadia was bad enough, but he'd *never* be able to overcome his distaste enough to do it with Agnes.

"There's already a comfortable alliance between our states," Agnes continued. "We have good trade agreements with each other, and there are very few strings attached. But if you and I marry, the balance of power between our states will change. We won't be quite so independent anymore, and we'll lose some of our more lucrative trade agreements with states that are your rivals. If the next heir to Paxco is going to be a Belinski, then the advantages outweigh the disadvantages, but if not . . ." Agnes shrugged. "The arrangement heavily favors

Paxco under those circumstances, and my father might decide he can make better use of me."

"By marrying you to that marketing director you told me about?" Nate asked incredulously. The idea that a man like that would make for a more favorable marriage prospect than Nate seemed almost insulting.

"It would be a financially advantageous match," Agnes said, "and would come with none of the same strings. So why would your father announce the existence of another potential heir *now*, of all times? If he'd waited just one more week, I'd have signed the papers to make our engagement legally binding and it would have been nearly impossible for Synchrony to back out."

Nate stared at Agnes in mute astonishment. He didn't think he'd ever heard her string so many words together before. And somehow, it had never quite occurred to him that Paxco might be getting the better out of their marriage arrangement. He'd focused on the relative size and wealth of their two states—and on Agnes's lack of personal charms—and decided Agnes was marrying above herself. He had never considered that in marrying above herself, Agnes might have been making her state into a vassal of Paxco, and that that might not be so advantageous for Synchrony. Never considered that Chairman Belinski might have been anything other than ecstatic about the match.

Maybe if he'd paid more attention to business and politics, instead of putting it all off until "later," he wouldn't be standing there gaping like an idiot.

Nadia was not similarly surprised by Agnes's assessment, but then she'd always been more politically aware than he.

"You're right," she told Agnes, nodding while her frown announced she was trying to figure out the mystery. "The timing is very strange. It seems like a serious blunder. But Chairman Hayes doesn't make blunders. Perhaps Dorothy or her mother have been putting pressure on him to bring her out in public."

Nate dismissed the idea with a shake of his head. "First of all, you know from personal experience how hard it is to put pressure on him." He immediately wished he could take the words back, even before he saw Nadia's warning look and the spark of interest in Agnes's usually dull eyes. He couldn't afford to be careless with his words. Agnes was shy, not stupid, although before now he'd been too hostile to notice.

"Besides, Dorothy can't really put pressure on him because she isn't really his daughter. Blackmail doesn't work unless you actually *have* something."

Once again, he braced himself for Nadia to argue about Dorothy's paternity, and once again, she didn't.

"Your father would hardly cave in to blackmail just to keep the world from knowing about an illegitimate child," she said. "And it wouldn't explain the timing, unless someone is hoping to sabotage the marriage arrangement."

"No one knows about it yet," Agnes pointed out. "No one who doesn't want it to happen, at least."

"Do you believe me?" Nate asked Nadia. "When I say Dorothy is an impostor?"

"Yes," Nadia said, without hesitation.

The relief that flooded him made him feel weak in the knees, and he finally decided it was time to sit down. He moved over to an armchair and practically collapsed into it.

"If Dorothy were the real thing," she continued, "your father would have been holding her over your head from the moment you were old enough to understand what you stood to lose."

"Exactly!" Nate exclaimed, sitting up straight once again.

He realized that, deep down inside, he'd worried his reasoning had been nothing but some form of denial, but hearing Nadia echo his own thoughts made it seem less outlandish.

"If she's not his daughter," Agnes asked tentatively, "then who is she?"

"I'm going to find out," he said, though he had no idea how. He wished like hell Nadia's family would let her come home, would let the two of them put their heads together to solve the mystery. Together, they'd been able to find Kurt, despite Kurt's vehement desire not to be found, but Nate could take very little credit for their success. Nadia, with her cool head and her sharp mind, had been the brains of the operation. He needed her if he was going to figure out who Dorothy was—and prove that she wasn't the Chairman's daughter.

"Maybe Agnes can help you," Nadia suggested.

Nate hoped his face didn't look as ridiculous as Agnes's when his jaw dropped and his eyebrows climbed, but he suspected it did.

Nadia turned to Agnes. "You immediately figured out the irregularity of the Chairman introducing Dorothy today. You obviously have a head for the twists and turns of politics." She flashed Nate a rueful smile, and he felt the heat rise in his neck. As the Chairman Heir of the most powerful of the Corporate States, *he* should have been the one to understand the implications at the drop of a hat. "And because you're so quiet and unobtrusive, I bet people would say things around you that they wouldn't say around Nate."

Agnes gave an undignified snort. "Quiet and unobtrusive?"

Nadia shrugged. "Well, you are." It was Agnes's turn to be on the receiving end of one of Nadia's knowing looks. "Tell me you don't spend a lot of time quietly listening to other people's conversations."

Agnes's familiar mottled blush gave her away. To his surprise, Nate found himself squirming in his chair, almost as uncomfortable as Agnes.

"You don't have to help me," he mumbled, taking a page from her book and staring at his shoes. "I've treated you like shit." Now it was his own turn to blush, because that was *not* the kind of language to use when speaking to an Executive girl. Agnes was not Nadia, and he couldn't allow himself to get so relaxed with her. "Sorry."

"For treating me like shit? Or for swearing?"

Blinking in surprise, Nate looked up and saw the faintest of smiles on Agnes's face. Nadia was grinning like a proud mama. Maybe she was right and there *was* a personality under Agnes's bland exterior.

"Both."

He couldn't tell from the expression on her face whether his apology was accepted or not. "I'll see what I can find out about Dorothy. If there's a chance she could be named Chairman Heir . . ."

She let her voice trail off, but Nate had no trouble filling in the blanks, especially when she couldn't hide the hope in her voice. He'd more than satisfied his initial aim to make her dislike him, and the thought that she might not have to marry him after all had her heart all aflutter.

Outside the parlor, there was a swell of sound—the porch door swinging open, footsteps, murmuring voices.

The service was over, and Nate had missed the whole thing.

CHAPTER FIFTEEN

nadia would have loved nothing better than to have
stayed in that quiet little parlor talking to Nate and Agnes
until it was time to return to Tranquility. She didn't want to
face her parents, didn't want to face the crowd, didn't even
want to face Gerri, who would almost certainly try to push
her into revealing what was on the recordings again, having
had a whole night to plan out a new argument. But with the
service over, there was no use trying to hide away anymore.

Nate allowed Nadia to do up his collar and tie while Agnes stashed the open whiskey bottle behind a tall ornamental
clock on the armoire. Not that anyone at this gathering would
dare rebuke Nate for drinking, but it was rather undignified
to swig straight from the bottle. Nadia didn't mention that
she could smell the alcohol on both Nate's and Agnes's breath,
because there was nothing they could do about it.

With a collective deep breath, the three of them opened
the door and plunged out into the crowd. Nate was instantly
swarmed by people desperate to convey their condolences.
Nadia wasn't sure what they made of his failure to appear at
the service. Perhaps they'd thought he was too prostrate with
grief to face it, and that was why they were so sure he was in
need of their sympathy.

Very few people even acknowledged Nadia's presence,
much less spoke to her. It was like there was an invisible

force field around her. Every once in a while, she caught someone sneaking surreptitious glances her way, and she felt sure she was the subject of more than one conversation. And this was how her fellow Executives treated her *before* they knew she was no longer destined to be Nate's bride. When that scandal hit, they'd do more than just ignore her—they'd flee her presence as if a leper had just stepped into the room.

Agnes, however, stayed by her side as the crowd cut both of them off from Nate. People greeted her easily enough, but they always seemed to spot someone across the room they absolutely *had* to talk to. Agnes's expression of long-suffering patience told Nadia she was used to such behavior, and she was making no effort to change things. Her body language and facial expression were both just this side of forbidding, and once she'd shared basic pleasantries with someone, she seemed to have nothing else to say. She'd seemed much more friendly, and less . . . sullen when they'd been in the parlor.

"Maybe the crowd is thinner out on the porch," Nadia suggested. If there were fewer people, maybe the two of them could hang out together and avoid the stilted and uncomfortable conversations Agnes's shyness and Nadia's disgrace brought on.

"My father will get mad at me for being 'antisocial,'" Agnes said, making air quotes. "I'm already in for a lecture if he saw me standing in the corner earlier. I'm supposed to mingle." She sighed heavily. "I'm not any good at mingling, but I need to at least pretend I'm making an effort."

Nadia decided then and there that she didn't much care for Chairman Belinski. There were ways to help draw Agnes out of her shell, but calling her antisocial and then ordering her to mingle wasn't one of them.

"Well, stick with me," Nadia said. "We can pretend to

mingle together. And if we see your father, we can bend our heads together and pretend to be having an earnest, important conversation."

That won her another of Agnes's rare smiles. "You're pretty cool."

Nadia grinned back. "I'm glad *someone* thinks so."

Nadia's grin faded when she spotted her parents threading their way through the crowd, headed in her direction. She met her mother's eyes across the distance and cringed internally. Esmeralda Lake was not happy with her, and Nadia suspected the two of them were about to have a pitched battle in the middle of a crowded room as they both smiled pleasantly so that no one would notice.

She was wrong.

nadia hated to leave Agnes alone in the midst of the crowd that so clearly made her uncomfortable. However, her mother wasn't about to give her a choice in the matter. Ignoring Agnes as if the girl didn't exist, she marched up to Nadia and said, "We need to talk. In private."

No hug, no kiss. Hell, no greeting of any kind. Nadia glanced at her father, who was trailing in her mother's wake. He met her eyes only briefly before looking away.

This didn't bode well.

Nadia was tempted to insist they have their private conversation right here and now. She was tired of being ordered around, and maybe if they talked in public, the conversation—or lecture, because Nadia knew that her mother would be the only one doing the talking—would be over sooner. The only thing that kept her from protesting was that she didn't want to subject Agnes to the unpleasantness.

"Fine," Nadia said, her voice no warmer than her mother's. "If you'll excuse me, Agnes?"

"Of course," Agnes said with a resigned slump of her shoulders.

"There's a place we can talk down this way," her mother said, turning toward a hallway off to the side.

"What's going on?" Nadia asked her father in a voice just barely loud enough to be heard over the chattering of the crowd.

This time, he wouldn't even make brief eye contact. "We'll talk when we have some privacy."

There was a flutter of panic in Nadia's stomach. Her father looked positively *guilty*, and she was struck by the premonition that he had lost his battle with her mother and she was to be sent away for good. Her chest tightened, and it was suddenly hard to draw a full breath.

Her mother led the way into a small sitting room, just big enough for a sofa, a couple of chairs, and a coffee table. There were a handful of retreat brochures on the coffee table, along with a box of tissues.

The sitting room door closed with a solid thunk, and Nadia noticed there was a second door located on the opposite side of the room. A door that had a discreet electronic card reader set into the frame.

"Sit down, Nadia," her mother said, putting her arm around Nadia's shoulders and trying to guide her to the sofa.

Nadia refused to budge. Her father was fidgety, his gaze darting nervously around the room, and her mother was stiffly dignified. The kind of dignity that felt forced and artificial.

"Tell me you're not sending me away," Nadia begged. Her voice was shaking, and there was nothing she could do to control it.

Her mother sighed heavily, and she lowered herself onto the sofa as if she were afraid the impact would break her. She blinked a couple of times, as if holding off tears. The only time Nadia had seen her mother show more emotion was when Mosely and his men had burst into their home to arrest her.

"We have to, sweetheart," her mother said, confirming Nadia's worst fear.

"No!" Nadia held back a scream of frustration and anger. "I've only been in Tranquility a little over a week, and I already feel like I've been buried alive. I need to come home. I can't live like this!"

Esmeralda firmed up her dignified veneer. "When the Chairman announces Nathaniel's new marriage agreement, you'll be ruined. *Completely* ruined."

Her father winced and made a calming gesture, as if that would somehow help the situation. "It's not your fault, and it's not even remotely fair, but your mother is right."

Nadia felt like she was holding herself together with little bits of tape and maybe a staple or two. "I know I'm going to be ruined," she said with as much calm as she could muster. "And I know it's going to be awful. But I will literally go insane if I have to stay locked up in a retreat much longer."

"Don't be melodramatic," her mother scolded. "A retreat is hardly a prison, and—"

"Yes, it *is* a prison," Nadia retorted. "At least for me it is. You know there isn't a single other teenager at Tranquility? I think the person closest to my age there is some woman who's about thirty and weighs about three thousand pounds. Her favorite activities are eating and sitting around staring into space, so we have a *lot* in common."

"Stop it, Nadia!" her mother said, standing once more.

"I'm sorry you're not enjoying your time in the retreat, but there's no place for you in polite society anymore."

Nadia shivered and hugged herself. "I can live at home even if I don't have a place in polite society. So I won't go out to parties or have a social life. At least I'll be free! I can . . . I don't know, go shopping, or go to museums." *Spend time with Dante.* "Keep myself busy."

"And every time you set foot out of the house, the press will be there to capture it on film and dredge up the dirt all over again."

"I don't care!"

"Well, I do!" There were twin spots of color high on her mother's cheeks, and for a moment Nadia thought her mother was going to slap her she was so angry. "It's not all about you, so stop acting like a spoiled child. Your father and I are going to be put through hell. So will your sister and your niece and your nephew. And the more you show up in public, the more photos the press prints, the more active and fresh they can keep the story, the longer that hell is going to last. Maybe you'd rather go through all that than stay in a retreat, but think about the rest of us."

Nadia was so angry she was shaking. "I've spent my whole life thinking about the rest of you, doing what you think is best. I never would have been in this position in the first place if I hadn't. So don't you dare make me into some kind of villain who's too selfish to live."

"Your mother isn't the villain, either," her father suddenly interjected.

Nadia turned to him, and there were tears burning in her eyes. "How could you?" Her father had always been the kind and nurturing parent, had always comforted her when her mother criticized, had always both told and shown her that he loved her. And yet he was going to allow her mother to lock her away.

Her father tried to give her a hug, but Nadia would have none of it. He lowered his arms, then wiped one hand over his whole face. "We're trying to do what's best. For everyone. Including you, whether you believe that or not. If I had it all to do over again, I never would have agreed to the match with Nathaniel in the first place. I knew it was a potential minefield, but I thought we'd be able to navigate it."

Nadia swallowed hard, forcing a torrent of angry words back down her throat. Her parents had agreed to the match out of unbridled ambition. With her marriage to Nate would come money and power and promotion. Making a match like that was the sole purpose in life of any Executive who was not an heir, as marriage was the only way they could further their family's interests. And she'd done everything in her power to make that match happen.

"We can't fix the past," her father continued. "All we can do is try to make the future as tolerable as possible. And the only way we can do that is to keep you out of the public eye."

"For how long?" she asked in a frightened whisper.

"As long as it takes," her mother answered.

"We'll come up to visit as often as we can," her father promised, and Nadia felt another trapdoor open up beneath her.

"Come up where?"

"Why here, of course," her mother said. "If the Preston Sanctuary is good enough for the Chairman Spouse, then it's good enough for you."

Oh God. They weren't *sending* her away. She already *was* away.

"Here," she said numbly. Here, where she'd be hours away

from anyone she knew. Here, where she would be too far away for Dante to visit her in the night, even if he *could* escape the notice of the guards in the watchtowers. Here, where she would be utterly cut off from anything and everything familiar. "I'm not going back to Tranquility tonight."

"We looked at them all," her father said, "and this seems to be the best. And unlike Tranquility, there are young people here."

Any "young people" who were at the Sanctuary would be suspect at best. Nadia might be here for reasons completely outside her own control, but mostly if someone her age ended up in a retreat, it was because of a drug problem, a mental illness, or severe behavioral issues. Just the sort of new friends Nadia was dying to make.

"Don't do this to me," she begged.

Her parents looked at each other, then at her. Her father looked miserable, and even her mother had a rim of red around her eyes. But right that moment, Nadia didn't much care how they felt.

There was a soft knock on the door.

When Nadia's mother said "Come in," the door opened, and two smiling women in navy blue uniforms stepped inside.

nadia desperately wanted to say good-bye to Nate before she was dragged off to the depths of the retreat, never to be seen again. And she wanted to see Gerri even *more* desperately. There was no way Gerri would have smiled at her so easily earlier if she'd known their parents weren't going to let Nadia leave the retreat. And she'd definitely have been up in Nadia's face trying to find out what was on the recordings.

Nadia ignored the two staff members who were trying to

introduce themselves to her and faced her mother, trying to keep the panic out of her voice.

"I have to speak with Gerri before she leaves," she said.

Her mother frowned almost imperceptibly. "That wouldn't—"

"Please, Mother. It's very, *very* important." She wished there were some way she could avoid telling Gerri about Thea, wished she could protect her sister from that very dangerous secret. But Gerri had promised to leave the recordings alone if and only if Nate didn't end up formally engaged to Agnes and Nadia didn't get sent upstate. The promise was now null and void, and Nadia knew her sister. Even though Nadia had told her there was nothing incriminating on the recordings, Gerri would want to listen to them, if for no other reason than that she hoped to read between the lines and figure out what Nadia was hiding.

"This isn't the time or place for a scene," her mother said. "I'll tell Gerri you want to see her, and she'll come on the first visiting day."

"No!" Nadia shouted, then tried to calm herself down. She was more likely to get her way by acting calm and reasonable than by getting hysterical. Even if the latter was awfully tempting under the circumstances. "You don't understand. This isn't something that can wait. I have to talk to her *today*."

When Gerri found out Nadia was to be confined to the Sanctuary, she would be furious, especially that their parents had made the decision behind her back. Despite all of Nadia's warnings, she doubted her sister would have the inclination to wait until the first visiting day to try to ferret out Nadia's secrets and use them against the Chairman. Five minutes after she heard the news, she'd be making a beeline for those recordings, and if the Chairman was watching her as closely as Nadia suspected . . .

She gave her father an imploring look, but he just shook his head and stayed silent, content to let Esmeralda take charge. As usual.

"I'm sorry, Nadia," her mother said firmly, "but you're going to have to settle for seeing her during visiting hours. We need this transition to happen as quietly as possible."

Nadia wanted to let loose an ear-piercing scream. Let her mother try to hide her away quietly after that! But of course, that wouldn't get her any closer to Gerri.

"I will be calm," she said, though her hands were shaking. "I will be quiet. I'll make no fuss whatsoever. But you have to let me speak to Gerri first. It's a matter of life and death."

Her mother gave her a look of exasperated disbelief. "Really, Nadia, there's no need to be quite so dramatic. It's better for everyone—"

"Screw what's better for everyone!" So much for maintaining her calm. Her mother blanched at her language, and her father looked at her like she'd grown a second head. Nadia had been able to remain calm and dignified when Mosely's men had arrested her, when she'd been convinced her future included imprisonment, torture, and execution, but somehow this was worse. This was being abandoned by the people who were supposed to love and protect her. This was being patronized like a child throwing a tantrum when she had never once given them any reason to believe she was some kind of drama queen.

"Perhaps it would be best if you and your husband said your good-byes now," one of the staff workers suggested. "We'll take good care of Nadia."

"I have to talk to Gerri," Nadia tried again. "Please, Mother. There are things that happened that you don't know about and Gerri does. I swear I'm not being melodramatic when I say it's a matter of life and death. Please trust me."

"I won't have you upsetting Gerri," her mother said. "Your father and I will sit down and talk with her about what we've decided *in private*."

For the first time, Nadia realized she wasn't the only one whose reaction her mother was worried about. She was worried *Gerri* would "make a scene." Bad enough for Nadia to do it, but at least she could be quietly dragged off into the depths of the retreat. If Gerri wanted to take it public—which she might, seeing as she wouldn't appreciate being blindsided—there would be no way to stop her.

"Good-bye, Nadia," her mother said stiffly. "We'll visit as often as we can, and I'll make sure to tell Gerri you want to speak with her when things settle down."

Her father took a step in her direction, raising his arms as if he planned to hug her, but Nadia wasn't about to accept any hugs, so she took a step backward and crossed her arms over her chest.

That was when she felt the faint bulge of her forbidden phone, tucked into her bra to keep it safely hidden. Maybe instead of continuing to butt heads with her mother, who had clearly drawn her line in the sand and was not prepared to back down, she should just wait until she had a quiet moment alone and give Gerri a call.

It would be dangerous. Much more dangerous than talking in person would be. Nadia knew the resistance would be listening in on anything she said on the phone, and she couldn't afford to let them find out about the recordings, or about the damning truth those recordings held. Not when she didn't know much about them or what their goals were. She wished she'd asked Dante more questions about them, but she'd let her loneliness and longing get the best of her. And she hadn't realized she'd be cut off from contact with him so soon.

Somehow, some way, she was going to figure out how to get the message across to her sister without betraying everything she knew.

Her eyes were watering, and she was practically choking on a toxic combination of hurt and anger. Her mother was implacable, and her father was too weak-willed to fight for her, and no one else even knew she needed to be fought for. She felt tears slipping from her eyes, and she made no effort to wipe them away.

"Don't bother coming to visit," she said hoarsely, knowing that someday she was going to regret the words. "I never want to see either of you again." She turned to the two prison matrons in their navy blue uniforms and their faux-sympathetic smiles. "Let's go."

Turning her back on her parents, she followed her new keepers to the key-carded door she'd noticed when they'd stepped in. One woman opened the door and gestured Nadia inside, while the other stayed behind her, as if ready to stop her if she tried to bolt.

Without another look at her parents, she stepped through the door.

JUST like at Tranquility, the first step of checking in to the Preston Sanctuary was for Nadia to change out of her street clothes and into a retreat uniform, this one a medium-blue belted tunic and pants. At least the color was more flattering to Nadia's fair skin, she thought as she changed in a curtained alcove while the matrons—who had now introduced themselves a second time without Nadia paying enough attention to remember their names—waited.

Only there was one crucial difference between the Preston Sanctuary and Tranquility, one Nadia had not anticipated or she wouldn't have gone as quietly as she had, would have pitched a screaming, hysterical fit and not cared who heard her or how embarrassed her family would be.

When the matrons guided Nadia through the back door of the changing room into the heart of the retreat, there was the distinctive beep of a metal detector going off. She froze in the doorway, feeling as if she'd just been kicked in the ribs.

One of the matrons gave her a smile that was both sheepish and sympathetic. "I'm afraid it's not uncommon for our new guests to try to smuggle things in. Please step back into the changing room and remove anything that is not part of the uniform."

Nadia shook her head, her lip quivering. The phone was the only link she had to the outside world, the only chance she had to warn Gerri not to attempt the blackmail.

"I-I don't have anything," she said, but it was a lame denial, and the matron just looked at her knowingly.

The second matron was less sympathetic. "Whatever you're hiding, we'll search you and confiscate it if we have to. You wouldn't be the first or the last rule breaker we've ever had to deal with. Make it easier on yourself."

Fighting it made no sense. But then, Nadia's life had stopped making sense a few weeks ago, and she had nothing else left to lose.

She didn't make it easy on anyone. But in the end, the matrons took the phone anyway.

CHAPTER SIXTEEN

nate couldn't get away from the Preston Sanctuary fast enough. The place felt gloomy and oppressive, especially with all the black-clad Executives milling about, always keeping their voices low and somber in respect for the sad occasion. People he didn't like, and who didn't like him, kept up a steady stream of insincere condolences, and he made only the barest effort to accept them graciously. Hell, sometimes he didn't make the effort at all, like when the Terrible Trio fought their way through to him and started cooing and batting their eyelashes. Their leader, Jewel, had always thought she was runner-up to Nadia, that if somehow he ended up not marrying Nadia, she would be the logical choice to step into the role.

Ordinarily, Nate tolerated, or sometimes even encouraged, Jewel's flirtation. The girl was stunningly beautiful, and if he didn't want people questioning his sexual orientation, he figured it was best to act dazzled by her. No matter how much he loathed her. Today, he just couldn't be bothered, so when Jewel put her hand on his shoulder and leaned forward, inviting him to look down her dress, he gave her his coldest stare.

"Surely even *you* have more class than to try to flirt with me at my mother's funeral," he said, and Jewel recoiled as if he'd slapped her. The other members of the Trio—Jewel's younger sister Cherry, and her best friend, Blair—both looked similarly shocked, although he thought he detected a hint of malicious amusement in their eyes.

"I wasn't—" Jewel stammered, her eyes wide with exaggerated innocence.

"Yes, you were," Nate said. "And for your information, I wouldn't marry you if I had a gun to my head, so why don't you just give up on flirting with me altogether."

His voice was rising dangerously, and the Trio were all gaping at him, pale and frightened-looking. This was a side of him they'd never seen. Not that he'd never been rude to people in public before—he was well known for ignoring the usual rules of propriety. But this was a whole different level. And if he wanted his father to disinherit him as soon as possible, acting like an asshole to girls from such highly ranked Executive families, in public where just about anyone could overhear, was a step in the right direction.

Nate couldn't bring himself to apologize for the harsh words, but he did manage to keep himself from spewing any more of them. He shook his head at the Trio, then moved away from them as briskly as he could manage with the crowd.

People tried to stop him to talk, but he ignored them all. He had to get out of here, no matter how bad an impression leaving now would make. If he stayed, he'd make an even worse one.

He looked for Nadia but couldn't find her. He wanted to say good-bye to her before he left, but he wanted to get the hell out even more. He spotted Agnes, standing alone with her back practically against the wall, and he made his way over to her. She looked alarmed at his approach, but she didn't try to avoid him, just stood there and waited placidly.

"Have you seen Nadia?" he asked as soon as he was within hearing range.

"Not for a while," she answered. "She went off to talk with her parents, and I haven't seen her since."

Nate grunted in frustration. He wanted to at least give Nadia a hug before they were separated once again, but who knew how long she'd spend closeted up with her parents, no doubt discussing their strategies for the future?

He couldn't wait for her. Not when his nerves were so sharply honed, not when just having someone look at him the wrong way could trigger him into an explosion. He'd made enough of a spectacle of himself already today by not show-ing up for the service, and if he had any hope of convincing his father that he could be a responsible heir, he had to avoid making any more waves than absolutely necessary.

He nodded at Agnes and turned to leave. He took one step away, eying the door across the room, then brought him-self to a halt and turned back to Agnes. She'd done nothing to deserve the horrible way he'd treated her, and he sus-pected she was at least as anxious to get out of here as he was.

"I'm going to head back to the city," he said, hoping Nadia would be proud of him. "You want to get out of here?"

Agnes bit her lip nervously, but it was impossible to miss the hope that flared in her eyes. "My father wouldn't like it."

Nate leaned forward and dropped his voice so that no one but Agnes could hear him. "But *you* would. Besides, our fathers have been shoving us together with both hands. Surely yours won't mind if you catch a ride back to the city with me."

Agnes raised an eyebrow. "When this reception is likely to go on for another hour, at least?"

Nate shrugged. "*I'm* the one you're supposed to be getting to know, right?" Though perhaps that would no longer be true, once the existence of the Chairman's "long-lost daughter" became public knowledge. Nate assumed his father hadn't dropped that particular bombshell yet, or the tone of the gossip and chatter in the room would have been quite different.

Nate held out his elbow to Agnes. Her lips curved into the tiniest hint of a grateful smile, and she slipped her hand through his elbow, her touch so light he could barely feel it. Then, he guided her out of the room toward the exit, ignoring everyone who tried to talk to him along the way.

He basked in the glow of his "good deed," right up until the door of the limo closed, leaving him alone in the back with Agnes. A privacy screen blocked the driver and Nate's bodyguard from view. The drive back to his apartment was going to take about four hours. Agnes might have more redeeming qualities than Nate had previously allowed himself to acknowledge, but that didn't mean he wanted to spend four hours shut up in a car with her.

What had he been thinking?

Agnes let out a soft sigh, pinching the bridge of her nose and closing her eyes. "If you don't mind," she said in her timid little-girl voice, "I'd like to close my eyes for a while. My head's been pounding ever since I had to come inside after the service."

Nate wondered if she really had a headache, or if she was just trying to give them both a graceful way out of trying to make conversation.

"Go ahead," he said, hoping he didn't sound too eager. "My head isn't feeling that great, either, to tell you the truth."

She opened her eyes briefly to give him a sympathetic smile, but she didn't try to console him with any empty platitudes.

He gave her credit for that. When she closed her eyes once more, he patted his pockets until he found the secure phone Kurt had given him, which he carried with him at all times just in case.

Obviously, he couldn't phone Kurt, not with Agnes in the car. Or even *without* her in the car, because the barrier that separated him from the driver and his bodyguard wasn't soundproof. But he could send a text. Kurt wasn't exactly an expert reader yet—the murder of the original Nate Hayes had put a stop to their reading and writing lessons—but Nate was sure his skills were up to deciphering the simple message he sent: *need to see u. come 2nite?*

If ever there was a time he needed to see Kurt, it was tonight. Not just because he needed the comfort of a lover's touch, though he did. But because the introduction of Dorothy meant his own lofty goals to make Paxco a better place someday might never come to pass. If Nate was going to make a difference in the world, it seemed it would not be as Chairman of Paxco after all. Which meant it was time to have a long talk with Kurt about this resistance movement of his, and whether it was something Nate might want to get involved with.

KURT didn't answer Nate's text, but Nate wasn't alarmed. Kurt's answer would be showing up at the apartment tonight. Or *not* showing up.

Thinking that the chances Kurt wouldn't show up were pretty slim, Nate decided to wait up for him. With a thermos of coffee by his side, he flopped on his bed in his pajamas and resolutely started reading up on the laws of succession, something he had never paid much attention to when he'd known he was the undisputed heir.

The laws themselves were impenetrable, of course. Nate suspected lawyers had been making up their own language from the beginning of time and would continue to do so for the foreseeable future. He read through the laws, just to be thorough, but then he went searching for a layman's explanation. Realistically, he didn't expect to find any convenient clauses that would prevent his father from naming Dorothy the Chairman Heir, but it wouldn't hurt to look. He wasn't going to sit idly by and watch his father hand their state over to some impostor. Especially not to one he'd handpicked to follow in his footsteps.

Nate had the best of intentions, trying to be more like Nadia and thinking about the future, planning for the challenges and hurdles that might present themselves. Unfortunately, he didn't have Nadia's single-mindedness or determination. His eyes glazed over almost instantly, and he had to read everything about three times before his mind would grasp even the simplest concepts. Not because he was an idiot, but because the layman's explanations of the laws of succession seemed all to have been written by lawyers, who had a different definition of *layman* than Nate did. And the reading was so dry and boring it made him want to scream.

He chugged coffee, but though he felt its buzz in his veins, it didn't make the reading any more interesting. His eyes dried out so that he had to blink all the time, and his head started aching. He laid his reading aside, telling himself he would just close his eyes for a few minutes . . .

. . . and woke up who knew how much later to find Kurt sitting on the bed beside him, squinting at his handheld as if he were trying to decipher hieroglyphics. Of course, the lawyer-speak had gotten the better of Nate, so it probably did look like hieroglyphics to someone like Kurt, who was barely literate.

"If you can make sense of any of that crap," Nate said in his sleep-roughened voice, "please enlighten me." He yawned hugely and rubbed his eyes.

Kurt grinned and tossed the handheld onto the night-stand. "I was looking for the pictures. What's the point of a book without pictures?"

Nate tried to grin back, but there was too much pressure weighing him down. His mother was dead. He'd met his father's "daughter," who just happened to be older than he and therefore a potential heir. And he'd been so distraught at the news that he'd managed to miss the funeral. Even a small smile was beyond him at the moment.

Kurt pried off the heavy black boots he was wearing and climbed onto the bed beside Nate, gathering him into his arms. Nate didn't think a hug had ever felt so good, and for a moment he allowed himself to bask in it.

"I'm sorry about your mother," Kurt said gently. "I know you had mixed feelings about her, but it's still hard."

"Yeah," was all Nate could manage to choke out.

There was a long silence, and when Kurt broke it, his voice was even softer and more gentle. "My ma used to beat the shit out of me when I was a kid."

Nate's whole body went on alert, and he practically held his breath. Kurt *never* talked about his family. In fact, he'd been so resolute about not talking about them that Nate had wondered if he even had any.

"I was maybe around eight when she introduced me to the family business."

Nate winced, but he bit his tongue to keep himself from saying anything sympathetic. He knew what Kurt meant by "family business," and the thought that Kurt had been subjected to it at such a young age turned his stomach. However, he doubted Kurt would appreciate the sympathy. And worse, it might cause him to clam up.

"Didn't like it at first," Kurt continued, his voice matter-of-fact. "I was little, and it hurt. So sometimes I'd try to say no. Some of the johns liked that, some didn't. But Ma punished me every time, said I didn't have to like it, I just had to do it."

Nate wanted to go back in time to kick the woman's ass. What kind of a mother would do that to her own kid? Suddenly, his own mom sounded almost saintly. Kurt's arms tightened around him.

"Relax. It was a long time ago, and she was trying to do her best for me, in her own way."

Nate couldn't take it anymore. He extricated himself from Kurt's arms and looked him straight in the face. "Doing her best for you? Are you out of your mind?"

"I grew up in Debasement, Nate. My career choices were drug running, smuggling, or whoring. Ma pointed me toward the one where I didn't have to join a gang so I was less likely to get killed. I didn't get it at the time, but I do now. You think I'm such a hard-luck case, but by Debasement standards, I was always one of the lucky ones. Even before you came along."

Nate knew he was right, but that didn't make it any easier to bear. Actually, it made it harder. It was unconscionable that *anyone* should live in the conditions Kurt was describing, much less innocent children. And it was unconscionable that the government of Paxco didn't give a damn, the attitude being, "We give them free food and shelter, what else could they possibly need?" Nate had always told himself he would fix it someday, but by introducing Dorothy, his father had neatly snatched his good intentions away.

"My point is, mothers are complicated. I didn't get along with mine, but I bawled my eyes out when she died. And sometimes I still miss her."

Nate reeled in his righteous indignation, remembering why Kurt had started this conversation in the first place. His throat hurt suddenly, and his chest ached.

"I must have had more than a hundred people tell me how sorry they were today," he said. "And you're the only one who has *any* idea what I'm feeling."

Nate was touched beyond words that Kurt had told him all this, had opened up to him about a past that he didn't like to talk about. They came from such different worlds, and yet Kurt understood him better than he had any right to. And Nate understood *Kurt,* too.

Kurt might have infiltrated his household as a spy for the resistance, but he did it because he thought it was the right thing to do. He had a heart of gold, and he'd never shown any sign that he resented Nate for his privileged upbringing. He'd never belittled Nate's problems, and he was always there when Nate needed him.

Nate didn't have the best track record when going with his gut, but that didn't mean he should forever ignore what it was telling him. There were two people in the whole world that he trusted with his life: Nadia and Kurt. Kurt and his resistance might have an agenda, but with Dorothy looming on the horizon, it was time for Nate to learn what that agenda was.

He blew out a deep breath, hoping he wasn't being the biggest sap in the universe. Then he met Kurt's eyes.

"If I tell you what really happened on the day Nadia was

arrested, will you promise me not to tell your resistance about it without my go-ahead?"

Kurt sat back and thought about it instead of volunteering a quick agreement. Nate gave him credit for that, and hoped it meant that he would be as good as his word, whatever he decided.

"You believed in me even when everyone around you was convinced I offed your original," Kurt said slowly. "Even when I tried to make you believe it myself. You risked your life to try to help me. I think I owe you a promise or two."

"Even though you wouldn't have needed my help if I hadn't gotten you into trouble in the first place?" If only Nate hadn't been so eager to give his father the virtual finger by screwing around at a state event, the two of them wouldn't have had to go looking for privacy, and they wouldn't have overheard what they should never have overheard.

Kurt shrugged. "It took both of us to get into that mess. So yeah, even though."

Nate nodded. And then he told Kurt the whole story.

CHAPTER SEVENTEEN

Kurt sat on Nate's bed, arms curled around his bent knees as he contemplated everything Nate had told him. There was a haunted, faraway look in his eyes, and Nate wondered if he might have lost anyone he knew to Thea's experiments. The Basement was an abysmally dangerous place, and people disappeared from it on a regular basis, which was how Mosely had kept anyone from noticing his depredations. Nate didn't have the impression that Kurt had left any good friends behind when he'd left the Basement to come work for him, but then there were a lot of things about his previous life that Kurt had failed to tell him. And that Nate had maybe been too squeamish to ask about.

"We've always known the government was corrupt," Kurt finally said, his eyes still lost. "But no one imagined anything like this."

"No, of course not. It's . . . beyond comprehension. And the worst thing about it is my father still doesn't think he and Mosely and Thea were doing anything wrong. He'd have happily killed me and produced another Replica who didn't know the truth so he could keep right on doing what he was doing. He said it was for the greater good of Paxco, and I think he actually believed it."

Kurt made a sound of disgust. "The greater good of the people in Paxco he thinks are worth a shit, you mean. He wouldn't shed a tear if every man, woman, and child in Debasement dropped dead. Hell, he'd probably throw a party. More money for the people who matter. Hurray!"

Nate wished he could argue the point, but he couldn't. His father had made it very clear that he thought the whole population of Debasement were leeches, sucking out the lifeblood of society. And he was far from the only high-ranking Paxco Executive to feel that way.

How many of Paxco's top Executives would have objected if Thea's experimentation had gone public? The Basement-dwellers would no doubt have risen up in violence, and much of the Employee class would probably have joined them, fueled by righteous indignation, but Nate bet many, if not most, of the Executives would have agreed with the Chairman that appeasing Thea by "sacrificing" certain unsavory elements of the population was the right thing to do. They wouldn't have been willing to give up the money and privileges Thea provided for them by making the Replica program possible. It made Nate ashamed to be an Executive.

"We put a stop to it," Nate said, reminding himself as much as Kurt. "Nadia and me." He made a face. "Well, mostly Nadia. But I did what I could."

Kurt whistled. "Kinda wish I could have been there to see it. Never thought the little mouse would have it in her." He smiled crookedly, and there was something that looked a lot like admiration in his eyes.

"She was never a mouse," Nate said, though he knew Kurt had always seen her that way, as someone timid and fragile and maybe even weak-willed. But then Kurt couldn't understand the burden she'd been carrying since she was four years old and promised to him. Nate had never truly understood it, either, not until everything had started to crumble.

"She was amazing. And now she's paying for it while you and I go on with our lives."

"Most times doing the right thing means taking risks," Kurt said. "You gotta be prepared for those risks to turn around and bite you. If you're not willing to face the consequences, you shouldn't be doing it in the first place." He reached out and squeezed Nate's shoulder. "I'm sorry Nadia got bit, but at least it's not fatal. It coulda been a lot worse."

"It still could be, if the Chairman ever finds those recordings."

Kurt acknowledged that with a nod. Nate didn't want to dwell on all the terrible things that could still happen, so he used the opening Kurt had inadvertently given him to broach a subject he hadn't been sure how to broach.

"So you're still . . . doing stuff for the resistance?"

Kurt gave him a puzzled look. "You know I am. I can't be their inside man anymore, but that doesn't mean I can't make myself useful."

"Like how?"

Kurt looked even more puzzled. "What do you mean, 'how'?"

"What kind of stuff do you do for the resistance?"

"Why do you want to know?" The puzzlement was replaced by something that looked more like suspicion.

Nate looked down at his hands, which he noticed he'd curled into tense fists. He forced his fingers to relax, not sure why he was suddenly feeling so vulnerable. "I've told you before I was going to change things in Paxco when I became Chairman." He had always noticed a hint of polite skepticism in Kurt's face when he'd done so, but he'd chosen to ignore it. "The stuff that's happened lately has made me realize that I shouldn't wait that long. I may be Chairman Heir, but I don't really have any power. Even if I were the perfect heir, with a keen mind for politics and a cool head, no one would listen to me because they think I'm just a kid. And forget about any-one listening to me now, after I've made everyone think of me as an irresponsible playboy."

"Where are you going with this?"

Nate cleared his throat. "I can't make any changes through official channels, but I can't just keep sitting on my ass and waiting for some mythical future where I have the power to make a difference. Especially since that future may no longer exist. I want to make a difference *now,* so I thought maybe I could do something to help out your resistance movement."

"The resistance movement you know squat about," Kurt pointed out.

"I know *you* believe in it. And I believe in you."

Kurt cupped Nate's face in his hands and planted a sweet, gentle kiss on his lips before shaking his head fondly.

"You know I love you, Nate," he said with a smile that was no doubt meant to ease the sting, "but the resistance is not for you."

Nate sat up a little straighter. "What's that supposed to mean?"

"It means you're the Chairman Heir, dumbass," Kurt an-swered, still smiling, making the insult sound affectionate. "You're the enemy."

"I'm not—"

"Not in my eyes. I know you. But the resistance is almost all Basement-dwellers and Employees. We're the have-nots, and you're most definitely one of the haves. When you say you want to make a difference, I believe you. But I don't have much more power in the resistance than you do in the gov-ernment. I'm just a kid, too, and no one's going to take my word for it that you're one of the good guys."

He understood Kurt's point, but that didn't make it any easier to swallow. "If every Executive in Paxco were to drop dead, would anyone in the resistance shed a tear?"

Kurt winced and drew back, answering the question without words. It seemed the resistance was every bit as class-conscious as the government they opposed. Nate shouldn't have been surprised. His education had been heavily weighted toward economics, political science, and history. He'd never been a great student, but he hadn't been a bad one, either.

"You know, when resistance movements like yours manage to topple the government they oppose, they tend to kill the opposition. I don't suppose you've ever heard of the French Revolution, but when the revolutionaries took over, they made being born to the aristocracy a crime punishable by death. And being seen as part of the 'establishment' wasn't too good for a lot of the Chinese during the Cultural Revolution, either. Is that the kind of regime change your resistance is hoping for?"

Kurt shook his head. "I don't know anything about those revolutions. We just want a voice in our government. The way we live in Debasement . . . It's not right. Not when Executives have everything they want just because they were born. We want a government that gives a shit about us. That doesn't mean we want to see a bunch of Executives' heads on pikes."

"And yet someone like me isn't welcome," Nate countered, trying not to sound bitter. His father was going to disinherit him; the resistance wanted nothing to do with him. What was he supposed to do with his life now? Go to parties and look pretty while being of absolutely no use to society?

"You're as welcome in the resistance as I would be in the board room. It's no lie: life sucks sometimes."

Nate swallowed a snappish response. If the resistance

wouldn't have him, then he'd just have to find some other way to work against his father and Dorothy. He wasn't going to lie down and let them win!

"I won't tell anyone about Thea," Kurt continued. "It won't do anyone any good, and it could do a lot of harm."

Nate couldn't resist issuing a challenge. "If your resistance is so peaceful, what harm could it possibly do?"

Kurt met his challenging gaze head-on. "I don't know the people who are in charge, but if they're Basement-dwellers, they're bound to have known and maybe even loved someone who disappeared. Probably had nothing to do with Thea. Probably they either disappeared themselves on purpose or are somewhere on the bottom of the East River. But once people get to wondering . . ."

Kurt let his voice trail off, and Nate couldn't help but get the message. The subject of Thea was too incendiary, too likely to hit nerves. He relaxed his shoulders, not having realized how much he had tensed up. Kurt might not be educated, but Nate had known from the moment he'd met him that he was smart. He understood just how dangerous the information about Thea could be if released into the wrong hands.

"You're sure Thea is dead, right?" Kurt asked with a shudder.

Nate remembered the sights and sounds and smells of his father destroying the living machine that was Thea. Remembered the shattering of the jars that had held Thea's biological components, blood-like fluid splashing onto the floor. Remembered the lumps of what looked like brain tissue those jars had concealed. Remembered the stink of blood and chemicals and gunpowder as his father had shot the jars one by one. Remembered the lights on Thea's nonbiological components going out as the world's first and only true artificial intelligence gave up the ghost.

"She's dead all right."

"Good."

There was a long silence as they both got lost in their own thoughts. Kurt snapped out of it first, shaking his head and blinking as if he'd just emerged from a trance. He reached out and planted a hand on the center of Nate's chest, pushing him firmly down to the mattress.

"After all that," Kurt said with a wicked smile, "I think we could *both* use some stress relief."

Nate couldn't have agreed more.

nadia rarely gave in to the desire to cry, and even when she did, she usually reeled herself in quickly and efficiently. But on her first night at the Preston Sanctuary, the first night of the rest of her life, she couldn't have stopped the tears if her life had depended on it.

Her room in the dormitory was perfectly nice, roomy and tastefully decorated with a comfortable bed and an array of lamps that would make up for the lighting deficiencies caused by the small window. There were bookshelves against one wall holding a small selection of books in case she was too lazy to walk up to the library on the third floor, and a small alcove with a coffee maker, a hot plate, and a tea kettle along with a basket of teas and prepackaged coffee.

But it might as well have been a prison cell as far as Nadia was concerned. Unlike at Tranquility, there were quite a number of rules here, so many that there was a booklet on her nightstand documenting them all. There was an eleven o'clock curfew, for one thing, and the staff checked each and every room to make sure that the inmates were accounted for. You needed a key card to open the doors at either end of the dormitory hall, and wherever you went, you had to check in and have your key card scanned. There were security cameras everywhere except inside the rooms themselves. You couldn't take a step without being tracked and observed. And instead of having visiting hours twice a week, there was only one visiting day each month, and Nadia had just missed it.

It would be a month before Nadia could set eyes on any of her loved ones again. A month before she had any chance to warn Gerri away from the recordings. And *forget* about seeing Dante. There was no way an Employee would be allowed to visit her, at least not without her parents' permission, which he'd never ask for and they'd never give. She was miserably, utterly, and truly alone.

And so she cried for everything she had lost, and she cried in fear for Gerri, and she cried because there was no one around to tell her she shouldn't.

CHAPTER EIGHTEEN

nadia doubted she got more than an hour or two of sleep on her first night at the Preston Sanctuary. The crying jag had exhausted her, and yet she was too worried about Gerri—and about her own bleak future locked away from public view—to fall asleep.

She rose from her bed shortly after the sun came up and tried to interest herself in one of the classic old novels on her prestocked bookshelf. She sampled four or five of them before she came to the inevitable conclusion that in her current state of mind, nothing was going to hold her attention. She felt so awful that she skipped breakfast, making do with a cup of tea and spending the morning in her room with the door closed.

By lunchtime, her stomach informed her in no uncertain terms that she had to eat, so she dressed and showered and headed down to the main dining room. There were several long tables in the center of the dining room, where the more sociable of the Sanctuary's inmates could gather and share whatever camaraderie and gossip was available for people who had no lives, but there were also tables for two and four dotting the edges of the room. Nadia stood in the doorway for a long moment, trying to decide where to sit.

As her mother had promised, there were a handful of teens among the inmates of the Sanctuary, and Nadia quickly spotted them, clustered together at one end of one of the long tables. Of course, they were all Executives, so even if they hadn't been seen in polite society in recent months or years, Nadia knew who they all were. There was Theresa Mallory, who was rumored to have a nasty habit of sleeping with the help—and then accusing them of rape when she got tired of them. There was Piper Cade, who was so jealous of her little brother that she'd pushed the boy down the stairs and practically killed him. That *wasn't* a rumor; Nadia had been at the party where the "accident" had occurred, and though she hadn't seen what happened, she *had* seen the self-satisfied look on Piper's face while the paramedics strapped her brother to a gurney to rush him to the hospital. And last, there was Sydney Sullivan, who was rumored to be mentally ill. Nadia had never met the girl in person—Sydney had been sent to the retreat years ago—but if the company she kept was any indication, Nadia was just as happy to keep it that way.

Ignoring her supposed "peers," Nadia chose a two-person table in the corner, her stomach tying itself in knots. Tranquility had been bad enough, but at least there hadn't been any psychos like Theresa and Piper there. Not that she knew of, anyway. She wondered how long it would take them to notice her and start trying to make her life more miserable than it already was. They were bound to be as aggressively jealous of her as the Terrible Trio, and because they were out of the public eye, there were no rules of polite society to keep their behavior in check.

Nadia was so busy chewing her lip, worrying over this new potential problem, that she didn't notice the older woman approaching until she pulled back the second chair at Nadia's table and sat down without an invitation.

"You don't have to worry about them," the woman said as

she snatched the elaborately folded napkin from her plate and smoothed it over her lap. "The staff here keep a very close eye on everyone, but particularly the known trouble-makers."

The woman smiled at her, creating crow's-feet at the corners of her eyes. "I'm sorry," she said, reaching out her hand for Nadia to shake, "I've been here so long I've forgotten my manners. I'm Athena Lawrence."

"Um, pleased to meet you," Nadia said, wondering if her own manners would disappear after she'd spent a few years here. "I'm Nadia Lake."

"I know," Athena said, giving her hand a mannishly hard squeeze as she shook.

"You do?" Nadia guessed Athena's age to be mid to late forties. Nadia had never heard of her, and that meant whatever scandal had sent her to the retreat happened long ago, before Nadia's time. Which meant Athena shouldn't know who she was.

Athena nodded, and her smile turned sad. "Ellie Hayes was my dearest friend for many years. I wasn't allowed to officially attend the funeral, but there were a couple of us who watched from one of the windows. I saw you with Ellie's son and made an educated guess about who you might be. You and Nathaniel were already promised to one another before I came to the Sanctuary."

Nadia wasn't sure what to say, especially when Athena's eyes misted with tears. The woman had done more than watch the funeral from a window if she had seen Nate and Nadia together. They had been indoors when they'd talked, and Nadia certainly hadn't been aware they were being observed.

"Apologies again," Athena said, dabbing at her eyes. "I'm

afraid I was spying a bit. I hoped to find a way to have a word with Nathaniel before he left, but my keepers here found me out before I could."

Nadia was intrigued despite herself, curiosity making her feel slightly more alive—and hungry. When a waitress came to the table, Nadia ignored the haute cuisine choices on the menu and went for a bacon cheeseburger instead. She had never eaten something so inelegant in public before, not wanting to see pictures of herself with her mouth hugely open and grease on her fingers plastered on the net, but if she had to be trapped at the retreat, the least she could do was eat what she wanted. Hell, it didn't even matter if she got fat.

"Why were you hoping to talk to him?" Nadia asked as soon as the waitress moved away.

Athena's blue eyes narrowed shrewdly as she regarded Nadia, her head cocked slightly to the side. "Do you mind me asking what your relationship is with Nathaniel these days? I don't suppose we'd be having this conversation if you were still his intended."

Nadia held her chin a little higher. The last thing she wanted to do was talk about her troubles with a total stranger. Even if that stranger had intrigued her. "Forgive me for being blunt, but that doesn't seem to be any of your business."

If Nadia had said something that blunt to an Executive out in society, the reaction would have been one of affront. There were subtle ways of avoiding conversation that were much more elegant and decorous, but she was done with being elegant and decorous. She reached for her glass of ice water, taking a drink to stop herself from apologizing.

To her surprise, Athena grinned at her. "A no-nonsense kind of girl, hmm? I like that. Reminds me a bit of what Ellie was like before that rat bastard husband of hers destroyed her."

Nadia choked on her mouthful of water, practically dropping the glass on her lap as she coughed. *No one* talked about the Chairman like that. Especially not to complete strangers. Nadia hastily put her glass down and held her napkin to her lips, trying to stop coughing.

Athena clucked her tongue. "You're not the only one who can be blunt. You'll find a lot of the fine manners you've been taught aren't terribly useful here."

Nadia nodded to indicate she understood. Her throat still itched, and the coughing fit had brought tears to the corners of her eyes. She was incapable of saying anything out loud.

"You're right that your relationship with Nathaniel is none of my business. I was asking because I wondered if there was a chance you would speak to him in the future. *I* certainly won't have that chance, but I promised Ellie I would do everything in my power to get a message to him."

A shiver traveled down Nadia's spine. Athena's face had gone grim and serious, no hint of her bright smile remaining. "But why would she have needed *you* to get a message to him? In ten years, she made no effort to contact him, not even once. If she had something she wanted to tell him—"

"Rat bastard husband, remember?"

Nadia wondered if lack of sleep had stolen her ability to think. She had no idea what Athena was getting at. She shook her head, unable to come up with a coherent question.

"It was the price she paid to avoid being arrested for treason," Athena explained, which only served to make Nadia more confused.

"Wait, what?" she asked, shaking her head again in case that would make her brain start working properly. "Treason?"

Athena frowned. "Why do you think Ellie spent the last decade of her life here? What does *society* think happened?"

"Umm. The rumor is that the Chairman cheated on her and she was so angry she locked herself away and refused to ever talk to him or Nate again." A rumor the Chairman himself had confirmed only the day before. Although it suddenly occurred to Nadia that if she agreed with Nate that Dorothy was an impostor, that made the rest of the Chairman's story equally suspect.

"Hmpf!" Athena snorted. "Leave it to him to cast himself as the cheater and still make himself come out looking better than Ellie."

"So that's not what happened?"

Athena shook her head. "Not hardly. It was *Ellie* who cheated. She and Rat Bastard had a polite arranged marriage, and they didn't hate each other. They got along well enough to produce the required heir, and after that they were married in name only. But Ellie wanted more out of life, and she fell in love. Rat Bastard was hardly celibate himself, but when he found out about the affair . . ." Athena's lips twisted in something between a sneer and a snarl. "Just sending her off to a retreat for the rest of her life wasn't punishment enough, not for him. He wanted her to suffer. So he told her that she was never going to see her son again. He said he would argue that cheating on him was an act of treason, and he would have her arrested if she ever made any attempt to see or even contact Nathaniel. She thought that maybe when they declared her terminal, he might relent. But no."

Nadia could hardly believe what she was hearing.

Treason.

Could the Chairman possibly have made a charge like that stick? If Nadia recalled her history correctly, Henry VIII had used similar charges as excuses to kill off inconvenient wives, but that was rather a long time ago. *Surely* such a charge wouldn't stick in modern times.

But if Nadia had been in Ellie Hayes's shoes, she very much doubted she'd have been willing to take the risk. Any reasonable person would agree that adultery was not treason, but the Chairman had ways of making reasonable people act unreasonably. After all, he'd been planning to torture and execute Nadia on a specious treason charge, and she saw no evidence that he wouldn't have gotten away with it if she hadn't managed to blackmail him.

"All these years . . ." Nadia said wonderingly under her breath. "All these years, Nate was convinced his mother was a selfish bitch who abandoned him. He thought she didn't love him enough to stay around and face her difficulties with his father."

Athena nodded. "That's what Rat Bastard wanted him to think. He wanted to build up the barrier high enough that Nathaniel would never bother trying to see through it. He's not a man you want as your enemy."

And yet that's exactly what he was to Nadia. It might have been her parents who had officially banished her to the Sanctuary, but it was the Chairman who had put them in the position where banishment seemed like their best option. Would he be satisfied with his revenge? Or would he want more?

Nadia shook off her worries about any future escalation of the Chairman's revenge. Her chief worry now was what would happen to Gerri if she went looking for the recordings. She regarded Athena Lawrence's open, friendly face, wondering if it would be foolishly naive of her to take anything the woman said at face value. For all she knew, the woman was clinically insane and was making up the whole story. Or was just someone who had an ax to grind with the Chairman and wanted to cause strife in his family.

But if anything she said was true, then she could potentially be Nadia's ally. An ally who'd lived at the Sanctuary for years and knew all its ins and outs. Who might be able to help Nadia formulate a plan to slip through the Sanctuary's security and get to a phone. She didn't quite dare imagine an escape attempt, not when she had nowhere safe to go and no access to money, but if she could at least talk to Gerri and warn her not to touch the recordings, maybe her imprisonment wouldn't seem quite so terrible.

"If you don't mind my asking," Nadia said, "how did you end up living here?"

Athena's smile turned crooked, and even bitter. "The man Ellie loved was my brother. I helped cover for the affair. My brother died in Riker's Island after the Chairman had him arrested on a trumped-up embezzlement charge. My family knew the true story and knew that I'd helped Ellie and my brother meet. They decided the whole disaster was my fault, and they sent me here. It didn't all shake out until more than a year after Ellie was sent away. I don't think the Chairman ever realized I was sent to the same retreat, or he would have looked for some way to have me moved elsewhere so Ellie wouldn't have a friend."

Nadia didn't know what to say. Even before the murder of the original Nate Hayes, she'd known the Chairman was a ruthless man and that he was not afraid of using and abusing his power. But though she'd thought herself a realist, she'd had no idea the depth of the corruption in his soul.

"Don't feel too sorry for me," Athena said. "At least I ended up here instead of in Riker's Island, like my brother. And it's not so bad, really, once you get used to it."

Nadia doubted she would *ever* get used to it. The living conditions were beyond reproach, and she remembered Dante's barbed comment about how luxurious life in a retreat would seem to a powerless Basement-dweller, living in squalor and deprivation and danger. But no amount of creature comforts could change the fact that she was a prisoner here, even if no one would ever admit it in those words. As an Executive, and as the presumed future bride of the Chairman Heir, her life had never truly been her own; but at least before, she'd had the illusion of freedom. Now, even that was gone.

"I imagine it's harder on someone your age," Athena said, giving her a motherly smile of sympathy. "But it gets better. You have my word on it."

Nadia tried to return the smile, but she suspected the expression looked more sickly than anything. Their lunches arrived, saving Nadia from having to respond. The bacon cheeseburger looked and smelled delicious, but there was an odd combination of hunger and nausea in her stomach that gave her pause.

How long did she have before Gerri acted? Was she already too late? How could she sit here and indulge in a hamburger when her sister's life was in danger?

"What's wrong, dear?" Athena asked, her fork poised above an elegant salad. "You've gone quite pale."

Nadia tried to pull herself together. Tormenting herself with her fears wasn't going to help anything. She had to do something more productive than that, had to channel her energy into figuring out a way to salvage the situation. She didn't have time for her usual caution, nor did she have time to sit and contemplate Athena's potential motives.

She needed help; she needed it now; and Athena was the only person she could imagine might give it to her. Swallowing her misgivings—and ignoring her food—Nadia clasped her hands together in her lap, leaned over the table, and spoke in a voice low enough she could be sure no one overheard.

"I have a desperate need to contact someone on the outside," she confided. "And I mean desperate as in life or death."

Athena nodded and frowned sympathetically, but Nadia could tell at once that she was having the typical adult response to a teenager saying something was life or death. The same response Nadia's own parents had had, that had kept them from letting her talk to Gerri before she was carted away.

"I swear I'm not exaggerating," Nadia said. Her voice rose, and she forced herself to lower it once more. She didn't know what might happen to her if her words were overheard, especially by a member of the retreat staff, but she didn't want to find out.

"Look," she continued, "my sister has reason to believe I have blackmail evidence on the Chairman." The spark of renewed interest in Athena's eyes suggested Nadia had chosen the right course to pursue. "It's not what she thinks it is, but I'm afraid she's going to try to use it to force the Chairman to reinstate the agreement between our families."

Athena leaned forward conspiratorially. "What is it you really have?" Her eyes were alight with the thought of sticking it to the man she called Rat Bastard.

"I can't tell you," Nadia said, because while she was throwing caution to the wind, she didn't dare let herself go too far. "I can tell you that I recorded him saying something incriminating, but I have to leave it at that. The problem is, the Chairman knows I have the recordings and knows I have them hidden. Right now, there's no way he can find them. But my sister can, and I'm terrified that she'll lead him right to them. I have to find a way to contact her and warn her away."

The skepticism was back in Athena's eyes. Nadia realized how outlandish her story sounded. Hell, for all Athena knew, Nadia had been shut up in the Sanctuary because she was a pathological liar.

"I *have* to get to a phone," Nadia concluded. "I thought maybe someone who's been here as long as you have might have some idea how I could do it. I don't care if I get caught or get in trouble, as long as I have a chance to make that call first."

Nadia swallowed hard, fighting back a rising tide of panic as her fears resurfaced one by one, tightening her chest and making a trickle of sweat run down her back. She was calling attention to herself, and one of the uniformed servers was heading toward the table. Her untouched burger was getting cold, and Athena had done nothing more than rearrange her salad on her plate as she listened to Nadia talk. Their eyes met across the table.

Athena shoved a forkful of salad into her mouth. Then she reached over to pat Nadia's hand, looking relaxed, if a little bit sad. Nadia's stomach was doing flips, but she took her cue from Athena and forced herself to take a bite out of her burger.

"Is everything okay over here?" the server asked. Her name tag identified her as "Susan," and she had the overly bright smile that Nadia was beginning to think was a prerequisite for retreat staff.

Nadia's mouth was so dry she could hardly chew, and the lukewarm burger felt like a lump of clay. Fortunately, Athena answered for both of them.

"We're fine," she said. "We were talking about Ellie, and it made us both a little sad. But life goes on for the rest of us, so we'll talk about something else from now on."

Susan gave them both sad eyes, then patted Nadia's shoulder. "If you need anything, please don't hesitate to let us know. And we do have grief counseling available, if you—"

Nadia managed to swallow the lump of burger and shook her head. "Thank you, but like Athena said, we're fine. I was very young when I last saw Mrs. Hayes. I'm sad about what happened, but I don't need a grief counselor or anything."

Susan nodded and patted her shoulder again. Nadia had to fight her desire to pull away. "All right, honey. But if you change your mind . . ."

Nadia nodded solemnly. "I will definitely let someone know."

She let out a sigh of relief when Susan wandered away.

"They mean well," Athena said with a roll of her eyes.

"Uh-huh." Sometimes, meaning well just wasn't enough. Knowing her stomach was going to protest, she took another bite of her burger, figuring if she ate, it was less likely there'd be another well-meaning intervention.

"Getting to a phone will be quite a challenge," Athena said, looking at her salad with great intensity as she speared a cherry tomato. "The staff are forbidden to bring phones with them to work here, so you'd have to get to one of the land lines in the business offices."

At Tranquility, sneaking into one of the offices would have been hard, but not impossible. But here, where there were key cards and curfews and security cameras . . .

"It can be done," Athena said. "Not without getting caught, though."

"What happens if I get caught?"

"They deactivate your key card for a while so you can't get out of the residence hall. No library, no gym, no movies, no classes. Nothing. And they'll deliver food to your room, because you can't get to the dining hall. Depending who's on duty at the time, they might also confiscate any books or paper you have in your room. It's death by boredom, and it's no fun."

"Sounds like the voice of experience."

Athena grinned, but neither confirmed nor denied Nadia's guess.

"So if I'm willing to pay the price, how would I go about sneaking into one of those offices to use the phone?"

Athena grinned again. "Well, if you happen to be lucky enough to know someone who knows the master override code for all the card readers . . ."

CHAPTER NINETEEN

waiting was pure hell. Nadia knew that every second she delayed was one more second for Gerri to get her hands on the recordings. But regardless of how urgently Nadia wanted to warn her sister, there was no way she was getting to a phone at the Sanctuary during the day. In fact, Athena had suggested she wait until 3:00 A.M. to have the least likelihood that anyone would be up and about to stop her. So she struggled her way through the day, trying not to act as if she wanted to crawl out of her skin.

She retired to her room shortly after dinner, which she could barely manage to choke down thanks to her nerves. And that was when the true waiting game began.

She had too much time to think. Too much time to imagine what Gerri might be up to, and to deride herself for not telling Gerri the truth in the first place. As long as she was dwelling on her worries, Nadia couldn't help wondering about Athena's motives in befriending her so quickly—and giving her the override code to the doors. When Nadia had asked her how she'd gotten the code, she'd blithely described how she'd seduced one of the retreat staff who worked the night shift in the dorm.

"She's quite a sweet little thing," Athena had said with a conspiratorial wink. "A little naive, perhaps, but she has an adventurer's soul and loves taking risks. Fooling around with one of her Executive charges strikes her as something excitingly dangerous, and she never noticed how closely I watched when she used the override code to open the doors without leaving a record."

"And your trysts aren't caught on the security cameras?" Nadia had asked.

"They would be if she didn't turn them off for the few seconds we need them to be off."

Athena's attitude had been careless to say the least, although her actions could have cost her lover her job—and possibly put the kind of black mark on her record that would make it impossible to find another. Nadia wondered if Athena would feel bad if her lover ended up in the Basement when their affair was over, and it didn't exactly make her feel confident that Athena was the compassionate friend she pretended to be. But Gerri didn't have time for her to indulge in second thoughts.

Time ticked away with exquisite slowness. The bed check happened precisely at eleven o'clock, and though she could stay up as late as she wanted as long as she was in her room, Nadia turned off the light to give any patrolling staff the impression that she was asleep.

And the staff *did* patrol the hall, whether they called it that or not. They wore soft-soled shoes, but as one by one the residents of the dormitory turned off their lights and went to sleep, the silence that descended made even soft footfalls noticeable. Nadia sat on her bed, fully clothed, listening carefully to those footfalls, getting a feel for how often the patrols occurred.

At first, it seemed that someone traveled the length of the hall every fifteen minutes. That lasted until about midnight, when the patrols started to happen less frequently, the intervals between them stretching to twenty minutes, then twenty-five, then thirty.

Adrenaline helped keep Nadia awake, even though she was sitting in the dark and hadn't gotten much sleep the night before. Thirty minutes was almost certainly enough time for her to slip out of her room, sneak downstairs, and slip into the office to make her phone call. When the two o'clock patrol passed by her room, it was all she could do not to set out immediately, wanting more than anything to get this over with. She didn't think she could possibly tough it out until three, no matter what Athena had advised, but she gritted her teeth and told herself to stay put.

Nadia sat on her bed, staring at the clock as her pulse began to speed up in anticipation. Sneaking out of the dorm and into the office seemed like a relatively small thing, compared to the other dangers she'd faced in recent weeks. She wasn't looking forward to facing the consequences of her actions, but she wasn't *afraid* of them.

No, what had her pulse racing and her hands going clammy was the thought that she might make it to the phone and be unable to reach Gerri. Of course, that wouldn't necessarily mean anything had happened to Gerri, but it would elevate Nadia's fear for her sister to epic levels.

Nadia muttered a curse under her breath when she heard the sound of footsteps in the hall at 2:15. If the patrols weren't as regular as she'd come to believe, it made her chances of getting to the phone before being caught lower.

But it didn't make sense for the staff to suddenly be making sweeps every fifteen minutes now, when they'd tapered off to every half hour. Why would anyone imagine there was more need for them at this time of night?

Come to think of it, the footsteps sounded different. Still

soft-soled shoes on a hardwood floor, but instead of the steady, march-like pace of the patrolling staff, these were slow, hesitant-sounding. *Sneaky.*

The hairs on the back of Nadia's neck prickled.

It could be she wasn't the only person planning to sneak out of bed tonight. The footsteps could easily be those of another inmate. Certainly in a facility completely devoid of men, Athena wasn't the only woman in the Sanctuary to be looking for love in alternative ways. With their reputations already in tatters, no one here had to worry about being forced into reprogramming, no matter how strong the Executive prejudice against homosexuality was.

Nadia closed her eyes and willed those footsteps to keep right on moving past her door, to prove themselves to be some harmless distraction having nothing to do with her. Maybe Athena had been right when she'd suggested Nadia wait until three. Maybe that was late enough that any nighttime trysts would be over and everyone would be back in their own rooms.

But the stealthy footsteps stopped right in front of her door, and she could see the shadow of two feet in the space between the floor and the bottom of the door.

Her doorknob began to turn.

nate had never hated the opera quite as much as he did tonight.

He'd gone to his first opera when he was about seven years old, when his mother had still been part of his life. It had been his first time wearing a tux, and he'd felt very mature and adult, even if people did keep telling him how "cute" he looked. That first time, he'd found himself bored before the overture had ended, and he probably never would have remembered anything about it if it weren't for the fact that it was Mozart's *Don Giovanni*. There was a terrifying scene at the end, when Don Giovanni got his comeuppance and was dragged down to hell. Between the loud and darkly ominous music, the special effects, and the costumes, Nate had practically peed his pants in fear, and he'd had nightmares for weeks afterward.

That, however, had been more fun than his current outing. One arranged by his father, of course, under the guise of entertaining the Belinskis during their visit to Paxco. Nate would have hated it under any circumstances, but since the news had finally trickled down to him today from Dante—who had officially begun work as his valet—that Nadia had not come back from the Sanctuary, he was in a particularly foul mood, and less inclined than ever to spend time with his father and the Belinskis. Unfortunately, it was his duty as the Chairman Heir to help his father play host to the visiting dignitaries, and with Dorothy lurking in the wings, shirking his duty was a very bad idea.

Agnes had tried to make herself look elegant and beautiful for the occasion, but the dress she'd chosen was absolutely *hideous*. There were probably some girls who would have looked stunning in a petal pink strapless number with a long poofy skirt, but Agnes wasn't one of them. Nonetheless, he had to act the gallant gentleman and escort her into the opera house, smiling and posing for the swarm of press who were lying in wait because outings like this were one big photo op disguised as leisure. Agnes looked more and more shell-shocked as each flash went off, and he could only imagine what kinds of deer-in-the-headlights photos were going to be gracing the gossip columns in the morning. Her hand was so clammy he could feel it clear through his jacket and shirt where she clutched his elbow. He felt bad enough for her that he tried to crack a joke or two to see if he could loosen her up, but it was a lost cause.

How the hell was she going to survive once their engagement was announced and the press became *really* interested in her? Her relief when they made it through the gauntlet and into the theater was palpable.

Nate sneaked a glance over his shoulder as he held out Agnes's chair in the front row of the Chairman's private box. Dorothy was hanging on his father's arm like a determined barnacle, smiling and batting her eyelashes. *She* had no trouble making herself beautiful, in a stunning dress of skin-tight red silk with a slit that would have men taking a second or third look.

The press had gotten wind of her by now, of course, and the gossip columns were all abuzz with her scandalous story. The Chairman was naturally taking some heat about it, but most of the press were too scared of him to be overly critical.

Nate noticed that although Dorothy clung to him, the Chairman didn't speak to her. In fact, he hardly *looked* at her, and there was a hint of stiffness in his bearing. Nate would have felt a glow of satisfaction at the evidence that there was tension between them, except Dorothy looked much too cheerful for it to be anything serious.

Chairman Belinski had brought his wife this time, but the poor woman was pale and wan, and Nate suspected she wasn't over her battle with migraines yet. He doubted she would hold out for the entire opera. Belinski was openly solicitous of his wife's health, but he kept darting speculative, worried looks at Nate's father and Dorothy. Rethinking the marriage arrangements, maybe?

Agnes had relaxed some now that she wasn't the center of

attention, but her posture was still unnaturally stiff and her hands were still clamped tightly together in her lap. Was it the aftermath of their time in the spotlight, or was she trying to brace herself for him to be cruel to her again? The more he thought about how he'd acted, the more ashamed of himself he was.

"Do you like opera?" he asked her, and she blinked at him in surprise.

Was this the first time he'd actually tried to draw her into a conversation? He wasn't sure, but it might well be.

"Sometimes," she replied.

He waited for more, but though Agnes looked like she was searching for something to say, she didn't find it. She hadn't been at such a loss for words when they'd been talking with Nadia at the funeral. Either Nadia had drawn Agnes out of her shell, or Agnes suffered from some kind of performance anxiety when faced with small talk. He was betting on the latter.

"If I asked you to tell me about the advantages and disadvantages to our states of an alliance by marriage, would you be able to find your tongue?"

She frowned at him in puzzlement. "But surely you already know all that."

"That's not what I asked."

Her eyes widened when she understood. "You mean am I more comfortable talking about something that matters instead of talking about what a lovely day it is or whether I like opera?"

He nodded.

"Yes," she confirmed. "Ask me about business or political strategy and I'll have no trouble finding something to say."

Nate grinned at her. "And I'm the exact opposite." The grin

faded, but he tried to keep the warmth in his voice. "Maybe we'll make a good team after all."

It was time to face reality: ending up married to Agnes was probably the best the future had to offer him. He was just going to have to suck it up.

Agnes didn't answer, but though he'd meant the words as a peace offering, he could tell by the look on her face that she didn't appreciate it. Perhaps she'd sensed his less-than-flattering resignation to his fate.

Nate breathed a sigh of relief when the lights dimmed and the overture began, saved from having to find a way to sound more enthusiastic about the future.

The feeling of relief didn't last long. He could tolerate, and sometimes even mildly enjoy, the old classic operas—though he would never be able to shake his prejudice against *Don Giovanni*—but modern crap put his teeth on edge, and this opera was about as modern as you could get. The composer was pretentious enough to go by the single name of Victor, and he had a love of dissonance to an extreme degree. Not only that, but the soprano had a shrieking nasal voice that made Nate want to stop up his ears.

A glance around the box showed him that Chairman Belinski and his father were paying no attention to the opera, deep in conversation with each other. A conversation on which Dorothy was obviously trying to eavesdrop, her head tilted slightly to the side to hear them better.

Beside him, Agnes looked like she was in physical pain listening to the atrocity the great Victor thought of as his triumphant work of art, and her eyes narrowed in a slight wince every time the soprano hit a high note. She caught him looking, and they shared a grimace of distaste that made them both smile.

His moment of sympathy with Agnes ended almost immediately when the phone in his inner jacket pocket vibrated against his chest.

It was his secure phone, the one Dante had given him. The one that would not be ringing unless there was some sort of emergency.

As casually as possible, Nate reached into his pocket and pulled out the phone, glancing at the text message it displayed from Dante. *Call me ASAP* was all it said, but it was enough to make Nate go cold. He leaned over toward Agnes.

"I'll be right back," he told her, though he suspected that was a lie.

She gave him a beseeching "take me with you" look that he pretended not to notice.

"Is everything all right?"

"Sure," he said. "Just have to make a quick call."

The way she was looking at him made him suspect she didn't believe him—he probably looked as worried as he felt—but she let it go. His father gave him a disapproving look as he excused himself, but Nate couldn't have cared less whether his father approved or not.

There were four bodyguards standing at attention at the back of the box, including Nate's personal bodyguard for the evening, Fischer. Fischer opened the door for him, and Nate slipped out into the Chairman's private lounge. Of course, Fischer couldn't let him out of his sight for even a moment, so he left his post to follow Nate into the lounge. The chances of mad assassins making it into the lounge were approximately zero, so Fischer's vigilance was a little over the top, but Nate knew better than to try to make the guy back off.

At least Fischer was respectful enough of his privacy to

remain just outside the door to the box while Nate pulled out his phone and moved to the farthest corner of the lounge to call Dante back.

Dante answered on the first ring, like he'd been sitting there with the phone in his hand waiting for the call.

"I think we have a problem," Dante said in a tight voice. There was traffic noise in the background, which meant he was not in the servants' quarters in Nate's building, where he was supposed to be.

"What's happened?"

"There's been an 'accident,'" Dante responded, and Nate could hear the air quotes in his voice. "Apparently Gerri Lake left her office this afternoon to go meet with some friend of hers out in Long Island. I don't know the full story yet, but somehow on the way back, her car ended up going off the Hayes Bridge into the East River. I haven't been able to get any details. I don't know if there were any witnesses or any survivors. But I'd guess no on the survivors part."

Nate kept his back fully turned from Fischer so his bodyguard wouldn't see the blood draining from his face. What had Gerri been doing *visiting a friend* in the middle of a workday? She would inherit her father's presidency eventually, and she was a far more dutiful heir than Nate could ever hope to be. So dutiful that nothing short of a crisis would cause her to take personal time on a workday.

Nadia had told Nate that Gerri had recruited a "trusted friend" to be the keeper of the recordings. A friend who would release them in the event that Nadia or Gerri were to die or mysteriously disappear. Was that the friend Gerri was visiting?

"I don't know what this all means," Dante continued, "but I have to ask: is Nadia in danger?"

"Why would you ask that?" Nate asked tightly while his mind wheeled.

"Gee, I don't know. Maybe it's because her sister was just *murdered* and you've both been living in mortal fear of *something* happening and this seems like it might be *something*."

Nate uttered a stream of curses he had learned from Kurt. He'd misinterpreted the tension he'd seen in his father's body language earlier. He'd thought it meant the Chairman had had a fight with Dorothy, but he had probably just been awaiting a progress report on his murder attempt. Or maybe *attempts*. If he'd had Gerri killed, could Nadia be far behind?

"Guess I was right," Dante said. "Wish that were a good thing."

Nate did, too. "Where are you?"

"On my way to the Met. I thought if I was right you might want to get out of there and maybe head out to that damn convent to see if we can get Nadia out. I'll go myself if you can't get away, but you might be able to open doors I can't."

Nate glanced over his shoulder at Fischer, who was still standing beside the doorway, his face devoid of expression as he looked straight ahead instead of at Nate. Trying to be unobtrusive. There was no way Nate was going anywhere without Fischer glued to his side, and though Fischer was a good man, his sole job was to protect Nate. He would not allow Nate to go rushing off to Nadia's rescue, even if he had a chance of understanding why she was in trouble.

Maybe Dante, with his resistance contacts, could get Nadia out of the Sanctuary—where she had to be a sitting duck—without Nate's help. But Nate wasn't about to let him be the hero. Despite all that had happened, protecting Nadia was *his* job, since he'd gotten her into this mess in the first place.

"I have to ditch my bodyguard," Nate said, "but I'll meet you out front as soon as I can. Are you close?"

"Be there in about ten minutes. But I can't afford to wait for you. I don't look like a chauffeur, and I'm not driving a limo, so I'm going to look out of place loitering near the Met."

Nate decided he didn't want to know what Dante was driving. Probably a loaner of some sort from the resistance, or maybe he'd just boosted the first vehicle he set eyes on. But Nate would worry about potentially having to get Dante out of being arrested for car theft later.

"I'll be there," Nate promised, hoping like hell it was a promise he could keep. He hung up the phone and took a quick look around the lounge, trying to figure out how he could leave without Fischer following him.

The prospects did not appear promising, and Nate wondered if he could somehow simply outrun the man.

But aside from the fact that Fischer would invariably beat him in a footrace, even if Nate did somehow make it into Dante's car and get away, Fischer would immediately raise the alarm. Nate needed a head start before anyone went looking for him.

He scanned the lounge one more time as adrenaline buzzed through his blood, urging him to *hurry, hurry, hurry* and making his mind work that much more slowly. Then he spotted the door to the men's room. Fischer was about the most thorough bodyguard Nate had ever met. If Nate headed to the men's room, there was an excellent chance Fischer would want to take a look inside before letting Nate go in. So, it was actually possible to get a closed door between himself and Fischer, if only for a handful of seconds.

Nate pretended to be texting to give himself an excuse to loiter while he surreptitiously checked out the door and its surroundings. The door opened inward, so trapping Fischer in there wouldn't be as simple as just blocking the door. And there was no lock on the outside.

Making a run for it the moment Fischer stepped through the men's room door wouldn't give Nate the kind of jump he needed, and he could see no way of trapping the man inside. Which meant he was going to have to stoop to something a little more . . . extreme.

The lounge was, naturally, luxuriously appointed, with antique furniture and works of art from the Chairman's own personal collection. Mostly paintings, but there were a number of bronze figurines as well as some priceless porcelain vases and ornate candlesticks. There was also a fully stocked bar. Plenty of potential weapons.

Nate shoved down a wave of guilt as he started toward the men's room. Fischer was a good guy, even if his overprotectiveness got on Nate's nerves occasionally. He didn't deserve what Nate was about to do—assuming he didn't lose his nerve—but if Nate was going to get Nadia out of the Sanctuary, he *had* to ditch Fischer.

On cue, Fischer saw where he was going and hurried over to cut him off. Nate rolled his eyes, trying to act as normal and nonchalant as possible. Then, as soon as Fischer was past him, Nate took a firm grip on a brass candlestick, plucking out the candle and dropping it to the carpeted floor. The damn thing was heavier than he'd expected, but if he wanted to get the jump on Fischer, he didn't have time to test out every potential weapon.

Gritting his teeth, Nate stalked forward, holding the candlestick behind his back. Fischer pushed the men's room door open. Nate surged forward, raising the candlestick high.

At the last moment, Fischer must have sensed something

was off—or Nate must have made some kind of noise. The bodyguard started to turn toward him, but it was too late.

Nate brought the candlestick down on Fischer's head, holding back as much as he dared because he didn't want to crush the man's skull. He expected Fischer to collapse in a heap, but his own squeamishness had perhaps taken too much off the blow. Fischer staggered, trying to catch himself on the doorframe.

"Sorry!" Nate said, wincing in sympathy as he swung again. Fischer let go of the doorframe to try to block the blow, but he was unsteady on his feet, and he started going down even before the candlestick struck him again.

Nate hadn't hit him any harder the second time, still trying to make sure he didn't seriously injure a good man, but apparently the second blow was enough to turn Fischer's lights out. His legs went out from under him, and he hit the floor in a boneless heap, half in, half out of the men's room. Nate had no idea how long Fischer would be unconscious, so he had to work fast. He put the candlestick down, then stepped over Fischer's body so he could drag him into the men's room by the shoulders.

And that was when he saw Agnes, standing by the door to the box, her eyes wide, both her hands clapped over her mouth.

CHAPTER TWENTY

ACTING on pure instinct, Nadia slid off the edge of her bed and rolled into the deepest shadows beneath it. The noise of the mattress springs seemed loud as a scream, and the thump of her body hitting the floor sounded like a gunshot, but she knew both were adrenaline-fueled illusions.

Nadia watched from under her bed as her door was slowly, carefully pushed open, letting in an ever-widening beam of dim light from the hallway. The light hit the edge of the bed, but couldn't penetrate the shadows beneath.

Nadia breathed out a sigh of relief when she saw Athena step through the door. She was letting paranoia get the best of her.

"Nadia?" Athena asked in a hushed voice as she frowned at the bed in puzzlement.

Nadia almost answered. But then she noticed that Athena was in her nightgown and robe, and her feet were bare. The stealthy footsteps that had triggered Nadia's internal alarm had definitely not come from bare feet.

There was someone else out in the hall.

"Nadia?" Athena asked again, knocking on the bathroom door and then peeking in when there was no answer. Nadia noticed that she used her left hand to knock and open the door, and that her right hand was buried in the pocket of her robe.

Hiding something?

Someone else stepped into the room, a tall, sturdy-looking woman dressed in the pants-and-blazer uniform of the Sanctuary staff. No one Nadia had seen before, but then she didn't usually see anyone who worked the night shift.

"You said she wouldn't leave until three," the staffer said in an irritated hiss, closing the door behind her and flipping on the light.

Nadia blinked in the brightness, the bed still shielding her from view—which it would continue to do nicely, right up until the moment it occurred to Athena and the staffer that Nadia was hiding. Apparently they had not factored her paranoia into the equation when they'd invaded her room. She might almost have convinced herself they were here to help, except they were being too sneaky about it. And, when Nadia's eyes adjusted to the light, she saw that the staffer was holding a stunner in her hand.

Nadia wasn't sure what the two women were up to, except that it was no good.

"That was the plan," Athena said, sounding equally irritated. "You didn't fall asleep while watching the security feed, did you?" She'd taken her hand out of her pocket, and Nadia saw that she was holding a small canister with a spray nozzle.

Nadia was a sitting duck under the bed, and it would be mere seconds before the women would think to look there. She had to do *something*, and do it fast, though both the stunner and the mysterious canister Athena held worried her.

Sucking in a deep breath and holding it, Nadia quickly rolled out from under the bed and snatched her pillow from it. Athena and the staffer were both surprised by her sudden appearance, which was the only way Nadia was able to get hold of the pillow before they converged on her.

Holding the pillow in front of her as a shield against the stunner, Nadia once again surprised the women by charging forward. The stunner made an electrical popping sound as it made contact with the pillow, but its charge couldn't penetrate the stuffing.

Out of the corner of her eye, Nadia saw Athena raise the little canister and point it in her direction. She pulled in a quick breath and held it, closing her eyes and shifting as the staffer tried to slip the stunner in around the pillow.

There was a hissing sound, which Nadia assumed came from Athena's canister. The Sanctuary staffer made a sound of protest, then gasped and collapsed.

Still holding her breath, Nadia cracked her eyes open tentatively. Athena was standing about five feet from her, the canister held out at arm's length. The nozzle made a hissing sound as she sprayed another fine mist of . . . something . . . in Nadia's direction. It wasn't pepper spray, because it wasn't making Nadia's eyes sting or burn, but it looked like it had knocked the staffer out cold.

Nadia used the pillow like a fan, hoping to blow the mist back in Athena's direction. She didn't know if it was working—the mist was only visible right when it was first coming out of the nozzle, but Athena took a couple of hasty steps back and stopped spraying. Continuing to fan the air, Nadia gave a brief thought to screaming and awakening the whole hall, but quickly rejected the idea. If she sounded the alarm, she'd *never* be able to get to the phone.

Her lungs were starting to protest the lack of air, and Nadia knew she couldn't hold her breath indefinitely. She dropped the pillow and ducked down to grab the stunner the Sanctuary staffer had been trying to zap her with. She had every intention of zapping Athena with it, but Athena was staggering woozily, having apparently gotten a lungful of her own knock-out gas.

Nadia darted for the door and bolted out into the hall, where she could finally draw a breath. Her first instinct was to run for the hall door and enter the override code, but she jerked to a halt after a couple of steps. She had no idea if the override code was even real. Plus, she had no idea how long her attackers would be out—or even if Athena had gotten a big enough dose of her own medicine to lose consciousness. If she took off running now, they'd catch her in no time.

Heart thumping heavily in her chest, Nadia turned back to her room. What had Athena and her accomplice been planning for her? Why had they snuck into her room in the middle of the night armed with a stunner and knockout gas? It was hard to believe their goal had been anything short of murder. Nadia tried to tell herself none of this had anything to do with the blackmail recordings, that it was some sort of vendetta against her family. They were more than powerful enough to have enemies, people who hated them just for existing. But really, what were the chances that the Chairman wasn't behind this? And he wouldn't dare try to kill her unless he'd found the recordings.

Nadia jerked her mind away from that line of thought. She couldn't afford to ponder the hows and whys right now. The only thing she dared think about was how to survive the night.

Taking another deep breath and holding it, Nadia stepped back into her room, the stunner at the ready, but she didn't need it. Both women were out cold. She closed the door and picked her way across the room to the window, sliding it open in hopes of clearing the air. After sticking her head out the window for another deep breath, she hurried over to Athena and took the canister away from her. Then she used the belt from Athena's robe to tie her hands together behind her back, tightly.

Nadia used the belt from her own robe, which hung from a hook in the closet, to tie the staffer's hands. The woman groaned softly, and Nadia took the precaution of gagging her with a pillowcase. It was a clumsy gag that the woman would probably be able to get rid of in time, but it would do for now. Nadia then patted the woman down, looking for anything that could be useful in her escape attempt.

What she found was chilling.

On the plus side, the woman—whose name, according to her ID badge, was Lily Hughes—had a key card that would no doubt be a big help in Nadia's escape. But she also had a handful of zip ties in one pocket, a ball gag in another, and a small snub-nosed gun on a holster strapped around her ankle. Worst of all was the sheet of white paper with a typewritten message on it, one Nadia suspected they'd have forced her to write by hand herself, once they'd subdued her.

It was a suicide note. Apparently, Nadia was so distraught at the turns her life had taken that she couldn't bear to live anymore. Nadia wasn't sure how the suicide was supposed to have occurred, but a precipitous fall from her window onto the flagstones below was a good guess.

They had really been trying to murder her.

The fresh air was beginning to bring Athena and Lily back to consciousness. Nadia used the zip ties she'd found in Lily's pocket to secure her hands more tightly. For good measure, she then used the belt to hog-tie her wrists and ankles. Satisfied that the woman who'd been sent to kill her wasn't going anywhere, Nadia turned to the one who had betrayed her.

Athena was blinking groggily, awake but not yet alert. Nadia had a zip tie left over, and she figured she might as well put it to good use. Brandishing the stunner, she cautiously approached Athena, who was waking up more every second.

"Call for help, and I'll make you wish you hadn't," Nadia growled, hitting the trigger on the stunner and causing an electrical spark. Athena's eyes widened, and she swallowed hard. Amazing how intimidating a sixteen-year-old Executive girl could be when she had a stunner in her hand and righteous anger in her heart.

"I'm sorry," Athena said, making no attempt to struggle as Nadia none-too-gently turned her over onto her stomach and fastened the zip tie around her wrists.

Like she cared about Athena's remorse or lack thereof. "What did they offer you?"

Athena sniffled, and there were tears leaking from her eyes. "They were going to set me free. Give me a new identity and enough money to start over."

Nadia snorted in disdain. Athena's wrists were now firmly fastened, so Nadia loosened the belt robe and retied one end of it with enough slack to secure the other end to Athena's ankles.

"And you believed them?" she asked incredulously, shaking her head at Athena's naiveté. "Ten to one you would have been dead and buried before the night was through, and your family would never know what had happened to you." Athena would have been a dangerous liability, and Lily probably wouldn't have lived much longer. The Chairman didn't allow people who posed a threat to keep breathing for long.

Lily had come to and was now struggling against her bonds. Nadia quickly finished tying Athena's ankles and pulled the canister of knockout gas from her pocket. She gave it a quick shake, and a liquidy sloshing sound told her she still had plenty of "ammunition."

"They'll try again," Athena said through hiccuping sobs. "You have to get out of here."

"Thanks for stating the obvious." Nadia didn't know whether

Athena was genuinely sorry for the betrayal, or whether she was just sorry to have lost what she thought was her chance at freedom. And she didn't care. Since Lily had conveniently provided a ball gag, Nadia decided to use it. "Open wide," she prompted, and Athena was so beaten down that she obeyed without hesitation.

Nadia stopped with the gag just inches from Athena's mouth. "Was anything you told me true?" she couldn't help asking, even though she knew she couldn't trust the answer.

"What I told you about the Chairman and Ellie was true," Athena answered. "If you ever get a chance to tell Nathaniel, please do. It was Ellie's last wish."

Nadia nodded brusquely, then went to stick the gag in the other woman's mouth, but Athena turned her head.

"The override code I gave you will only work for the hall door," she warned. "Plans changed this evening, but originally I was just supposed to be cozying up to you for future use. There isn't usually an override code—they just programmed it into the door for tonight so I could gain your trust. Take Lily's key card."

Apparently, Athena didn't think much of Nadia's intelligence if she thought there was a chance she *wouldn't* take the key card.

Having said her piece, Athena allowed Nadia to insert the gag and tie it firmly into place. Nadia made sure she had everything she needed tucked into her pockets, then rose and shut the window. Lily was struggling more vigorously now, and though Nadia thought she'd done a pretty good job of restraining her attackers, she would not take any chances.

Holding her breath one more time, Nadia sprayed both of them with another dose of the knockout gas, then slipped out of the room, closing the door behind her.

CHAPTER TWENTY-ONE

shit. He was busted.

Nate froze where he was, bending slightly forward in his interrupted attempt to grab onto Fischer's shoulders and drag his considerable weight into the men's room. He held his breath, meeting Agnes's eyes across the distance.

Would she bolt back into the box and raise the alarm? It seemed like the logical thing for a mousy Executive girl to do.

And yet, instead of bolting, she took a couple of steps closer to him and dropped her hands from her mouth. Her face was white, her eyes wide enough to show white all the way around.

"What are you doing?" she asked, her voice so soft he could barely hear it.

There was no good explanation for it. Nothing except the truth, that is. Nate didn't feel up to coming up with a convincing lie.

"Nadia's in trouble," he said simply. "I have to help her, and I can't do it with a bodyguard on my heels."

"What kind of trouble?"

He didn't have time for this. "The kind of trouble that's bad enough to do this," he said, gesturing at Fischer's limp body.

Agnes processed his words for what felt like five minutes. He figured he was lucky she was taking a moment to think about it before sounding the alarm. She'd probably never broken a rule in her life, and the very thought of standing by and letting him do something so obviously against the rules probably made her feel faint with horror. Nate wondered if he was enough of a bastard to try to knock *her* out as he had Fischer.

If that was the only way to get to Nadia, then yes, he was. He only hoped that thought didn't show on his face, because the last thing he needed was for her to become even *more* frightened. Then she would run for sure, and he wouldn't be able to get close enough to knock her out.

"I know I'm asking a lot," he said, "but please go back to your seat and forget you saw me." Letting her go would probably be foolishly trusting of him, but he wasn't going to hit a girl unless there was no other choice.

To his surprise, perhaps even *shock,* Agnes nodded to herself and then started coming toward him.

"I'll take his feet," she said, bending down and grabbing Fischer's ankles.

Nate stood there for a moment, blinking stupidly. "I'm not asking you to *help* me. I'm just asking you to keep quiet."

Something flashed in Agnes's eyes, and he realized that had been the wrong thing to say.

"That's probably the first time anyone's ever told me to keep quiet. Usually, they're badgering me to talk, then looking down their noses at me when I can't think of what to say. If Nadia's in trouble, then I want to help. She's the only person in all of Paxco who hasn't treated me like a pitiful dimwit."

Nate winced, realizing he'd treated her even worse than that.

"Besides," she continued, "just because I'm shy doesn't mean I'm a coward. Now let's hurry, before he wakes up."

Nate could see he'd gotten her back up and he was stuck with her help whether he wanted it or not. Which was probably just as well. Fischer had to weigh about 250 pounds, so dragging him anywhere wasn't going to be easy.

Keeping a careful eye on Agnes, Nate stuck his hands under Fischer's shoulders and heaved backward. Agnes picked up Fischer's feet and pushed. Hauling Fischer's dead weight took all of Nate's strength, and he was sweating and panting by the time they got the bodyguard all the way into the men's room. He stood up to leave; then, on a whim, he bent and removed the gun Fischer always wore in a shoulder holster. He doubted he would need it, and didn't actually know how to use it, but it couldn't hurt to be prepared for any eventuality.

No doubt Agnes thought her part in this was over now except for a little fibbing to cover for his absence. But really, he couldn't let her go back to her seat. His only chance of getting to Nadia was if his father didn't know he was trying it. Maybe Agnes wasn't a coward, exactly, but she *was* timid. If his father started leaning on her even a little bit, she'd tell him Nate had run off to help Nadia, and there'd probably be a whole security team waiting in ambush at the Sanctuary when he got there. No, he had to buy himself some time, and that meant she had to come with him.

Nate jumped over Fischer's body and grabbed Agnes's wrist, dragging her out of the men's room. Her skin was cold to the touch, and he felt a shudder run through her. Perhaps she was already having second thoughts about getting involved.

"Come on," he said, as if she'd already agreed to go with him. "We have to hurry."

He started toward the door to the Chairman's private entrance, expecting Agnes to resist his pull. But she didn't.

"How are we going to get past the man at the door?" she asked instead.

Nate hadn't given his plan a whole lot of advance thought,

and until Agnes mentioned it, he'd forgotten that there would be a guard outside the door. Of course, that man wouldn't be Nate's personal bodyguard, so it wouldn't be his duty to follow Nate, or to stop Nate from leaving.

"I guess I'll just order him to stay put," Nate said, though he didn't like it. Too much chance the guard would find his behavior suspicious enough to report on it.

Agnes took him by surprise and snatched her hand from his. He made a startled sound of protest and prepared to lunge after her, but she wasn't heading for the box. She was heading for the bar, where she picked up the first bottle of wine she could lay hands on and grabbed a couple of glasses. She came back to him and handed him the bottle.

"We just want to have a private drink with no one watching us," she informed him. "The door to the outside is locked anyway, so we'll be perfectly safe."

Nate was sure he looked like an idiot with the way he was gaping at her, but who would have guessed she had this in her? Not only was she willing to break about a thousand rules of polite society to help a girl she barely knew, but she had plotted their escape in about two seconds. She still looked pale and frightened, but she showed no signs of balking. And she hadn't even batted an eyelash at his assumption that she was coming with him.

Color blotched Agnes's cheeks, and her shoulders slumped in a defensive posture as she lowered her gaze. "I-I know I'm not the kind of girl . . . er . . . that I'm not someone you'd . . ."

If it were physically possible for Nate to kick himself in the ass, he'd have done it. Agnes was taking his obvious shock as distaste for the idea of implying he felt any kind of romantic attraction to her. And why wouldn't she, when he'd made no effort to hide that he found her unappealing?

"Don't be silly," he told her with a dismissive wave of his free hand, trying to be casual. "I was just surprised again that you're willing to go out on a limb for Nadia. And the idea is perfect."

Agnes smiled tentatively at the praise. Nate shifted the bottle of wine to his left hand and then held out his right elbow to Agnes. She squared her shoulders and raised her chin as she slipped her hand into the crook of his elbow and allowed him to lead the way.

nate was only mildly surprised to find that Agnes's plan worked. People were certainly used to him being reckless and irresponsible, and they were also used to taking orders from him. The man guarding the door to the Chairman's lounge gave Nate a funny look when he glibly repeated Agnes's lie, but he made no attempt to stop them from leaving. Agnes leaned into him and uttered a completely fake-sounding giggle as they descended the stairs. Nate cringed a bit at her bad acting, but there was no sign that the guard found it suspicious.

When they reached the first-floor entrance, Nate glanced at his watch and saw that the ten minutes Dante had given him were almost up. He wanted to burst through the door and sprint out to the car, but if he wanted a clean getaway, he couldn't afford to attract attention. And if he wasn't careful, the guard at the top of the staircase would hear the opening and closing of the heavy door and know that Nate and Agnes weren't cozying up in some safe, private corner as they'd claimed.

He put the wine bottle down, and Agnes put the glasses down beside it. Then he pulled on the door, trying to be quiet and gentle about it.

Even the Chairman's private entrance had to conform to the city's fire code, so the door opened freely from the inside even though it was locked. There was a soft electronic beep as the lock disengaged. Nate hoped that high-pitched sound hadn't been loud enough to be heard from the top of the stairs.

The door weighed a ton. Nate motioned Agnes through, then slipped out himself, easing the door shut behind him. However, it was impossible to close a door that heavy without making a thunk. He would just have to hope the guard either didn't hear it or didn't think it was his business to investigate the Chairman Heir's activities.

There wasn't a whole lot of traffic, either on foot or by car, at this hour, but it *was* Manhattan, which meant there were still people around to observe Nate and Agnes's exit. Even if their faces hadn't been famous, they were pretty conspicuous in their elegant opera clothes.

Together, they hurried toward the curb just as a nondescript brown sedan pulled up. Agnes's steps slowed.

"Keep moving," Nate urged, giving her arm a little tug. "That's our ride."

She looked over her shoulder. Nate supposed it was natural for her to have second thoughts at this point, but he didn't have time for them.

"It's not like you can get back inside anyway," he said, tugging a little harder. "Too late to change your mind now."

"I'm not changing my mind," Agnes said, and she sped up again.

Nate could see Dante, staring at them with a fierce glare as they approached. Nate was afraid Dante might see that Agnes was coming and decide to floor it and go off on his own, but despite the pissed-off look on his face, he waited. Nate opened the back door for Agnes, and she slid in. He went to get in the back himself, then thought better of it and took the front passenger seat because he didn't feel like talking to the back of Dante's head.

Dante hit the gas before Nate had finished closing the door, and he was pleasantly surprised he didn't fall out.

"What the *hell*?" Dante shouted at him, then glanced at the rearview mirror and said, "Excuse my language, Miss Belinski," in a much more measured tone of voice.

Nate buckled his seat belt hastily, because Dante was driving like a maniac. "She wanted to help," Nate said, figuring it was best to keep it simple. "I didn't have time to talk her out of it, and I didn't want anyone asking her questions about where I'd gone." He half-turned in his seat so he could see Agnes.

"Agnes, this is Dante. He used to work for the Lake family, and now he works for me."

Out of the corner of his eye, Nate saw the glare Dante shot his way. He'd accepted the job on Nate's staff because it was convenient, but he was never going to let Nate forget how little he liked working for him.

Agnes rearranged the preposterous pink flounces of her dress, her restless hands betraying her nerves though her face looked relatively composed. "You don't have to lie to me, you know. If there are things you don't want to tell me, well, just don't tell me."

Nate opened his mouth to protest that he wasn't lying, but for once he decided to actually think about his words before he spoke. A hasty, indignant protest would just cement her conviction that he was lying to her, and considering how testy the dynamic between himself and Dante was likely to be over the course of the long drive ahead, she'd have a lot of trouble swallowing the idea that Dante was his servant.

"I'm not lying," Nate said. "I'm just leaving a whole lot out. Dante *does* work for me, but for reasons I can't explain, he knows I won't fire him, so he feels free to treat me like an equal."

"Uh-huh," Agnes said, clearly unconvinced.

Nate expected Dante to get out of the city as fast as possible, so when the car made a sudden turn into a parking garage, he turned his attention away from Agnes.

"What are you doing?" he asked Dante.

"We have to change cars," Dante explained. "Too many people saw the two of you getting into this one. We don't need anyone tracking us. And both of you, take the batteries out of your phones."

Nate uttered a curse. He should have thought of that himself. The secure phone wasn't a problem, because no one who'd be looking for him knew he had it, but his personal phone was. He fished it out of his pocket, keeping an eye on Agnes to make sure she followed suit. Her phone was in one of those silly little clutch purses ladies carried, and when she took the battery out, she handed it to him. He raised his eyebrows.

"I don't want you thinking I'm going to put it back in the minute your back is turned," she explained.

He accepted the battery, though if Agnes were going to betray them, it seemed like she'd have done it by now. Then he pulled out the secure phone. This was just the kind of emergency he'd had in mind when he'd asked Dante to smuggle a phone to Nadia, so he punched in the number and held his breath.

"Who are you calling?" Agnes asked.

"Nadia, I hope," he said. He had no way of knowing if she still had the phone, but he had to try. He cursed when he reached voice mail.

"Try again later," Dante suggested. "She may not be free to answer right now."

Nate resisted the urge to bite the asshole's head off for stating the obvious.

The garage was deserted, and though most of the spaces on the lower floors were filled, as they climbed, there were fewer and fewer parked cars. When they were near the top, Dante pulled up beside another bland-looking sedan, this one blue.

"You must pay your servants awfully well," Agnes commented. "Not just one car, but *two*. I'm impressed."

Apparently, when she wasn't in some kind of fraught social situation, Agnes wasn't quite so shy about speaking up. He didn't know how to explain the cars. Dante certainly wouldn't be able to afford a car on a servant's wages, and the cars were both too cheap for Nate to claim them as his.

"Please stay in the car, Miss Belinski," Dante said as he turned off the ignition and opened the door. "I need a private word with Mr. Hayes."

Amazing how much contempt Dante managed to get into his voice while technically addressing Nate in a proper fashion. Nate thought Dante was as surprised as he was when Agnes said, "No, I think not."

She opened her door, but remained in the car, clearly planning to get out if they did and stay put if they didn't.

"It'll just be for a minute," Nate said, figuring Dante wanted a chance to let him know how displeased he was at Nate's decision to bring Agnes along.

"No, it won't," Agnes countered. "He's going to suggest sticking me in the trunk while you two ride off to the rescue."

The mingled surprise and guilt on Dante's face proved she had guessed right. And Nate supposed it made good sense. She would be nothing but a liability on this mission, but they couldn't just let her go because of what she might tell people. It would be a really shitty way to treat her after she'd helped him, but it was logical. Of course, since she had guessed what Dante had planned, there was no way they were getting her into the trunk quietly.

Agnes sniffled and lowered her eyes, and Nate felt like a bastard. She opened that little purse of hers, and he assumed she was looking for a tissue to blot her eyes. He practically swallowed his tongue when she pulled out a gun instead.

"You are *not* putting me in that trunk," she said, pointing the gun at Dante, who glared at Nate as if this were all his fault. Which, come to think of it, it was.

"Where did you get that?" Nate asked, shaking his head. There was no way Agnes habitually went to the opera with a gun in her purse.

"It was in your bodyguard's ankle holster. I was holding his ankles, remember?"

She sounded calm enough, but there was a slight tremor in her hands. Obviously, she'd had an inkling she'd be coming along from the moment she'd helped him with Fischer, but she probably hadn't given herself enough time to think it through.

"You're not really going to shoot anyone, are you?" Nate asked. Five minutes ago, he'd have been *saying* that, not *asking*, but he had obviously underestimated Agnes.

"Not unless someone tries to lock me in the trunk."

Nate and Dante looked at each other.

"I thought she was supposed to be shy and quiet," Dante said. There was a thread of anger in his voice, and the look he was giving Nate was anything but friendly, but it didn't seem like he was particularly bothered by having a gun pointed at him.

"I did, too," Nate said, then turned to Agnes again. "You don't even know what's going on or why we think Nadia is in danger, nor do you know what we plan to do." Actually, Nate didn't know what the plan was, either, and it would be rather hard to discuss it if they couldn't ditch Agnes.

Agnes let out a shaky breath. "I know something extremely fishy is going on in Paxco, and I'm damn well going to find out what it is before I find myself locked into a marriage agreement. I agreed to the match because I thought it was for the good of my state, but now I'm not so sure. No one's going to tell me the truth, so I'm going to have to learn whatever it is firsthand."

Nate couldn't blame her for not wanting to be locked in the trunk, and he supposed the whole situation had alarm bells clanging in her head. The haste with which the marriage agreement was reached, the "hiatus" in the Replica program, the introduction of Dorothy, and now this. She was more than prepared to take one for the team, but the match probably wasn't looking so ideal right about now.

"You have no idea what you'd be getting yourself into," he told her. "The less you know about it, the safer you'll be."

"Perhaps you should have thought about that *before* you dragged me out of the theater," she said quite sensibly. "I'm now thoroughly involved anyway."

Dante scowled at her in a way that probably would have been intimidating if she weren't holding him at gunpoint. "You don't get it. You come with us, you could get *killed*. This isn't some stupid game, and we don't need you coming along for the thrill."

It was hard to tell in the darkened car, but Nate thought Agnes's face lost some of its color, and he was sure Dante had made his point. Her hand wavered, but she regained her resolve before the muzzle lowered enough for anyone to try to take the gun away.

"I'm coming," she said firmly. "And we're wasting time here. Stop trying to figure out how to get around me and let's go."

"She has a point," Nate admitted reluctantly. "We don't have time for a long standoff. Unless you're willing to gamble that she won't shoot."

He felt about 90 percent certain she wouldn't, but she'd surprised him so many times tonight he wasn't about to rely on his instincts.

Dante shook his head in disgust. "Fine. We'll take her along. And when she gets us caught before we get to Nadia, it'll be all your fault." He got out of the car and slammed the door behind him, then stalked over to the blue sedan and unlocked it.

Nate followed suit, as did Agnes, who kept a careful distance between them and didn't actually get into the sedan until Dante did. She stopped pointing the gun at Dante's head when they were all in the car, but she didn't put it away, and Nate knew she was poised for any attempt to wrest it away from her.

Wondering what the hell he'd gotten them all into, Nate buckled in as Dante started the car and pulled out of the space.

CHAPTER TWENTY-TWO

nate didn't realize what a complete disaster his situation was until he'd had a few quiet minutes to think about it. He knew he and Dante needed to talk about the plan to get to Nadia, but it was hard to even begin discussing it with Agnes sitting in the backseat and listening to every word they said. She'd as much as said that she was considering this her own personal recon mission, and letting the daughter of a foreign Chairman find out there was a sizable, organized resistance movement in Paxco wasn't such a hot idea. However, Nate was pretty sure they were going to need inside help to get Nadia out of the Sanctuary, and he was dying to ask Dante about his resistance contacts.

Unable to think how to start a conversation, Nate sat quietly in the passenger seat as Dante drove through the streets of the city, going as fast as he dared when it was imperative they not draw attention. And in that quiet time, Nate realized that his life would never be the same.

If he was right, and Gerri's death meant she had led the Chairman to the blackmail recordings, that meant there was nothing to stop the Chairman from killing Nadia. Before his mother's funeral, Nate had assumed he himself wouldn't be in any real danger, because his father needed an heir and no longer had Thea around to make a blissfully ignorant Replica if he disposed of Nate. But now the Chairman had Dorothy, whom he had publicly acknowledged as his daughter. He could get rid of Nate and still have an heir.

Did his father hate him that much?

Sure, the man had already had Nate killed once, but knowing he could create a Replica—one who hadn't overheard the Chairman and Dirk Mosely talking about Thea's human experimentation and therefore wouldn't make waves—must have made it feel like he wasn't *really* killing anyone.

Nate's father had been angry with him for almost as long as Nate could remember. And Nate had taken every opportunity to foster more anger, acting like a spoiled, selfish brat for the sheer pleasure of pissing his father off.

But did that anger lead to actual *hate,* into something so toxic it would drive him to murder his own son?

The fact was, Nate couldn't be sure. And that meant that once this adventure was over, even if everything went perfectly and they got Nadia out of the Sanctuary without a hitch, he couldn't go home, couldn't go back to his old life.

The realization was like a brutal kick to the chest, forcing all the air out of his lungs and triggering a moment of sheer panic. He closed his eyes and clenched his fists as he tried to fight it off, but he felt the sweat beading on his forehead and upper lip. He thought for a moment he was totally going to lose it, right there in the front seat of the car with both Agnes and Dante as witnesses.

"We'll get her out," Dante said gruffly, making the natural assumption that Nate was freaking out because he was worried about Nadia. But Dante didn't have a clue what was really happening.

And then what? Nate wondered. Neither he nor Nadia could set foot in their homes. Nadia would have no money, no access to money, and nowhere to go. Nate might be able to get hold of some scrip before his father came up with an excuse to freeze his account, but even that would be dangerous, giving those who might be hunting him a bead on his location, even if it was just for a short while. So he might have a temporary supply of scrip, but that would be it. Like Nadia, he would have nowhere safe to go. In fact, the only place he could even *imagine* going was the Basement. He at least had some experience there from the jaunts of his reckless youth, but a sheltered Executive girl like Nadia might as well have the word "victim" tattooed on her forehead in a place like that.

"Maybe now is a good time to tell me what's really going on," Dante prompted when Nate failed to pull himself out of his panic nosedive. Dante frowned at the rearview mirror, once again letting Nate know how unhappy he was about Agnes's presence.

Nate turned in his seat so he could meet Agnes's eyes. "Can I trust you not to repeat everything I say?"

"Will you believe me if I say yes?" she countered.

Good point. He still didn't quite know what to make of her. Clearly, she wasn't the meek little pushover he'd thought, but he had no clue what she was really made of. Hell, for all he knew, she was a spy planted on him by the Chairman to try to eke out his secrets. Though surely if she were meant to act as a spy, she would have better-developed social skills.

"You know, it doesn't matter," he said. "Tell anyone you think should know." His neck was getting stiff from the awkward position, so he shifted in his seat and faced forward once more. Maybe it would be easier to talk about what had happened if he didn't have to look into someone's face anyway.

"Nadia was arrested on suspicion of treason a few weeks ago," he started.

"Yes, I know," Agnes said. "But she was cleared of all charges."

"Well, yeah, but it's the why of it all that gets us into trouble." He sneaked a glance over at Dante, who was watching the road with studious concentration.

"She was wearing a transmitter when she was arrested," Nate said. "I went to try to help her, and got into a big fight with my father and our late chief of security, and they said some things they would never have said if they'd known about the transmitter. They said things so incriminating that once they found out Nadia had been transmitting to a secret location, and that she'd set it up so that the recordings would be released if she died or disappeared, they had to let her go."

Nate stalled out, remembering the horror of seeing Nadia strapped to a table with Thea poised to vivisect her. Nadia had been gagged, unable to reveal that she had the transmitter on her and therefore unable to use the information to save herself. If Nate hadn't figured it out . . .

"I don't understand," Agnes said. "You got into a big fight and they said 'incriminating things.' In front of you. I mean, I get that they didn't expect Nadia to be able to tell anyone about it, but what about—" She interrupted herself with a gasp.

"You're a Replica . . ."

Dante frowned and looked at Agnes in the rearview mirror. "Surely you already knew that."

Nate couldn't help turning in his seat again, despite the stiff neck. Agnes's shocked expression told him that whatever she might lack in social graces, she had one hell of a sharp mind. She was making all the connections, despite having very little information to go on.

"He felt free to talk in front of you because he was planning to kill you," she said in a horrified whisper. "Then he was going to use an old backup to make a new Replica who hadn't heard any of his secrets."

Nate nodded, but Agnes wasn't finished making connections yet.

"What happened to the original Nathaniel Hayes?"

Nate and Dante shared a look. Dante knew the answer to that question because Kurt had witnessed the murder. It had been passed off to the public as the work of Dirk Mosely acting alone. But after everything Agnes had figured out so far, she was never going to buy that story.

"He was in the wrong place at the wrong time," Nate answered grimly. "The only reason my father didn't kill me the second time was because of those recordings. And the only thing that's kept him from killing Nadia is that she had those recordings hidden and had arranged for them to be released if anything happened to her."

Nate had turned to face front once more, so he couldn't see Agnes's reaction to the news. "I got word during the opera that Nadia's sister had just died in an 'accident.'"

"And you think she led your father to the recordings and now he's going to go after Nadia," Dante finished for him.

Nate nodded and chose not to mention the likelihood that *he* was on the Chairman's hit list as well.

There was a long silence as everyone stewed in their own thoughts.

"What do you know that's worth killing so many people over?" Dante asked.

"I can't tell you that." Even if he trusted Agnes and Dante completely, he doubted he'd tell them about Thea. She was dead and gone, and telling people about her would serve no good purpose.

"Did you tell Bishop?"

"Not that it's any of your business, but no."

"Who's Bishop?" Agnes asked.

Nate didn't consciously intend to answer that question with any real honesty. He could tell her Kurt was his old valet, and it would be completely true. But his subconscious had other ideas.

"He's my boyfriend," Nate blurted, then blinked in surprise. But really, what was the point of keeping that particular secret any longer? Under the circumstances, he had no choice but to flee his Executive life anyway, so why should he keep pretending? He'd always hated having to hide that side of himself, hated having to live a lie.

Nate didn't look to see how Agnes was taking the revelation. Dante shrugged, as if it were no big deal—which to an Employee, it wasn't.

"I must admit," Dante said, "I'd wondered about you two. You seemed way more attached than an Executive would normally be to his valet."

"Well, now you know." Nate resisted the urge to squirm. He felt like Agnes was probably staring daggers at him from the backseat, but he didn't have the guts to check. It wasn't like she'd been hoping for high romance in her marriage with him anyway, but he supposed the news still had to come as something of a shock. Maybe she was now regretting having helped him. He was certainly regretting his impulse to bring her along in the first place. When he and Dante had tried to leave her behind in the trunk, Nate had tried to warn her what kind of danger she was walking into, but he hadn't fully appreciated it himself at the time. It wasn't just her reputation she had ruined by running off with him; it might well be her very life. What were the chances his father would believe

Agnes didn't know any damning secrets after all this? Finding out the truth about his sexual preferences was the least of her troubles.

Nate reached up and rubbed his eyes, as if he could somehow wipe away everything that had happened in the last few hours.

"When were you planning to tell me this?" Agnes asked, her voice cold for the first time he could remember.

Nate sank down a little lower in his seat. "I wasn't. I'm sorry if that makes me dishonest, but I couldn't risk you outing me. I have no interest in being 'reprogrammed.' But hey, look on the bright side: I'm going to be either dead or in hiding when this is over, so you won't have to marry me after all." He didn't have the heart to break it to her that she would be in the same boat.

"You think your father would really kill you?" Dante asked. "Now that the Replica program is on hiatus?"

"Let's just say I wouldn't put it past him. Now why don't we talk about something more important, like how we're going to get Nadia out of the Sanctuary, and once we work that out, where the hell we're going from there."

They'd finally reached a highway, and Dante gunned the motor. A warning light on the dashboard came on, telling him he was exceeding the speed limit. With a growl of frustration, he slowed down. If he didn't, the car would automatically send out a signal to the highway patrol, and he would have a hell of a time explaining why he had Nate and Agnes in the car with him if they were pulled over.

"I don't suppose you know how to disable that sensor?" Nate asked, and Dante shook his head.

"I'll get us there as fast as I can without drawing attention.

When we get there, can you use your status to talk the re-treat guards into delivering Nadia?"

Nate gave Dante an incredulous stare. "*That's* your rescue plan? We just drive up to the gates and ask them to hand her over?"

Dante's hands tightened on the steering wheel, and a muscle in his jaw twitched. "I've never tried to break someone out of an Executive retreat before, so excuse me if I'm a little out of my depth."

"Can't your . . . contacts help somehow?" The resistance had been able to get to Nadia at Tranquility, so surely they had someone on the inside at the Sanctuary, too.

Dante clenched up even more, anger radiating from him in waves. "No," he said through gritted teeth.

At first, Nate thought the anger was directed at him, for asking uncomfortable questions, but then he realized he was being an idiot. The resistance had been willing to help get a message to Nadia at Tranquility in return for the information Nate had promised them. He had nothing left to bargain with, except for information he didn't dare share. Though perhaps Dante's resistance bosses didn't have to know that . . .

"Don't bother," Dante said, as if reading his mind. "They have zero interest in getting involved. This is too dangerous, and she's too high-profile. It wouldn't matter if you offered to solve the mysteries of the universe for them, they wouldn't bite."

Nate did a double take. "But you're going after her anyway. And you're using one of their cars . . ." He was talking too much again, giving Agnes more clues than it was safe to give her. If she went blabbing to someone about this conversation, Dante could very well find himself brought in for questioning.

Then again, who would she have to blab to? Her life was as ruined as his.

Dante nodded grimly, watching the road. "I'm disobeying direct orders. But I am *not* abandoning Nadia. I promised I would get her out of there . . ."

Nate wondered when that had happened, but he kept his curiosity—and the habitual pulse of jealousy that came with it—tightly leashed. Right now, he had to concentrate on coming up with a plan. Even though he kind of sucked at planning. He was more of a "charge in and hope everything works out" kind of guy, but that wasn't going to be enough tonight. He tried calling Nadia's emergency phone again, but was again dumped into voice mail.

"The place is guarded out the wazoo," Nate muttered, hoping that maybe thinking out loud could help. "The fence is electrified, and they have freaking watchtowers!"

"And security cameras," Agnes added from the back. "I noticed those when we went through the gates for the funeral."

"Not only that," Dante contributed, "but it'll be almost three in the morning when we get there, and we don't know exactly where Nadia is. If we don't get through to her on the phone, she'll probably be fast asleep and have no idea she's in trouble or that we're coming."

Nate told himself not to panic, no matter how insurmountable the problems seemed. But in all honesty, he had no idea how they were going to pull this off without getting themselves captured and condemned to a fate worse than death.

CHAPTER TWENTY-THREE

The constant flow of adrenaline through her veins made Nadia want to run as fast as she could, but her best chance of escape was to move slowly and cautiously. She tiptoed down the dormitory hall and used Lily's key card to unlock the hall door. The door made a soft beep when it approved the key card, and Nadia winced. But though this place *felt* like a prison to her, it wasn't one. There were no guards posted to keep the inmates locked in, no one to come running to investigate the unexpected sound.

Nadia cast a wary eye on the security cameras as she slipped out the door. She had to assume that Lily had disabled them so as not to catch the planned murder on them, but how many of the cameras had she disabled? All of them? Or just the ones that might have caught her doing something incriminating? If any of the cameras were active, Nadia's escape attempt would end before it truly began.

Closing the door behind her as softly as possible, Nadia cautiously stepped out of the dormitory hall and went for the main staircase. She had to pass through another security door to get there, but Lily's key card once again did the trick.

The main staircase and the lobby it led to were both dark, only a few dim night-lights offering any illumination at all. That was a good sign, Nadia decided. It meant the staff of the night shift didn't frequent this area. Nadia suspected they used a service stairway to gain access to the second floor, where the dormitory was located.

Creeping forward, listening for any sign that she was not alone, she headed toward the office, where she could use the phone to call for help. She hated to put anyone else in danger, but escaping the Sanctuary penniless, on foot, and in uniform wouldn't do her a whole lot of good. She held her breath as she passed a door with a discreet placard declaring it to be the security center, but, though she heard voices, no one leapt out at her.

Like just about everything else in this damn place, the office was locked, with entry allowed by key card only. Nadia put her ear to the door, trying to guess whether anyone was inside. She didn't hear anything, and the longer she lurked in the lighted hallway, the more likely someone was going to happen along, so she quickly ran her key card through the reader and pushed the door open, canister held out in front of her like a gun.

She needn't have bothered. The room was dark and empty. She let out a sigh of relief as she closed the door behind her. She leaned her back against it and closed her eyes, trying to calm the frantic beating of her heart and take a deep breath. She still had a long, long way to go before she was out of here. There was no time to indulge in relief or search for calm.

Nadia plucked the nearest phone from its cradle, glad that she'd had the foresight to memorize the number for Dante's secure phone instead of depending on the address book in the phone he'd given her. A quick check of the time showed her that it was past 2:30 A.M., and she hoped and prayed that Dante was a light sleeper and would hear his phone ringing.

Her knees went a little weak when he answered on the second ring, and she had to sit down on the edge of the desk to stay upright.

"Nadia?" he asked, sounding not at all like someone who'd just been woken up at 2:30 in the morning. "Is that you?"

"Yeah," she said. There was a quaver in her voice, and the hand that held the phone was shaking slightly in delayed reaction. But she was still in dire trouble, so she ordered herself to delay the reaction even longer. It didn't stop her hands from shaking.

"I'm in trouble," she said. "I need help."

"What's happened?"

"Someone just tried to kill me." Her voice was shaking more now instead of less. She had to get ahold of herself. "I'm fine, but I have to get out of here before they try again. I didn't know who else to call." And she didn't know what she was hoping Dante could do for her. He was at least a four-hour drive away. It wasn't like she could afford to wait for him before making her move.

And that was when her mind finally processed the fact that there was noise in the background on Dante's end of the line, noise that didn't sound like it belonged in a bedroom.

"Where are you?" she asked.

"About fifteen minutes out from the Sanctuary. Hold on and I'm going to put you on speaker. I've got Nate and Ag—Miss Belinski with me."

Nadia was glad she'd already sat down or she might have collapsed in shock. "What?"

The background noise became louder and tinnier. "We're coming for you, Nadia," Nate's voice said.

It should have been good news. They were only fifteen minutes away instead of four hours, and that greatly increased her chances of escaping. But they wouldn't be coming for her in the middle of the night unless something gave them reason to fear for her life. The dreadful suspicion she'd been trying to hold off crashed through her mental barriers.

"Has something happened to Gerri?" she asked, willing them to tell her no.

There was a silence in the car, and she imagined them looking at each other, each waiting for someone else to answer. It was Dante who finally did.

"Her car went off the bridge into the East River."

Pain stabbed through Nadia's heart. "No," she moaned, pressing her free hand against her sternum as if that would somehow ease the pain. It didn't.

"I'm so sorry," Dante said softly.

Nadia wished he were here with her, wished she could throw herself into his arms and sob until her eyes could produce no more tears. But she didn't have time to lose herself in grief. Not here, not now.

There was a mother lode of anger beneath the grief. Anger at her parents for not letting her talk to Gerri. Anger at the retreat staff for taking her phone away. Anger at herself for not having told Gerri the truth in the first place. But most of all, anger at the Chairman, who had ordered both her death and Gerri's. Nadia tapped into that well of fury to hold the grief at bay.

"Are you all right?" Nate asked, though he had to know the answer was no. "It's not a coincidence that you're calling right now, is it?"

Nadia remembered she hadn't been on the speaker yet when she'd told Dante what had happened. She hoped Nate would take the news as calmly as Dante had.

"Don't get hysterical," she answered. "I promise you I'm fine, not a scratch on me. But someone just tried to kill me."

"We don't have time for you to freak out," Dante said, and Nadia presumed he was talking to Nate based on the sharpness of his voice.

"I'm not freaking out, and I'm not getting hysterical!" Nate snapped. "I'm just so pissed off I want to punch someone. Maybe it doesn't bother you that someone just tried to kill Nadia, but it definitely bothers me."

"Don't start, guys," Nadia said, wondering how the two of them had managed to survive a four-hour car ride together. And what had Dante said about Agnes being with them? She'd have asked about it, except she didn't think they had the time to waste. She'd get them to fill in the many details she was missing when she got out of here.

"We, uh, still haven't exactly figured out how we're going to get you out," Dante said. Nadia was glad he wasn't rising to Nate's bait and was keeping focused on the problem at hand.

Nadia chewed on her lip. There was no way she was getting out the front entrance, not with the little guard station they had there. She doubted even the Chairman Heir had the authority to order them to let her go—only her parents or the Chairman himself could do that. The fence was electrified, so there would be no fence-climbing as there had been at Tranquility—even if Nadia thought she had the upper body strength required to get over a fence.

"The watchtowers," she murmured under her breath, visualizing the retreat's grounds with the towers set into the fence. The towers themselves wouldn't be electrified, and Nadia doubted there was more than one guard manning each one.

"Huh?" Dante asked.

"They're the weak spot," she explained. "I can get over the fence by jumping from a watchtower."

"Umm, aren't there *people* in those watchtowers?" Nate asked.

"My guess is that there's a single guard in each," Nadia said, reaching into her pocket and fingering the canister of knockout gas. "I've got some handy supplies thanks to the people who tried to kill me, so I ought to be able to get into one of the towers and subdue the guard. Then I'll just have to jump down and hope I don't break my legs." She hadn't ever gotten an up-close view of the towers and wasn't sure how high they were, but out with broken legs would be better than inside in one piece.

"Meet me at the second tower from the right of the entrance, and make sure no one sees the car driving up."

There was a silence on the other end of the line. Despite everything, Nadia couldn't help smiling just a little, imagining the looks on their faces when they heard her, a sixteen-year-old gently bred Executive girl, claiming she was going to take out an armed guard all on her own.

"It won't be as hard as you think," she assured them. "I've got a key card and some knockout gas. And these aren't prison guards braced for trouble. I doubt any of them has seen any action *ever,* so they won't be prepared to deal with me."

Still silence.

"Unless you have a better idea . . . ?"

Someone—or maybe multiple someones—let out a heavy, frustrated sigh that she took for a no.

"All right, then. I'll see you in a few minutes." She crossed the fingers of her free hand, knowing there were about a thousand things that could go wrong, no matter how easy she had made her escape plan sound.

"Be careful," Dante said, as if there were any doubt that she would.

"You too. And thanks for coming for me." Her throat tightened with grateful tears, but as with everything else, she didn't have time for them right now.

Bracing herself for another plunge into danger, she hung up the phone.

nadia exited the building onto the back porch where people had gathered for the funeral. Unlike at Tranquility, there were no discreet little lights marking the edges of the walking paths here. During the day, there was a clear view from the porch straight to the fence, though it was at least a quarter mile away. At this time of night, however, there was nothing but an intimidating pool of darkness out there. The fence itself and the watchtowers were well lighted, but getting there would require a nerve-jangling run in the dark.

There was no sign of the moon or the stars, which Nadia took to mean it was overcast. The air had a wintry bite to it, and she could see her breath steaming. Spring took its own sweet time to visit upstate, and Nadia shivered with a combination of cold and nerves as she took off across the lawns. The overcast sky would work to her advantage, she told herself even as she stumbled over the decorative rock edging of one of the paths. It might make for a stubbed toe here and there, but it was far less likely anyone would see her as she ran toward the tower.

Nadia forced herself to slow down when she approached the band of light that stretched out from the watchtower. She stood still under the protection of the darkness and took stock of the situation.

The tower was narrow and circular, a utilitarian concrete

cylinder with a glass-enclosed control room at the top. As she'd expected, there was a single guard stationed in the control room, sitting on a tall stool and facing out over the fence. But he wasn't actually *looking* out, or even looking at the feed from the security cameras on the various screens built into the console; his attention focused instead on something he held in his lap. From his jerky, urgent movements and the occasional flashes of colored light, Nadia guessed he was playing some kind of game on his handheld.

He was exactly as alert as Nadia had hoped he would be. She watched for a minute or two and saw that he spared the console a brief glance every once in a while. Nadia couldn't see the images on the console, but she was pretty sure the cameras were pointing outward, designed to find people trying to sneak close enough to get forbidden photographs of the Executive residents.

Getting her key card and the canister of knockout gas ready, Nadia sprinted toward the tower, her whole body tense with nerves when she stepped into the light. She half expected lights to start flashing and sirens to start blaring, but nothing happened, and the only thing she could hear over the pounding of her heart was the thump of her feet hitting the turf.

She made it to the base of the tower without being seen. Sure enough, there was a card reader at the base of the tower by the door. Nadia cursed in a way that would make her mother cringe when she tried Lily's card and it didn't work. Apparently, the security crew had their own access cards.

So much for *that* plan.

But Nadia had to get into the tower. It was her only hope of escape, and she was painfully aware of every agonizingly slow second that passed by. Surely Lily and Athena were awake by now, probably had been for a while, and were making noise in an effort to attract attention. Though come to think of it, they'd be pretty hard-pressed to come up with an explanation for what had happened, so maybe they weren't in such a great hurry to raise the alarm after all.

Reminding herself for the millionth time that the man in the tower was a night watchman, not a trained, paranoid prison guard, Nadia took a gamble and pounded on the door with her fist.

"Help!" she cried. "Open up! Help!" She let out a muffled sob that sounded forced to her own ears, but that she hoped sounded real to the guard.

An elongated man-shaped shadow formed on the grass behind her as the guard stood up and stepped to the window to investigate, but he couldn't see her where she stood in the protection of the doorway.

"Help!" she cried again, and gave the door another pound for good measure.

"Who's there?" the guard called out. "What's wrong?"

Nadia just sobbed and gasped, making as if she were so panicked she couldn't even talk. If the guard called for backup, she was in big trouble, but she was gambling it wouldn't even occur to him.

He called out again, but she kept making incoherent sobbing sounds. Sure enough, she soon heard the clank of shoes hitting metal stairs as the guard came down to investigate. She readied the canister of knockout gas.

The moment the door opened, she stuck her foot in the gap to stop it from closing and discharged the knockout gas straight into the guard's face.

He had about two seconds to register surprise before his eyes rolled into the back of his head and he collapsed. He was too heavy for Nadia to move, so she merely stepped over him to get inside. Because another weapon couldn't hurt, she relieved the unconscious man of his sidearm before she sprang for the stairs. She held her breath to avoid accidentally breathing in any gas until she made it to the top.

The windows around the control center allowed the room to be climate controlled, which Nadia supposed was only reasonable, considering how fierce the winters could be. But it didn't make sense to station an armed guard behind windows if he couldn't open them to shoot, so she fiddled around with the center panel until she found a catch and popped it open. She swung her legs out and sat on the ledge, looking down. She was definitely up higher than she'd like to jump from, maybe ten feet or so, but she didn't have a choice.

Ahead of her, just outside the reach of the lights, shadows moved in the darkness. Thinking that she was quite literally making a leap of faith, Nadia jumped.

CHAPTER TWENTY-FOUR

aBout half a mile shy of the Sanctuary, Dante pulled the car into the parking lot of a small grocery store that was closed for the night. He parked around back by the delivery entrance so that no one driving by would see the car. Not that there was any traffic out in the middle of nowhere at this time of night, but you couldn't be too careful.

According to the map on Dante's handheld, if they forged ahead on foot through the woods behind the store, they would eventually emerge right near the Sanctuary. It was still chilly at this time of year upstate, and the woods looked relatively easy to navigate with most of the undergrowth still dormant. Even so, the moment they stepped out of the car, Nate realized they had a couple of problems, both centered around Agnes's opera finery. For one, she had on high heels that would make it impossible for her to even *walk* through the woods, much less run. For another, since she hadn't been planning on an excursion outside, she hadn't even brought the gossamer, ineffectual wrap she'd worn into the theater. If Nate felt the cold through his tux, she had to be freezing in her strapless gown.

"I think you'll have to wait with the car," he told her as she crossed her arms over her chest and shivered. "You'll never get through the woods in those shoes."

She looked down at her feet as if startled to find she was

wearing heels. "Damn," she said, her breath feathering in the cold air.

"We can't leave her here alone," Dante protested, eying Agnes with suspicion.

"Oh, come on!" Agnes said with an exaggerated roll of her eyes. "What do you think I'm going to do? Steal your getaway car? You have the keys, and you have my phone battery."

Dante ignored her and focused on Nate. "You should stay here with her."

Nate laughed with no humor. "Yeah, right. Not gonna happen."

"She could run off the moment we have our backs turned," Dante argued. "Just because she doesn't have a working phone on her doesn't mean she can't find one. No offense, Miss Belinski, but I still don't get why you're 'helping' us, so I'm not about to take any chances."

"I'm not helping *you*," Agnes said with disdain. "I'm helping Nadia. And in case you've forgotten, I'm already in this up to my neck by now. Plenty of people saw me leave the theater with Nathaniel—willingly. Once they figure out what he's up to, they'll know I was an accomplice. I don't know what's going to happen to me, but it's not going to be anything good."

Her eyes shimmered with tears. It was a rare Executive girl who couldn't conjure up crocodile tears in an attempt to get her way, but even so, Nate believed her. In the heat of the moment when she'd insisted on helping him, and even when she'd refused to allow them to lock her in the trunk, Agnes might not have fully comprehended what the consequences of her actions would be. But she'd had more than four hours to think things through, and she was not stupid. It was far too late to change her mind now, and she knew it.

"I'm coming with you," Nate told Dante, "and Agnes will wait with the car."

Dante bristled, drawing himself up to his full height and shifting his weight onto the balls of his feet in a posture that screamed of aggression and intimidation. He was an imposing specimen with muscles on his muscles, and Nate had no doubt he knew how to fight. He probably learned all kinds of useful skills like that in spy training school.

"Stay with Agnes," Dante ordered, as if ordering around the Chairman Heir were business as usual for him. "Or I'll make you."

"He's your servant," Agnes put in drily, nodding. "Ri-ight."

Nate was sure he'd come out the loser if he got into a fistfight with Dante, but he wasn't about to let the bastard ride off to Nadia's rescue while he sat around in the car and twiddled his thumbs. Internally wincing, pretty sure he was about to get the crap kicked out of him, he raised his fists and gave Dante his fiercest glare.

"Fine. Make me."

"We don't have time for this," Agnes said before any punches were thrown. "Put me in the trunk if that will satisfy both of your overblown egos. Stop acting like kids on a playground and get moving."

Nate's face flushed with heat as he realized how right she was. What possible reason could he have for refusing to back down except that his ego was too big to let Dante be Nadia's hero? Childish *and* selfish. He was really on a roll.

Nate forced his fists open and straightened up from what he was sure was a pathetic imitation of a fighter's crouch. Conceding to Dante was harder than it should have been, and he chose his next words carefully, trying to get his point across without escalating hostilities once more.

"If you really think I'm more useful sitting in the car with Agnes than coming with you as backup in case anything goes wrong, then I'll stay here. But we're not putting her in the trunk." She deserved better than that.

Dante looked back and forth between the two of them, then sighed and scrubbed a hand through his hair. He stared at the pavement at his feet for a moment, then looked up again.

"Do you know how to use that gun you took off Fischer?"

"Um, I assume I just point and shoot."

Dante grimaced as he held his hand out and made a give-it-to-me motion. Nate handed over the gun, and Dante took a quick look at it.

"This is a semi-auto," he said, "so it *is* basically point and shoot. Just make sure you have the safety off before you do." He turned the gun over and pointed at a toggle switch beneath the grip, then handed the gun back.

"Is it on or off right now?" Nate asked, even though it made him sound like an idiot too ignorant to be allowed around a deadly weapon.

"On. And keep it that way until I tell you."

Nate swallowed a protest, knowing that objecting to Dante's tone was just petty. If Dante was the one who knew what he was doing, then Nate was just going to have to be a man about it and listen to him. Even when he insisted on giving orders.

"I'm getting back in the car," Agnes said, her teeth chattering with cold.

Nate slid his tux jacket off and handed it to her. "It won't be much warmer in the car," he said. He might have tried to talk Dante into leaving the keys so she could turn on the heater, but he didn't want to start another argument.

"You'll need it," Agnes said, trying to hand the jacket back.

"With all this adrenaline pumping through me?" he asked with a grin. "I won't feel a thing. Besides, we'll keep warm by running."

Reluctantly, Agnes slipped the jacket over her shoulders. "Good luck," she said. "Bring her back safe."

"That's the idea," Nate said under his breath.

And then he and Dante were jogging through the darkness of the woods, using Dante's handheld as a half-assed flashlight and trying not to trip over roots and underbrush.

It didn't take long for Nate to realize his occasional forays into the gym for a bit of exercise had not prepared him for real-world physical exertion. He was huffing and puffing in no time, even though they weren't running terribly fast. Dante, of course, wasn't even breathing hard. If Nate wasn't careful, he was going to give himself an inferiority complex. He wasn't used to feeling inferior to *anyone,* and he couldn't say he much cared for the experience.

Eventually, they saw the glow of the Sanctuary's lights in the distance, and they slowed down, picking their way much more cautiously through the woods. When they got close enough that they could catch glimpses of the fence, Dante came to a complete stop and crouched behind a tree.

Nate had no idea where they were in relation to the tower Nadia was planning to escape from, and he knew even the superspy couldn't have figured out their position based on the tiny expanse of fence they could see through the trees.

"Why are we stopping?" Nate asked, his breath still short from the run.

"You need to stay here while I go on ahead and figure out where we are." Nate started to protest, but Dante cut him off with a sharp gesture of his hand. "That white shirt of yours glows like a beacon. You don't dare get too close to the fence, or someone might see you."

Nate cursed as he looked down at himself and the crisp white tux shirt. He supposed he could take it off, but aside from the fact that it was freezing out, he didn't think his pale skin would be that great an improvement. Dante, of course, was wearing all black, and his complexion was naturally darker, even though he'd lost the unfashionable tan he'd had when they'd first met. It only made sense to let him scout things out by himself, no matter how much it galled Nate to be left behind.

"Fine," he said. "Just hurry."

Dante gave him a look that managed to convey *no shit* without words. Then he began creeping forward, keeping low and darting from tree to tree. Even knowing where he was, Nate had trouble picking his form out of the darkness, and that had to be a good sign.

Dante was gone long enough that Nate wasn't out of breath anymore when he returned. Nate knew that caution was absolutely necessary under the circumstances, but curbing his impatience was damn hard when urgency kept beating at him. It was possible his father had figured out Nate was going to show up here in an attempt to get to Nadia. Unlikely, given how impossible it seemed that he could get her out of there, but if his father *did* guess, pursuit wouldn't be far behind.

"Looks like Nadia's tower is about half a klick that way," Dante said, waving to his right. "Let's go."

Nate didn't know how far a *klick* was—a kilometer, maybe?—but he wasn't about to admit his ignorance by asking. He wondered if Dante had used the term just to be annoying, or if he'd had military training before becoming a spy for Paxco security.

Nate reminded himself that he didn't actually care how far half a klick was, that he'd run another five miles if that was what it took to get Nadia out of the Sanctuary. He took off after Dante.

It felt to Nate's burning lungs and leg muscles that they had run at least a mile when Dante called a halt again. This time, he allowed Nate to get a little closer to the circle of light surrounding the Sanctuary's fence, but he still made him stop before Nate could see much of anything.

"If you could see the guy in the tower," Dante reminded him, "then he could see you. The last thing we need to do is put him on alert before Nadia gets there."

Nate looked at his watch. It had been a good thirty minutes since they'd talked to Nadia. "She should be there already," he said as his heart rate jacked up on a fresh surge of adrenaline. It felt like it had taken him *forever* to get here, and Nadia had had much less ground to cover. If the Sanctuary staff had caught her trying to escape . . .

"She's cautious, Nate," Dante said with a hint of impatience. "It takes a while to get from place to place when you're cautious. Not that *you'd* know about that."

Nate closed his eyes and ordered himself not to rise to the bait. And not to get testy that Dante insisted on calling him *Nate* when they were far from friends. "You really want to pick a fight *now*?" Talk about your bad timing.

"I'm not picking a fight. I'm just telling it like it is. I'm going to get closer, and you're going to wait here. Might be a good time to get out the gun and turn the safety off. If things look like they're about to go to hell, I'll whistle. Keep your finger off the trigger until you're sure you have something to shoot at. And try not to shoot Nadia or me if it comes to that."

Nate's self-control was definitely getting better. He refrained from making a smart-ass reply. He was never going to like Dante, but he had to grudgingly admire the guy. By being here, he was defying not only his official bosses in the security department, but his unofficial ones in the resistance. It took major guts to do that.

Nate withdrew the gun that he'd stuck in the back of his pants. He couldn't see the safety in the oppressive darkness of the trees, but he found it by feel and flicked it off as Dante crept forward once again.

nadia hit the ground with a thump that rattled her teeth. Her ankle buckled on impact, sending a stab of pain up her leg. She choked off a cry of pain as she fell to her hands and knees. The lights of the guard tower felt like a spotlight, picking her form out of the darkness and screaming "she's trying to escape" to anyone nearby. Her ankle throbbed, but she felt too vulnerable in the light to wait for it to ease up.

Hobbling as fast as she could, she half-walked, half-limped toward the trees. She caught a flash of motion, nothing more than a patch of shadow darker than its surroundings, and she came to a sudden halt, panting with exertion and pain.

"Dante?" she called in a breathless whisper, her hand straying to the canister of knockout gas, in case it wasn't him.

"Keep moving!" Dante said abruptly, stepping into the fringes of the light.

Nadia wanted to throw her arms around him and weep, but Dante was all business, grabbing her and dragging her toward the trees. She stumbled along behind him, her ankle screaming in protest. Once they left the circle of light, she could barely see anything. The cloudless night and Dante's black clothes made him practically invisible.

As soon as they were safely under cover of the trees, Dante hauled her into his arms and hugged her so tight she could barely breathe. Not that she had the slightest inclination to complain.

"Are you all right?" he whispered in her ear, and the brush of his lips against her skin made her shiver.

Her sister was dead, her life was in ruins, someone had just tried to kill her, but other than that . . .

Nadia pulled back from the embrace so she could look up into Dante's eyes and drink in the sight of him.

"I thought I would never see you again," she whispered.

He gazed down at her, opening and closing his mouth a couple of times as if he couldn't quite decide what to say. In the end, he settled for kissing her, his lips hot, hungry, and almost desperate against hers. He pulled away sooner than she wanted, his hands cupping her face.

"I wish we had time for a proper hello," he said, "but we have to get moving."

Nadia agreed on both counts. She had no idea how long she had before the alarm was raised, or even what the Sanctuary staff would do about it when it was—and she didn't want to find out.

"Just give me your arm for a bit," she said, slipping her hand into the crook of his elbow. "I'm a little gimpy."

Dante swept her off her feet so fast she gasped in surprise. Her arms settled around his neck by instinct, and she held on tight as he made his way through the darkened trees. She couldn't help cuddling against him, noticing the firmness of his chest and the breadth of his shoulders. He carried her with an effortless strength that was undeniably sexy, and she felt way safer in his arms than she had any right to feel under the circumstances.

"Where's Nate?" she asked, though she was reluctant to let anyone else intrude on this moment. "And Agnes?"

"I left Nate a little ways back," Dante answered, "and Agnes is with the car. We'll have you out of here in no time."

And then what, she wondered, but didn't ask because she doubted Dante had any more answers than she.

nate's breath frosted in the air, and the cooling sweat on his skin made him shiver. He stared intently at the little slice of the fence and tower he could see from his position.

The shivering got worse and worse, and Nate regretted his moment of gallantry in giving Agnes his jacket. It felt like the sweat from the long run was freezing against his skin, and he held the gun with great care, afraid his shaking fingers might get him into trouble.

The wait seemed to last forever, and it took all of Nate's willpower to keep himself planted in position. He would never forgive himself if he crept forward to see what was taking so long and someone spotted him and sounded the alarm. He hoped the lack of commotion meant nothing had gone wrong at least.

Eventually, he saw movement in the trees coming toward him. He gripped the gun with both hands, then let out a shuddering breath when he saw Dante approaching, carrying Nadia like she weighed about two pounds. She was cuddled intimately against his chest, one arm locked securely around his neck.

Nate turned the safety back on and stood up. Jealousy stirred in his gut, an instinctive reaction he couldn't will away, no matter how much he wanted to.

Throughout his life, Nadia had always been there for him. She'd understood him like no one else and just generally been his rock. He genuinely wanted her to be happy, and he wanted her to find love, just as he had found it with Kurt. That didn't make it any easier to accept the changes a burgeoning romance would make to their friendship. Somehow, he had to train himself to stop relying on her so heavily, to get used to the idea of her being someone else's rock now.

"Why did it have to be *him* of all people?" Nate muttered to himself. Couldn't she have fallen for someone who wasn't such a dick?

A dick who could have pulled off this whole rescue without any help from Nate, thank you very much. It was Dante who'd gotten word of Gerri's death and warned Nate. It was Dante who'd provided the transportation. And it was Dante Nadia had called for help. Nate was merely tagging along, proving himself to be exactly the kind of useless aristocrat Dante thought he was.

Nate shoved his self-pity to the side. He could bemoan his uselessness later. Nadia was out, but they were hardly out of the woods—har, har—yet.

As soon as Nate stood up, Nadia raised her head from Dante's shoulder and stopped cuddling against him. Nate wondered if she was trying to spare his feelings. Then he wondered why he always seemed to think everything was about him.

Damn, he needed to get out of his own head.

"Nate!" Nadia cried with a smile that would have lit up the night if it weren't for the shadows in her eyes. She held out her hand to him. "I'd give you a hug, but this caveman refuses to put me down."

Nate clasped the offered hand and squeezed it firmly. "Are you hurt?"

"Just a twisted ankle," she assured him. "I just need to walk it off."

"We need to hurry," Dante said, not about to put her down. "We'll move faster with me carrying you than with you limping."

Nadia shot a pleading look Nate's way, but he shook his head, reluctantly agreeing with Dante. "For the duration of Operation Rescue Nadia, he's in charge. Let's get the damn thing over with before I kill him."

There was one and only one benefit to having Dante carry Nadia the whole way back to the car: even the superspy couldn't run through darkened woods while carrying someone, at least not indefinitely. Which meant that not only could Nate keep up, he didn't have to do all that panting and sweating in front of Nadia.

CHAPTER TWENTY-FIVE

Despite Dante's suspicions, Agnes was in the car, huddling in Nate's jacket, when they burst through the woods and into the grocery store parking lot.

No one had spoken throughout the course of the hike, aside from a couple requests from Nadia to be put down, which Dante ignored. They were probably about as quiet and subtle as a herd of elephants crashing through the underbrush, but it didn't seem like there was anyone around to hear.

Agnes leaned over and opened the car door before Nate could reach it, and Dante laid Nadia carefully on the seat as if she might break if he put her down too hard. He closed the door behind her, and he and Nate both climbed in the front. Nate didn't know about the others, but he didn't feel remotely safe, even though they seemed to have gotten away cleanly.

Dante pulled out of the driveway and hung a right, pushing the car up to the speed limit fast enough to look suspicious to anyone who was watching.

"So, where are we going?" Nadia asked from the backseat after having exchanged a brief greeting with Agnes.

Nate looked at Dante, hoping he had some suggestion of what to do and where to go now, but he looked as clueless as Nate felt.

"We're still working on that part," Nate said. "We figured we needed to concentrate on getting you out first." Which was certainly true, but he wondered if any of them had *really* thought they were going to succeed. Until Nadia had called them, their rescue plans had been vague at best.

He doubted his answer was what you'd call satisfying, but Nadia took it in stride, as she seemed capable of doing in even the worst situations. "Why don't you start by telling me the whole story," she prompted. "Including why you and Agnes dressed up so much to break me out of the retreat."

As Dante drove resolutely *away* from the Sanctuary but not *toward* anywhere in particular, Nate filled Nadia in on everything that had happened from the moment he'd received Dante's call at the theater.

nadia was still shaking with cold and residual nerves as she listened to Nate's recounting of the night's events. She raised her eyebrows at Agnes a couple of times, surprised and touched that the timid girl had put herself at risk as she had. Though it would have been better for all if Agnes weren't with them. She knew too many of their secrets already, and the more time she spent with them, the more she would learn—and the deeper a hole she would dig for herself. Nadia wondered if the girl had any clue how catastrophic her decisions tonight were going to turn out to be. Had she figured out yet that she couldn't go back?

"There's something I don't understand," Agnes said after Nate had finished explaining everything.

Nadia was looking at Agnes, but out of the corner of her eye, she saw the face that Nate made. There was actually *a lot* Agnes didn't understand, but she didn't seem to know that.

"What's that?" Nate asked.

"You said your father can afford to kill you now because he has Dorothy."

"Yes."

"What does Dorothy have to do with it? I thought once he found the recordings, your father was free to eliminate anyone who knew too much."

Nate looked puzzled. "Well, yeah. But he couldn't kill me because he needed an heir, and now he has Dorothy for that."

Agnes looked just as puzzled as Nate did. "But he still has a backup of the original Nathaniel Hayes, and that backup scan was done before you learned any of his secrets. Why couldn't he just create a new Replica and start from scratch? I mean, it would be really expensive and all, but . . ."

Nate squirmed a little in his seat. "I know you've heard that the hiatus in the Replica program is temporary, but that's a lie. There won't be any more backups or Replicas. Ever."

Agnes's eyes went wide, and her mouth dropped open in shock. Nadia could only imagine the girl's dismay at discovering how she and her father had been played. With Paxco's chief source of revenue gone, Nate as its Chairman Heir became a considerably less appealing marriage prospect. Would Chairman Belinski really have wanted his daughter tied to a state on the verge of economic collapse? Nadia was quite certain Chairman Hayes had never mentioned that little issue during the marriage negotiations.

Agnes opened and closed her mouth a few times with false starts before she took a deep breath and shook her head. "There's obviously been a lot of lying going on. More than you know about, apparently. Remember I said there was something fishy going on?"

She was talking to Nate—she'd had no such conversation with Nadia—but a lump of dread was steadily rising in Nadia's throat.

Nate nodded cautiously.

"Well, the first fishy thing that happened was the announcement about the Replica program."

Nate grinned wryly. "You mean you don't believe my father when he says the press was exaggerating and it's just a temporary glitch?"

Agnes shook her head. "It's not that. At least not exactly. My father and I were sworn to secrecy—for obvious reasons—but part of the appeal of the marriage agreement was that my father and I would both have backup scans. We freaked out when we heard the news, but your father assured us the Replica program is still up and running. It's just that he's running low on storage space for all the backups so he's picking and choosing who he'll use it for."

Nate shook his head. "That's not true. It *can't* be true."

Nadia found she was gripping the seat in front of her so hard her fingers were going numb. She hadn't even realized she'd reached out to grab it. "He's just stringing you along," she said with more hope than conviction. "After you sign the agreement, he'll regretfully tell you—"

"My father and I had our scans done on Friday."

"No," Nate said again, as if denying what he didn't want to hear could make it not true.

"Maybe it's all a scam," Nadia said. "Maybe he just pretended to make backups." But she didn't believe her own theory.

"That *has* to be it!" Nate said.

Somehow, without meaning for it to happen, Nadia's hand had found Nate's, and their fingers twined together. Whatever else kept them apart, in this they were together.

"What is it?" Agnes asked. "Why is this . . . upsetting you so much?"

Still holding on to Nate's hand, Nadia let herself think back to that dreadful day when she had been arrested. Thought back to the deal she'd made with the Chairman. She remembered Thea somehow messing with the electronic lock so that they couldn't get into her vault. Remembered the Chairman going back to the other room to retrieve a key from Dirk Mosely's dead body. Remembered him walking back to the vault with blood on his hands.

And remembered the moment before he'd finally gotten the vault door open, when all the lights had suddenly dimmed.

Just like they did when a Replica was created.

"Thea's not dead," Nadia murmured in horror. "She made a Replica of herself before the Chairman destroyed her."

And if Thea was still alive, that meant that everything Nate and Nadia had gone through had been for nothing.

CHAPTER TWENTY-SIX

nadia had been so shocked by the realization that Thea was still alive and kicking that she didn't immediately realize she had spoken aloud. Not until Dante and Agnes asked, "Who's Thea?" in concert.

Nadia blinked and shook her head as her mind continued to reel. Chairman Hayes had tricked her. All this time, she'd been comforting herself with the knowledge that no matter what bad things had happened to her, she had made a difference in the world by destroying the monstrous machine/creature that was Thea. She thought she had saved lives. She thought her own sacrifices were worth it. And all along, the Chairman had been laughing at her behind her back, biding his time until he located the blackmail recordings so he could do away with the pesky little threat she offered him and return to business as usual.

"Nadia?" Dante prompted. "Who's Thea?"

"Someone who shouldn't be alive," Nate answered for her. "And that's all we can say about the subject, so don't ask any questions."

"I'm the one with the car, asshole," Dante retorted. "You in the mood for a walk?"

"Cut it out," Agnes said to the boys before they could escalate hostilities. She turned to Nadia with both worry and sympathy in her eyes. "So this Thea person being alive is bad, isn't it?"

Nadia nodded. "Very, very bad."

"And you and Nate weren't supposed to know about it, because Chairman Hayes thought you'd release your black-mail recordings if you did."

This time, Nadia didn't respond, as if by now going silent, she could stop Agnes's agile mind from putting more puzzle pieces together and figuring out stuff she had no business knowing.

"And I tipped you off that she was alive by letting you know the Replica program is still active," Agnes continued.

Nate muttered a curse under his breath. "You can shut up now, Agnes."

But the lid was already off Pandora's box.

"Which means the Replica program isn't possible without Thea," Dante said, taking over the chain of thought. "Which means Thea is the person who invented it—and she's the only one who knows how it works."

"But how can that be?" Agnes asked. "Surely Chairman Hayes isn't stupid enough to let the entire program hinge on a single person. I mean, she could get hit by a bus and then poof! It's all gone."

Nadia's gaze locked with Nate's. Agnes had figured out so much already. And the truly incendiary truth about Thea, the truth that they *had* to keep hidden from the public if they didn't want to risk a violent uprising, was her human experimentation—and the Chairman's willingness to provide her with test subjects.

Nate's mind seemed to travel the same direction as Nadia's, for he nodded slightly, and she knew without exchanging any words that he was giving her the go-ahead to tell Dante and Agnes a little more about Thea.

"Thea's not a person," Nadia said. "She's an A.I., an artificial intelligence. She's this bizarre mixture of biological . . . stuff and machinery. And she's smart enough to know that she can use her unique ability to take scans and create Replicas as leverage. I don't know if a human mind can comprehend whatever it is she does, but she isn't about to explain it to anyone even if it can."

"Maybe *especially* if it can," Nate said. "As long as she's the only one who can do it, she's invaluable, one of a kind."

"But you think it's better for her to be dead and the Replica program with her than for her to still be alive," Agnes said.

"Yes," Nate replied. "She is very, very bad news. And she has my father twisted around her little finger. Even though she doesn't technically *have* a little finger."

There was a long silence, which Agnes eventually broke with a long, low whistle.

"I knew there was some cloak-and-dagger stuff going on, but nothing like this. Wow."

"Yeah, but as creepy and disturbing as this all is," Dante said, glancing at them quickly in the rearview mirror, "we have a more immediate problem. Like, where the hell am I going to take you guys? I can't just drive around indefinitely. And you can't go home."

"Not even me?" Agnes asked in a small voice, tears shimmering in her eyes. Her expression was bleak, suggesting she already knew the answer. Nate had explained why he'd brought Agnes along—Nadia wished she could have seen the boys' faces when meek little Agnes had pulled a gun on them—but she wished there had been some alternative.

"I'm sorry, Agnes," Nadia said gently. "But no, not even you."

Agnes closed her eyes and nodded, her lower lip quivering.

"I wish you hadn't dragged her into this," Nadia said to Nate, though it wasn't fair of her to blame him.

"It was that or let her shoot Dante," he responded. "It was kind of a tough decision, actually."

Dante took a hand off the wheel to make a rude gesture that he probably thought Nadia and Agnes couldn't see.

"It's my own fault," Agnes said. "They tried to tell me how dangerous it was, but I wouldn't listen." She plucked at the ruffles on her gown. "I wanted to feel brave, just this once." Her eyes flicked briefly to Nate then away, and Nadia read between the lines easily. Agnes had been trying to impress Nate, fighting against the contempt her future husband had shown her from the moment they'd met.

Impulsively, Nadia leaned over and gave Agnes a quick hug. "You *were* brave," she said. "I just wish you hadn't gotten sucked in with the rest of us."

"Well, she has," Dante said, sounding like he was pretty fed up with all the touchy-feely stuff. "And the only place I can imagine you being able to hide for any length of time is in the Basement."

Nadia shuddered at the thought. The Basement wasn't safe for adult gangbangers with years of experience on the gritty streets. It certainly wasn't a safe place for a handful of Executive teenagers and a Paxco security spy. However, it *was* the one place where it was possible to live entirely off the grid. Not only that, but the Basement "dress code" meant they could easily disguise themselves to the point of being unrecognizable. Wigs, masks, face paint . . . All were used in abundance in the Basement.

"Somehow, I don't see us wandering into the Basement with me in this tux and Agnes in her evening gown," Nate said. "Not if we want to make it in one piece, that is."

"We'll make a pit stop first. The apartment I grew up in is in one of the crappy fringe neighborhoods. I moved my folks out as soon as I could afford to, and I haven't set foot in the place since I got my first assignment. We ought to be able to hole up there for a little while. I'll put in a call to Bishop and see if he can meet us there with some new wardrobe options."

"*I'll* call him," Nate corrected.

Nadia didn't much care for this plan. It would be daylight by the time they reached their destination, and she and Nate and Agnes were hardly inconspicuous. And if anyone in Nate's household realized Dante was missing and told the authorities, they might guess that Dante and Nate were together and check out Dante's apartment. Even if everything went right and they made it safely to the Basement, how were they going to survive there?

But the fact was, with the kind of enemies Nate and Nadia—and their friends by extension—had gathered, they had very few options. So for now, hiding out in the Basement was the best they could do.

Dante's apartment was in a seedy neighborhood within sight of the first line of identical concrete high-rises of the Basement. Everything was dingy and run-down, and there wasn't a ground-floor window in sight that didn't have bars or metal mesh protecting it. There was graffiti on the scaffolding leading up to the elevated train. The scaffolding was a dreary shade of green, but lighter patches gave testament to the neighborhood's ongoing attempts to combat the graffiti.

The apartment itself was cramped, and its aging fixtures looked like they would fall apart if someone breathed on them. There was a coating of dust on everything, and the air smelled stale.

"You said you moved your folks to a better place," Nadia commented as she looked around the dismal living room with its faded wallpaper and threadbare couch. "Why didn't you go with them?" Dante was eighteen and striking out on his own, but it was hardly unusual for an eighteen-year-old to still live with his parents. Not that Dante really seemed to be *living* in this apartment, at least not while he was posing as a live-in servant.

Dante hunched his shoulders. "They don't approve of my career choice. My dad especially. People 'round here don't think too highly of Paxco security goons."

"So they don't know . . . ?"

Dante glanced over his shoulder at Agnes, who had a dazed expression on her face as she looked around and didn't seem to be listening to them. He lowered his voice anyway. "That I'm with the resistance? Hell no. The less they know, the safer they'll be if I ever get caught. Not that that's too likely anymore. I doubt the resistance will have much use for me after I disobeyed direct orders. And used one of their cars to do it."

"I'm sorry," Nadia said, reaching out to touch Dante's arm. Everyone had given up so much to try to help her. "I—"

"Shh," he said, putting a finger to her lips and stepping closer. "It was my decision to make. And I wouldn't change a thing."

Nadia wanted to wrap her arms around him, hold him tight, maybe even kiss him. But she couldn't do that with Nate and Agnes around. She didn't have a reputation or status left to protect, but a lifetime's worth of caution and propriety didn't evaporate overnight, so instead she gave him a brief squeeze and a peck on the cheek. Even that had her blushing as she stepped back and put proper distance between them.

nadia paced the length of the living room while Dante scrounged in the cupboards of the kitchen in search of some canned food that hadn't expired. He came up with two large tins of beef stew and dumped them into a pot. Nadia had never eaten canned beef stew in her life. It would make a spectacularly unappetizing breakfast, but who knew when their next meal would come?

Nadia suspected hers wasn't the only stomach to do a backflip when Dante distributed four bowls of brown slop. It smelled like dog food, and looked like . . . Well, never mind what it looked like.

"Sorry," Dante said, with an edge in his voice. "I gave my chef the day off."

He'd probably grown up eating this stuff, and having three Executives turn up their noses at it was putting the habitual chip back on his shoulder. Nadia couldn't blame him, though based on the spark in Nate's eye, he wasn't as forgiving.

"So what are we going to do now?" Nadia asked, then shoved a spoonful of stew into her mouth and tried not to make a face at the taste. She gave Nate a pointed look, and he meekly obeyed by taking a bite. Agnes was still stirring the stuff around, looking a little green.

"I suggest we all try to get some sleep until Bishop gets here," Dante said, with his mouth full.

According to Nate, Bishop was planning to show up with costumes in hand around nightfall.

"And then we go to the Basement," Nadia said.

Dante nodded.

"And *then* what?"

That was a question no one had a good answer to, so they all spooned up some stew and chewed in silence. Even Agnes, though she seemed to chew the tiny nibble she'd taken far longer than necessary, as if she couldn't quite force herself to swallow it.

"Then I guess we just try to stay alive," Nate said grimly, when no one else spoke.

"That's it?" Nadia asked. "We just turn a blind eye to everything we know? We let the Chairman get away with murdering my sister and trying to murder me?" Nadia had spent most of the previous night feeling helpless and afraid; now she gave in to fury. "And what about Thea? Do we just figure she's someone else's problem now? We have to *do* something."

Nadia looked around at her friends' faces and didn't like the expressions of defeat they all wore.

"I don't like it any better than you do," Nate said, "but what can we do?"

She knew he had a point, but she kept pressing anyway. "I bet your plan to get me out of the Sanctuary seemed impossible at first, but you didn't let that stop you. And you got me out."

"Getting you out of an Executive retreat is one thing," Dante argued. "Going up against the Chairman is another."

"Isn't that what your resistance is all about?"

Dante gave her a pointed look and jerked his head toward Agnes. Nadia would bet her right foot that Agnes had already figured out Dante was involved in some kind of resistance movement, but even if she hadn't . . .

"She's in the same boat as the rest of us," Nadia said. "Who's she going to tell? Now how do we sign up?"

"What?" Dante asked, his voice just short of a yelp.

Nadia had been hesitant to dub the resistance the good guys in the past, afraid of their plans and their motives. But that was before she'd known Thea was still alive. Even if the resistance hoped to spark a civil war, it might be worth it if that's what it took to stop Thea. The A.I. had no moral compass and no regard for human life. She was a menace to society, and the longer her research was allowed to continue, the more dangerous—and more powerful—she would become.

"The resistance," Nadia said. "I want to *do* something instead of running away and hiding. So how do we sign up?"

Dante shook his head. "You don't."

Nadia opened her mouth to protest, but he wasn't done.

"They'll kick me out on my ass once they know what I've done. They don't like loose canons. And there's no way in hell they'd want anything to do with the Chairman Heir or either of his supposed fiancées."

"But we *know* things—" Nadia started.

"Doesn't matter," Nate interrupted. "I already had this conversation with Bishop a while back. Executives are the enemy to them, and the three of us are as Executive as you get."

"So they've never heard of *the enemy of my enemy is my friend*?"

"Even if they believed you were their friends, they wouldn't have you," Dante said. "You're all way too high-profile. Too dangerous to touch."

Nadia wanted to hurl her bowl of cooling, congealing stew across the room. "So that's it? We're just going to cower in the Basement and hope for the best?"

"No," Nate said. "You're right: we have to fight back somehow. If the resistance won't have us, then screw them! We can be our own resistance movement, just the four of us—and Bishop, if he wants in."

Dante gaped at him. "You can't be serious."

"Why not?" Nate asked. "We're all smart, and resourceful, and highly motivated. Nadia and I managed to beat Dirk Mosely against all odds. And Nadia escaped the retreat after surviving a murder attempt. We're not pushovers, no matter what my father may think."

Something fierce and proud stirred in Nadia's heart. They were *not* going to accept defeat. They were going to do something more than run for their lives. And she was personally going to make the Chairman pay for what he'd done to her sister.

Dante still looked skeptical. "That all sounds great, but I don't think—"

"You were so committed to your cause you joined the Paxco security department to spy on them," Nate interrupted. "You were ready to take a cyanide pill to keep from being captured. Are you seriously telling me you're too chicken to keep fighting?"

Dante bristled, clenching his fists. "I am *not* chicken! And I didn't say I didn't think we should keep fighting."

Nadia suppressed a smile. Nate had always been a skilled manipulator. Just this once, she was glad for it.

"So who's with me?" Nate asked. He thunked down his bowl of stew and held out his hand, palm down, fixing Dante with a challenging glare.

Nadia quickly crossed the distance and put her hand on top of his. Dante made a low growling sound in the back of his throat, but he followed suit.

Nadia expected Agnes to balk. After all, she couldn't have had a clue what she was getting into when she left the theater with Nate last night, and never in her wildest dreams would she have considered she might be joining some half-baked Paxco teen resistance movement. But she raised her chin high and stuck her hand in the circle with barely a hesitation.

"We are a force to be reckoned with," Nate said with conviction, "and we're going to win."

And for that moment, Nadia allowed herself to believe it.

Тне plan to spend the daylight hours sleeping made perfect sense. They were all exhausted, and if anyone had slept at all on the ride back from the Sanctuary, it had been for scant minutes at a time.

Nadia and Agnes shared the bed that had once belonged to Dante's parents, while Dante slept in his own bed and left the couch for Nate. If Dante was trying to needle Nate by relegating him to the couch, it didn't work. Nadia felt oddly proud of him for his lack of reaction.

It was actually Agnes who felt the most obvious discomfort at their surroundings, looking at the double bed she was to share with Nadia with distaste.

"Beggars can't be choosers," Nadia told her as she pulled back the covers. "And right now, we're beggars."

"I know," Agnes said, chewing her lip. "But . . . I've never slept in someone else's bed before. I mean, in a guest room, sure, but, you know . . ."

"There's a first time for everything," Nadia said, because apparently she was too tired to speak in anything other than clichés. She couldn't think of a time when *she'd* slept in another person's bed before, either, but that didn't stop her from sliding under the covers and laying her head on the lumpy pillow with a groan of relief. She hoped she was tired enough for sleep to overwhelm her quickly, rather than leaving her trapped with her own thoughts.

Agnes clearly wasn't as adaptable. She took off her shoes and earrings, and she took down the elaborate updo she'd worn for the opera, but she couldn't quite bring herself to get into the bed, so she merely lay on top of the covers instead. In her strapless evening gown, which likely had hard metal stays in its bodice. How was the girl going to survive the hardships of the Basement? She had been remarkably brave and cool last night, but she had been raised to slavishly follow the rules of Executive society, and to say she was now a fish out of water was an understatement.

Then again, Nadia had been raised the same way, had long lived in dread of taking a single misstep. Defying authority was hardly in her blood, but necessity had changed her. Maybe it would change Agnes, too.

Discomfort from the evening gown aside, Agnes seemed to fall asleep about five seconds after she lay down, her breathing growing deep and even while Nadia found she couldn't even keep her eyes closed. Instead, she lay on her side and stared at a hairline crack in the paint of the far wall. And with no immediate threat bearing down on her, with no decisions to be made right this moment, she couldn't stop herself from thinking about Gerri.

Tears ran sideways down her face and soaked into the pillow, pain wrenching her heart. Gerri had died because she'd wanted to save Nadia from a lifetime in the Sanctuary. And because Nadia had refused to tell her the truth about what was on those recordings. Because Nadia hadn't trusted her own sister to do the right thing.

Nadia's shoulders started shaking, and she stifled a sob.

The last thing she wanted to do was wake Agnes and have to deal with a near-stranger's pity. Unfair, perhaps, when that near-stranger had very possibly destroyed her whole life in an effort to help her, but feelings don't care whether they're fair or not.

Swallowing convulsively, trying not to gasp too loudly for air that suddenly seemed thin and inadequate, Nadia slipped out of the bed. The pain of guilt and loss doubled her over, and she put her hand over her mouth to try to hold it all in. Agnes didn't stir, but Nadia knew it was only a matter of time. She staggered out into the hall, planning to lock herself in the bathroom and sob her heart out, but when she turned to close the door, she saw Nate draped awkwardly over the living room couch.

As if he felt her gaze upon him, Nate turned his head and opened his eyes. Her face must have looked awful, because he sat up quickly and held his arms out to her. The idea of crying in the bathroom lost its appeal, and Nadia quickly crossed the distance between them and practically flung herself into his arms. She tried her best to muffle her sobs against his chest while he held her tightly and rocked her back and forth, an anchor in her storm of emotion.

She cried until her throat was raw and her head felt swollen to twice its normal size. Her eyes burned and her chest ached. Mingled with the devastating grief was a rage so enormous she didn't know how she could ever manage to hold it in, and if Chairman Hayes were to appear before her, she knew she would happily kill him with her own two hands.

"I'm so sorry, Nadia," Nate said into her hair, his own voice choked with sympathy. "There's nothing I can do to make this right, but I swear to you, if it's in my power, I will make my father pay for what he did."

Nadia squeezed him tightly, grateful for his steadfast support. Cold logic told her that their impromptu teen resistance movement was just a pretty fantasy to hang their faltering hopes on, but she didn't voice her doubt.

"Thank you."

And although she figured she should wash her face and get back to bed, Nadia found she needed the warmth of Nate's friendship too much to go anywhere just now. She'd bask in it just a little longer before she made another attempt to sleep . . .

CHAPTER TWENTY-SEVEN

nate's foot was going numb, but he didn't have the heart to move and risk waking Nadia. She had fallen asleep on the heels of her violent burst of emotion. He considered picking her up and carrying her back to her bed, but figured that if she'd found rest in his arms, he ought to leave her there. He closed his own eyes and hoped he'd drift off, but there was little chance of that. The couch hadn't been that comfortable to start with, and it was even less so now that he was semi-sitting up and had Nadia sleeping on him.

In truth, Nate didn't think there'd been much chance of him sleeping anyway. He was mentally and physically exhausted, but not enough to make his mind shut up.

It was all well and good for the four of them to run to the Basement and hide out with Kurt somewhere. Certainly it would lower the chances that they'd be apprehended by Paxco security officers. But it was hardly what you'd call a permanent solution. After all, even in the Basement, you needed money, and they didn't have any. And how were three Executive teens and a Paxco security spy going to survive in the Basement? All well and good to declare they would set themselves up as their own resistance movement, but the *real* resistance movement had money and connections and resources . . . It was hard to put up much of a fight without any of that.

If Paxco security didn't track them down and arrest them

all for treason, then the more predatory of the Basement-dwellers would probably pick them off one by one as they tried to adapt to a life they weren't suited for. Hell, for all he knew, Dante's resistance buddies would be after them, too, wanting to eliminate the potential danger they could represent if they were arrested. Unless they could somehow, impossibly, beat the combined forces of his father and Thea, the future was looking far from bright.

Nate sighed and shifted around a bit on the couch, drawing a sleepy protest from Nadia.

No matter how he looked at it, he couldn't see a way out. His father had all the resources and power of Paxco at his fingertips; Nate and his friends had nothing. How could they possibly hope to do battle with, or even hide from, the Chairman of the richest, most powerful state in the world?

As the day crawled endlessly by, Nate kept chewing the problem over, his mind going in endless circles until eventually, the pull of sleep became too strong.

nate awoke to the feel of a warm hand resting on the side of his face and an even warmer pair of lips brushing against his. He blinked his eyes open to find the living room cloaked in darkness. Kurt was squatting on his heels next to the couch, a fond smile on his face barely illuminated by the streetlight that shone right outside the closed blinds.

"Time to wake up," Kurt whispered.

Nate had to blink a couple more times to orient himself. He was still reclined on Dante's couch, with Nadia lying half on top of him and deeply asleep. He could hardly feel the left side of his body, and his back and neck were throbbing steadily to the beat of his heart. He stifled the urge to explain away Nadia's presence. Kurt's smile and affectionate greeting made it clear he wasn't subject to inappropriate jealousy like Nate was.

"What time is it?" Nate asked, wondering if he could move without accidentally dumping Nadia to the floor.

"A little after six," Kurt replied, no longer whispering. "You all sleep like the dead. I knocked, but no one answered. I had to let myself in."

Nadia stirred against Nate's chest, trying to roll away from him, still half-asleep. There was nowhere for her to roll to, so Nate tightened his arms around her to keep her from falling to the floor. She jerked fully awake, and they might both have ended up on the floor if Kurt hadn't reached out to steady her. She sat up with a groan.

In the dim light, she barely looked like the Nadia Nate had known for most of his life. Her hair was tangled and stuck to the leftover tear tracks on her face, and her eyes were sunken. Sleep had given her some respite from grief, but he could almost see the realization that Gerri was gone creeping over her face. She swallowed hard and started brushing her hair away from her face, subtly scrubbing at the crust around her eyes.

"I'm so sorry about your sister," Kurt said to her with genuine sympathy.

She nodded a thanks but seemed unable to muster any words.

"Guess I'll go roust Dante out of bed," Kurt said, standing up. "I'll leave the Executive chick to you guys, 'cause she'd probably run screaming if I was the first thing she saw waking up."

Probably so, Nate thought with a smile. Kurt's hair was definitely growing back, but it looked like he was cultivating a Mohawk. He was wearing a silver mesh shirt that showed off his tattoos, along with pleather pants cut so low you could probably see his butt crack when he bent over. Add to that the three tons of metal in his ears and the facial piercings, and he looked like an Executive girl's version of the bogeyman.

"I'll get Agnes," Nadia said, her voice gravelly and rough, though Nate wasn't sure if that was from sleep or the remnants of her tears.

"Don't turn on any lights," Kurt warned. "This apartment has been dark for months. We don't want any neighbors noticing it's not empty anymore."

Nadia nodded, and she and Kurt headed toward the bedrooms to deliver their wake-up calls while Nate stretched and winced and shook his extremities in an effort to restore feeling to them. He was so stiff he felt about ninety years old, and his leg muscles were embarrassingly sore after last night's run. His joints popped and crackled, and in that moment when he wasn't really thinking about anything except his own physical discomfort, he finally realized what he had to do to protect himself and Nadia and their friends from his father's wrath and malice.

This morning, he'd come to the conclusion that they couldn't defeat or hide from a man who had all the resources of Paxco at his fingertips. The only reason Nathaniel Hayes Sr. had all that power at his fingertips was because he was the Chairman. Therefore, to remove the threat to himself and to his friends, Nate had to make it so his father wasn't Chairman anymore.

Nate stood stock still and pursued that line of thought as the others shuffled into the living room, all except Kurt looking decidedly worse for wear. Agnes was still wearing her ridiculous pink evening gown, only now the ruffles were all wrinkled, making it even uglier. She recoiled when she caught sight of Kurt, and though she quickly gained control of herself, she was still visibly tense and ready to bolt when Nadia introduced them.

"I have an idea," Nate announced, his heart pounding as

he anticipated stating his idea out loud. Somehow, he didn't think anyone was going to like it very much. He couldn't say *he* was all that fond of it himself, come to think of it. But even a bad idea seemed better than no idea.

"Glad to hear it," Kurt said, "'cause this lot won't last a week in Debasement. I could hide one of you, maybe even two, though that would be a stretch. But four?" He shook his head. "Not happening, least not for more than a day or two."

Nate reached up and rubbed his still-stiff neck. Kurt was actually being more diplomatic now than he had been this morning when Nate had called. He'd been eager to help Nate, willing to help Dante, and grudgingly willing to help Nadia. Agnes—a highborn Executive he'd never met—had been a real sticking point, but Nate wasn't about to abandon her now. He still couldn't say he liked her, but he didn't *dis*like her anymore, and it was his fault she'd gotten sucked into all this.

"I know hiding us is going to be hard and that it's just temporary," Nate said. "Why don't you all sit down and I'll tell you what I have in mind."

He was greeted by expressions of polite skepticism, which he might have found insulting if he weren't so aware of his own shortcomings. He had spent many years painting himself as the feckless playboy who was well short of a rocket scientist on the intelligence scale. He doubted even Kurt and Nadia, who knew him best, expected him to come up with a viable plan.

And maybe they were right. Maybe his was the stupidest idea in the universe. If so, he was sure the others—especially Dante—would be happy to let him know.

Nate remained standing while the others all sat. Dante, unable to resist the urge to be a prick, sat beside Nadia on the couch and put a possessive arm around her shoulders. Nate was predictably irritated—and Agnes looked like she might faint in shock at the impropriety—but he kept his irritation to himself. He had more important things to concentrate on, like how he was going to present his idea without the others thinking he was a dangerous lunatic.

Nate rubbed his hands together, then abruptly stopped when he realized it was a nervous gesture. "So, um . . ." *Brilliant start. Way to fill everyone with confidence.* "As long as my father is the Chairman of Paxco, we're all basically screwed." That was a fact no one could argue with. "Nadia and I know something that he would kill to keep from getting out." He looked at Nadia's pale face and gentled his voice. "Actually, he *has* killed for it." More than once, in fact, seeing as he'd had the original Nate killed for discovering the truth. "Last night, he tried to have Nadia murdered in her sleep, and I doubt it would have been long before I met with some kind of 'accident' myself."

So far, he wasn't telling them anything they didn't know, and they all watched him with varying degrees of interest—except for Dante, whose expression said he was just humoring the useless aristocrat who liked to hear himself talk.

"Because my father can't be sure we haven't told all of you what we know, he'll want to eliminate you, too."

"Eliminate, as in kill?" Agnes asked. "I'm the daughter of a foreign Chairman; surely—"

"He has no compunction about charging teenage girls with treason," Nate interrupted. "You're in Paxco, not Synchrony, and *my* father is in control here, not yours. Hell, he might even charge your parents with something just to get them out of the way."

Agnes was deathly pale and seemed on the verge of tears. He felt bad for her, he really did. This was not the kind of trouble she'd bargained for when she'd come with him last night. But it was too late to go back now.

"So, like I said, as long as my father is Chairman, we're screwed. Which means if we don't want to live the rest of our short lives in miserable hiding, looking over our shoulders and waiting for the ax to fall, we have to make it so he's not the Chairman anymore."

That went over about as well as Nate expected. Lots of wide eyes and gaping mouths, and Agnes even gasped in shock.

Dante looked like he was fighting off laughter. "Man, when you said we should start our own resistance, you really weren't kidding!"

Kurt recovered the fastest, cocking his head and regarding Nate as if he'd never seen him before. "Are you suggesting we assassinate your father?"

"No," Nate answered quickly. He still had a lot of complicated feelings to work out about his father, but no matter how much he hated the man, he couldn't see himself stooping to cold-blooded murder. "I'm likely the only one who can get close to him, and I don't have it in me to just walk up to him and shoot him." Not to mention that if he murdered his father, Dorothy would have a legitimate reason to contest any attempt he made to seize the Chairmanship himself. He knew next to nothing about Dorothy, but he *did* know he didn't want her being the next Chairman of Paxco.

"So what do you mean when you say you want to make it so he's not Chairman anymore?" Nadia asked.

And here was where it was going to get really dicey. "My father wants to kill us because he wants to make sure his secret doesn't get out. He'll do just about *anything* to prevent that from happening. We don't have concrete proof in the form of recordings anymore, but we do have two eyewitnesses."

"Oh!" Nadia exclaimed as the virtual lightbulb went on over her head.

"If Nadia and I were to reveal what really happened on the day she was arrested, there would probably be people who wouldn't believe us without proof. But there would be a lot who *would* believe us, and the Chairman knows that. He wouldn't be so anxious to silence us if he weren't worried that we could do him damage."

"You know you're going to have to tell us what the hell this big secret is, right?" Dante said.

"Let me finish first," Nate said, locking eyes with Nadia. "My plan involves telling you what we know, but I'm not going to do it unless Nadia agrees."

"Go on," Nadia said. Her expression was perfectly neutral, giving him no clue as to what she thought.

"My idea is that we make our own recording. A video of me and Nadia talking about exactly what happened on that day and what we found out. We make five copies of it, and each of us hides our copy. Then I go and confront my father and tell him that if he doesn't step down, we'll release the video. With five copies out there, each individually hidden, it would be damn near impossible for him to find them all before at least one of them got out."

There was a moment of stunned silence, and Nate felt like he was dreaming, everything taking on a blurry feeling of unreality. Could any of this really be happening? Could he really be talking about taking over the Chairmanship? He'd been irresponsible and negligent as a Chairman Heir. How could he possibly handle become a freaking head of state? He was obviously nuts.

Kurt shook his head and looked at Nate with open shock. "What the fuck is this secret you think is big enough to make your father resign?"

"Language," Nate reminded him automatically, then wanted

to kick himself. Kurt wasn't his valet anymore, and it was no longer important that he learn to act socially acceptable in the Executive world. If he wanted to curse, he had every right to, despite the way it made Agnes squirm. Nadia, at least, had been around Kurt long enough to be inured to his fouler moments.

Kurt arched an eyebrow at him and affected an upper-crust accent. "I beg your pardon, Miss Belinski, Miss Lake."

"Oh, stuff it!" Nadia said while Agnes looked around as if in search of a place to hide. Nadia spared Kurt only a brief scowl before turning her attention back to Nate. "Your plan is to take over as Chairman of Paxco."

It sounded so . . . ridiculous when said out loud like that. Nate had to resist the urge to duck his head and hunch his shoulders in embarrassment.

"Um, basically, yes," he said, no doubt cementing everyone's opinion of him as a firm and decisive leader. He cleared his throat. "I couldn't be much worse than my father right now. Especially if Thea's still got her hooks in him, which she obviously does. And if I'm Chairman, I can make sure Thea is shut down permanently."

The loss of income Paxco would suffer without the Replica program would no doubt make Nate the most hated Chairman in his state's history, but it was the right thing to do. And surely their economy would recover eventually. Maybe it would even become more healthy, no longer relying so heavily on a single source of revenue.

"I know it sounds crazy," Nate said. "But if you accept what I said about us not being safe as long as he's Chairman, then I think the rest naturally follows."

A long, meditative silence followed. Kurt and Dante and Agnes were all obviously bursting with curiosity, dying to know what secret was so massive the Chairman might step down rather than letting it get out. And though it was Nate who was proposing he take over as Chairman, it was *Nadia* everyone looked to for a decision.

She thought about it for a long time, her brow creased with concentration. Nate kept expecting her to poke a hole in his plan, to point out something obvious that he'd overlooked, or even just to tell him that the idea of him being Chairman before he'd had at least another decade of training under his belt was too ridiculous to contemplate.

"Do you really think he'll step down?" she finally asked.

"I don't know," Nate replied, because it was the only answer he could give. His father was convinced that if the truth about Thea got out, it could spell doom for all of Paxco. Basement-dwellers would riot; dissidents would revolt; anyone who had a friend or relative die in prison would wonder if they'd been one of Thea's subjects. And possibly worst of all, other states that coveted their territory—and that already had serious moral qualms about the Replica program—might decide this was a good excuse to stage the kind of hostile takeover that left thousands of bodies in its wake. "If he thinks we'll really follow through on the threat, then maybe."

Nate didn't think the Chairman's ego could withstand the total devastation of his legacy that would come if the public ever learned about Thea. "I tried to blackmail him into not changing the marriage agreement, but he called my bluff. He said there would be no upside to releasing the recording, either to me or to Nadia, and that was why we wouldn't do it. But if he tries to call our bluff this time, then releasing the video would be our only chance of stopping Thea. And he knows that's something we think is worth doing."

"I have to come with you to confront him," Nadia said. "I

won't have any trouble convincing him I'd release the video, not after what he did to Gerri." Her voice was cold and hard, and the intensity in her eyes was chilling. "I don't care what I have to do to make him pay. If I have to shoot him dead, I'll do it. And if I have to release the video, I'll do that, too. Tell me there's any chance your father could see me now and not believe I mean it."

Everyone was looking at her with a kind of wary caution, Nate included. She didn't look at all like his childhood friend right now. She was an avenging angel whose eyes glowed with fury and hatred.

Nate dried his suddenly sweaty palms on his pant legs. She was right, and his father would believe her threat when he saw her face. But he wanted his gentle-natured, kindhearted friend back, wanted the girl with the easy smile and the rapier-quick wit. He didn't want to think that his own father's cruelty had destroyed what she had once been, but everyone had their breaking point.

Nadia met each of their gazes in turn, then gave a nod of satisfaction. "I didn't think so. Now, let me tell you exactly what Chairman Hayes is so desperate to make sure no one finds out . . ."

CHAPTER TWENTY-EIGHT

nadia's costume was relatively simple, if uncomfortably revealing, and it appeared to be the same one she'd worn on her one and only previous foray into the Basement: a skintight catsuit, a pink wig, and a band of black face paint over her eyes. Agnes helped her out with the paint, but was twitchy enough that she managed to get as much paint on her pink gown as she did on Nadia's face. Of course, ruining that gown was an act of mercy.

Agnes's costume was more of a challenge, the first part of which was getting Agnes to agree to wear it.

"I can't wear that!" she squeaked when she opened the package Kurt had brought her and found the neon-blue vinyl bodysuit with high-cut legs and enormous silver epaulets.

Nadia sympathized, but she kept her opinion to herself. "This is how people in the Basement dress," she said firmly, as if she made a habit of sightseeing in the Basement in her spare time. "I'm sure it will look better on than it does in the bag."

Agnes's eyes pooled with tears. "You can't be serious."

Nadia couldn't be sure in the dark, but she suspected Agnes's cheeks were crimson with embarrassment. "Bishop knows what he's doing," she soothed. "The most important thing is to make it so people don't recognize you, even if the outfit makes you feel uncomfortable. You don't imagine I feel comfortable in *this*, do you?" She indicated the catsuit with a sweep of her hand. She'd been mortified the first time she'd put it on, though she'd felt better about it when Dante had looked at her as if she were the hottest girl in the universe.

Agnes was never going to be the hottest girl in the universe, but Nadia could clearly see where Bishop was going with the costume. The epaulets and the lack of Agnes's habitual pleated pants or fluffy skirt would change her shape entirely, evening out her hips and shoulders. True, he *could* have just given her tightly fitted pants instead of the bodysuit, but Basement-dwellers did not go for subtlety.

Agnes picked the bodysuit up with two fingers as if afraid it would bite her. Shaking her head, she turned her back on Nadia and worked her way out of the pink monstrosity she'd worn to the opera. Nadia tactfully looked away while Agnes changed.

When she was ready, Agnes held the pink dress up against her as if to shield herself, and Nadia fought for patience. Getting this worked up over modesty when their lives were in danger was just plain silly. And the longer they took getting ready, the more risk that the authorities would show up to check out Dante's apartment.

Agnes dropped the dress, and Nadia rolled her eyes before she could stop herself. Luckily, Agnes was too sunk in her own misery to notice.

"Sweetie, you can't wear panties with that," she said with as much patience as she could muster.

Agnes looked down at herself, startled, and saw that the edges of her panties were showing all around the high legs of the bodysuit. Nate had described her as acting brave and calm the night before, but whatever courage had seized her during the rescue had clearly been used up.

Agnes shuddered, but started to take the bodysuit off again. Nadia didn't tap her foot, but she was sure her impatience was showing no matter how hard she was trying to hide it.

When next she turned around, Nadia found that Agnes had put the costume on properly and was now sticking her feet into the thigh-high platform boots that came with the outfit. The last item in her bag was a tube of blue gel, which neither of them knew what to do with. With Agnes as decent as she was going to get for the night, Nadia called Bishop in, and he explained the gel was for Agnes's hair. He made Agnes sit down—which was clearly hard to do in the stiff bodysuit—and squirted the entire tube of gel into her hair, using it to plaster her hair to her head in a hard blue cap.

"Don't worry," he assured Agnes, holding up his bright blue hands, "it washes off." He ducked into the bathroom to wash his hands, then displayed them for Agnes's benefit.

She was still teary-eyed and uncertain-looking, but she nodded.

The blue-haired Amazon looked nothing like the Agnes Belinski Nadia had known. Agnes would never be beautiful, but right now she was strikingly exotic. Sexy even, though Nadia doubted Agnes would think of herself that way. "You could walk by your own father and he'd never recognize you," Nadia told her.

"If you say so," Agnes mumbled, rubbing her hands up and down the thin mesh sleeves of her bodysuit. "I'm just glad there's no press to see me like this."

Nadia smiled. "Ditto."

"You both look great," Bishop said, "now let's get the fuck out of here before it's too late."

"Always such a gentleman," Nadia said, but she had long

ago developed an immunity to his foul mouth. And she was more than ready to get going.

The trip from Dante's apartment to the Basement could only be described as *harrowing*. While the five of them were all dressed in their best imitation of Basement regalia, they didn't fit in nearly as much as Nate would have liked. He—and presumably Dante, though Nate didn't know for sure—had spent enough time in the Basement not to be struck by culture shock the moment they crossed its border, but the same could not be said of the girls. Nadia had only set foot in the Basement once in her life, and that had been in a secluded, disused underpass where there were no Basement-dwellers except Kurt in sight. And Agnes . . . Well, Agnes couldn't have looked more screamingly uncomfortable and out of place if she were stark naked.

Agnes's vulnerability was so great—and so obvious—that Kurt and Dante flanked her as they made their way through the Basement fringes. Whether because they feared she would bolt, or because they were afraid she would attract predators, Nate didn't know.

The buildings in Debasement were all identical, bland concrete high-rises with cookie-cutter apartments that were available rent free. At least in theory. There was approximately zero security presence in Debasement, which left the gangs and other predators free to claim whatever territory they wanted and charge people whatever they wanted—whether in the form of money, goods, or services—for the privilege of living there.

The first few blocks of the Basement were a kind of borderland between polite society and the heart of Debasement. During the day, this was where respectable Executives and Employees went when they wanted to dabble in the black market. During the night, it was where respectable Executives and Employees who were too dumb to know better came as tourists to enjoy the bars, the clubs, the drugs, and the prostitutes. A chance to take a walk on the wild side and see how the "other half" lived. Nate knew because he'd been one of those dumb Executives himself, treating trips to the Basement as joyrides, completely blind to how he and others like him were exploiting the misery of their fellow human beings.

The apartment Kurt had claimed for his own was right at the edge of the neighborhood, perilously close to Debasement's gang-controlled heart, where even the bravest of tourists knew better than to set foot. He led them all inside, where they had to climb five flights of fire stairs to reach his floor because the elevator was broken. Nate didn't want to think about how people on the highest floors coped.

Nate had never been inside one of the buildings that was used as an actual residence before. He'd always stuck to the clubs, whose owners had gutted the interiors for their own purposes. Considering everything he knew about the Basement, Nate shouldn't have been shocked that the building was such a pathetic dump, but knowing something and seeing it with your own eyes were two different things.

The enclosed stairway reeked of urine, old smoke, and sweaty bodies. There were several places where the walls were pockmarked with what Nate figured had to be bullet holes, and only one out of every three fluorescent light fixtures was working.

Kurt's actual apartment wasn't much better, though at least it looked relatively clean and didn't stink. There was no furniture in the living room, only a scattering of sofa cushions that looked like they had been pillaged from the trash. The floor was covered in stained gray linoleum, which was peeling up in numerous places, and when Kurt switched on the lights, only a couple of the fluorescent bulbs overhead came on.

"You *live* here?" Nadia asked in amazement.

"You were expecting a palace?" Kurt countered as he closed the front door behind him. The array of shiny locks on the door, as well as the grid of metal reinforcements that crisscrossed it, were by far the newest and most sophisticated things in sight. Kurt saw Nate looking at them and gave him a crooked smile. "Security is priority number one around here," he said, patting the door like it was a favored pet. "I'll get shit like furniture and whatever eventually, but this had to come first."

Nate would have felt ridiculous bugging Kurt about his language here, so he didn't. He also tried really hard not to think about what Kurt was going to do if Nate's grand plan failed. The dollars Nate had given him obviously didn't stretch as far as Nate would have hoped if he was still at the point of considering furniture optional. And if Nate didn't manage to have himself named the new Chairman of Paxco, he would most likely end up dead and unable to funnel any more money to Kurt. Which meant Kurt would have no choice but to take up his prior occupation.

The thought made Nate shudder.

"We need to record the video and get this over with as soon as possible," he said.

"Agreed," Dante said. "You and Nadia need to get washed up and back into normal clothes."

"Those *are* normal clothes," Kurt said in mock offense.

"Back into *your* normal clothes," Dante corrected smoothly. "You need to look as respectable as possible for the video."

Nate wasn't sure how respectable either of them was going to look. He'd be wearing a stained, wrinkled, and generally worse-for-wear tux, and Nadia would be stuck wearing her retreat uniform. But if he wanted his father to take the threat seriously, they couldn't record the video in their Basement disguises, so their rumpled, slept-in clothes were the next best thing.

"Bathroom's down the hall to the right," Kurt said. "You're lucky to get five minutes' worth of lukewarm water, so wash up quick if you don't want to freeze your nuts off."

Nate gave him his best dirty look, sure Kurt was actively trying to offend the girls with his language. Either that, or keeping his potty mouth tamed had been more of an effort than Kurt had ever let on when he'd been working as Nate's valet.

"Why don't you hit the shower first," Nadia suggested to Nate, "since I don't have any nuts to freeze off if you use too much hot water."

Nate grinned. He should have known better than to think Nadia was that easily offended. And from the looks of her, Agnes was still too uncomfortable about her costume to pay much attention.

"I'll hurry anyway," he assured her, then headed toward the bathroom.

Debasement came alive at night, its streets teeming with forbidden pleasures and unseen dangers. Looking down at the crowded streets from Kurt's fifth-floor window, Nate was filled with a guilty yearning for the nights when he had traveled those streets as the Ghost, his Basement alter ego, with Kurt by his side. Nights when he'd been willfully oblivious to the squalor around him, blinded by the exotic trappings and the sense of being someone other than the Chairman Heir of Paxco for just a few hours.

How different the world had looked to him then. And how different his *future* had looked. His life had changed so much in the last handful of weeks, he could hardly comprehend it.

Nate turned from the window at the sound of a door opening behind him. He suffered another pang of guilt as he looked at the mattress that lay on the floor, covered with a yellowed sheet and a ratty blanket. While Nate had bedded down in silk sheets with a mound of down pillows, this was where Kurt had been sleeping.

"I've lived like this all my life," Kurt said from the doorway, naked except for the towel wrapped around his hips. "Doesn't bother me near as much as it does you."

Nate nodded, knowing it was true. But it didn't make him feel any better. The sorriest fact of all was that Nate would be more comfortable tonight than Dante and the girls. The mattress was the only bed-like piece of "furniture" in the apartment, and the others had to make do with the collection of mismatched sofa cushions that were scattered on the living room floor. Nate would have joined them to share in the misery, except this could very well be the last time he and Kurt ever saw each other.

Tomorrow morning, he and Nadia were going to Paxco Headquarters to confront the Chairman with their ultimatum. There were about twelve zillion things that could go wrong, and some of them could happen before Nate and Nadia ever reached the Chairman's office. Dante had checked the news feeds on his handheld after they'd made their video, and he'd seen that Nate was a wanted man, accused of having kidnapped Agnes Belinski. The chances that he would be spotted and arrested before he got in to see his father were way higher than he would like.

To reduce the risks as much as possible, Nate and Nadia planned to arrive at Headquarters well before business hours. There would be security officers on duty, but between the remnants of Nadia's knockout gas and the four guns they had between them, Nate figured there was a reasonable chance he and Nadia could get past those guards. Then all they'd have to do was ride the elevator to the top floor—assuming his father hadn't changed the access code, but Nate saw no reason why he would have. Surely he wouldn't guess that Nate would be so bold as to march into Paxco Headquarters.

By the time he and Nadia got into the Chairman's office, someone would have notified the Chairman of their presence, and it would turn into a wait-and-see situation.

Kurt dropped the towel, instantly pulling Nate back into the present. Tomorrow might turn out to be hell, but at least for the few short hours until dawn, he would lose himself in Kurt's arms and try to forget the rest of the world existed. His heart quickened at the thought. And wouldn't you know it, when he slipped under the ratty covers and lay on the lumpy mattress, it felt better than the finest bed when Kurt slid in beside him.

nadia was way too wired—and too uncomfortable—to sleep. She'd never slept on the floor before, and she hoped she'd never have to do it again. The pair of mismatched sofa cushions she was using for her "bed" were woefully thin and harbored the faint scents of smoke and mildew.

Eventually, she gave up the effort, sitting up and wrapping her arms around her knees. On one side of her, Agnes was fast asleep, her body curled into a protective ball on her nest of cushions. On the other side, Dante sprawled in what looked like total comfort, although he'd only taken one cushion for himself and most of his body lay on the hard floor. Sleep softened some of the harsher angles of his face, making him look warmer and more approachable, despite his Ninja-warrior-black outfit. Nadia wondered what it would feel like to curl up against his body, to let him wrap those powerful arms of his around her.

The temptation to find out was so strong she forced herself to her feet and moved away, tiptoeing to one of the windows on the far side of the room. Turning her back on Dante, she leaned against the sill and peered out.

It wasn't what you'd call a picturesque view. The bland high-rises of the Basement formed a wall of solid gray that kept visibility to a minimum. The street below was crowded and noisy, despite the fact that it was well after midnight. From above, the Basement-dwellers in their colorful, outlandish regalia looked rather like a group of seedy circus clowns gathering for a block party. Except when she looked more closely, the resemblance to clowns faded. The clothing, both on the men and on the women, was way too revealing, for one thing. And no one seemed to be having any fun, despite the occasional raucous bursts of laughter. Everyone out there was doing business of one sort or another, and their eyes were always searching their surroundings for a hint of danger. Danger one unfortunate man seemed to have found, as three Basement-dwellers descended on him and started beating him. No one paid them any mind, stepping around the altercation without sparing it a glance.

"There but for the grace of God . . ." Dante whispered, and Nadia swallowed a yelp of surprise.

She put her hand to her chest as if the touch could calm her suddenly racing heart. "You scared me," she said.

"Sorry," he murmured, sidling up behind her and putting his arms around her waist.

Her heart thumped for a different reason as Dante's body pressed up against hers and he nuzzled her neck. It had been a while since he'd shaved, and his whiskers scratched in a way that was surprisingly sexy. She glanced over her shoulder to reassure herself that Agnes was still asleep.

"Behave," she told Dante breathlessly, as his lips brushed against her skin.

"Why?" he countered. "If tomorrow goes badly, we may never see each other again. You don't suppose Nate and Bishop are 'behaving' in that bedroom, do you?"

Nadia had no desire to speculate about what Nate and Bishop were doing. "But they *have* a bedroom," she said, though despite her halfhearted protest, she found herself leaning into his warmth and stretching her neck to give him better access. They had had so little time together, so little opportunity to explore. She'd experienced her first real kiss with Dante, and she very much wanted more. But not when they had an audience, even if that audience was currently asleep. There was no guarantee she'd stay that way. "With a door that closes."

Dante nipped lightly on her earlobe, and her breath caught in her throat. "There *is* a second bedroom," he murmured. "And its door closes, too." She swallowed hard. "Of course, there's no bed in it, but we can improvise."

Nadia shivered and her skin prickled with goose bumps. It was very possible she might die tomorrow. Tonight might be the only chance she ever had.

Dante's arms tightened around her. "I'm not trying to

pressure you," he assured her. "I just don't want you to let Agnes get in the way of what you want. Er, if you want it, that is."

Nadia smiled, glad to know Dante wasn't quite as smooth and confident as he'd been making himself out to be. But at least he knew what he wanted, which was more than she could say for herself.

Actually, that wasn't true. She knew *exactly* what she wanted, and it was something she didn't have: time. Time to take things slowly and see where they led. Time to figure out just how she felt about Dante and ease into the kind of relationship she'd never allowed herself to think about having when she'd been promised to Nate. Time to make a decision based on mutual desire instead of desperation.

Dante turned her around and cupped her face in his hands. "Sorry," he said, then pressed a light kiss to her lips. He sighed. "I'm pressuring you whether I mean to or not."

"No—" she started, but he silenced her with another kiss.

"If suggesting tonight might be the last time we see each other isn't pressuring you, I don't know what is. I'm being an asshole."

Nadia smiled up at him. He was the perfect antidote to all the pain and ugliness that surrounded her, someone strong and thoughtful and honorable. The warm glow in her chest told her she could easily find herself falling in love with him. Or maybe she'd done that already.

"I've known more than my fair share of assholes," she said. "You're not one of them."

Dante took both her hands in his and squeezed so tight it almost hurt. "Promise me you'll come back to me. Promise . . . Promise you'll win." His voice was choked. "You have no idea how hard it is for me not to beg you to let Nate go alone."

"Would it make it any easier to resist if I told you nothing's going to change my mind?"

He sighed. "I already knew that."

"I have every intention of winning," she told him, putting every ounce of confidence she could muster into her voice. "This is *not* the last time we'll see each other. I won't let it be."

Dante enveloped her in a hug, and Nadia prayed with all her being that she would be able to keep her promise.

CHAPTER TWENTY-NINE

NOW that Dante was in the resistance's doghouse, he no longer had access to a car. Nate and Nadia didn't dare take public transportation to get to the Headquarters building—way too much chance of being spotted and recognized. That left car theft as the only feasible alternative.

There were very few cars in the Basement—only the gang lords and drug kingpins could afford such an extravagance—which meant they had to obtain their vehicle from the low-rent Employee neighborhood that bordered the Basement. Nadia didn't like that part of their plan one bit. Anyone living in that neighborhood who drove a car had either sunk his or her life savings into it or was driving a company-issued car and would have his or her pay docked if it went missing.

"We'll just be borrowing it," Dante assured her as he set out just before five in the morning to procure their ride. "The owner will have it back in one piece by the end of the day. And if Nate's plan works, you'll have enough money to more than make up for the inconvenience."

Nadia didn't mention that she also didn't like the risk Dante was taking upon himself in venturing out to steal the car. However, he was the only one of the five of them who had the skills to pull it off.

"Be ready when I get back," Dante said. "We have to move super fast."

"Just go already," Nate said irritably from the living room, where he'd taken to pacing like a caged animal. He didn't like depending on Dante any more than Nadia did, only she suspected it was for different reasons.

Dante didn't respond to Nate's prodding, unless you could call the heady kiss he gave Nadia in farewell a response. Nate said something she was sure wasn't complimentary under his breath.

"See you soon," Dante said, and then he was gone.

Bishop parked himself by the window, leaning on the sill and looking out. Dante would signal with his headlights as he drove up, and Bishop would let Nate and Nadia know it was time to go. Agnes was back in her pink dress, huddled in a corner half-asleep. She had torn out a layer of petticoat from beneath the skirt and was using that petticoat as a makeshift shawl to keep her shoulders warm. The gel had not washed out of her hair as cleanly as Bishop had claimed it would, so her hair was baby-blanket blue. Nadia was desperately worried about what would happen to the girl if she and Nate failed. Dante and Bishop were both tough and strong-willed, with a heavy dose of streetsmarts to boot. They had a decent shot of protecting themselves if everything went to hell. Agnes, on the other hand, was spectacularly ill-equipped for a life on the run.

"Kurt and Dante will take care of her if need be," Nate said practically in her ear, and Nadia jumped. She'd been so focused on Agnes she hadn't even noticed him approaching.

Nadia slipped her hand into his and squeezed. "Let's hope they don't need to." She met his eyes and saw the same combination of fear and determination that she suspected he saw in hers.

Nate resumed his pacing, and Nadia resumed her pointless

worrying, until a few minutes later, when Bishop came to attention at the window.

"Showtime," he told them, grabbing the thin sheet that he'd bundled up by his feet. The chances that anyone in Debasement would see them getting into the car, recognize them, and report them were incredibly low, but why risk it? They'd look weird running around with a sheet draped over them, but weird was better than recognized.

Nadia looked away, not wanting to intrude while Bishop gave Nate a kiss good-bye. Then Bishop helped drape the sheet over them so that it would hide their faces and as much of their bodies as they could manage, and they hurried down to the first floor to be ready when the car pulled up.

They made it into the backseat of the car without incident.

"Stay down," Dante ordered them unnecessarily. They had already been over the plan about twenty-five times, and it involved eliminating any chance of anyone seeing and recognizing them before they reached Headquarters.

Nate squeezed himself into the tight space on the floor behind the passenger seat, while Nadia lay down on the backseat. They kept the sheet draped over them for maximum anonymity, even though it made the air feel stuffy and close. Or maybe that was just Nadia's nerves.

"Are we completely insane to try this?" Nate muttered as the car bumped its way over the poorly maintained streets of the Basement.

Nadia shrugged. "Maybe. But I didn't come up with any new options overnight, and I guess you didn't either, so we're kinda stuck with it."

That was the last of the conversation. The ride soon smoothed out, the car having crossed the Basement's border.

It seemed to take forever to get to Headquarters, though Nadia supposed it wasn't much more than twenty-five minutes with the thin traffic of early morning. She couldn't wait to get out from under the suffocating sheet and actually *do* something. The worry and anticipation were surely going to drive her insane if she had to stay still any longer.

"We're only a couple of blocks away," Dante said, breaking the long silence. "Get ready."

Nadia patted the pockets of her much-loathed retreat uniform, making doubly sure she had her canister of knockout gas and the small gun she'd taken from Lily within easy reach. She heard Nate similarly patting himself down, then heard a soft click, which she gathered was the sound of him turning off the safety on Fischer's gun. He was also carrying the gun Nadia had taken from the tower guard as a backup. She closed her eyes and prayed they didn't have to shoot people who were just trying to do their jobs. But if that was what she had to do to protect herself and her friends, she was determined to do it.

"One block," Dante counted down. Then, several seconds later, "I'm about to pull up to the curb. There's one guy stationed by the door, and I see another sitting at the security kiosk."

The Chairman's private entrance was located at the back of the building, far from the public entrance and the historic art deco lobby. If the Chairman were inside, the security presence would be more substantial and visible, although even if the entrance were unmanned, the place was the next best thing to impenetrable. It would take a rocket launcher to get through the high-tech glass doors—unless you were the Chairman Heir and had access rights.

"Are you ready?" Nate asked.

"As ready as I'll ever be," Nadia answered.

"Yeah. Me too."

The car slowed, and Nadia helped Nate pull the sheet off them so they wouldn't get tangled up in it when they tried to get out. It was still dark, but the streetlights were momentarily blinding, and Nadia had to blink a few times to clear her vision.

Then the car came to a complete stop, and Nate sprang up from the floor and opened the door.

nate might have found the look of shock on the security guard's face funny if his heart weren't beating from somewhere in the vicinity of his throat. Behind him, he heard Dante gun the engine of his stolen car. Nate didn't want the guard to pay attention to the car or try to get its license plate, so he pulled his keys out of his pocket, making it obvious he planned to enter the building with or without any assistance. He'd never had to unlock the door before—he barely showed up during working hours, much less when the building was locked up—but he knew he needed the physical key before he could trigger the retinal scanner, the fingerprint scanner, and the voice-recognition software. He would probably have looked more authoritative if he actually knew which key it was instead of shuffling through them indecisively.

The guard, looking totally flummoxed, called something over his shoulder, alerting the guy at the kiosk that something was up. Between the two of them, they would eventually scrape up the nerve to try to detain him, but right now they were both too stunned. There were three keys on his ring that Nate couldn't identify, but before he decided which one to try first, the guard opened the door for him. Either he was being habitually polite to the Chairman Heir, or he thought it would be easier to arrest him if he let him in.

The guy at the kiosk was on the phone when Nate stepped inside, Nadia close on his heels.

"I wish to speak to my father when he gets in," Nate told the door guard, keeping his voice calm and easy, as if nothing out of the ordinary were going on. "I'll just go on up and wait for him in his office."

The guard blinked, still looking confused, but the confusion gave way to determination before Nate's eyes. The guard's hand started moving toward his gun, but Nate pulled his own out of his pocket first. He pointed it at the door guard while angling his body so that the guy at the kiosk wouldn't be able to see.

"No one has to get hurt here," Nate said. "All I want to do is talk to my father. If he wants me arrested after we've talked, then you'll arrest me. But right now, you're going to walk with me to the elevator and stay between me and your friend over there." Nate jerked his chin toward the kiosk, where the second guard was just hanging up the phone.

Nate grabbed the door guard's arm to make sure he didn't bolt, and Nadia relieved him of his sidearm. The second guard was leaving the kiosk, reaching for his own gun as he came toward them.

"Let's go," Nate said, putting his gun to the door guard's head and jerking him toward the elevators. "And tell your friend to back off and put his gun down."

"Give it up, Mr. Hayes," the other guard said. He had his gun drawn, but wasn't pointing it yet. Nate suspected the man didn't much like the idea of pointing a gun at the Chairman Heir, wanted man or not. "There's no way out of this."

Nate laughed, hoping he sounded confident instead of

scared. "In case you didn't notice, I'm trying to get *in,* not out." Being very careful to keep his hostage between himself and the other guard, Nate started moving toward the elevator, Nadia right behind him. "Like I told your buddy here, all I'm going to do is go up to my father's office and wait for him. You can apprehend me afterward."

"That's not the way it works, son," the other guard said, his gun finally coming up and pointing in their direction. If worse came to worst, Nate could use the door guard as a human shield, but he really hoped it wouldn't come to that. "Put the gun down and put your hands up."

They had reached the bank of elevators, and Nadia hit the call button. "We're both armed, officer," she said, holding up the massive gun she'd taken from the door guard's holster. "And believe me, after all the crap we've been through, we're both dangerous, too. Just stay back and let us go up to the Chairman's office. As you said, we're not getting out of here. No reason to start a shoot-out when you've got us surrounded."

A couple of other security guards had emerged from other parts of the building, and Nate heard the sound of sirens approaching. It was definitely time to hurry the hell up.

The elevator dinged. Out of the corner of his eye, Nate saw Nadia turn and point the gun toward the car as the doors opened. Which was a good thing, because there were two guards inside, ready to charge out at them.

"Hold your breath, Nate," Nadia said.

There was a hissing sound that could only be her little can of knockout gas being discharged, and then the thump of two bodies hitting the elevator floor. Nadia walked into the elevator, gingerly stepping over the limp guards, and held the door for him as he backed in. She disarmed the unconscious men, then took Nate's keys from his pocket and inserted the appropriate one in the elevator's control panel. Nate told her his clearance code, which she entered into the keypad, and the doors began to slide closed. Nate considered shoving the door guard out, but decided to keep his human shield instead.

The elevator rose with stomach-rolling speed. Nate wanted to take a deep breath to help calm his nerves, but the faint medicinal scent in the car suggested there might still be enough knockout gas in the air to make a deep breath inadvisable. His ears popped hard enough to hurt, and within seconds the doors opened onto the building's top floor.

During business hours, there would be at least three security guards in the reception area alone, but not now, before dawn. Nate stepped aside so that Nadia could get out of the elevator first, holding her gun at the ready as if she were well trained in the art of using it. Which, of course, she wasn't, but Dante had given them both pointers on how to project an aura of competence.

Nate backed out of the car, still dragging the door guard with him. Just as the doors started to close, Nate gave the guard a hard shove back into the car. Nadia sprayed another dose of knockout gas for good measure, and by the time the car started back down, there were three unconscious guards on its floor.

Nate finally took the deep breath he'd been craving. "So far, so good," he said, and Nadia smiled at him gamely.

"Now all we have to do is live through the hard part."

CHAPTER THIRTY

The most secure location in the entire Paxco Headquarters Building was, naturally, the Chairman's office. Nate let himself and Nadia in, then engaged its entire series of locks, meant only for emergencies. Two of those locks were good, old-fashioned dead bolts—locks that would still do their jobs in the event of a power outage.

The front door was the only way in, but there was a hidden emergency exit behind a decorative bookcase, filled with leather-bound antique tomes so pristine they'd probably never even been opened, much less read. There would be no getting *in* through that door, but Nate figured it wouldn't hurt to check it out anyway while they were waiting for his father to arrive. He put his shoulder to the bookcase, prepared for heavy labor, but found it was on rails and slid aside with relative ease to reveal the door behind it.

"What's that?" Nadia asked.

"It's an emergency exit," Nate replied as he opened the door into a small, concrete-lined stairwell. This door was fitted with even more locks than the front entrance, and was reinforced with steel. Nate didn't know if it had once been a fire exit, or if it had been created from scratch when the Empire State Building had been gutted and repurposed as Paxco Headquarters.

He stepped out onto the landing and peeked over the edge

to see the endless flights of stairs leading down. He supposed the stairs were necessary for certain kinds of emergency situations—like, say, when there was a fire or a power outage that made the elevators unusable—but it made his body ache just thinking about going down them. The office was on the 102nd floor, and that was a whole lot of stairs to descend.

"If things go to hell," Nate called over his shoulder, "we'll use this exit to run for it."

Nadia peeked in and gave him a doubtful nod. They both knew that if things went to hell, they weren't getting out of here. That didn't mean they wouldn't try.

Since the door wasn't that hard to open, Nate went ahead and closed it and slid the bookcase back into place. There was no reason to broadcast their escape plan, even if it wouldn't be anything like a surprise to his father. They both knew the exit existed, and it was the only logical way for Nate and Nadia to try to get out, if it came to that.

The phone inside the office rang, and both Nate and Nadia jumped at the sound. Their eyes met across the room. The phone rang a second time.

"I guess that's for us," Nate said, because there was no way a call for his father was coming in to the office at 6:00 A.M.

"Are you going to answer it?"

The phone rang a third time, and Nate couldn't think of any reason not to pick up. It wasn't like security could arrest him over the phone. He grabbed the receiver.

"Yeah?" he said, because *hello* just didn't seem right for the occasion.

"I hear you want to talk to me," his father said.

The calm, cool voice of the man who had raised him made Nate shiver. Nate was sweating with nerves, and his father sounded about as worked up as he would be if he took a sip of his coffee and found it had gone cold.

"That's right," Nate said. He sounded like a scared little boy to his own ears, not at all the bold rebel who planned to demand the Chairman step down in his favor.

"I'm on my way. But son, the smartest thing you can do is use the emergency exit and get out before I get there."

Nate snorted. "Yeah, right. You think I'm going to make it that easy for you?"

"There are things going on you don't know about." Maybe Nate was imagining things, but he thought he heard an uncharacteristic edge of worry in his father's voice. Not that Nate gave a damn.

"You mean things like you murdering Gerri Lake and trying to have Nadia killed?"

"That wasn't me."

Nate laughed. It was either that or scream. That his father would try to deny he was behind it all was positively maddening. How stupid did he think Nate was?

"You know what, Dad? Fuck you. We'll talk when you get here."

Nate hung up the phone with a resounding bang, his heart pumping hard enough he figured Nadia could hear it from her perch across the room. She was chewing her lip anxiously and looked pale and fragile, but even so, she looked more together than he felt. He'd come here certain he wasn't capable of cold-bloodedly killing his own father, but judging by the intensity of his rage, he was no longer so sure.

"You're going to have to do most of the talking," Nate said. "A few sentences on the phone were enough to make me want to kill him with my bare hands."

"You expect me to be more reasonable?" Nadia asked. "He

had my sister killed, Nate. It's going to take everything I have not to shoot him the moment he shows his face."

She had a point. Negotiations of the kind they were about to attempt were best carried out with a cool head. Shouting expletives and broadcasting uncertainty weren't the best ways of establishing themselves as negotiating from a position of power. Nate closed his eyes and wished it weren't too early in the morning for a drink. He probably had too much adrenaline in his system for alcohol to even take the edge off unless he drank it in larger-than-advisable quantities, but the illusion that he was doing *something* to steady himself would have been nice. Something other than pacing a rut in the floor, that is.

The phone rang again within seconds of Nate having hung up, but he felt no inclination to answer. Voice mail picked up, but a different line started ringing almost instantly. Nate turned the ringer off, because the sound was getting on his nerves.

The good news was that his father had been telling the truth when he said he was on his way. The room was well soundproofed for privacy, but, even so, Nate and Nadia could hear the evidence of people gathering outside, if only because they themselves were so quiet. Of course the Chairman wouldn't show up without a large entourage, including bodyguards. Even to meet with his own son.

There was a knock on the door, and then Nate heard his father's voice, much muffled by the soundproofed door.

"I'm here, son," he said. "Let me in."

"Only you!" Nate shouted. "Your bodyguards and the rest of your entourage stay outside."

"Understood."

Just because the Chairman said "understood" didn't mean he was planning to comply. Nate raised his gun and positioned himself so it would be the first thing his father saw.

"Do me a favor and open the door, would you?" he asked Nadia. "And stay behind it until he's safely in."

She nodded and unlocked the locks one by one as Nate listened to the sound of blood rushing in his ears and tried to ignore the sweat he felt beading on his brow.

The last lock snicked open, and Nadia looked at him for a signal. He nodded, and she opened the door just enough for someone to slip in.

Nate half-expected the security team to rush the door. After all, for all he knew, his father had stepped aside the moment he'd heard the locks opening. There was no peephole to show them what was just outside the door. There were surveillance cameras that his father could access from his desk, but Nate didn't know his password so couldn't get to the feed. His finger tightened on the trigger in preparation.

But when the door opened, only his father stood there. Nate had the vague impression of maybe ten or twenty more guys milling about, but the Chairman was blocking his view.

The Chairman had sounded like his usual calm, dispassionate self on the phone, but in person he didn't seem to be quite so calm after all. His face was paler than usual, and his body screamed with tension. And not because Nate had a gun to his head. Nate doubted his father believed he would shoot, though he would be cautious on the off chance he was wrong.

"Come on in," Nate said, backing up to give him space while keeping the gun firmly pointed at his head. "Move slowly. And if anyone else tries to come with you, I'll shoot."

His father hesitated on the threshold, and Nate had the strangest impression he was trying to convey some kind of silent message with his eyes. It was no doubt a ploy of some sort, but it didn't work, since Nate didn't get whatever it was his father was trying to communicate.

"Are you coming in, or aren't you?" he prodded. The gun was surprisingly heavy, and Nate's muscles already felt a little shaky holding it up. Of course, holding a gun to your father's head was somewhat unnerving, even when you hated the bastard.

With a look of resignation, the Chairman crossed the threshold.

Nadia heaved the door shut the moment the Chairman was clear, but she wasn't fast enough. Another figure darted in behind Nate's father. A tall, auburn-haired beauty Nate belatedly recognized as Dorothy, the impostor.

Nate was startled enough that he almost pulled the trigger by reflex as he jumped backward, trying to stay out of reach of the attack he was sure was coming. But as the door slammed shut behind Dorothy, he saw something that made his blood run cold and that turned his understanding of the situation sideways.

Dorothy had a gun. And it was digging into the small of his father's back.

when she saw an unfamiliar woman push her way into the room behind the Chairman, Nadia had a split second to decide what to do. She went with locking the door to make sure no one else came in, even though that left her with danger at her back. She slid the last lock home as quickly as possible, then pulled her gun and whirled.

She and Nate had discussed a lot of potential scenarios as they'd talked over their strategy for this morning. This was not one of them.

The woman who'd forced her way in had a firm grip on the back collar of the Chairman's shirt and jacket, fingers pulling the fabric tight enough to make him bend his head backward. She also had a small pistol in her other hand and was pointing that pistol at the Chairman's back.

Nate had backed off several steps, but was still pointing his gun at his father. Nadia supposed she could point hers as well, but it would most likely be redundant.

"I'd advise you to put down the gun, Nathaniel," the woman said, smiling smugly. "Daddy has already declared me the new Chairman Heir after you went and kidnapped a foreign Chairman's daughter. You don't want to make me Chairman so soon, do you?"

"Dorothy," Nadia muttered under her breath, realizing who the mysterious woman had to be even though they had never met.

"You'll want to put down your weapon, too, Miss Lake," Dorothy said without taking her attention away from Nate. "You've been quite the thorn in my side, and my first act as Chairman of Paxco would be to order your death."

Nate had not lowered his weapon. His eyes swam with confusion, and there was a fine sheen of sweat on his brow, and yet he still gave the impression he had no intention of backing down.

"This is some kind of trick the two of you cooked up together," he said. "You think if you pretend to hold my father hostage, I'll go from hating his guts and wanting him dead to giving myself up to save his worthless life. Well, it won't work."

The explanation sounded plausible, but it seemed rather more extreme than necessary. Surely the Chairman wasn't *afraid* to confront the two of them, even though they were armed. He was arrogant enough to think he could talk his way out of any problem.

Dorothy shrugged. "If you think it's a trick, then call my bluff. Shoot him."

The Chairman tried to say something, but Dorothy tightened her grip on his collar and choked the sound off. Nate wavered, sending a quick glance Nadia's way. Asking for her help figuring things out, no doubt, but Nadia didn't have a clue.

"What is it you want, Dorothy?" Nadia asked, because it seemed like a reasonable question.

"That's 'Miss Hayes' to you," Dorothy corrected. "I don't suppose we are destined to become friends." She paused as though expecting Nadia to rephrase her question more politely. She had a long wait ahead of her.

The look on Dorothy's face hardened, her eyes going cold with malice as she stared Nadia down. There was *hatred* in those eyes, but why would Dorothy hate someone she had never met? Come to think of it, why had she said Nadia had been a thorn in her side? What had Nadia ever done to her? She'd been imprisoned in a retreat since before Dorothy's existence had even been made public.

"I want both you and Nathaniel to put down your guns and back away," Dorothy said through gritted teeth. "Do it now, or Chairman Hayes will regret it."

"I fail to see how putting our guns down is going to improve the situation for Nate and me," Nadia said. "I presume the next step after that is arrest and execution, and that doesn't sound so good."

Dorothy smiled broadly. "What if I told you I had every intention of allowing you both to walk out of here unharmed?"

"I'd say you're full of shit," Nate snarled. He was still pointing his gun, but his arm was shaking from the strain.

Once again, Chairman Hayes tried to say something, but

Dorothy shook him by the collar. "Hush now, Daddy. You don't have a speaking role in this little drama of ours." She returned her attention to Nate and Nadia. "You will serve my purposes better if you're on the loose, wanted for the possible kidnapping of Agnes Belinski, than if you're in prison awaiting trial—or even awaiting one of those unfortunate accidents that tend to occur in prison."

"And what purposes would those be?" Nadia asked.

"Put down your guns, and I'll tell you."

Nate and Nadia shared a look of confusion. None of this was making any sense. Nadia could understand why Dorothy wanted them to put down their guns, of course, but obviously she wanted something more than that. Nadia just had no clue what it was.

"Let's put an end to your concern that Daddy and I are just trying to fake you out, shall we?" Dorothy said. In a lightning-fast motion, she lowered her gun from the small of the Chairman's back, angled it toward his butt, and fired.

The shot made so little noise, Nadia thought it was a bluff of some kind. Except the Chairman's face squinched up with pain and he tried to force a scream past Dorothy's choke hold. Then there was the blood that was pooling on the seat of his pants. His legs seemed to go weak, but Dorothy held him up by the collar, displaying a strength that seemed incongruous with her delicate build.

Nate had gone pale, and he'd lowered his gun, though he hadn't dropped it.

"Shall I have Daddy turn the other cheek?" Dorothy asked with a predatory grin. "Or are you going to be good little children and put those nasty guns down so we can have a civilized conversation?"

Nadia didn't like the idea of putting the gun down, not

one bit. However, as much as she hated the Chairman, she couldn't stomach standing there and watching Dorothy torture him before her eyes—and before Nate's. Nate's skin had gone from pale to a sickly green, and Nadia couldn't even imagine the riot of emotions he must be sorting through.

Moving slowly so as not to startle Dorothy, Nadia shifted her grip so she was holding her gun by the muzzle, then slowly bent and put it on the floor. She still had Lily's gun in her uniform pocket, as well as the canister of knockout gas, though it was perilously close to empty. Nate wouldn't be disarmed if he put *his* gun down, either, so Nadia hoped he'd follow her lead—and that Dorothy would think the guns they'd taken from the guards were the only weapons they had.

Still looking almost sick to his stomach, Nate put his own gun down. The bloodstain on the Chairman's pants was spreading, and his face was bathed with sweat as he gasped for air.

"How about you loosen your hold enough so the Chairman can breathe?" Nadia suggested as she stood up.

"How about you each kick your guns toward me. Nathaniel, I'll need your other gun as well, and I'll need that knockout gas from you, Miss Lake."

Damn it. Dorothy must have watched the security feed from the lobby and seen their other weapons before coming upstairs to confront them. Surely *now* she would assume she'd completely disarmed them. They were just a couple of kids, after all. How much firepower could she expect them to be packing?

Reluctantly, Nadia did as Dorothy ordered, and Nate followed suit. Dorothy forced the Chairman to his knees so she could keep easy control of him while she gathered up the weapons. The guns were too large to fit in the pockets of her skirt suit, so she stuck them in the waistband instead, one in front, one in back. The knockout gas *did* fit in her pocket. She rose from her crouch, dragging the Chairman with her, keeping him between herself and Nate and Nadia as if she still needed his services as a human shield.

"So what happens now?" Nadia asked quietly. Dorothy seemed to have painted herself into a corner by shooting Chairman Hayes. If she let the security officers in now to arrest Nate and Nadia, how would she explain the gunshot wound?

"Have you figured out who I am yet?" Dorothy countered.

"We've figured out you're not my sister," Nate snarled.

Dorothy looked at him with an expression of smug condescension. "But I *am*, Nathaniel. Ask any geneticist you like to examine my DNA, and he will tell you I am the daughter of Chairman Hayes."

Nadia's head spun as an awful, terrifying idea came to her. "Thea," she whispered barely above her breath, not expecting anyone to hear her. But Dorothy did.

"In the flesh," Dorothy said with another grin. She certainly wasn't making any attempt to hide how much fun she was having. "Literally."

"What?" Nate cried.

"I was rather further along in my research than you were led to believe," Dorothy said. "Even Daddy didn't know about the most recent breakthroughs I'd had before you meddling children got in the way. I've had to move up my timetable a little bit to make sure my remaining research is secure. I couldn't stand the thought of coming as far as I have and then being cut off just before achieving full success."

Thea had claimed to be researching the mind/body connection. Her ultimate goal had been to fully separate the two, so that she could combine a person's mind—more specifically, Chairman Hayes's mind—with a younger version of that person's body. To protect herself from any change that might lead to her deactivation, she had determined that Chairman Hayes had to remain in power forever, his mind forever reimplanted into a new body when old age got the best of him.

"So you've succeeded," Nadia said breathlessly, unable to stop herself from looking Dorothy up and down with both awe and revulsion.

"I'm very close," Dorothy corrected. "As you can see, I have mastered the construction of a human body. Minds, however, are harder to create. Fascinating thing, the human mind. Give me an original to work with and a perfect duplicate of the body, and I can bring it fully to life. As I did when I created this Replica of Nathaniel." She jerked her chin toward Nate. "A perfect likeness. But as of this moment, I can only transfer that mind to the exact physical duplicate of its original."

Dorothy's brows drew together in obvious frustration, her fingers tightening on the Chairman's collar.

"Obviously, there's something about the human brain I am failing to understand properly," Dorothy continued. "There is no such thing as what you humans call a soul, no mystical, magical entity that makes you who you are. It is all scientific and physical, or I would not be able to produce such perfect Replicas. Somewhere in that science, I will be able to isolate the specific differences in brain chemistry or biology that make a human being into a unique individual, and I will be able to sculpt a fully functioning brain in a fully functioning body."

"You seem to have had a lot of success with that already," Nadia pointed out, her mind reeling at the implications of what Dorothy was saying. It didn't sound so much like she was trying to find a way to make a human mind immortal by implanting it in a younger body; it sounded more like she was trying to create a human being from scratch. A human being whose mind would be exactly what Thea wanted it to be, who would think exactly as she wanted it to.

Dorothy sighed, an expression of frustration crossing her face. "I am close. As you can see, I've created a fully functional body that is not a Replica of any living human. The brain is capable of controlling motor functions, and it *should* be capable of handling all the other jobs of a human brain. But I'm still missing something. There is no mind here. This body would be nothing but a worthless vegetable if I hadn't implanted receptors in its brain that allow me to control it. It is a vessel, not a person."

Her expression brightened. "But it's an achievement nonetheless. A step in the right direction. With more research, I'll be able to figure out how to create an independent, functioning mind."

Nadia didn't want to think about what Thea's idea of research entailed. "What is it you hope to accomplish, exactly?" she asked, because keeping Dorothy talking couldn't possibly be a bad idea. Whatever Thea was up to, it seemed that Chairman Hayes was no longer on board with it. Nadia remembered when the Chairman had first introduced Dorothy to the world and Agnes had speculated that it had been an odd time to introduce a potential heir. Perhaps that hadn't been the Chairman's idea at all.

"I was created for the purpose of research," Dorothy said. "It is the end-all, be-all of my existence. I cannot rest until I understand the workings of the human mind. I will not give up, nor will I settle for anything less than perfection."

Thea had made a similar claim when she'd been eagerly awaiting permission to vivisect Nadia. Nadia had taken it as nothing but the truth then, but this time, she found it harder to swallow. There were any number of ways Thea could have used her hunger for research for the good of mankind, and yet she was focusing on the mind/body connection with single-minded resolve. She wanted more than just research for the research's sake.

"Wants to be goddess," Chairman Hayes choked out, then gasped when Dorothy twisted her hand in his collar and cut off his oxygen. He reached up to claw at her hand, but she poked her gun into his back.

"Stop that," she commanded, and though his eyes were unnaturally wide and his lips were turning blue, he let his hand drop.

"Please let my father go," Nate begged Dorothy. "There's no need to torture him. We gave up our weapons like you asked. You don't need to use him as a hostage anymore."

"I am rather angry with Daddy right now," Dorothy said, but she loosened her hold slightly. "He has allowed you children to interfere with my work. He destroyed me to appease you. Yes, he made a Replica of me, but tell me, Nathaniel, do you forgive him for killing your original just because he made a Replica? Does it make the original Nathaniel any less dead?"

Nate didn't answer. But then, he didn't have to.

"I dedicated my entire life to making him immortal," Dorothy continued. "I've been unfailingly loyal to him. And he was willing to destroy me rather than let the world know I existed."

Still using the Chairman as a shield, Dorothy moved toward the door. "Be a dear, Daddy, and unlock the dead bolts for me. Leave the electronic locks engaged.

"In a way," Dorothy continued as the Chairman followed her orders and opened the dead bolts, "I should be grateful to you for revealing exactly where I stand in Daddy's heart. I might never have understood it if it weren't for you. But I now also understand what humans mean when they say ignorance is bliss.

"Here are some things you should know. One is that as Thea, I can undo the electronic locks anytime I feel like it. Two is that if something were to happen to this body, I can make another one, and it will still be genetically identifiable as the daughter of Chairman Hayes. And three is that there is a great deal of digital surveillance available in this room, and it's child's play for me to make it record *my* version of what has happened here.

"In my version, there was a heated verbal altercation between the two of you and the Chairman." Moving faster than seemed humanly possible, Dorothy tossed her little gun into the far corner of the room and drew one of the guns she'd confiscated earlier. "Miss Lake was unhappy with the Chairman, accusing him of causing her sister's death, and she fired that little gun, hitting him in the buttocks. After which the altercation escalated. I tried my best to protect my dearest father now that we have finally been united."

"No!" Nadia screamed, figuring out what was coming a bit too late.

"But Nathaniel went crazy and shot his own father in the head."

The sound of the gunshot was deafening.

CHAPTER THIRTY-ONE

nate couldn't move. Couldn't think. Couldn't breathe.

Dorothy let his father's limp body fall to the floor.

It didn't seem real. *Couldn't* be real.

Dorothy aimed the gun that had just killed his father at him, and Nate felt no inkling of alarm, his nervous system too tied up in knots to react. His ears were ringing from the explosive gunshot in the enclosed room, and when he managed to drag in a breath, the air stank of gunpowder and blood.

The Chairman's blood.

His *father's* blood.

"I'm sorry, Nathaniel," Dorothy said. The face of Thea's puppet put on the requisite sad expression, but Nate could have sworn he saw through those eyes into the heart of Thea's malice and madness. "I didn't want to do this. I truly didn't. But I know our father as well as you do. Probably better, actually.

"You see, I have always monitored the net for security purposes. I found one of the copies of the video you and Miss Lake made while you were in hiding. You were going to use it to blackmail Daddy into stepping down, weren't you?"

Nate was too numb and too horrified to acknowledge the question, much less answer it. He'd come here thinking he'd been almost angry enough to kill his own father, but seeing his father lying on the floor in a pool of blood disabused him of the notion.

"Daddy would have been furious, of course," Dorothy continued without waiting for a response. "And he would have asked me to go looking for the videos to destroy them, just as he had me looking for the recordings you made when last we met. But until I found them all and destroyed them, he would have felt obligated to accede to your demands, no matter how furious it made him. And that would have been unacceptable."

"But *you* don't care if those videos are released," Nadia said in a small, shaking voice. "You don't care that it could cause a war."

"I wouldn't say I don't care," Dorothy said with a thoughtful frown. "I have dedicated my whole life to the well-being of my state and would hate to see it jeopardized. However, I believe that only the lower classes would be outraged enough by your claims to object with any great violence, and they don't have the means to stage a long-term insurrection. There would be violence and there would be casualties, but the Executives of Paxco would quickly gain the upper hand.

"In other words, unlike Daddy, I don't think it would be the end of the world if the truth got out." She glanced down at the body at her feet with a fond smile. "Of course, I also don't think anyone will believe your claims after they learn the two of you conspired to assassinate the Chairman. You can be certain the video I release will be playing on the net all around the world and will be far more convincing than your quaint little confessional."

Nate shook himself from his trance and looked at the monster his father had created. The monster who thought it would be no big deal if Paxco's lower classes were to take up arms against the government. So thousands of people would die. So what? As long as the government won in the end, she was okay with that.

And she was also okay with killing the man she'd once claimed to want to make immortal.

There were people pounding on the office door and yelling, though the soundproofing made their voices indistinct and their words indecipherable. The Chairman's personal phone rang from inside his pocket, but no one was inclined to answer it. Nate imagined his father's bodyguards must be frantic out there, but they would need a bomb or something to get into this well-defended room.

Nate was shaking, and he wasn't sure if it was from rage or grief or maybe even fear. He felt the weight of the still-hidden gun tucked into his pants at the small of his back. His odds of getting to it, flipping its safety off, aiming, and firing before Dorothy put about ten holes in him were slim at best, but he was so, so tempted to try it. Even though killing Dorothy would be a pointless gesture. *Thea* was the one who needed to die, and killing Dorothy wouldn't accomplish that.

"Don't get any funny ideas, Nathaniel," Dorothy warned. "I told you before that I was going to let you go, and I meant it. But not if you turn this into a gunfight."

"Why?" Nadia asked. "Why would you let us go?"

"Because dead, you might take on martyr status. In prison, you might start oversharing with anyone who will listen, and there will be people who *want* to listen despite the evidence I present. But on the run, wanted for the assassination of the Chairman, you remain exactly what you are and what you should be: powerless children."

Nate shuddered. There was always a lot of political maneuvering that went on when the Chairmanship changed hands, and Dorothy, as an unknown who had only been introduced into Paxco society a few days ago, would have her hands full. Nate had no immediate family left, but that didn't mean he didn't have relatives who would see any political unrest as a chance to further their own interests, maybe even seize the Chairmanship for themselves. Dead or alive, Nate might be able to help their cause, or at least become a symbol they could rally around. The same could be said of Nadia, whose family was almost as powerful as his own. But if he and Nadia were missing, and wanted for murder and treason and any number of other crimes . . .

Dorothy wasn't going to let them go. Not really. She just wanted them to run so she could kill them somewhere else, where no one was looking and their bodies would never be found.

"You know where the emergency exit is," Dorothy said, gesturing. "I suggest you use it. The video will show that you and I wrestled for the gun, and you eventually hit me over the head with it and knocked me out. I will be 'unconscious' long enough to give you a nice head start."

Nate stared at his father's body. He couldn't just let Thea get away with this, could he? Couldn't run away like a common criminal and thereby convince everyone that he was as guilty as Dorothy claimed.

"My preference is that you be on the run," Dorothy said when he didn't immediately move for the exit. "My second choice is that you both be dead and silent. More inconvenient for me, and a little harder to stage convincingly for the video, but I'm sure I will manage if I have to. And I'll start with Miss Lake."

The gun shifted, pointing at Nadia's head. Nate's body moved without conscious thought, and he found himself stepping in front of Nadia to shield her.

"Nate, don't . . ." she said, putting her hand on his shoulder as if to push him aside. But he wasn't budging.

"Go ahead and open the emergency exit, would you," he said, his eyes locked with Dorothy's. "It's not as heavy as it looks."

"Are you sure?" Nadia asked.

"I'm sure. We have to get out of this alive. We're the only ones who know who and what she is, and that makes us the only ones who can stop her."

Dorothy laughed, and Nate had to admit that the idea of him and Nadia being able to stop her seemed absurd. They had no resources, no power, no money. They had a fledgling resistance movement that consisted of five teenagers on the run from the law. Not exactly a force to strike fear into Thea's heart. But the odds had been against them from the very beginning, and they'd kept fighting. They would keep fighting until the bitter end.

Nate straightened his shoulders and glared at Dorothy as she continued to chuckle over his threat and Nadia pushed the bookcase aside to reveal the exit. She might laugh now, but there was no doubt in Nate's mind that the moment he and Nadia were out of sight, she'd be planning how she could track them down and kill them.

Nadia opened the emergency door. It was time to go.

Nate looked at his father's crumpled body one more time. His eyes misted over, and his heart ached. Despite everything that had happened between them, Nate realized now that he'd always harbored a secret hope that, someday, they might reconcile their differences. Now, thanks to Dorothy, that hope was gone.

"You could make a Replica." His voice came out hoarse, and he hated that he was betraying any of his emotions.

Dorothy shook her head. "But I won't. Even if I started over with an earlier version of him, we would eventually reach an impasse. I loved our father, but like all human beings, he was resistant to change, and he could not share my vision of Paxco's future.

"Now go," she commanded. "Your time here is up."

Vowing to himself that he would be back, that he would not allow Dorothy to win, Nate followed Nadia into the stairwell and shut the door behind them.

acknowledgments

First and foremost, I'd like to thank my fans, especially those of you who reach out to me through e-mail, or Facebook, or Twitter. The writing business can be truly grueling and often frustrating, and some days, it is only your enthusiasm and kind words that keep me going.

I'd also like to thank my editor, Melissa Frain, who gives me the perfect blend of constructive criticism and encouragement, and who helped make this a better book without making me any crazier than I already was. Thanks also to the Tor Teen art department, which has done such a wonderful job with the covers, and all the other great people at Tor who've worked on this book behind the scenes!

And then there are the "usual suspects," without whom writing would be a far lonelier and less enjoyable endeavor: my agent, Miriam Kriss; my husband, Dan; and the Deadline Dames, Devon, Jackie, Kaz, Keri, Lili, Rachel, Rinda, and Toni. Thanks for all your support!